P.C. CAST

DIVINE BY CHOICE

www.LUNA-Books.com

DIVINE BY CHOICE

ISBN-13: 978-0-373-80251-7
ISBN-10: 0-373-80251-X

First printing: December 2006

Author Photo by Kim Doner

This edition published by arrangement with Harlequin Books S.A.

www.LUNA-Books.com

Printed in U.S.A.

Praise for P.C. CAST and her Partholon novels…

"A mythic world of humor and verve."
—*Publishers Weekly* on *Goddess by Mistake*

"Fantasy lovers…are going to have a great time with this book. A fun read."
—Christopher Moore, bestselling author of *Bloodsucking Fiends—a Love Story*

"One of the most innovative fantasy romances I've read. From beginning to end, the surprises in P.C. Cast's new page-turner never stopped. Its poignancy resonates with both whimsy and fantasy, leaving the reader with a childlike believability in the impossible. I loved it!"
—*New York Times* bestselling author Sharon Sala on *Goddess of the Sea*

"Watch out for this author, she's sure to rise to the top of the romantic fantasy genre."
—*Rendezvous*

"Cast's tales of Partholon are truly magical. The world is an intriguing mix of Celtic folklore and Greek legend, peopled with an astonishing range of unique races.... Cast once again challenges readers to look beyond outward appearances and, simultaneously, crafts an exciting adventure that will appeal both to romance and traditional fantasy fans."
—*Romantic Times BOOKreviews* [4-star review]

"Ms. Cast has again served up a great story. There is a wonderful blend of characters and she makes you believe that all things are possible."
—*Rendezvous* on *Brighid's Quest*

"I cried and laughed....
I was drawn into Partholon and sad to leave it.
I eagerly await P.C. Cast's next installment."
—*Fallen Angel Reviews* on *Brighid's Quest*

This is another one for my dad,
Dick Cast (Mighty Mouse—the Old Coach).
With all my love (Bugs).

ACKNOWLEDGMENTS

Thank you to my wonderful LUNA team (especially Mary-Theresa Hussey, Stacy Boyd and Adam Wilson) for producing such a beautiful book! It's a pleasure to work with all of you.

Much appreciation to my agent and friend, Meredith Bernstein.

Thank you, Dad, for letting me use your terrible break-through-the-ice-and-almost-die accident, even though seeing it in print gave you the heebie-jeebies.

And a special and loving THANK YOU to the *Goddess by Mistake* fans who have been waiting five long years to get this sequel. My fans are the best!

PART I

Like ink running down a sheet of black paper, the darkness at the edge of my vision wavered, sending a chill of foreboding shivering across my skin. What the hell? I peered into the shadows. Nothing. Just an empty, starless night that had turned cold and windy.

Clearly I was losing my friggin mind.

The Fomorian War had been over for months. No winged demons lurked about waiting to pounce on me. I mean, please, I was in the middle of my own temple, which, despite its beauty, had been built as a fortress. Even had some kind of freaky monster been loose upon the world (and in this world, one never knew), I was more than perfectly safe. Seriously, I was in more danger of being pampered and adored to death than I was being monster-grabbed. Yet I still had the awful "someone just walked over my grave" feeling. And tonight wasn't the first time I'd felt as if something was wrong.

As I followed the marble path that led to the monument I thought about the weird sense of foreboding I seemed to be carrying around with me. Had it been weeks? Damn! Now that I really thought about it I realized that it had been at least two or three weeks that I'd been feeling off. I'd definitely been off my food, which was bizarre in its own right because I seriously love food. But a lingering stomach virus and/or stress could account for that. What was most odd was the way I'd been jumping at shadows. And the shadows seemed dark and thick and filled with something definitely malevolent.

Okay, yes, I'd just been through a truly awful war in which the good guys (naturally, the ones on my side) had to battle horrid demonic creatures and save the world from enslavement and annihilation. Literally. And yes, that could make a girl slightly jumpy. Especially if the girl was really a high school English teacher from Oklahoma who had accidentally been exchanged for the Beloved Incarnate of a Goddess in a world that more closely resembled a weird mixture of ancient Scotland and mythological Greece than Broken Arrow, Oklahoma (a lovely suburb of Tulsa). All true. But the war was over. The demons extinguished, and (supposedly) all was right with the world. So why did I feel like the damn booger monster was out there in the darkness waiting to leap on me?

Jeesh, I had another headache.

When I got to the MacCallan's memorial I tried to still my roiling thoughts by breathing deeply and savoring the peace and serenity that always blanketed me when I visited it. Tall, graceful columns ringed a three-stepped marble dais, whereon an ornately carved pedestal stood as the resting place for a weighty urn that was kept perpetually filled with sweet-scented, forever-burning oil.

Tonight the silver-gray smoke curled lazily up through the circular hole in the domed roof. I walked slowly toward the urn, enjoying the way the brilliant yellow flame contrasted with the backdrop of the starless night's sky. I had specified that the monument be built with no walls, just columns, a dome and this ever-burning flame. I believe the man memorialized here would have liked the freedom it symbolized.

A breeze stirred my hair and I shivered. The cool air was almost moist. I was glad I'd let Alanna bully me into wearing my ermine-lined cloak, even though the memorial was only a short walk from my chambers.

"Lady Rhiannon!" A young maiden rushed between the columns on the far side of the edifice. She paused long enough to drop almost to the floor in a fluid curtsy. "May I bring you some warmed wine? The night has become chilly."

"No." Distracted, I barely glanced at her, quickly searching my memory for her name, "Maura. I don't need anything. You may go back to bed."

She smiled at me shyly. "Yes, my Lady." Then she blurted, "But you will call if there is anything you require?"

I returned her smile with a tired one of my own. "Yes, I will call."

She bounded away.

I looked sardonically at the urn and rolled my eyes. "The

annoying exuberance of youth," I muttered at the smoking flame. "But I'm probably preaching to the choir here. Heck, you'd probably consider *me* filled with youthful exuberance." Getting no audible answer, and, of course, expecting none, I climbed to the top level of the dais and sat down with a sigh, tucking the thick folds of my cloak around my knees before I rested my chin in my hand. "But then I don't *really* know what you would think. I never actually knew you." I sighed again, plucking irritably at the escaping curl that was tickling my cheek.

I had hoped visiting the monument would lift my spirits as it usually did, but tonight I couldn't shake the depression that threatened to engulf me. I rubbed my right temple where the needle prick of a headache throbbed with each beat of my heart.

Another wisp of breeze ruffled my cloak. Again, the hair on the back of my neck lifted eerily. I turned my head to check the leather tie that knotted my thick tresses back from my face, and my eyes caught the movement of something liquid and dark as it skittered just outside the line of my sight. Forgetting the escaping hair, I sat up straighter, ready to chastise whoever was encroaching upon my privacy.

"Who is it?" I demanded imperiously.

Silence.

I studied my surroundings. The low-hanging clouds curtained the night sky. The only illumination came from the flame burning steadily before me. I could see nothing out of the ordinary—except that the darkness of the night mirrored my mood. Nothing sinister stirred or skulked or crept in the dim non-shadows.

Jeesh, Shannon. Get a grip, girl!

It was probably just the wind in the nearby trees, mixed with a healthy dose of my always-active imagination. That was probably it. Nothing was *really* wrong…

…Then another movement caught at the edges of my vision. I turned my head quickly, but all I could see was darkness on darkness—more ink running across a page of black paper. I shivered again and my memory stirred. What was it Alanna had told me not long after I'd come to Partholon? Something about dark gods who were better left unnamed. My stomach clenched in an unexplained spasm of fear. What was wrong with me? I definitely didn't traffic with dark gods. Hell, I didn't even know anything about them. Why should just the thought of such beings cause me to be afraid?

Something was definitely not right.

As it had been for weeks, a feeling too deep to call sadness and too thick to call loneliness nagged at the edges of my mind. I put my face in my hands, stifling a sob.

"I wish you were alive, Dad. I need to talk to you about what the hell is going on inside of me."

He's not really your father. My errant thoughts taunted me. *And this is not really your world. Interloper. Usurper. Fraud.*

"It's my world now!" I yelled before I spiraled down into an endless wash of tears. My voice split the night with its strength. The sound echoed eerily off the columns like a tolling bell, which made me start in response. My unexpected reaction caused me to laugh out loud at my own foolishness.

"What the hell am I doing sitting here yelling at myself and imagining the booger man in night shadows?" The humor in my voice helped to ease my morose mood. As I wiped the tears from my eyes and took a deep breath, I watched the almost full moon suddenly break through the misty sky and appear over the trees. I smiled in pleasure at the ethereal beauty of the timeless orb.

"I don't care if I wasn't born into this world. I love it here. This is where I want to be, and it's where I belong." I said resolutely.

And, of course, it was true. Rhiannon, the original Incarnate and Beloved of the ancient Celtic horse goddess Epona, had jerked me out of twenty-first century America—Broken Arrow, Oklahoma, to be specific—where I had been content to be Shannon Parker, an incredibly attractive, witty and broke high school English teacher. Rhiannon had succeeded in casting a spell that caused us to exchange places. Almost six months ago I had awakened from what I'd thought was a horrible car accident to find myself in Partholon, a parallel world where mythology and magic lived. To add to my initial confusion, some of the people of Partholon mirror those of my old world. In other words, people looked familiar, they even sounded and maybe acted familiar, but in actuality they weren't. Which is where the monument to the MacCallan (my dad/non-dad) came in.

For a moment I felt a wave of sadness, not just because my beloved father was a world away, but because his mirror image in this world, Rhiannon's father the MacCallan, had been brutally killed not long after I had arrived here. The power of my Goddess had allowed me to witness Rhiannon's father's death so that I could warn this world of an encroaching evil. My mind told me that the man whose death I had witnessed, Lord MacCallan, Chieftain of his Clan, was not actually my father, but my heart whispered something else. The MacCallan had been a leader and a warrior. My father, too, was a leader of men—mostly young men. His chosen field of battle was the football field. I couldn't help feeling unalterably bonded to the dead man who so closely resembled my father.

"It's damn confusing sometimes," I said as I rose and gave the side of the urn a pat. MacCallan's body wasn't entombed here. He lay with his men within the charred ruins of MacCallan Castle. I had felt the need to erect this monument to him, to show him the respect I would want accorded to the memory of Richard Parker.

There were a lot of things I had learned about Rhiannon that mortified and embarrassed me, but her love for her father was not one of them. Now I enjoyed having the status of Lady Rhiannon, High Priestess of Partholon, Beloved of Epona and Goddess Incarnate in her place. And I supposed that she "enjoyed" being an underpaid Oklahoma public-school teacher.

The thought made me laugh as I walked toward the path that would lead me back to Epona's Temple.

"Yeah," I whispered sarcastically. "It was obvious how much she had been *enjoying* her change of status when she attempted to re-exchange places with me a few months ago."

The memory of that failed attempt sobered me. Even though I hadn't been born to this world I had become bound to it. Partholon was my home now; these people my people—Epona my Goddess. I closed my eyes and sent a quick prayer to her. *Epona, please help me to stay.*

My stomach lurched and I swallowed hard. Maybe that was what was wrong with me. Maybe Rhiannon was up to her old tricks and was trying to pull me away from Partholon and back to Oklahoma so that she could return here, and this creepy, bullshit sick feeling was Epona sending me a premonition of trouble so that I'd keep my eyes open. Ugh. Just thinking about losing Partholon—and the husband and people I'd come to love here—was enough to cause another wave of sickness to wash over me. Damnit! I was completely tired of feeling like this! I shivered again as a breath of chilled wind caressed my cheeks and slipped within my cloak. I thought of the weird, running darkness I kept imagining around me. Now it seemed I had started hallucinating.

Great—my husband was gone for one month to make sure the land was recovering from battle and I go totally nuts.

Squaring my shoulders, I told myself to knock it off. Rhiannon was in Oklahoma. I was here in Partholon, which was how things were going to stay. I'd just be on my guard against unusual weirdness (easier said than done, but still). And about the sick feeling in my stomach...well...I had probably just caught a nasty flu bug, which was adding to a bad case of the I'm-a-newlywed-and-my-husband-went-on-a-trip blues. Anyway, he was due home any day. Things would get back to normal then.

At least that's what I told myself as I ignored the crawling night shadows. The lights of the temple beckoned and I picked up my pace, whistling the theme to *The Andy Griffith Show*. Loudly.

2

Unfortunately, the next day didn't get any damn better.

"Oh, yuck!" I spit the piece of chocolate-dipped strawberry into my hand. "There's something wrong with it." I sniffed suspiciously at the semichewed lump in my palm. It looked disquietingly like a hunk of raw flesh. I grimaced at my friend, who also served as this world's equivalent to my girl Friday. In other words, Alanna knew about everyone and everything in Partholon, which helped me look less like a fish roosting in a tree and more like a real Goddess Incarnate. "I think it's rotten." After spending yet another sleepless night, what I didn't need was a tragic and messy episode of food poisoning on top of my already weird upset stomach.

Alanna chose a different strawberry from the artistically displayed setting, sniffed it, then nibbled carefully.

"Mmm..." She licked her lips and threw me a quick, cream-filled kitten smile. "It must have just been that one—this one tastes wonderful." She popped the rest of it into her mouth.

"That figures," I grumbled. "The one I grab is the only yucky one on the whole damn plate." I picked around the platter until I found an especially lovely, plump chocolate-dressed berry, then I bit carefully into the delicious-looking end of it.

"Ugh!" The half-chewed tip joined the other piece of mush in my hand. "Okay, this is getting ridiculous! This one is nasty, too." I offered the unchewed part of the offending fruit to Alanna. "Please taste this and tell me I'm not crazy."

Alanna, being a good friend and, coincidentally, the person who was in charge of the upcoming gala celebration, gingerly took the strawberry from me, sniffed it and nibbled a bite from its sun-kissed side. I waited for her expression to change and for her to spit the berry into her own hand (I pulled my yuck-filled hand out of her range of fire).

And waited.

And waited.

She swallowed and looked at me with doe eyes.

"Don't tell me it tastes fine."

"Rhea, it tastes fine." She offered it back to me. I got one whiff of the rich chocolate/berry smell and cringed.

"Uh, no, keep it."

"Obviously you are still unwell." Alanna's eyes were filled with concern. "I am pleased that Carolan returns with ClanFintan tonight. This stomach sickness of yours has gone on entirely too long."

Yeah, I'd look forward to our "doctor" checking me out—sans penicillin, blood tests, X-rays, etcetera, etcetera. Of course, I couldn't share my trepidation with Alanna because not only was Carolan this world's leading doctor, he was also her husband.

A little nymphet-servant scampered up to me.

"My Lady..." She dipped down in an adorable curtsy. "Please allow me to clean your hand!"

"Thank you," I took the wet linen cloth from her, "but I think I can clean my own hand." Before she could give me a look that said I had just crushed her little ego, I added, "I would really appreciate it if you could run and get me something to drink."

"Oh, yes, my Lady!" Her face radiated pleasure.

"Bring a goblet for Alanna, too." I shouted at her back as she (literally) ran across the room to do my bidding.

"Of course, my Lady!" she shot back over her shoulder before she disappeared through the arched door that led to the kitchens.

Sometimes it was just damn nice to be Goddess Incarnate and Beloved of Epona. Okay, I'll admit it—it was more than *sometimes* nice. Please—I was surrounded by opulence and loved by the populace. I had a veritable herd of eager handmaidens whose sole purpose in living was to see that my every need was met, not to mention wardrobes filled with exquisite clothing and drawers brimming with (be still my heart) *jewelry*. Lots of jewelry.

Let's face it—I was living well beyond the means of an Oklahoma high school teacher's salary. Big surprise.

I finished wiping my hand and turned back to the table to find Alanna watching me closely.

"What?" My tone said I was exasperated.

"You have been looking decidedly pale lately."

"Well, I've felt decidedly pale, too." I realized I sounded grumpy, and attempted a smile and a lighter tone. "Don't worry about it, I just have a touch of the…the…" (think Shakespeare) "the, um, ague." I finally finished, pleased with my grasp of the vernacular.

"For two seven-days?" I swear she sounded more like a mother than a best friend. "I've watched you, Rhea. Your eating habits have changed. And I believe you've lost weight."

"So, I've had a cold. And this weather hasn't helped."

"Rhea, winter is almost upon us."

"And to think when I first arrived here I thought that it must never get cold." I looked pointedly at the wall closest to us, whereon a lovely painting depicted someone who looked exactly like me riding a silver-white mare, breasts bared to the world (mine, not the mare's), while a dozen scantily clad maidens (or at least they were supposed to be maidens) cavorted around me, indiscriminately strewing flowers.

Alanna's good-natured laughter tinkled. "Rhiannon always chose the frescoes to be painted from scenes of spring and summer rituals. She reveled in the lack of clothing."

"She reveled in more than that," I muttered.

I hadn't been here long when I realized that even though many of the Partholonian people who mirrored people from my old world were alike in personalities (like Alanna and my best friend, Suzanna), Rhiannon was, quite frankly, not a nice person. Alanna and I surmised that one of the reasons she and I were so different could be because Rhiannon was raised as an indulged, totally spoiled High Priestess, and I was raised to act right by a dad who would have knocked the Oklahoma crap right outta me if I'd acted like a brat. So I'd grown up to have some self-discipline and a pretty decent set of morals. Rhiannon, to put it in twenty-first century terms, had grown up to be a raving bitch. Everyone who knew her either loathed her or feared her, or both. She had been self-indulgent and amoral.

And, yes, it had been a mess to step into her friggin ruby slippers (so to speak).

There were only three people in Partholon who knew I was not the original Rhiannon: Alanna, her husband, Carolan, and my husband, ClanFintan. Everyone else just thought I'd made an amazing personality change several months ago (about the same time I'd adopted Rhea as the shortened version of my name). I mean, it really wouldn't do to let the masses know their object of worship had been snatched from the twenty-first century. And not only that, to my utter and complete surprise this world's Goddess, Epona, had made it clear that I was, indeed, her choice as Beloved of the Goddess. Huh.

The delicate clearing of a throat swung my attention back to the present.

"The maidens said you spent more than your usual amount of time at MacCallan's tomb again last night." Alanna's voice sounded worried.

"I like it there. You know that." Thinking of the skittering, inky darkness, I couldn't meet her eyes. "Alanna, do you remember that you told me that Rhiannon's lackey, uh, I think his name was B-something."

"Bres," Alanna said distastefully.

"Yeah, Bres. Didn't you say something about him worshipping dark gods?"

Alanna's eyes narrowed with concern. "I do remember. Bres had powers granted him by evil and darkness. What would make you think of him?"

I shrugged, trying to sound nonchalant. "I don't know. I guess something about the cold, cloudy night must have creeped me out."

"Rhea, lately I have been concerned that you—"

Thankfully, Alanna was interrupted by the sound of approaching feet pattering against the marble.

"Your wine, my Lady." The nymphet had returned bearing a tray on which rested two crystal goblets filled with what I assumed was my favorite merlot.

"Thank you," I mentally searched for her name as I took one of the goblets and handed the other to Alanna, "Noreen."

"You are most welcome, Epona's Beloved!" She skipped away—her red hair flying in a breeze of her own making.

God, she was perky.

"To our husbands returning." I offered the toast, hopeful that it would change the subject. Alanna clicked her glass to mine as she blushed a sudden, dazzling pink.

"To our husbands." She smiled softly at me over the top of her glass as she took a drink.

"Ugh!" I could barely swallow my own sip. "This stuff is awful!" I sniffed at the glass, and cringed as the scent of rancid wine met my nostrils. "Does being Beloved of Epona not mean anything anymore? Why do I keep getting everything that's rotten?" I realized I sounded uncharacteristically petulant, and somewhere inside my mind I was shocked at my own outburst. Why in the hell did I constantly feel on the verge of tears?

"Rhea, let me taste it."

Alanna took my goblet, smelled the wine, then took a long drink.

And another.

"Well?" My voice reflected my frustration.

"It is fine." Alanna's eyes met mine. "There is nothing wrong with the wine."

"Oh, shit," I collapsed onto a chaise that sat near the laden banquet table. "I'm dying. I have cancer or a brain tumor or an aneurysm or something." There was a burning in the back of my throat that signaled I was close to tears. Again.

"Rhea—" Alanna sat next to me and took my hand gently in hers "—perhaps you have become choleric. You have gone through much in the time you have been in our world."

Oh, sure, "choleric." What the hell was that? Next she'd want to bleed me or drill holes into my skull to let out the "bad humors" or something equally medieval. My mind frantically tried to recall how penicillin was made from bread mold.

"Carolan will know what to do to help you." She patted my hand, trying to comfort me.

"Yeah, Carolan will know what's wrong." Like hell. There was no technology in this world. That meant no medical schools. He would probably want to chant some kind of off-tune song over me and make me drink something made from frog snot.

I was friggin doomed.

"A long bath always makes you feel better." She stood, pulling me up with her. "Come, I will help you choose a lovely gown—with matching jewelry." She paused as I got reluctantly to my feet, then added, "The jeweler was here this morning while you were busy with Epi. I had him leave all of his new pieces. I think I remember seeing a lovely pair of diamond earrings and a gorgeous golden brooch."

"Well, if you insist." We smiled at each other as we left the banquet room. Alanna knew my weakness for jewelry and knew that it could coax me out of just about any dreary mood, almost as easily as could spending time with my extraordinary mare, Epi, who I had nicknamed after the Goddess, Epona, and rightly so. Epi was the horse equivalent of me. She, too, was Beloved of the Goddess. She and I had a connection that was as magical as it was strong.

"Hey!" Inspiration hit me halfway to the bathing chamber. "Maybe I'm having a bizarre reaction to what's going on with Epi." The mare was going to be bred on Samhain night, the eve of the first day in November, as was traditional each third year. In Partholon three is a "magic" number, as Alanna had explained to me, and when the third year rolled around, the equine incarnation of Epona was bred to insure the land's fertility in the coming harvests. November first was in a couple days, and Epi had been acting fretful and uncharacteristically temperamental ever since the arrival of her future mate the week before.

"Rhiannon never behaved any differently during Epi's breeding cycles."

"I wonder if that was the norm for Epona's Chosen, or was Rhiannon such a selfish hag that she wasn't sensitive to the mare's moods?" Before Alanna could answer, I continued, "Or maybe since Rhiannon was always in heat herself, she didn't notice a difference."

We both laughed and I felt a little of my tension release. The door to the bathing room was guarded by two of my scrumptious warriors. There were several positive things about the Goddess I'd begun to serve, the fact that she was a warrior goddess, and had a hundred handsome, virile men "on staff" was just one of the perks of my new job. I noticed that the guards had added leather tunics to their hot-weather uniforms of, well, virtually nothing except well-filled loincloths. I couldn't help sighing in disappointment at the thought of all of those muscles being covered.

Yes, I'm married, but I'm not a corpse. Jeesh.

The warm-mineral smell of the candlelit room enveloped me. Steam rose invitingly from the deep, clear bathing pool. The bubbling of the water as it continually filled the bath, and the gentle sound of the waterfall as the overflow left the pool coupled with the moist warmth, beckoning me to relax in its depths and soak away the soreness in my unusually achy body.

I ducked my head out of the cowled robe I wore to keep out the prewinter's damp cold, and winked my thanks at Alanna as she unwound me from my silky underwrap. Slowly, I immersed myself in the warm mineral bath, reclining against the smooth sides of my favorite rocky ledge. I closed my eyes and listened to Alanna send another nymphet for a cup of herbal tea—then felt my face grimace in self-disgust at my sudden unfortunate aversion to wine—until recently, a glass of rich, red wine had been one of my favorite things.

Maybe I was getting old.

No, thirty-five and a half couldn't be old, and anyway, I had always planned on being one of those eccentric old ladies who wore lots of big jewelry, had chic, funky hair, drank wine knowingly and died suddenly of an Old White Woman's Disease (preferably a painless aneurysm after an especially sumptuous dinner). I enjoy practicing for my future golden years.

I tried to convince myself for the zillionth time that I just had a stubborn flu. It was making me depressed and making me imagine things. Of course, now that it was daylight, last night's dark images seemed distant and more than slightly ridiculous. ClanFintan would be home tonight. Just thinking about being with him again made me feel better, or at least that's what I told myself. He'd been gone almost a month, and this world's lack of telephones and e-mail had really worn on me. We'd been married less than six months, but with him gone I felt strangely hollow, like a bell without a clacker. Which was a disconcerting feeling for someone who had changed worlds recently. Actually, it made me feel a little like I was trapped in one of the alternative-dimension *Star Trek* episodes (minus Kirk and whatever alien bimbo he would be boinking).

"Try this." Alanna handed me a thick mug filled with fragrant tea. "It will settle your stomach."

I sniffed at it hesitantly, waiting for it to turn rancid in my hands (kind of a twist on the Midas touch thing), but the soothing scent of herbs and honey thankfully stayed enticing. I sipped at the mixture and let it comfort my rebellious stomach.

"Thanks, girlfriend, I feel better already." If I said it, it would be true... If I said it, it would be true... If—

"The maid said the sentries have spotted ClanFintan's warriors," Alanna's chatter was comforting. "They should arrive soon. I knew they would be on time. Carolan said they would return within the days that prelude Samhain—it is two days before and he will be here today." Her voice was washed with the expectation of a newlywed.

I knew exactly how she felt. I let visions of my husband's strong, sexy torso drift through my mind as I soaked.

"Man, I've missed him."

"As I have missed Carolan."

We shared girlfriend smiles.

"Better hand me that sponge. I want to be sweet smelling and well dressed when they arrive." Well, for a little while I wanted to be dressed.

I poured my favorite vanilla nut–scented soap from its delicate bottle, and started scrubbing with the thick sponge. Alanna began rummaging through one of my overfilled wardrobes.

"It'll be nice to see Victoria again, too." I had missed the Lead Huntress the past couple months. Her nomadic duties caused her to travel almost constantly, and I was happy to hear (by way of centaur runner—a little like the Pony Express, only with the rider built in) that she had joined with my husband's band of warriors and would be returning with him. We had become close friends, and I was hoping that Epona's Temple would be a second home to her.

"Perhaps we will see Dougal smile again." Alanna's eyes sparkled with mischief.

"He's smiled, you bad thing."

"Is that what that expression was?" Her musical lilt intensified as she teased. "And here I was sure he must have caught part of your stomach upset."

"Poor Dougal, between you and ClanFintan teasing him about his thing with Vic it's a wonder his face isn't permanently pink from blushing."

"Which reminds me, what exactly do you think happened between the two of them?"

"Well, I thought it was just a crush he had on her, but before she left I noticed they were both absent from the temple quite a bit—at coincidentally the same time. Add that to his misery since she's been gone, and his pink face whenever Vic is mentioned, and I do believe we have a pair of lovers."

Alanna giggled. "He really is a sweet blusher, isn't he?"

"Oh, look who's talking!" I splashed some water at her, which she neatly sidestepped.

"I do not blush."

"You don't blush like I don't cuss." We giggled at each other. "Toss me that towel, please." I began drying myself vigorously, determined that tonight, surrounded by my friends and my husband, I would feel well again. "I'm glad ClanFintan had Dougal stay here and take charge of the construction of the new centaur quarters. It's kept him too busy to do much moping." Dougal had lost a brother a few months earlier, and then the centaur he had apparently fallen for, Ms. Lead Huntress Victoria, had broken off their budding relationship and left him to go back to her old life. He was definitely a young centaur who desperately needed diversion.

"You know, Rhea, perhaps it is not a coincidence that

Victoria just *happened* to meet up with our warriors. Perhaps she was looking for a reason to return here—" she raised her eyebrows suggestively (which made her look like a blond bunny) "—to Dougal."

"I hope so." I finished drying myself and ran my hands appreciatively over the shining length of fabric Alanna presented to me. "I think they make a great couple, and who cares that he's younger. Something tells me any centaur who Victoria loves is going to need to be young *and* highly athletic."

We laughed in agreement. I wrapped the towel around myself and sank down onto the padded seat of my vanity chair, relaxing into Alanna's expert hands as she tried to tame my wild red hair.

"I seriously need a trim." I mentally calculated... I'd been in this world for almost six months, and I hadn't had my thick curls trimmed for several weeks before I'd been yanked over here. Man, my hairdresser, Rick, would have an apoplectic attack if he could see me now. Rick always said, "Girlfriend, I don't know why you'd ever let a *woman* touch your hair. They're in competition with you, so they just *look* for hateful little ways to make y'all look like shit. *I* don't mind if you look *fabulous*. We're not, shall we say, dipping out of the same punch bowl." You have to admit he had a point.

"Women do not cut their hair."

I snorted, remembering ClanFintan saying something very much like that several months ago.

"Let me clue you in, my friend." I spoke to her reflection in the mirror. "There's nothing wrong with a little snip-snip once in a while. I swear I've seen more split ends in the past six months than I have in the past decade. You'd think we were at a Pentecostal retreat."

Alanna didn't say anything. She was becoming used to my out-of-this-world babblings. Apparently she enjoyed the excitement now that she trusted me not to bite her head off. And, yes, I mean that literally. I'm telling you, Rhiannon was not a nice girl.

I contemplated silently how I was going to go about mass hair trimmings while Alanna finished my hair and makeup. When I had first awakened in this new world, I had felt awkward about Alanna waiting on me. Because she is the mirror image of my best friend (in any world), Suzanna, it felt somehow, I don't know, blasphemous, to allow her to coif me, clothe me and coddle me. But I have come to the realization that I am Alanna's job. She's technically my slave, but that's ridiculous and I called bullshit on that as soon as she told me about it. So now I tell myself, and everyone else, that she's my personal assistant and I let her have her way with me.

Okay, I admit I like the attention.

And Suzanna always was great at everything that had to do with being a Lady. She had to be. She's Southern Mississippi born and raised, transplanted in adulthood to Oklahoma (which they don't consider a part of the True South). And being a Lady of the South must be some kind of crossdimensional-genetic-imprint, because Alanna definitely did Dixie proud.

Alanna squeezed my shoulder, signaling that she was done with my coiffure. I stood and held my arms out while she wound a shimmery piece of golden silk around my body until it hung in beautiful folds, accentuating my deep curves and long legs.

"Hold this while I find that new brooch."

I held the slick material together at my left shoulder while Alanna dug through a pile of gold and sparkles that pooled on my vanity.

"Here is it..." She held a brooch out for my inspection. "Is it not exquisite?"

"Ohmygod, it's beautiful!" I breathed a long, sincerely jewelry-loving sigh.

It was a golden miniature replica of my husband—a plunging, centaur warrior—complete with a diamond-handled claymore, which he held before him in both hands, streaming hair (or mane, whichever way you wanted to look at it) and plenty of muscles (both horse and human). It looked so lifelike that for a moment I thought I felt it quiver. And in this world, you never know.

"Wow—" I peered down at the brooch as Alanna pinned it into place "—it even looks like him."

"That is what I thought." She turned and retrieved a new pair of hoop earrings that were encrusted with diamonds. "And I thought these would lighten your spirits, too."

The earrings flashed with clear fire as they caught the reflection of the candles.

"I'll bet these weren't cheap." I put them in my ears, loving their weight.

"Of course they were expensive. Only the—" we finished the familiar sentence together "—best for Epona's Chosen."

Alanna handed me a thin golden coronet, decorated with an ancient piece of polished amber, and I slid it in place on my forehead. It rested comfortably there—like it had been made for me—like I had been born into this position and Chosen by a Goddess for special favors (*and responsibilities*, my mind reminded me). Little wonder I had grown to love this world. My husband was here; my friends were here; people depended upon and trusted me; and (incidentally), the position of Goddess Incarnate does carry with it a decidedly better salary than Oklahoma public-school teacher (well, let's face it, a burger-flipper has a better salary than an Oklahoma teacher, as I'm sure the real Rhiannon is finding out).

"You look lovely. Pale, but lovely."

"Thanks, Mom." I pulled a face at her.

Two firm knocks sounded against the bathing room door.

"Come on in!" I called.

The perky little Noreen nymphet rushed into the room.

"My Lady! The warriors have been sighted over the western ridge," she gushed.

"Well, let's go welcome them!"

"Rhea, your wrap." Alanna reminded me of the encroaching cold as she helped me into an ermine-lined cloak (no animal rights activists here). Then she wrapped herself in a similar cloak, and we were ready to roll. I felt my heart pound in expectation as the two women stood aside so that I could lead the way from the room.

A quick left turn took me through my private hallway, which led to the main inner courtyard of Epona's Temple. One of my warriors opened the door, and the three of us spilled out into the crowded courtyard.

"Hail, Epona!"

"Blessings upon you, Lady Rhiannon!"

"Blessed be Epona's Chosen!"

I smiled and waved cheerfully at the throng of maidens and guards who made a path for me through the courtyard, out past the plunging-horse fountain that smoked with bubbling mineral water, to the smooth, ivory-colored marble wall that enclosed the temple. Outside the front entrance I was pleased to see a nice-size crowd of locals had gathered to welcome home the warriors.

Epona's Temple had been built on a plateau, and the raised entrance to the temple faced a westerly direction. I looked up from the crowd that spread before me and felt my already hammering heart leap in response to the magnificent sight. The setting sun had left the sky a watercolor of dramatic violets and pinks, which shaded to deep, sapphire blue near the horizon. Against that amazing backdrop came the warriors. Plunging over the western ridge the army moved as one, a liquid tide of strength tempered by grace. At first they were just darker shadows within shadow, bodies silhouetted by the setting sun, centaurs intermingled with humans on horseback. The closer they came the more individuals emerged. Beading on the centaurs' leather vests shimmered and glinted with the movement of their long strides. The bridles of the horses ridden by the human men winked brilliant shards of color as the fading evening light caught its reflection in well-adorned headdresses. They galloped in a tight formation, the banner of Partholon, a silver mare rearing against a regal purple background, snapped and curled above them.

As they came to the strategically cleared area that surrounded Epona's Temple, the army executed a neat flanking movement. Rippling like water, they separated into two neat columns that split to surround the group of joyously waiting spectators who cheered their maneuvers appreciatively.

Unexpectedly, I was reminded of my father's football practices. His team had become so successful that a crowd that outnumbered the total fans at most Friday night high school games consistently gathered to watch their practices. He had decided it would be good for morale to entertain his loyal fans, so he had his boys enter the practice field in intricate formations. The football players feinted and moved around each other like they were in a well-choreographed play.

The loneliness of having no father in this world with which to share this amazing sight felt especially poignant as I watched my centaur warrior husband break rank and move fluidly toward me.

Dad would have liked him.

I mentally shook myself free from my morose thoughts, swallowing back a wave of nausea that threatened to overwhelm me. Throwing back my shoulders in an attempt to look Goddess Incarnate–like, I stepped forward to greet my mate. As he approached, the cheering died to an expectant hush.

ClanFintan closed the space between us quickly, but time seemed to suspend long enough for my eyes to be filled with the being that was my husband. He moved with a grace and strength that I had come to realize was unique to his species—centaurs. You might imagine that melding horse and human would create a creature that was either a monstrously confused apparition, or a gawky, uncomfortable attempt to mix worlds, but neither was true. Centaurs were, perhaps, the most exquisite creatures I had ever encountered. And my husband was a prince among them. He was tall. His human torso towered above my five-foot-seven frame. His hair was dark and slick, reminiscent of Spanish Conquistadors, and it was tied back into a thick braid, from which a few tendrils escaped to play a teasing game around his well-defined face. Seeing him after a month's absence with new eyes, I was struck by how much he reminded me of a muscular Cary Grant, complete with chiseled cheekbones and a deep, romantic cleft in his chin.

I let my eyes slide down his body, and I felt my lips form an appreciative, welcoming smile as I took in his muscular torso, which the traditional leather vest of the centaur warrior left enticingly semi-bare. As I already knew, centaurs had a body temperature several degrees higher than a human's. Obviously, the chill in the air wouldn't bother him. Not for the first time I appreciated the muscular view his hot (in all senses of the word) body afforded me.

From his human waist back, his body was that of a well-muscled stallion. He stood easily sixteen hands tall at the withers. His coat was a rich bay, the color of ripe acorns that had been polished until they gleamed. This glistening bay deepened to black on his legs and tail. With each stride, his muscles rippled and tensed. As he approached me, he looked very powerful and suddenly—unexpectedly—very foreign.

He came to a halt directly in front of me, dwarfing me with his physical presence. I had to force myself not to take a nervous step back. My eyes lifted quickly from his body to meet his gaze.

ClanFintan's eyes were large but vaguely slanted, almost

Asian in shape. They were the color of a starless night, so black I couldn't distinguish his pupils. I found myself trapped in their darkness, and the nausea I had felt earlier fluttered to life in the back of my throat.

I suddenly remembered my first response to the thought of being intimate with this amazing being. I had been more than a little uneasy at the prospect—even after I had learned he could shapeshift into human form at will.

Then he smiled, and the lines at the edges of his eyes crinkled into familiar patterns. In one swift movement, he stepped forward and took my hand. Turning it palm up he raised it to his lips and kissed me softly. While his lips still touched my skin, his eyes again met mine, and he playfully took the meaty part of my palm between his teeth, nipping my hand gently.

"Hail, Epona's Beloved," he said in a deep voice that carried throughout the crowd. "Your husband and your warriors have returned."

His voice washed over me, reassuring me with its obvious affection. I blinked once, and my trepidation blew away like autumn leaves. This wasn't some gigantic stranger. This was my husband, my lover, my mate.

"Welcome home, ClanFintan." As any good teacher can, I raised my voice so that it carried. My smile grew as I spoke. "High Shaman, warrior and husband." Stepping into the warmth of his embrace, I was vaguely aware of the cheer that escaped from the watching crowd.

"I have missed you, my love." His voice resonated throughout my body as he bent to capture my lips.

His kiss was brief and hard. Before I could return the kiss as enthusiastically as I'd like, he grasped me around the waist and swung me up onto his broad back. As if responding to a signal, the cheering crowd swept around us as individuals were welcomed by family and friends, and a tide of well-wishers pushed us joyfully toward Epona's inner courtyard. From the corner of my eye I caught a flash of silver-blond, and turned my head in time to see my friend, Victoria, accepting the restrained greeting of Dougal. They stood close to each other but not touching, letting the crowd swirl around them. To a stranger, it appeared that Victoria's classically beautiful face was serene and unaffected by Dougal's presence. In the time I had known her I had come to understand that she masked her emotions well and, as Lead Huntress and provider for her people, that was only proper. But she could not conceal the emotions in her eyes, and right now they blazed with a desire that I hoped Dougal could read as clearly as I could.

ClanFintan moved forward with the crowd and Victoria and Dougal were soon blocked from my view. Sighing, I rested one hand lightly on his shoulder while I waved greetings to the warriors I recognized as we moved forward. Still a little shaky from my initial reaction to ClanFintan, I concentrated on being welcoming and goddess-like. This, at least, was a familiar drill. I had become accustomed to playing the benevolent Goddess Incarnate.

You are not playing, Beloved.

The words whispered into my mind, and I jerked in surprise like I'd brushed against an electric fence (jeesh, I hate those things). ClanFintan glanced back at me in alarm, and I squeezed his shoulder reassuringly. No doubt he could feel the tension transmitted from my body into his.

Epona had not spoken to me for months, yet I recognized the Goddess's voice as surely as I would my own.

We entered the courtyard and ClanFintan came to a halt, turning so that we faced the pressing crowd. He glanced briefly over his shoulder at me, covering my hand that rested on his shoulder with his own.

Hastily I cleared my throat, trying to regain my scattered thoughts.

"Um, I…" The people silenced themselves as I looked out at the crowd, and for an instant it seemed that behind the joyously gathered group I saw something dark. Something that lingered and watched and waited, but when I tried to look directly at it, disappeared. I cleared my throat and mentally shook myself. "I…um…I mean…" My gaze flitted around until it found Alanna. Her arms were wrapped intimately around her husband, but her eyes were on me. A frown hovered on her lips as her confusion at my uncharacteristic hesitance registered.

I started again.

"We would like to invite you to join us, all of Epona's servants and their families, for a feast to welcome home our brave warriors." The strength of my voice grew as I spoke. "Please share with us the joy of their return with food and wine!"

The crowd cheered, milling expectantly, eager to follow us to the Great Hall. At the same time, ClanFintan twisted around, pulling me down from his back and setting me gently on the ground beside him. We moved forward through the entrance side by side, his arm resting protectively around my shoulder, his gait slowing to match my much shorter steps.

"Are you well, Rhea?" he asked softly.

"Yes, I'm fine." I tried to smile up at him, but a new wave of nausea left me feeling clammy and weak.

The warriors who guarded the huge intricately carved doors saluted as I approached. In a move that made them look like muscular shadows of one another, they pulled the doors open and the smells and sights from the Great Hall escaped, spilling over us in a welcome of the senses.

ClanFintan led me to our familiar chaises, which to me always evoked the image and opulence of ancient Rome. He folded himself down into one after bowing me toward my own. As was customary, we reclined for our meals as did the ancient Romans (minus the stuffing puking stuffing puking part). The heads of our chaises were almost touching, and a narrow pedestaled tabled rested within arm's reach. I smiled at him, feeling slightly uncomfortable with the intense way he was studying me. Then the hall quieted and I cleared my throat before I began the blessing. Taking a deep breath, I felt myself relax. Not only was I used to public speaking/teaching/scolding/whatever, I enjoyed it.

"We thank you, Epona, for the safe return of our brave warriors." I noted a murmur of agreement rustling through the crowd. I closed my eyes and tilted my chin back, raising my arms over my head as if I was focusing my blessing upward and within at the same time. I continued. "I have only to close my eyes and in memory I see the hardships we have overcome this past season." I had learned early on that in Partholon time wasn't measured by months, it was measured by seasons and the changing moon. "But our Goddess was near us then, as always. We can hear Her voice in the sounding of the rain, and the trilling of the birds. It is in the rhythm of the moon, the brush of the breeze, the sweet, living scent of the earth. We are reminded by the changing of the seasons that blessings are not to be had singly. Instead, they come to us in a mixture, and sometimes must be discovered as sifting gems from sand. Tonight we are thankful for our gems." The walls of the Great Hall echoed my closing words, "Hail Epona!"

I opened my eyes and smiled at my wonderful audience before I sank gratefully into my chaise.

"Please bring me some herbal tea, and take away this wine," I whispered to an attentive servant. She gave me a confused look, and who could blame her? I was definitely acting out of character, but she complied without question.

"What is wrong, Rhea?" Although he kept his voice low, ClanFintan's worry was obvious enough to cause several of the people and centaurs in chaises near us (which included Alanna and her doctor husband) to send me concerned, questioning looks.

"Oh—" I tried to make my voice sound light "—I've had some kind of stomach upset that doesn't want to go away." I met my husband's steady gaze with my usual slightly sarcastic grin. "It's almost as stubborn as I've been known to be."

Several of our eavesdroppers chuckled. I noticed that Alanna, Carolan and ClanFintan did not join them.

"You look pale..." He hesitated, studying me again. "And thin."

"Well, you can never be too rich or too thin," I quipped.

"Humph," he snorted through his nose, making a sound that was very horselike.

"Alanna," I called, "I thought some of the maidens were going to play music during the feast."

"Yes, Rhea." Her smile was tinged with concern, like she thought I was hovering at the edge of a nervous breakdown. "They await your signal, as always." She pointed to a raised platform in the corner of the hall where six young women sat with various instruments resting against their silken-clad laps. They were all looking expectantly in my direction.

"Oh," I said, feeling doltish. What in the hell was wrong with me? Brain tumor. Had to be. I raised my hands and clapped twice. Immediately the hall was filled with the opening notes of a single harp. When the others joined in, I was enthralled anew with the music, which seemed to me an intoxicating mixture of Gaelic melody and Partholonian magic. Unexpectedly, I felt my eyes tear up at the lilting sadness of the song, and I had to fight the urge to curl up for a good cry.

Okay, something was REALLY wrong.

I'm not a crier. I mean it. Weak women who dissolve into tears make my ass hurt.

The clattering of plates brought my fragmented attention back to the table. Something chicken-like and dripping with a buttery garlic sauce was being placed before me. As the smell wafted over me, I had to press my lips together and swallow hard.

I grabbed the arm of a startled servant. "Take this away and bring me…" I spoke through clenched teeth as I struggled to think of something that sounded like it might be palatable. Remembering the BRAT rule (upset stomach = Banana, Rice, Applesauce, Toast) from my college stint as a hospital unit secretary, I brightened and released my vise-like grip. "Rice! Bring me some plain white rice."

She blinked in surprise. "Just rice, my Lady?"

"Uh, and some warm bread," I added with an attempt at a smile.

"Yes, my Lady."

She hurried off and I looked up to meet my husband's worried gaze. Before he could begin the interrogation, I began chirping questions, merrily attempting to change the subject.

"So, fill me in—I want to hear everything." I sipped my herbal tea, willing my stomach to stay still. "Are the people all settled into Guardian and Laragon Castles? Did you have any luck tracking the Fomorian survivors?"

"Rhea, I sent weekly reports keeping you apprised of our actions."

"I know, love, but they were just the bare facts. I want to hear the *details*." I smiled my thanks to the servant who deposited a plate of warm white rice before me.

"As you wish," He took a deep breath and, through bites of his nauseatingly delicious-looking food, he began a summary of the past months. "Because the work crews had already cleaned and repaired both castles, settling the new inhabitants was actually simply accomplished..."

While ClanFintan talked, I kept an attentive look on my face as I gingerly forced small spoonfuls of rice into my resisting mouth, sipping tea between chews.

"...so the settling of Laragon went smoothly, and we have Thalia and the rest of the Muse Incarnates to thank for that. Many of the students who were near graduation volunteered to stay at Laragon, helping to get the new warriors and their families established." He smiled. "I believe several of the young disciples of the Muse will not be returning to their Goddess's temple."

Laragon Castle was situated near the great Temple of the Muse, which was really a Partholonian version of an all-female university. Exceptional young women from all over Partholon were chosen to be educated there by the nine Incarnate Goddesses of the Muse. Women who had been educated at the Muse's temple were the most highly revered women in Partholon. No wonder the warriors had little trouble settling into Laragon.

ClanFintan's face became troubled as he continued. "But the women who were to settle Guardian Castle, at first, were noticeably uneasy about living there, which is why I decided to delay the departure of our troops for several weeks. It is only natural, after the atrocities committed at Guardian Castle, for the new inhabitants to feel unusually vulnerable."

His words sent a shiver down my spine, and I remembered all too well the atrocities to which he referred. Shortly after my arrival in Partholon, a race of vampire-like humanoids called Fomorians began an attempt to subjugate and destroy the people of this world. Perhaps the most horrible aspect of their invasion was that the male Fomorians were capturing, raping and impregnating human females. The human females, in turn, gave birth to mutated creatures that were more demonic than human. I shuddered as a "birthing" scene I had witnessed, through the power of Epona sending me on a spirit journey, replayed in my head. Suffice it to say that the human mother didn't survive the birth. Fomorians considered human women as disposable living incubators for their spawn.

Though the Fomorians had destroyed Laragon Castle and its inhabitants, the attack had been quick, and the end came suddenly. Worse had happened at Guardian Castle. It was there that the Fomorians had infiltrated Partholon months before we were aware of their invasion. It was at Guardian Castle that they made their headquarters, and there that so many women endured the horrors of repeated rape until impregnation. It was also there that the women were housed until Fomorian young clawed from their swollen bodies.

"I am grateful you stayed until the new women of Guardian Castle felt secure." And, for the zillionth time I sent up silent thanks to Epona that the Fomorians had been defeated, and ironically enough, for the smallpox epidemic that helped weaken them and led to their annihilation.

"I knew you would have expected no less." His eyes were warm pools.

"You're my hero," I sighed romantically.

"As is only fitting," he verbally sparred with me, relaxing as I acted more like myself.

Too bad it was an act. I forced myself to swallow another spoonful of the bitter-tasting rice.

ClanFintan continued with his report. "Tracking the surviving Fomorians was more difficult than seeing Guardian Castle settled." His voice became grim. "During our search, we found many human women. As their captors died, or fled, they left clusters of pregnant women in their wake." He shook his head grimly. "Some had been infected with the pox, and were so weakened they died quickly. To those who survived and were still within the first months of their pregnancies, Carolan administered his potion. The potion worked every time, causing the women to miscarry, but almost half of those women perished during the ordeal." His jaw clenched. "There was little Carolan could do for the women we did not find until they were well along in their pregnancies. He could only dull their pain and ease their passing." ClanFintan's gaze shifted to find the Healer, and he lowered his voice. "It was hard for him to bear, Rhea, this inability to save so many."

My gaze followed his, and I noticed new lines around Carolan's expressive eyes, and the way he constantly touched Alanna, almost with desperation, like she might fade away from him if he didn't stay physically connected to her.

"I'll make sure Alanna has plenty of *free* time." I winked suggestively.

"That will help him." His warm eyes locked with mine. "I, too, was hoping my wife would make some *free* time—" he mimicked my wink "—for me."

"Well, it just so happens that I know your wife." I tried for a sexy purr, but a wave of nausea threw my timing off. "And, uh, she assured me— Oh, shit!"

Leaning over the side of my chaise (fortunately, the opposite side from which ClanFintan faced me), I heaved and like an explosive volcano spewed a mixture of white rice and herbal tea all over the marble floor, and (unfortunately) a young servant who didn't leap out of the way quickly enough.

I knew the hall had gone very still, but I was busy sucking air and wiping my mouth. I couldn't seem to tear my eyes from my puke. Lots and lots of little white kernels all splattered across the floor (and the maiden). They looked…they looked disturbingly like something familiar…like, oh, no! Maggots!

And I projectile vomited all over Victoria and Carolan as they rushed to my side.

"Oh! I'm s-so sorry!" I stuttered and shook, trying to blink thick tears from my eyes. For some ridiculous reason I thought I should stand up, and immediately the hall began to gray around the edges; it was almost impossible to breathe. I had no control over my body as my knees gave way.

"I have you, Rhea!" Victoria's voice penetrated the fog and I realized she had somehow beat ClanFintan to my side, because she was laying me gently back onto my chaise.

My eyes fluttered open, but I still couldn't catch my breath. I was dying. Puking myself to death in front of everyone. God, what a tragically unattractive way to die…

Then ClanFintan was beside me, reaching down to lift me into his arms, and I was doubly terrified by the pallor of his usually bronze face.

"No, wait, I have to tell Vic…" My voice sounded eerie and somehow detached from my body. I reached blindly out, and the centaur huntress grasped my hand with her own puke-spattered one.

"Just love him," I whispered, noting how her eyes widened. "Who cares what people say—who cares about the age thing." I clung to her hand when she tried to pull away. If I was dying she was damn sure going to listen. The terminally ill have certain inalienable rights. Or, perhaps, death just scares most people shitless, so they listen to the soon-to-be-dearly-departed. Whichever was the case, I was going to get said what needed to be said. *Then* I could continue puking myself to death in peace. "You need him. Stop running and accept the amazing gift you have been given."

She had grown very quiet, and her expression didn't change. The only external reaction she showed was that her usually proud, erect shoulders suddenly drooped, like she couldn't keep them lifted a moment longer.

I squeezed her hand before freeing it and then let my sticky head fall onto ClanFintan's chest. "I feel so sick." I murmured.

"Healer, follow me," his stone voice ordered as he strode from the silent hall.

"She has been like this for more than two seven-days." Alanna sounded like she was tattling, and I threw her an ugly look, which didn't stop her. "Except, never before has she been sick in public."

"I'm feeling better already. I just needed to lie down." Of course, I hadn't needed to puke in front of my people (and on my friends), have my husband rush to my side, pick me up and practically run (well, gallop) to my bedchamber with Carolan and Alanna following closely behind. I groaned. "I've ruined the celebration." Before she could say anything, I interrupted. "Alanna, you have to go back to the hall and reassure everyone that I just have some kind of…of…" I looked at Carolan for help, but he didn't offer any medical terminology. "…Of stomach distemper-thing, and now that Carolan and my husband have returned, I'll be fine."

Alanna opened her mouth to argue, but I played my trump card.

"I need you to do this for me. The people will be so worried."

"Of course." Her tight smile said she knew my tactics. "But I will return as soon as the people have been reassured." She kissed me quickly on my damp forehead, then patted ClanFintan's arm in a motherly gesture before kissing Carolan on the lips and whispering, "Please, my darling, find out what is amiss with her."

"I heard that!" I yelled weakly at her departing back. She ignored me.

My attention shifted back to the two males who were watching me like I was an egg ready to hatch.

"Why did you not send word of your illness?" ClanFintan sounded more hurt than angry.

I started to protest that I was really okay, but his expression told me I was definitely done playing that game.

"I didn't want you to worry. And I guess I thought if I didn't admit something was wrong, nothing would be wrong."

His grunt said he thought I was a moron.

"I will need to examine you, Rhea." Carolan's voice was soothing.

"Ok-k-kay..." My voice shook.

"ClanFintan, I will call for you when I have completed my examination." Now Carolan was the general giving orders as if he expected to be obeyed.

"I prefer to stay with Rhea." My husband sounded stubborn.

Before I could chime in, Carolan spoke with the quiet surety of experience. "It would be better for her if she had some privacy. Trust me, my friend." His hand grasped the centaur's muscular shoulder and their eyes locked.

ClanFintan broke their gaze first. Abruptly, he leaned down and kissed me on my damp forehead. "I will be just outside. Call if you have need of me." His exit was quick.

I tried to smile bravely at Carolan. "Thanks. I love him, but this whole thing is very awkward for me, and, well, you were right about my need for privacy."

He returned my smile as he sat next to me, making the huge down-filled mattress fluff up.

"This is an interesting sleeping arrangement you have here." His gesture took in the enormous mattress that rested directly on the floor of my spacious bedchamber.

"Being married to someone who is part horse demands some creative solutions to things you wouldn't otherwise think about. I mean, really, how the heck does a horse comfortably fit into a traditional bed? And *I*, the Beloved of Epona, certainly need more than a pile of sawdust or a bale of straw." I patted the mattress. "This works for us."

"Alanna says you have a unique name for it."

"A marshmallow." I grinned. "It's named after a sweet, sticky mound of white fluff from my old world that can be eaten as a dessert." Carolan, Alanna and ClanFintan knew my true identity. Sometimes it was a relief to be able to relax and make references to my prior life without worrying about betraying myself. Relaxation, I suddenly realized, must have been Carolan's reason for getting me to chatter. Being on the receiving end of his much renowned bedside manner was a new and not totally unpleasant experience.

"So, now that I'm not hyperventilating anymore, what's next?"

"Nothing too horrible," he reassured me. "Just some questions first, then I will examine you." The confidence in his voice soothed my puke-frazzled nerves. "Tell me how long you have been feeling ill."

I started to reply with a quip, but he held up his hand, cutting off my words.

"You must be honest, Rhea. If you are not totally truthful, I will have a difficult time being of any aid to you."

I sighed. "Almost three weeks, or, as Alanna would say, three seven-days. It's just been so obvious for the past two weeks that I couldn't hide it from her." I shared a pretended long-suffering look with him. "You know how nosy she is."

He rolled his eyes as he began feeling the glands in my neck. "You need not tell me how tenacious she can be when it comes to the welfare of those she loves." He began taking my pulse. "How long have you been purging yourself?"

"Purging?" I was confused. Bulimia had never interested me. I've always been strictly an "eat everything in sight and work out like a fiend" girl when it came to weight management.

"Relieving yourself of what you've eaten. Vomiting," he clarified.

"Well, I certainly haven't been doing it on purpose."

"Of course you have not!" He paused in his examination, giving me a shocked look.

For an instant a sarcastic remark rose to my lips, then I reminded myself that he wasn't pretending to be shocked at what my twenty-first century peers would consider a norm. I know it sounds hard to believe, but sometimes I forget I'm no longer in a world where beauty is defined by anorexic, strung-out models with boob jobs.

"Right, well, I've been actually vomiting for a little over a week, but I've been feeling like I could puke any second for almost three weeks." Before he could get confused I added in a teacherly, informative voice, "To puke is to vomit."

"To puke," he pondered as he opened a huge leather bag that seemed to always be with him. "That is an interesting term."

We smiled at each other.

"Have you had any other symptoms besides your stomach upset?" He asked.

"Well," I said hesitantly, "I've been feeling kind of weird and depressed and jumpy." I figured that about covered everything from my emotions being all out of whack to the possible hallucinations last night.

He patted my arm reassuringly as he pulled out of the bag a long, funnel-like object that seemed to be made of construction paper. "Please sit up and breathe deeply," he said, and I complied as he used the funnel as a sort of crude stethoscope.

He appeared okay with what he heard, because he put the funnel-scope away and continued with the examination, gently probing, prodding and looking all over (and within) my body as he questioned me. He asked me everything from what kinds of flowers my maidens had been cutting for the daily arrangements that filled my bedchamber with fragrance, to how often I'd been pooping.

Finally, he finished. Patting my nervously folded hands, he began, "I am very certain you—"

"Have a brain tumor!" My stomach rolled in revolt and I felt my palms dampening.

Carolan chucked. "You have no tumor, Rhea, but you certainly have something within your body now that was not there just a few months ago." His eyes sparkled, and I wanted to choke him until they bulged out of his face.

"A friggin aneurysm. I knew it. Somehow I was exposed to something radioactive when Rhiannon the Bitch traded places with me." I fell back on the pile of pillows, trying unsuccessfully to stop my eyes from filling with tears.

"By the Goddess, Rhea, will you not listen!" Carolan's voice was frustrated but definitely tinged with humor. "You are not dying. You are not ill. You are, quite simply and blessedly, pregnant."

"I'm…I'm…I'm…"

"I estimate you will give birth mid-spring."

"A baby?" I realized I sounded like a dolt, but my mind had literally become mush.

"That would certainly be my experienced diagnosis." He smiled as he collected odds and ends and fed them back into the mouth of his doctor's bag. "A girl," he added.

"A girl? How do you know?" My hands unclasped themselves and crept down to cup my deceptively normal-looking abdomen.

"The firstborn of Epona's Chosen is always a girl child. It is a gift from your Goddess to you and your people."

I felt stunned. Sure, I had missed a period, but I hadn't given it much thought. I'd chalked it up to stress. A new world in a different dimension where mythology lives. Becoming Goddess Incarnate. Battling demonic hordes. Stuff like that was bound to throw off anyone's system a little, to say the least. I noticed that Carolan suddenly seemed in a big rush to leave.

"What's your hurry?" I sounded on the verge of a crying jag, which, at least, now made sense. Hormones.

"Alanna will want to announce the wonderful news to the people. The celebration will continue all night!" I blanched and he laughed. "No, you will not be required to attend, but there will be many toasts to your health and the health of your child." He turned to face me one last time before he opened the door. "Congratulation, Rhea. Let me be the first of many to wish your daughter health and happiness!"

I could hear him telling ClanFintan he could come in now as he rushed past my still worried-looking husband. The centaur approached me, folding his legs and settling fluidly to the floor by my side. His expression was grim as he studied what I realized must be my glazed, Barbie-exposed-to-math-word-problems expression.

"What is it, love? What has happened to you?"

"You!" A semi-hysterical giggle escaped from my lips.

His brow furrowed in concern. "I? I have injured you?"

I reached up and touched his cheek. "You haven't injured me, you've impregnated me."

He blinked twice, his expression blank. Then realization folded over his face.

"A child!" His deep voice resonated with joy. "We are to have a child?"

"Yes…" I knew I sounded reticent, but I had gone from tumor to baby in just a few heartbeats.

ClanFintan took my hands in his, kissing both my palms before leaning down and kissing me softly on my lips.

"Ugh." I pulled away. "I taste like puke."

"I do not care."

"Well, I do."

He pulled back and studied my face. "Rhea, are you not pleased?"

"I'm scared." I blurted out before I took time to think.

His face softened and he pulled me into the warmth of his strong embrace. "Do not be afraid. Epona will always care for her own."

I rested my cheek against the butter-soft leather of his vest and murmured my fear. "I don't want to hurt your feelings or anything, but, well, what am I going to have?"

He remained silent, and I bit my lip. I loved ClanFintan, and I didn't want to cause him pain, but the facts were that he was part horse and he was the father of my child. I couldn't help but be concerned about the meshing of our two gene pools—especially when I would be the one giving birth—in a world without C-sections or epidurals.

"She will have your form, Rhea."

"And what will she have of yours?" I whispered into his chest.

He paused for just a moment, then quietly said, "My heart. She will have my heart."

My arms tightened around him while my eyes filled. "Then she will have everything."

His warm lips briefly pressed against the top of my head. Then he shifted his hold on me so that he had me scooped up in his arms. Rising to his feet in one fluid motion he started toward the door.

"Oh, please don't make me go back there with all that food and all those people." I futilely tried to wipe at speckles that clung to my soggy dress.

"No, I am taking you to your bathing chamber. Tonight I will care for you, and our daughter." He beamed down at me as he shouldered our way through the door and turned down my private hall in the direction of my bathing room.

The temple guards leaped out of his way, saluting me and calling, "Blessings on you and your child, Lady Rhiannon!" as they opened the door to the steamy chamber for us.

For a world that didn't have TV or the Internet, it never failed to surprise me how fast news could travel.

I grinned mischievously at them over ClanFintan's shoulder and winked. "Thanks, guys!" I didn't "know" my guards (yes, I do mean in the biblical sense) as the original Lady Rhiannon had, but I did appreciate them.

"Do not encourage them." ClanFintan chided good-naturedly.

"Soon I'll be too fat and pregnant to get a second look from them."

"Humph," he commented eloquently as he deposited me near the edge of the deep pool.

One of the many benefits of being Goddess Incarnate was that a veritable plethora of overenthusiastic maidens considered it an honor, as well as a duty, to keep me in the lap of ancient luxury. Which meant I had all the best wine, food, clothes, jewels, horses, warriors...on and on, but no television, telephones, computers or cars. In return I had to care for the spiritual health of Epona's people: conduct ceremonies (albeit bare-breasted, which took some getting used to, especially as the weather had begun turning cold), serve as figurehead, you know, do whatever it was my Goddess asked of me to the best of my ex–high school English teacher abilities.

I was pretty sure I'd gotten the best part of the deal, which included having an opulent bathing chamber that was perpetually kept in a state of ready-for-me-to-use.

"Let me help you with that." ClanFintan's deft fingers took over for my pukey ones, which were struggling upside down to unclasp my diamond-encrusted brooch.

"New brooch?" he asked as he studied the mini replica of himself.

"Yes, today is the first time I've worn it. Do you like it?"

"I like that it rests near your breast."

"Talk like that, if I recall correctly, is how I got into this condition." I swatted at him playfully.

"I have suspected your old world wasn't as, shall we say, knowledgeable as our world, and if you think talking impregnated you, then we should—"

"Oaf!" I swatted at him again, causing the once-lovely, now-crusty fabric of my bodice to slide down, exposing the very bosom to which he had been referring. I watched his expression change as he reached one hand out to gently cup my breast.

"You already appear changed. Your breasts are more full, more welcoming." His voice was hypnotic as he framed my rib cage with both of his hands, softly caressing the sides of my weighty breasts with his palms.

Even after being married to him for half of a year, the heat of his body still had the ability to surprise me. A centaur's natural body temperature is several degrees higher than a human's body. ClanFintan's touch was always erotically warm, and, although I knew it was simply the state of his physiology, his heat worked on me like an aphrodisiac.

I shivered in anticipation, pleased the queasy feeling in my stomach had subsided.

"You are chilled..." His sensuous touch was replaced by a matter-of-fact unwinding of the rest of my soiled dress. "Start soaking," he ordered.

"Not very romantic," I muttered, trying to bend seductively and slip out of my teeny thong, but he had already turned toward the shelf near my vanity and was searching, opening bottles and sniffing.

"The vanilla-almond one is in the gold-colored bottle." I called to him over my shoulder as I lowered myself slowly into the clear, bubbling mineral water, and made my way to my favorite rock ledge.

ClanFintan turned back with a triumphant smile, golden bottle in his hands. "I like the scent of this one."

"I know you do—that's why I use it." We grinned at each other.

His hooves clicked on the marble floor as he approached the edge directly across from where I was submerged. In one swift movement, he divested himself of his leather vest, and placed it and the bottle of perfumed soap on the floor.

"Do I need to remind you that you must not speak?"

"Oh!" I blinked in surprise. "No, but, I, uh, didn't—"

"Shh..." He put a finger to his lips.

I closed my mouth, preparing myself for what I knew would come next—the Change. As a High Shaman, ClanFintan had the extraordinary ability to shapeshift from his centaur form. I didn't think it would ever stop amazing me. I watched in awe as his concentration turned within, and I felt a shiver of bittersweet desire. We could only mate as husband and wife if he Changed, thus the fluttering of passion I felt as his chant began. But the Change did not come without cost. He could only maintain a different shape for a temporary amount of time, approximately eight hours, and he was never truly comfortable in any form but his centaur shape. The shapeshifting itself caused him terrible pain, and after he shifted back into his centaur form it left him in a weakened state for hours.

Every time he called the Change so that he could shift into human form, he proclaimed the depth of his love and commitment to me.

His chanting was becoming louder, and I could distinctly hear the magic in the Gaelic-sounding words ClanFintan's velvet voice spoke over and over again. He began lifting both arms, until they were directly over his head, which was flung back. His long hair fell free down his human back, which did nothing to obscure his tensed, quivering muscles. Then it seemed that his skin had begun to sparkle and shimmer as if he was being beamed through a *Star Trek* transporter. His glowing skin rippled, like it was about to liquefy. I knew I should close my eyes and protect them from the blast of light that would come next, but I couldn't pull my gaze from my husband's face. It was set in a grimace of agony. Light burst from him, making my eyes blink and tear even though I closed them in response to the explosion of silver-white brilliance.

I could hear his harsh breathing in the quiet darkness that always seemed so complete after the light of his transformation.

"ClanFintan?" I couldn't help the edge of fear in my voice. It wasn't that I was afraid of his magic, or of his Change. I was afraid of what it cost him, scared that someday he would not recover from the pain.

"I have—" his voice was raspy as he struggled to regain his breath "—told you not to worry so."

I rubbed my eyes, trying to blink away the sunspots that kept me from seeing him.

"I know, but I hate how much it hurts you."

"It is a price I will never regret paying."

My vision cleared and I could see that he was still on his knees, where the Change had caused him to collapse. With one hand he raked his hair out of his sweat-streaked face, with the other he pushed himself slowly up into a standing position. He stood still for a moment, and I knew he was gathering his energy and accustoming himself to this much smaller, less powerful human shape.

Not that he was a small man (in any sense of the word). Actually, he was a beautifully proportioned human male. He was tall and well muscled, and he retained the breadth of shoulder and chest that was so impressive in his true body. His human hips were sleek; his ass and legs were tight and well shaped. As was everything else that protruded from his very naked body. And he did appear quite happy to see me, if you know what I mean.

He raised an eyebrow at me, reminding me of a randy, naked Spock (imagine that!). "Is everything—" he glanced down at his body "—where it should be?"

I felt my breath catch in shock. "You mean things can get moved around when you Change?"

"Of course not." His laughter reassured me, as did the strong, confident way he began striding toward the edge of the pool. "I was simply—how do you put it—*messing at you.*" He attempted to mimic my Oklahoma drawl with his deep, lyrical voice.

"It's messing *with*, not *at*, you silly thing." I flicked some water at him while he bent to pick up the bottle of soap. Then, using the stone steps that led down into the water, he joined me. "And you know I've been trying to get rid of my Okie accent." Thankfully, one of the many things being Epona's Beloved entitled me to was the ability to be eccentric without having the populace question me. Partholon had simply gotten used to the weird way I talked. I'd even heard some servants whispering, "It is more of Epona's touch," after I'd y'all-ed and yep-ed them one too many times.

"Do not lose your accent. I like the long, lazy way you can make words sound."

"Anythin' for you, darlin'," I twanged. And I was serious. A month was a long time, and I was *really* glad he was home. (And doubly pleased that my stomach had quieted enough for me to contemplate doing more than puking.)

"Good." He reached past me and plucked a thick sponge that was resting close to the edge of the pool. He poured a generous amount of thick soap onto it before setting the bottle back on the floor. "Then what I would like you to do for me is to relax and let me care for you." He paused and his eyes slid down to where the water obscured, but did not conceal, my reclining body, "both of you."

His words brought back the reality of my "condition," which effectively silenced me. I numbly let him begin soaping up my shoulders with a slow, circular motion, while I contemplated the fact that I was carrying another life within my body.

ClanFintan stayed silent, letting me think as he brought the soapy sponge down one of my arms, being careful to wash all of the crusty, leftover rice from my hands. Then he followed the same path down my other arm. His touch was soothing, and I felt my numbness dissolve with the last vestiges of the rice. Gently, he slid the slick sponge around my neck and lower, until its softness brushed my sensitized nipples.

"Tell me if I do anything that you find uncomfortable."

"Everything you're doing is just fine." I sounded out of breath.

"Good. Then I will continue." The sponge followed a path down to my thigh, calf and foot, where he set it aside briefly so that he could massage the bottom of my foot. The heat and strength of his touch made me groan with pleasure. "I have not forgotten how much you love having your feet rubbed." He exchanged one foot for the other, and continued his soothing ministrations.

"Thank you, Goddess," I whispered, meaning every syllable of it. There are few things a teacher loves more than a great foot rub (a pay raise, perhaps, but a foot rub is easier to come by—at least it is in Oklahoma).

Too soon he picked up the sponge and lathered his way back up my other leg. By the time he reached my shoulders again I was feeling excessively clean for a woman who was having such dirty thoughts.

Pulling myself up from a reclining to a sitting position, I watched as his eyes caressed my wet, soapy breasts.

"You are a beautiful woman."

"And squeaky clean." I let my body slide forward until my legs were straddling his lap. Wrapping my arms around his neck, I rubbed my breasts against the seductive heat of his chest, loving how my nipples puckered against his skin.

"Alanna better watch out. You make one heck of a bathing assistant."

He replied by devouring my mouth with his, pulling me hard against him. My hands explored the curve of his back and hips, and I felt pleasure thrill through my body at the wonderful textures of his muscles. His familiar taste flooded my senses, and my body felt so hot and wet I couldn't tell where I ended and where he began.

"I've missed you so much, my love." His voice was rough with lust, and the sound of it had desire tugging hot and heavy low in my stomach.

"How could I have forgotten about your heat?" I moaned, and nipped his shoulder.

"Ah, Goddess! I should be gentle with you, but I—"

"Don't be gentle. I promise I won't break."

With a growl of raw desire his hands cupped my butt. He lifted me and in one smooth motion, plunged himself inside me. I met his thrust with my own. I clung to him, sucking and nipping at his tongue. We came together like we were starved for each other, like the month apart had been a lifetime. Our tempo escalated quickly, and before either of us could think about math problems or taxes my orgasm built and exploded as I felt his release pumping heat into me.

Still breathing hard, ClanFintan traded places with me, pulling me onto his lap as he reclined upon my ledge. We clung to each other, allowing our bodies to remember how well we fit together.

"I meant for that to happen after I had bathed, dried and returned you to our marshmallow." I felt his chest vibrate as he spoke.

"I love the way you say marshmallow. You make it sound like it's a magic carpet, something special and mysterious."

"It is special and mysterious to me." He reached down and tapped the end of my nose with his finger. "I have never seen a real marshmallow."

"I should try and figure out a recipe so that I could explain how to make one to the pastry cook. It would be fun to roast them over an open fire."

His eyes widened in shock. "It would certainly take an enormous fire."

"An eatable marshmallow is smaller than my fist. It's just our mattress that's huge." I started to giggle, but I interrupted myself with a rather large and embarrassing belch right into his face. "Oops!" I covered my mouth with my hand. "Sorry, I didn't—"

And I belched again.

"Your stomach?" His concern made me feel somewhat less humiliated.

"I think maybe I should dry off and drink some more of that tea Alanna's been pouring into me." I was feeling a little queasy again.

He easily pulled himself out of the pool, then reached down and lifted me out beside him. We padded wetly over to a pile of thick towels and he began vigorously drying me.

"Hey! You're rubbing off skin!" I squeaked, and grabbed the towel from him.

"I thought you might be chilled out of the water."

"I'm fine, really. You just dry yourself." I was suddenly feeling kind of touchy, like my skin was too sensitive to allow any handling. Hormones were certainly strange things.

"The Change will dry me." His smile said he understood my shift in mood, and that he wasn't offended. I just hoped his patience would last the rest of the nine months. Who knew what else my body was going to do to me?

"Thanks, I—"

"Shh," I hadn't noticed that he had taken several steps from me, and had begun muttering the words that called the Change to him.

I closed my mouth before the "I'm sorry" could escape. Shading my eyes with the end of my towel, I watched as he retransformed. The Change back to his centaur form always seemed to happen more quickly than when he shifted into the alien shape of a human male. His skin glittered and rippled. This time I pressed my eyes closed before the starburst of color. When the light against my closed lids disappeared, I knew it was safe to look (and to talk).

"I have really missed you." The words tumbled from my mouth as I looked up at the magnificent being who was my husband.

"And I you. I was born to love you." He smiled as he came to me, dwarfing me with his size while he encompassed me within the love of his embrace. He held me gently in his massive arms, and looked into my eyes, saying simply, "I am not complete without you. It is good to be home."

I had witnessed enough of this world's magic to know that he spoke the truth. Through some wondrous twist of fate, my Goddess had fashioned him as my mate, even before I was a part of this world.

"Yes," I repeated his words. "It is good to be home."

"Come!" He swept me off my feet and up into his arms

like I weighed no more than a child. (Uh, let me assure you, I weigh more than a child!)

"You know, I really can walk." But my complaint was only halfhearted. I liked the safety I felt in his arms.

"Humor me. I have only just returned."

He kicked the huge door, his hoof ringing dully against the oak like a living doorbell. My warriors immediately pulled it open for us. I noticed how they diverted their eyes from my towel-clad form. No doubt they were trying to avoid a scowl from my husband. But I made a point to wave gaily at them over ClanFintan's shoulder, and was rewarded by their quick grins.

"You spoil them."

"They're adorable. And anyway, you know you have nothing to worry about. It's that other Rhiannon who felt the need to sleep with all of her warriors, and then some."

"I do not believe she did much sleeping."

"You know what I mean." I flicked his shoulder. "As you already are very well aware, I am a faithful wife. Shoot, my middle name's Faithful!"

"I thought your middle name was merlot." His laughter boomed at his own joke.

I blanched. "Don't mention that word." My new aversion to wine must be Epona's way of making sure I didn't pickle my unborn daughter. I supposed I should be grateful—and I would be, as soon as I was purged of this pathetic puking. (Pardon the pun. And the alliteration.)

My chamber had obviously been freshened since we had been gone. The down-filled marshmallow mattress that served as our bed had been made, and a small dinner for two had been set on the table in the alcove that sat before the velvet-curtained glass doors that led to my private garden. I sniffed the air suspiciously, afraid that any wafting aromas would set off my puke reflex. When I didn't catch the scent of anything objectionable, I hesitantly approached the table. My husband's attempt at smothering his chuckle caught my attention.

"What are you laughing at?" I asked.

"I never thought the day would come when you would approach a table of food with trepidation."

My love of a good meal had been a constant source of amusement to my husband. Actually, more than once he has commented that I have the appetite of a centaur Huntress, which somehow is endearing to him.

To me it's less endearing, and more like the reason I force myself to exercise regularly.

"Very funny. Keep in mind I've already puked on one centaur tonight." When I got to the table I breathed a sigh of relief. Alanna's delicate hand and unerring ability to manage me was evident. There was a steaming tureen filled with an almost clear broth that had a light, vaguely chicken-like aroma. A cloth-covered basket held thin pieces of toasted bread and sliced bananas. A pot of hot herbal tea waited invitingly for me to pour. For ClanFintan she had fixed a platter of cheese and cold chicken. Not a scrap of rice or anything that reeked of fried food, spices or (yeesh) dripping butter.

"Alanna is very wise," ClanFintan said as he settled into his chaise and began to happily dig into his chicken.

I ladled myself some broth and nibbled hesitantly at the toast. "Knowing her, she's probably already making baby clothes." He and I smiled at each other.

I sipped the broth slowly, allowing time for my easy-to-upset stomach to accustom itself to food.

"So, you would say the trip was a success?" I asked as I blew at the hot tea.

"Laragon Castle was thriving when we departed. In the spring their fields will once again yield the healing crops and flowers they once did. The reinhabiting of Guardian Castle went well after the women settled in. The new warriors are vigilant." He cleared his throat as if what he was about to say was lodged there uncomfortably. "As we had thought, there were signs that the prior inhabitants had been lax in their duties as watchers and defenders."

It had been a shock when it was discovered that the demonic Fomorians, Partholon's ancient enemy, had broken though the supposedly impenetrable Guardian Castle, which defended the only pass through the mountains. Much speculation had been gossiped about regarding how the invasion had begun. I gave him a curious raise of my eyebrows, prompting him to continue.

"Their weapons were rusted, broken and untended. Tournament fields were overgrown with weeds, proving that no practice in weaponry or those skills needed in warfare had been kept at ready." His frown deepened. "But there was no shortage of wine and ale, and even before we unpacked the supplies brought with us, we found the kitchens were filled to overflowing with stored delicacies."

"So, they ate and drank and that was about it?"

"We also found many *disturbing* paintings depicting…" His voice trailed off.

My curiosity was certainly piqued. My own temple was filled with bigger-than-life-size frescoes of my image clad in not much more than a slip, and that only from the waist down. Not to mention the zillions of cavorting maidens who frolicked seminude (in the paintings and around the temple). I couldn't image what kind of images had shocked a centaur who was so used to the casual nudity and open sexuality of a clearly matriarchal world.

"Okay, give. What was in the pictures?"

"They enjoyed inflicting pain upon one another." I guess my face didn't register much shock (keep in mind, he's never been exposed to MTV, as I, unfortunately, have been), so he continued. "They inflicted pain during sexual acts. And there was evidence that they had been dallying with a dark god."

I had the unnerving feeling that maybe my question to Alanna earlier that day had been prompted by more than a random thought. I swallowed, not particularly liking where this might be taking me, but knowing that I had to follow my goddess-touched instincts. "A dark god? What do you mean?"

He looked as disgusted as he sounded. "Amidst the paintings of their perversions there were drawings that showed the Triple Face of Darkness."

"Wait, I don't understand what you mean. What's a Triple Face of Darkness?"

He lowered his voice, which only heightened my feeling of unease. I mean, we were totally alone. Why was he lowering his voice?

"I do not like to speak of such things. One should not name a dark god without care—even if he is a High Shaman, or the Chosen of a Great Goddess. But as Epona's Beloved you have the right to know exactly what the Fomorians, and the decadence of the Guardian Warriors, allowed to enter Partholon."

"Tell me." I sounded much braver than I felt.

"Pryderi is the Triple Face of Darkness. Ancient stories say that he was once a god, like Cernunnos, only he chose the mountains and the Northlands in which to reign. Legends also say that he was Epona's consort and that she loved him. Then he began to lust for more power—power to subjugate Epona to his will."

I felt the wrongness of Pryderi's attempt to usurp Epona in the depths of my soul. Partholon was a matriarchal world. There were gods who were worshipped as consorts to the goddesses, but their place was definitely secondary. Men were not bullied or repressed in Partholon. They respected the Goddess as birth-giver and creator; therefore, they respected women. Anything else would ultimately destroy the beautiful balance that made Partholon such an incredible place.

"What did Epona do?" I asked, even though my heart already knew the answer.

"The Goddess's anger and hurt were terrible. She cast him from Partholon with such wrath that his aspect fragmented, much like a soul can be shattered if it is too traumatized, which is why the depictions of him show three faces." ClanFintan looked away from me when he said this and I could tell he didn't want to explain further, but I needed to know, so I prompted, "What do the faces look like?"

He sighed deeply. "One face has nothing but eyes. The mouth has been seared closed. The rest of it is featureless. Another has only a gaping, fanged maw, terrible to behold. The eyes of that face are hollow holes. The third is unbelievable in its beauty. That face is said to look exactly as he did before he betrayed Epona."

I sipped my tea, trying not to notice that my hand was shaking. "And there are people in Partholon who worship him?"

"No. Or at least if there are they are only in the most obscure parts of the nation."

"But Guardian Castle isn't an obscure part of Partholon."

"No, it's not. But the people there had been corrupted, whether by the Fomorians or by greed and sloth before they infiltrated the castle—the sequence of events have never been entirely clear. What is apparent is that Pryderi had been influencing them for some time." He touched my cheek reassuringly. "Don't worry, love. People must be open to Pryderi's poisonous whisperings for him to gain a hold on their souls, and Epona's Partholon will not so easily open itself again to such darkness. We need not fear that the new Guardian Warriors will forget their duties."

"Good." Purposefully I shook off the creepy feeling discussing Pryderi had begun to give me. "So, you think my idea is going to work?"

He smiled. "Yes, your orders to make Guardian Castle a working school to train warriors resonated with its new inhabitants."

"Vigilance and education—always an excellent mix."

"It is certain that Guardian Castle will not fail Partholon again," he said soberly.

"You don't think enough Fomorians survived to attack us again, do you?" Those creatures were evil, vampiric beings that belonged in hell. Yes—the thought of them plotting to come back through the mountain pass Guardian Castle had been built to guard definitely made my skin crawl.

"I believe the pox and their losses in battle weakened

them to the point of annihilation, but we must remain prepared for their resurgence."

"You think they took pregnant women back over the pass with them?" I asked, horrified.

"I pray they did not."

Which really didn't seem like a positive answer to me.

"So we stay prepared and keep our eyes open."

"Yes," he acknowledged.

"Okay." I yawned and his ears pricked (not literally).

"When your body tells you to rest, you must rest," said the father-to-be.

"For a change, I won't argue with you." I stood, stretching like a cat. Even after the rather morbid dark god subject, the warm broth and tea, and the absence of worrying that I might have a fatal illness, had made me feel more than ready for a long night's rest. Not to mention the wonderful orgasm.

"Perhaps your not arguing with me will be a nice side effect of your pregnancy," he said as he followed me to our bed.

"I wouldn't count on it," I retorted through another yawn.

He folded himself down onto our mattress first, then I settled into a position curled comfortably against him. I realize it should be an awkward pairing, a being who was half horse, half man, sleeping with a human woman, but it wasn't. No matter how I lay, one of his hands would find the small of my back, or the curve of my leg, and rub gentle circular patterns over my skin. His warm caress was like a sleeping pill. I loved that his touch could lull me to sleep. My eyes were already closed when his voice interrupted my foggy thoughts.

"It surprised me that you did not use the Magic Sleep to visit me." He paused, then added, "Or did you come to me, and I failed to feel your presence?"

"No…" His question brought me fully awake. "I have not had the dream-thing since your battle with Nuada."

Except for a quick grunt of acknowledgment, he stayed silent. I knew we were both thinking back to that terrible last battle when Nuada, the leader of the Fomorians, almost killed ClanFintan. I had been knocked unconscious, and my Goddess had called my spirit free from my body so that I could distract Nuada. ClanFintan had killed the creature, causing the Fomorians to react in confused panic, and the tide of the battle to turn in our favor. Before then, Epona had used my dreams to call me out of my body and send me on what amounted to spiritual reconnaissance trips to spy on our enemies and taunt them into falling into our traps.

But since the Fomorians had been vanquished, I had not been called by Epona to go on any nighttime spirit trips, even when I had tried to will myself on one after ClanFintan left. Nor had I heard the whisper of her voice, which I had become strangely accustomed to hearing, until today when she had breathed into my mind the words *You are not playing, Beloved.* It took hearing her voice again for me to realize how much her silence had bothered me.

"I tried to send my spirit out of my body to visit you, but it didn't happen. I asked Epona to let me visit you. It was such an easy thing before—I even traveled so much that I got really tired of it."

"Yes, I remember." I felt him nod his head.

"And she hasn't been talking to me, either," I said in a small voice.

"Rhea, your Goddess would not leave you. You must believe that."

"I don't know, ClanFintan. I don't really know anything

about this Goddess Incarnate stuff. Remember, I'm not Rhiannon."

"Yes, and I thank your Goddess daily that you are not." His voice was firm. The truth was, no one had liked Rhiannon. Okay, more accurately, most people who had known her had loathed her, which was—at first—an almost constant source of irritation to me. Plus, it was confusing to look like someone who had evolved into such a different kind of person.

"Sometimes I wonder if I just imagined that I was meant to be Epona's Chosen."

"Do you think so little of Epona?" He didn't sound angry, just questioning.

"No." My answer came easily. "I've felt her presence and experienced her power."

"Then it must be yourself of whom you think so little."

I couldn't answer that. I had always believed I was a strong woman with a healthy ego and excellent self-esteem. But maybe my husband was right. Maybe I needed to look inside myself for doubt and weakness, and not Epona.

Could that be part of why Rhiannon and I were so different? I knew self-doubt could be destructive and life altering, but wasn't some self-reflection healthy? Had Rhiannon become so spoiled and willful that she was immune to any kind of self-questioning? Mix that with the power that went along with being Epona's Beloved and maybe, like Shakespeare's Julius Caesar, she had become "as a serpent's egg which hatched, would as his kind grow mischievous." Had Epona done what Brutus contemplated, and by switching me with Rhiannon, smashed her shell before her hatched evilness could destroy Partholon?

Or was I just letting the useless literature that tended to clutter my English teacher brain freak me out?

"Rest now." Once again his hand began a hypnotic caress, and ClanFintan's familiar touch helped to quiet my jabbering mind. "Your Goddess will answer your doubts."

"I love you," I murmured as a wave of weariness closed my eyelids and I fell softly into a deep sleep.

I was nibbling Godiva dark chocolates while I lounged on a down-filled, violet-colored divan, which was situated in the middle of a field of waving wheat. At the end of the divan sat Sean Connery (dressed in 007-era black tie). My feet were in his lap, and with one strong, firm hand he rubbed erotic swirls across my instep, and with the other he held open a book of poetry entitled Why I Love You. *As he read to me in his sexy Scottish burr, he kept glancing at me with looks of undisguised adoration…*

…And I was suddenly sucked out of my fabulous dream and through the ceiling of Epona's Temple.

"Whoa! Feeling sick!" My spirit voice held a familiar ghostly resonance and I gulped the night air. The rush of exhilaration I felt as I realized my Goddess was once again directing my spirit warred with the revolution in my stomach. My spirit hung over the middle of Epona's Temple, remaining very still while I got my bearings and reaccustomed myself to the Magic Sleep—which wasn't actually sleep at all, but the traveling of my soul, and was therefore exceptionally magical.

As my vertigo receded, I was able to relax and enjoy the incredible view. The moon was almost full, and its clean silver light kissed the walls of the temple until they seemed to come alive, glowing with an inner blush of illuminated marble.

Below me I could see that the feast must be coming to a

close. Sleepy shapes moved in groups of twos, threes and fours, and were stumbling a little amidst good-natured jesting and merriment as they emerged from the front entrance of the temple, heading back to their neat homes outside the temple walls. I smiled as several of the pairs seemed to have a hard time moving out of the shadows, and when they did continue on their way home, their arms remained entwined suggestively around one another.

I guess my people had been inspired to emulate my condition.

As I continued to play spiritual voyeur, I noticed a centaur couple standing apart from the departing crowd, some way from the path taken by the other people. My body drifted in their direction, until I was hovering above the female's back—far enough above her that my presence was not noticed, but not so far that I could not easily see that the two centaurs below me were my friends, Victoria and Dougal.

I could not see Victoria's face, and I could not hear what was being said, but I could see that Dougal was speaking, and that his words held rapt the Huntress's attention. (I realize I should not be eaves-watching, but, well, my spirit body wasn't moving away—which gave me a great excuse to pry.) As I watched, Victoria held up one of her hands and pressed a finger against Dougal's lips, stopping his speech. Then she stepped forward, and in one graceful movement, she rested her head against his shoulder and nodded once, yes.

The radiance in Dougal's face made the light of the moon appear sallow in comparison as he wrapped his lover within his arms.

I grinned, thinking that I couldn't wait to tell Alanna that whatever had been keeping Dougal and Vic apart appeared to be totally fixed.

Slowly, my spirit form began moving forward, leaving my friends their privacy and me a happy knot in my throat. I traveled in the night's sky toward the road, which led past the western ridge of the temple plateau. Once over the ridge, I picked up speed and began moving with purpose toward a tidy-looking home that was situated north of the road amidst a rolling field of well-tended grapevines. The main house was flanked by a sturdy barn with a matching corral, as well as another large structure, which was probably used for the fermenting and storage of wine (may-the-Goddess-bless-them-and-keep-them-till-I-give-birth-and-regain-my-love-for-the-fruit-of-the-vine).

For an instant I hovered directly over the house, then the bottom fell away beneath me and I dropped through the thick thatched roof.

"I wish you would warn me before you do that," I mumbled to my Goddess, but my grumbling stopped as I beheld the sight beneath me.

I was floating near the ceiling of a nice-size bedchamber that was lit by what must have been hundreds of brilliant white candles. A large bed sat against a windowed wall, and an intricately carved wardrobe and matching vanity had been pushed against another wall. Small stools and tables hugged the other two walls—all of the furniture was covered with soft, draped material and pools of lighted candles.

Women clustered below me, surrounding a naked female, who was standing, but leaning heavily against the top of a cushioned chaise lounge, much like the ones we used at the temple. The naked woman was obviously very pregnant. Her head was bowed, and her eyes were screwed shut in con-

centration. I watched as her ripe stomach rippled and her breathing became more pronounced.

As I observed the scene beneath me, I realized that the other women were a single, focused unit. One woman gently pressed against the laboring woman's lower back with the palm of her hand. Another woman crouched before her, breathing in concert with each of her panting breaths. Two women fanned the air so that a light breeze continually bathed the laboring woman. The other women either hummed or sang softly.

My body drifted closer, and the woman's contraction ended. Instantly, her head came up, and I was amazed to see a satisfied smile curve her full lips. She wiped a loose strand of damp hair from her face.

"It is almost time!" Her voice was joyous, not filled with the pain and strain I had expected.

Cheers and laughter greeted her announcement.

A tall, handsome woman approached the soon-to-be mother, offering her a sip from a goblet. Another woman, this one a teenager, wiped her brow with a thick cloth. All of the women were smiling, as if they were taking part in an event filled with such wonder that it was impossible to contain within them, and the happiness came spilling out of their bodies.

"Help me into position..." The pregnant woman's voice was soft, but it carried throughout the room. Three of the older women stepped forward. One woman knelt before her. The other two supported her on either side as she moved into a squatting position. The next contraction took hold of her body. I could see her muscles tense as she took a deep breath and began pushing.

The women surrounding the group formed a circle, clasping each other's hands while they hummed a wordless tune, which reminded me of something Loreena McKennitt would sing.

"I see the head!"

The woman's bulging belly relaxed for just an instant, then she drew an even deeper breath and bore down again.

After another round of concentrated pushing a wet, writhing form slipped from between her legs and was caught deftly by the waiting woman.

"Your daughter is born!" the matron cried.

And the other women caught up the cheer.

"Welcome, young one!"

I found my voice somewhere between my tears, and I echoed their joyous cry. Only occasionally can my presence be sensed when I'm on a spirit journey, so I was surprised and delighted when the new mother's head snapped up in response to the sound of my ethereal voice. Her eyes glistened through tears of happiness and I felt the change in my spirit body that told me my hovering form had become visible to her.

"Epona's Beloved has witnessed my daughter's birth!" Her tired voice was rapturous.

The other women began laughing and clapping—some even started an impromptu dance, twirling and spinning with their hands painting intricate patterns in the air. I found their joy infectious, and as the women cleaned the newborn and the mother, I felt my spirit body moving in time to their song of new life.

And a thought struck me. The miracle of birth was and should always be a moment of empowerment for all women—as it had been in the scene below me. Perhaps this ancient world had lessons it could teach the modern one from which I came. C-sections and epidurals should be blessings to women, but I suddenly wondered if they had become a means from which to steal the magic of the power of birth away from a generation of mothers.

As this thought formed in my mind, I could feel my spirit body begin rising. The new mother's head lifted from its resting place and she waved at my departing form.

My heart felt full and at peace as I floated contentedly back to the temple, and down through the ceiling of my bedchamber. As my spirit rejoined my body and I fell back into a deep sleep, Rest now, my Beloved, and know that I am always with you…*whispered through my mind.*

4

Morning peered a bit too intently through a gap in the thick drapes that covered the floor-to-ceiling windows leading to my private flower garden.

"Uhf," I muttered, just about to pull the covers over my head when I noticed a movement and looked across the room to see Alanna and Victoria sitting on my chaise watching me with bright eyes and wide grins.

I blinked and rubbed my eyes, hoping they were figments of my not yet awakened imagination.

They did not disappear. Actually, their annoyingly wide grins became wider.

"What are you two doing?" I grumped, glaring at my guests and running my tongue over my lips. My mouth tasted like the bottom of a birdcage.

I am not a morning person. Never have been—never want to be. As a matter of fact, I am vaguely distrustful of people who bound out of bed early like demented puppies. It's barbaric to wake up before 9:00 a.m.

"We are here to wish you joy at the blessed news of your daughter!" Alanna chirped.

"Yes, we tried to wait for you to awaken, but it is almost midmorning and we could not wait any longer!" Even Victoria's lovely voice sounded shrill this morning. "And," she added shyly, "I have some news I wanted to share with you."

"You and Dougal are getting married," I said as I reached for a long, silky nightshirt that lay across the bottom of the bed. I pulled it over my head in time to see Victoria's startled-sparrow expression.

"How…"

Sheepishly, I gave my standard answer, which covered everything. "Epona."

"Ohhh," the two of them said together, nodding their heads in unison.

"I think it's wonderful, Vic. You two are going to be great for each other." I winked at Alanna, who giggled in response as I added, "And it'll be nice to see poor Dougal smile more often. He was one miserable centaur after you dumped him."

It was hard to believe, but Victoria, Ms. Sure of Herself Huntress, actually blushed, which made her look shy and girl-like.

"I brought your tea, Rhea." Alanna offered me a steaming mug of fragrant tea. I took it and perched on the chaise across from them.

"Thanks." I blew at it and sipped.

"Your words forced me to listen," the Huntress explained slowly. "I finally really listened to what he had been trying to get me to hear for quite some time. He does love me. Me." Her face was radiant. "He does not wish I was younger. He does not want me to change and be a mate who stays close to his hearth. He understands that my position as Lead Huntress is, and will continue to be, my life." The happiness that suffused her face made my breath catch. "He simply wants me."

"Uh, Vic," I said. "That's what Alanna and I have been trying to tell you for ages. I guess I should have tossed my cookies on you sooner."

This obviously reminded Alanna of the original purpose of their visit. "A daughter!" she shouted joyfully.

"A child! What a blessing," Victoria chimed in.

"You two can quit grinning at me now. You're making me nervous."

Two quick knocks sounded against my door.

"Come in!" I commanded. Three silken-clad maidens rushed into the room, carrying trays laden with what looked suspiciously like breakfast. All three of them began gushing at once.

"Congratulations, my Lady!"

"We are so very pleased!"

"The news is joyous!"

When I had first arrived in this world the general populace had treated me like a person who should be revered and honored, literally placed on a pedestal. The people who were close to me and used to dealing with Rhiannon on a daily basis treated me like I was a live bomb. They handled me carefully, but acted as if they expected me to explode at any moment into a goddess-level tantrum. It had taken a lot of consistent effort to convince the people I came in contact with on a regular basis that I had changed (unfortunately, I couldn't tell them I was literally a different person). Although it made me happy that over the past six months I had been able to coax my maidens into being at ease around me, this morning their familiar affection was making my head hurt. I felt dizzy as they milled around me, touching me reverentially after they set out my morning meal.

"Thanks, girls." I tried to smile at them. "You may leave now."

"Yes, my Lady!" They melted into graceful curtsies. As they scampered to the door, I heard one of them whisper to the other, "Our Lady is *not* a morning person."

"They give me a headache," I said after the door closed.

"They adore you," Alanna corrected me.

"They still give me a headache," I grumped.

"Eat something. It will improve your humor," Alanna said.

"We hope," Victoria added.

I wrinkled my nose at her, then shifted my gaze to the food. There was a lovely fresh-fruit salad, some bran muffins that looked like they were still warm from the oven, thin sliced bread that had been toasted to a golden brown, as well as another pot of my herbal tea and pitchers filled with cold water and milk.

"I don't know if I can eat." My stomach lurched dangerously.

"Try the toast first, then eat the bananas that are in the

fruit salad. I directed the cook to bake these particular muffins because they are simple and healthful. Many times the key to controlling the sickness in the first months of pregnancy is to discover what soothes the mother's stomach," she lectured in her musical voice.

I took a deep breath and picked up a piece of toast. After a sniff I started to nibble. My stomach stayed inside my body, which I took to be a good sign.

"Actually, the muffins are from a centaur recipe," Vic said as she grabbed one off the platter and broke it open.

"Do centaurs go through this sickness thing when they get pregnant?" I asked Vic. As always my curiosity was piqued by these incredibly interesting beings.

"No." She smiled at me apologetically. "But we carry our young within us through four full seasons."

My eyes flew to Alanna. "That doesn't mean I'll have to—does it?" I sounded panicky (because I felt decidedly panicky).

"No," Alanna reassured me, and I let myself breathe again. "ClanFintan only mates with you while he is in his human form."

"Your gestation and birth will follow the same rules as any other human female's would," Vic added.

Her words reminded me of last night's spirit journey and I felt a smile spread over my face.

"Epona let me witness a birth last night during the Magic Sleep." I explained to my friends. "It was amazing."

"It is truly a blessing." Alanna beamed at me.

"A wondrous miracle," Vic said through a mouthful of centaur muffin.

"I really am hap—"

Without warning my stomach revolted. I turned my head in time to miss my friends and spew semi-chewed toast and herbal tea all over the floor.

"Oh, yuck." I wiped my mouth with a shaky hand, looking desperately at Alanna as she hurried to my side. "Are you sure I'm not dying?"

"I am sure," she said as she poured some water from a pitcher into a goblet and offered it to me.

I drank gratefully, rinsing the nasty taste from my mouth.

"Come along." Alanna pulled me to my feet. "You will feel better when you have bathed and dressed." She handed me a muffin and my mug of tea. "ClanFintan told me that he could be found around the temple grounds overseeing the building of the new centaur quarters, and checking the winter supplies."

"I have business near the new quarters, too." Vic gave me a quick hug, then she wrinkled her nose. "You smell, Rhea."

"Thanks for mentioning it." I purposely breathed heavily in her direction, and she retreated hastily to the door. "I will see you after have recovered and returned to your goddess-like self," she threw over her shoulder.

"You may have to wait till spring for that!" I yelled at her hind end.

I turned back to catch the surreptitious smile Alanna was trying to cover with a cough. "You know," she said, "the ill feeling usually only lasts for a small part of a pregnancy. And," she continued, ignoring my malevolent look, "I have noticed that women who are very ill in the beginning have the healthiest, happiest of babies."

"Well, I suppose that's something." I was still grumping,

but it did make me feel better. I sniffed at the muffin in my hand, and realized I suddenly felt hungry. Taking a bite, I was happily surprised by the wonderful, nutty taste that suffused my mouth. "Do you think there's a limit on how often a pregnant woman can puke in one day?" I asked hopefully as we headed down my hall to the bathing chamber.

"No," Alanna replied brightly.

5

"Brr!" I pulled the folds of my ermine-lined cloak closer, glad I had chosen to dress in my riding clothes—butter-smooth leather breeches, lace-up leather shirt and knee-high boots, complete with stars carved into their soles, so that wherever I walked I left behind beautiful footprints. It's seriously good to be Goddess Incarnate. "It's really getting cold." Alanna and I walked side by side through the rear courtyard, which was situated between the stables and the temple proper. The day was misty and damp, which only added to the chill in the air (and the frizz in my hair).

"Congratulations to you, Lady Rhiannon!"

"Blessings upon you and your daughter, my Lady!"

Everyone who passed us shouted well wishes. It was

like being wrapped in a thick blanket of care and warmth and love…

…It was suffocating, and it was making my headache return. Although Alanna had been right, I did feel better after bathing and dressing (and eating three delicious muffins).

The new centaur quarters would be situated on the northern side of the temple, just to the east of the stables, but still well within the temple walls. As I had learned months ago, Epona was a warrior goddess, so her temple was built in a fashion that reflected the priorities of protection and defense. The temple walls were beautiful, but they were also thick and high. The grounds around Epona's Temple were well manicured and maintained, but they were also kept clear of any obstruction that could aid an attacking army—as was evidenced when the Fomorian army attempted unsuccessfully to overrun the temple, and we had to battle for our lives on the cleared grounds surrounding it.

I shook off the unpleasant memory, and looked around at the focused energy before us. Centaurs and humans were hard at work cutting and fitting stone. The skeleton of the new building was already clearly visible, even through the maze of bamboo-rigged scaffolding that seemed to be everywhere. It gave me a feeling of timelessness to watch the construction of this marble edifice, like I was being afforded a glimpse into Caesar's Rome and the building of the Forum.

"It's amazing how quickly it is taking shape." I confided to Alanna in a whisper. "Without the help of technology, I would have thought that a structure like this would take decades to build."

"We do not have your old world's *technology*—" she struggled over the pronunciation of the alien word "—but we do have those who are linked with stone, as well as the Sidetha."

I gave her a startled look. "What do you mean by linked? And what the hell is a Sidetha?"

Alanna laughed. "The Sidetha are a race of miners. They live in the far northeastern part of the Tier Mountains, which is where the most exquisite marble can be found. Epona's Temple is made of marble that comes from the mines of Sidetha."

"Huh. I had no idea."

"They are a shy, secretive people who rarely leave their caves."

"Huh," I said again, thinking that except for being shy they sounded a lot like Tolkien's dwarves. "What did you mean the linked with stone thing? Is that why the Sidetha are such good miners?"

"Well, I suppose some of the Sidetha could be linked with stone, but in general I think they are just experienced miners—it's their life. No, I mean that some people in our world have an affinity for certain animals or spirits or elements. For instance, you have an affinity for horses—especially the mare chosen by Epona as her equine incarnation."

"Okay, I understand that." Epi and I shared a bond that went beyond normal human–horse relationships. I nodded at her to continue.

"It can be the same for spirits. ClanFintan is a great Shaman, which means he has a special link with the spirit world. He can touch the spirit world in a much more intimate fashion than you or I can. It also enables him to transform his physical shape—as you know only too well."

My hand lifted to caress my (relatively) flat stomach, and we shared a knowing girlfriend smile.

"Sometimes people are gifted with an affinity for the elements. On the Centaur Plains humans who can hear the call of hidden water are revered. They have an affinity for the water element, and always know the perfect spot in which to dig a well. Our blacksmiths feel a special link with metal. Very often, women who have gifts in music or dance can touch and mold the wind with their spirits and have an affinity for the spirit of flame."

"So some people feel something special for stone?" I asked.

"Yes, but usually the people who are linked to stone are also linked to the earth itself. They are attuned to the land and everything that it produces. Some of these earth-linked people have special talents in the carving and shaping of stone. They dedicate their lives to the art of masonry. Through them the shape hiding within the stone lives."

"And we have one of these people working for us?" I squinted at the workers, wondering what a stone-linked person would look like.

"Yes, he traveled deep into the mines of the Sidetha to find the perfect stones for the new construction and now he has returned here with it where he will remain for the duration of the building. I would have presented him to you sooner, but you have not been feeling well."

"Tell me about it," I muttered. "Well, introduce me to him now. I'm curious to meet this stone guy."

As we arrived at the work site, the construction temporarily halted so that the men and centaurs could greet me and shout their congratulations. The shouts caught the attention of a small group emerging from the infrastructure of the building. The tallest of the group was my husband, who was clapped on the back several times and included in the builders' congratulatory frenzy. Dougal and Victoria were with him.

Alanna nudged me and waggled her eyebrows. "'*I have business near the new quarters, too,*'" she said, mimicking the Huntress's throaty voice.

"She's becoming shameless," I whispered back at Alanna.

With ClanFintan, Dougal and Vic was a tall gangly man who I didn't recognize. As the group approached and he got closer, I realized he was way younger than I'd first thought. His thick brown hair was tied back in a cropped ponytail, which gave him a randomly artsy look that clashed surprisingly with the fact that he was clearly no older than sixteen.

"Good morning, love." ClanFintan took my hand in his, then bent to kiss me softly on the lips. "How are you feeling this morning?"

"Better," I said, my smile warm and meant to reassure him.

He squeezed my hand.

"Congratulations, my Lady!" Dougal's face was alight, and I knew it wasn't just my news that was making him shine. I thought how wonderful it was to see him so happy. I had been worried that his naturally gregarious personality would morph into something dark and sad after his beloved brother had died in his arms several months ago, but now I could see the sweet openness that reflected his love of life mirrored in his expressive face.

"Thank you, Dougal. And congratulations yourself on finally talking sense into Victoria's hard head."

Vic snorted at me, but her arm slid intimately through Dougal's, and he gave her an adoring smile.

"We would like you to perform the handfast ceremony, Lady Rhiannon." Dougal asked.

"It would make us very happy." Vic smiled softly at me.

I felt a rush of emotion and had to blink back tears. Hormones acting up, no doubt. "I can think of nothing I'd like better."

The pair beamed at me. I swallowed the knot in my throat. Alanna sniffed happily. We were disgusting. No wonder I was puking.

"Lady Rhiannon," Alanna said after she finished sniffing. "May I present to you our lead mason, Kai. Kai, the Lady Rhiannon, Incarnate of Epona," she finished with a flourish.

The tall, young man stepped forward and executed a low, respectful bow.

"Lady Rhiannon, I am pleased to be in the service of Epona."

His voice was unique—not deep or unusually loud, and way too youthful to be particularly manly, but it had a quality that intrigued me. It made me think that I would enjoy listening to him read.

"Perhaps more important are the stones pleased to be in the service of Epona?" I asked, finding it impossible to contain my curiosity (mentally crossing my fingers that I was not committing a faux pas in asking).

"Absolutely, my Lady!" His face brightened and became animated with an eagerness that I wish my students could have emulated. Of course, they wouldn't have known what emulated meant. Sigh. "I searched the mines of the Sidetha until I found the marble vein that spoke the Goddess's name. It is from that marble that the support columns of the structure are being formed."

"I would love to see that marble," I answered, intrigued at the notion that stone could have a preference.

"Follow me, my Lady. I would be honored to show you."

"Rhea, Dougal and I are through here. We need to see to the winter supply of grain." ClanFintan lifted my hand to his lips.

"Okay, I'm going to check out this stone stuff, then I need to look in on Epi. She's been restless lately. I'd like to take her out for a ride. Exercise seems to calm her." I'd known too many Oklahoma women who kept riding through most of their pregnancies to worry about whether it would be safe or not in my supposedly delicate condition. Plus, Epi was not like other horses. I knew she would be extra careful with me.

"I will meet you back at the stables."

"Good day, Lady Rhiannon," Dougal gave me a quick bow, and then he touched Vic's cheek in a gentle caress before he followed my husband.

"If you wait here, my Lady, I will have the workers clear some scaffolding in order to accord you a better view of the main support column." Kai said, his voice breaking endearingly, as he hurried away, obviously excited at the opportunity to share his love of marble. I nodded at him encouragingly.

After he was gone, Alanna elbowed me and jerked her head toward Vic. The Huntress was still standing there, gazing after Dougal's departing form like a lovesick teenager. I caught Alanna's eye and we quickly surrounded the Huntress.

"Girl, you've got it bad," I teased.

Victoria blinked and brought her eyes back into focus.

"I have no idea about what you are speaking." She sounded like Miss Priss, but her cheeks were pink.

"All I can say is that it's a good thing he's young." I grinned at Vic.

"They do say the young have boundless energy." Alanna mused.

"He is not *that* young." Vic tried to sound offended, but I could hear the smile that was lurking behind her proper Lead Huntress facade.

"So, tell me," I leaned into her side and spoke conspiratorially. For months I'd been dying to ask Vic about centaur sex. Now seemed like the perfect opportunity. After all, we were females, and females like to talk about sex. (Try not to be shocked.) "Just what kind, and how much energy, will poor Dougal need?" I nudged her and winked. "On your wedding night."

Vic looked down at me, a little grin pulling at the edges of her full lips.

"Yes," Alanna's deceptively innocent voice trilled, "tell us."

"Well..." Vic motioned for us to lean even closer to her, which we did (gleefully). "Have you ever seen horses mate?"

We nodded.

"Then you know they bite and squeal and kick when their passion is ripe?" Her voice suddenly reminded me of Mae West.

We nodded enthusiastically.

"You know that sometimes their desire is so fierce that

the mating is filled with violent, uncontrolled lust?" Her voice shook with intensity.

We nodded very enthusiastically.

Breathing heavily, she paused. Looking from Alanna to me, her smile widened. "Well, it is nothing like that."

With that, a flippant guffaw burst from her mouth, and she spun away from us, twitching her tail haughtily.

"She is not going to tell us, is she?" Alanna sounded wistful.

"Doesn't look like it," I sighed. "Damn."

Alanna sighed in mirrored frustration. (Note to self: it's about friggin time I asked ClanFintan to explain centaur sex.)

"My Lady, if you will come this way." Kai had returned and was gesturing for me to follow him into the center of the construction area.

As Alannna and I caught up with him I whispered to her, "Is it normal that he's so damn young? I mean, he's a friggin teenager. He can't even be sixteen! Barf."

"The spirit of stone speaks strongly within him. It does not care that he is young, only that he is willing to listen. You will see."

We joined him atop the marble stairs that had already been completed. It was an enormous area that was littered with massive chunks of marble, some of it raw and some already carved and smooth. Around the circumference of the structure were the bottoms of thick columns. These columns weren't fully formed yet, and they looked like broken teeth in a giant's mouth, but as we moved farther into the building site I could see that several central columns were already completed. They stood tall and proud, as if they were concentrating on setting a good example for the others. We stopped directly in front of the center-most column, which was so broad there was no way the three of us could touch fingertips if we stood around its base, arms outstretched. The marble was a luminescent, pearlized color with deep, smooth grooves etched into its expansive length. Its top was intricately carved in a circular pattern of interwoven knots framing plunging centaur warriors.

"This is the central support piece," Kai said. His unusual voice had a faraway sound as he looked adoringly at the newly constructed column. "Each individual piece of stone I used to construct it spoke Epona's name. I brought it home."

"You hear a voice in the marble?" I couldn't stop myself from asking.

He smiled at me. "It is not a sound—not exactly. It is more like a whisper in my mind."

I thought about Epona's voice and nodded. "It's a feeling, but you can hear it like it has been spoken."

"Yes!" he said.

"Can you still hear its voice?" Alanna asked before I could.

"Of course—the marble will always speak to me." He placed his work-toughened hand, which looked much older than the rest of him, against the column and closed his eyes. As his hand met marble, it seemed the stone quivered. We watched, and he caressed the column. For a moment the massive stone appeared to liquefy under his palm. It looked as if his hand sank into the stone, as if his touch made it claylike and malleable. I studied him, and saw an outline of shimmering radiance surrounding his body, much like the magical illumination that enshrouded Clan-Fintan as he called the Change to him. Then Kai took his hand from the column and opened his eyes. The glow faded as if it had only been a figment of my imagination.

"The marble greets you, Incarnate of Epona." His voice was wonderfully serene.

"Really!" I breathed. "May I touch it?"

"Of course, my Lady," he said, obviously pleased by my request.

I stepped close to the column and placed my hands gently against its smooth surface.

"Uh-hum..." Nervously I cleared my throat. "Hello," I offered, feeling very small beside the huge stone.

I was surprised by how soft the marble felt beneath my palms. And this close I realized its appearance changed. I could see that it was not one color but a mixture of many different shades and veins, all blending together to create the distinctive pearl hue. While I studied it, I suddenly sensed a sentience, almost a listening presence, and my hands detected warmth that came from within the stone itself. Then I was enclosed in an astonishing swell of feelings, like I had been immersed in a warm pool of emotion, or had been wrapped in a mother's embrace. My hands shook—not from fear, but from the sheer wonder of it.

A line from Shakespeare flitted through my mind and I whispered, "'Beauty too rich for use, for earth too dear!'"

Then the feeling dispersed, and with a parting caress I pulled my hands from the column and turned to find Alanna and Kai studying me intently.

"It spoke to you!" Kai said.

"Not really." I let my eyes linger on the amazing marble.

"But I felt something," I didn't know how to describe it. "Something wonderful," I ended lamely.

"When is the day of your birth?" He sounded excited.

"The last day in April," Alanna answered before I could—and I was surprised that she answered correctly.

A flash of understanding came over Kai's expressive face. "Ah, a Taurean. Of course! You must be linked to the earth as well as to your goddess."

I had no idea what he was talking about. I mean, I knew I had been born under the sign of the bull, and I'd suffered through pretending to listen to several discarded lovers lecturing me about my stubbornness (who really listens to guys after you fire them?). But I'd never paid much attention to horoscopes and that kind of stuff. Well, up until six months ago I hadn't.

Alanna was nodding happily in agreement.

"Well, that's nice to know," I said a little lamely.

The clatter of hooves announced the arrival of a male centaur I recognized as being one of my husband's couriers.

"My Lady..." He executed a graceful centaur bow. "ClanFintan asks that you join him in the stables."

"Is Epi all right?" Concern flashed through me.

"She is very restless, and the Shaman believes your presence will soothe her."

"Tell him I'll be right there." I turned to Kai. "Thank you for sharing this—" I faltered, not wanting to choose the wrong words "—magic with me."

"It was my pleasure, my Lady." His smile said I had chosen correctly.

I started to turn away, then stopped and reached out to pat the smooth stone in farewell. It still felt warm.

"Rhea," Alanna said as we made our way back through the maze of construction, "I should go see to the preparations for the Samhain feast. There is still much to be done, and I do not think you will want to oversee the choosing of the food."

"Ugh," I agreed. "Go ahead. Just be sure there are plenty of those centaur muffins and some boiled rice. I'll see to Epi and meet you and Carolan around midday for lunch." I grinned at her. "That is, if you're willing to chance eating around me again."

"I will chance it." She smiled back. "But I will not sit near you."

"Smart aleck," I muttered at her. Then I thought to add in a low voice, "Hey, how did you know April 30 is my birthday?"

"It is the date of Rhiannon's birth, too," she whispered through a wry smile.

"Weird coincidence," I said.

"It is only one of many," she replied thoughtfully.

"Huh," I said succinctly before I turned to the waiting centaur. "Lead on," I told him, and we headed briskly to the ornate entrance to the stable.

The stable of Epona was an incredible building, like nothing I had ever seen before. It, too, was made of luminous marble carved and fitted into place by master masons. With newly educated eyes I gazed at the massive columns that supported the beautiful domed edifice, suddenly wondering if the sense of serenity and acceptance I had felt since the first time I had entered this building had been caused by more than the presence of the wonderful horses. I made a mental note to come back and do some marble feeling after Epi had calmed down.

The center aisle was wide and long. On either side of it were situated roomy, immaculate stalls, each tenanted by a mare unique in beauty and temperament. As I hurried down the aisle, I was greeted by throaty whinnies. I called to each of them by name, wishing I had time to stop and caress their shinning faces.

"Hello, Pasiphae, you wonderful girl."

"Lilith, you sweet thing, stop trying to pull down that hay net."

"Heket, baby girl, you're much too beautiful to look at me with such sad eyes."

And on and on and on—stall after stall held mares that were examples of the very best of their breed. As I neared the end of the hall, the aisle took an abrupt turn to the left. But before I entered that special area reserved for Epona's equine incarnation, I could already hear the restless squeals and pawings of the mare that stood out as exceptional, even in this group of the finest horses in Partholon.

Taking the left turn I entered an enormous rounded room that held a huge stall to which a private corral was attached. My husband and Dougal were standing in front of the closed stall, as were several rumpled-looking stable maidens. Their attention was focused on the neurotic-acting mare who paced from one end of the spacious stall to the other.

Epi's beauty was ethereal. Her coat was a mixture of gray and white, that blended to form an incredible silver color, which glistened like pooled mercury until it shaded to coal around her eyes and down her delicate legs. She was a nice-size mare, probably about fifteen hands high, and her confirmation was beyond perfect. I adored everything about her.

As if she had the ability to sense my presence (which, truthfully, she does) she spun around and locked her bottomless eyes on me. A full-throated neigh split the air between us.

"Hello, my darling." I laughed joyously and hurried toward her. "I hear you are causing quite a stir."

"We are pleased to see you." ClanFintan sounded as relieved as everyone else looked. The small group parted so that I could pull back the half-door and enter the stall.

"She's been like this since Ouranos arrived," I said as I stroked her beautiful head and kissed her velvet muzzle. "Even though he's housed across the temple, she knows he's here and hasn't been herself for days." Epi rubbed her head against me and lipped the edge of my cloak.

"She needs her mate," ClanFintan said.

"Well, she'll have him, but not until tomorrow night." I had been preparing for the Samhain ceremony for several weeks, and I, too, was nervous about the intricate mating ritual that was supposed to insure the next three years of fertility for this land and its people. I rested my forehead against hers. "How about a ride? Think that will make you relax a little?"

Epi lipped the shoulder of my cloak and blew softly in my face. I took that for a horsey yes.

One maiden was already scrambling to strap her soft saddle blanket to her back, while another slipped an ornately detailed hackamore over her head. Even though she was unnaturally nervous, I was pleased to see she didn't fidget or throw a typical horse fit. Epi knew what was going on, and she behaved with her usual good manners.

"Here..." ClanFintan came up behind me and offered to give me a leg up onto the mare's back.

Epi held still until I had my seat, and then she started determinedly toward the gate in the corral, which a maiden was already opening. ClanFintan followed close behind us. I just had time to wave over my shoulder at the stable maidens and Dougal before Epi broke into her smooth canter, heading in a northerly direction.

"I guess we're going this way." I called over my shoulder to my husband, who was loping easily near my side. "She's driving." I nodded at Epi and he smiled. I could feel that she was eager to stretch her legs, so I took a deep seat, gripped her smooth sides with my thighs, leaned forward and whispered, "Let's go, gorgeous."

She flicked an ear back to catch my words, then I felt her stride lengthen. We entered the edge of the wooded area that framed the temple grounds, but the wide, level path that led into it didn't cause Epi to slow, nor did it cause me to worry. She was no ordinary scatterbrained horse. She would slow when necessary, and not before. All I had to do was sit back and enjoy the ride.

The day had become cooler as it had progressed, and even though it wasn't actually raining, a mist hung low over the land, obscuring our surroundings and giving the trees a weird, ghostly appearance. I noticed most of them had already lost their leaves, and realized, with disgust, that I had been too busy worrying about my mysterious puking sickness to appreciate what must have been a lovely show of changing leaves.

The path split ahead. I knew the left branch led to the upper vineyards, and the right branch would eventually take us to the outskirts of Ufasach Marsh. Not a pleasant place. ClanFintan and I had had to use the marsh as an escape route from the Fomorians, and it had almost cost us our lives. Unfortunately, Epi chose the right branch.

If she wanted to visit Ufasach, I'd have to exert my veto power. I did take solace in the knowledge that the beginnings of the marsh were several miles away, and I was pretty sure Epi would tire before then. And if she didn't, I would.

ClanFintan edged up so that we were galloping shoulder to shoulder. He looked relaxed and fresh, and I knew that he could go on for hours without visibly tiring at this ground-eating pace.

"How are you feeling?" he asked without even breathing hard.

"*'I feel good!'*" I sang to the tune of the old James Brown song, which made my husband roll his eyes and heave a long-suffering sigh. (I'm not really very musically inclined, although I'd like to be, so I keep trying.) Then my mind caught up to my automatic response and I realized it was true. I still had a funny, heavy feeling in the back of my throat. Kind of like you feel when you're fighting off the flu, but my stomach was definitely better since I'd filled it with muffins. Actually, now that I knew the hormonal cause of my illness and weird imaginings, I was decidedly more relaxed and more like my only sometimes grumpy self.

"Do not wait to feel tired to stop. We should go back before you become fatigued."

"Okay, okay." I mimicked his eye-rolling. "I'll be careful."

I think he snorted at me, but his hooves covered the sound.

We rode on silently, and Epi's rapid gallop turned into her more rolling, leisurely canter. I enjoyed the change of her gaits, which were as smooth and flawless as her liquid-silver coat. Then the rolling canter turned into a rapid trot, which I found I could only tolerate for a short time.

"Whoa," I said without needing to pull back on the reins. Epi's ears rotated back at the sound of my voice, and she immediately dropped out of the trot and into a brisk walk. ClanFintan looked at me with questioning eyes.

"It jiggles me too much," I explained.

He snorted again. So did Epi.

"Just wait," I said into her listening ears. "You'll be in my condition pretty soon yourself."

She didn't say anything, but ClanFintan unsuccessfully tried to hold back a chuckle.

Suddenly, Epi surprised me by coming to an abrupt halt. Her ears were no longer cocked back listening to me, but were pointed to the right side of the path. ClanFintan had gone ahead a few paces before noticing that we had stopped, and he trotted back to where Epi stood, statue-like.

"What is she looking at?" he asked.

"Beats me." I squinted, trying to peer through the swirling fog. "What's up, Epi?" I asked, but the mare made no response. All of her attention was focused on a spot to the right of the path.

"The birds are silent." ClanFintan's voice was grim, and I heard the deadly hiss of his ever-present claymore being unsheathed. "Stay here." His deep voice was harsh with the command.

"I don't want to stay here by myself!" My hormones must have been acting up (again), because I couldn't seem to stop myself from feeling very helpless. It was like I had suddenly turned into Doesn't-Have-a-Prom-Date-Barbie.

"The mare will protect you," he said as he crossed before us and entered the edge of the forest. "And if I tell you to move, you move." The fog swallowed him in sticky gray and I had an uncomfortable flashback to the skittering darkness that had haunted me at my father's tomb. I shivered and wanted to call after ClanFintan that Epi wasn't moving, let alone protecting, but I didn't want to mess with his concentration. Nor did I want to give whatever booger thing that might be lurking within hearing distance a clue that Epi had turned into Stone Horse.

"What the heck is out there?" I whispered to Epi, and I was encouraged when one of her ears swiveled quickly back at my words. "Booger monster?" I inquired in a conspirator's whisper.

She didn't answer.

"Ghost?" I asked.

She snorted, but it didn't sound like a yes snort. It sounded like a be-quiet-and-pay-attention snort.

I sighed and waited. It had probably only been minutes, but in the middle of the fog and the forest it felt like we had been abducted by The Little People. I started to worry about the intricate aspects of time and Rip Van Winkle and...ClanFintan's body materialized out of the fog. I breathed again.

"I found nothing threatening." He gave Epi an exasperated look. "The mating must be affecting the mare's judgment. A short distance from the trail there is a small clearing. A stream runs through it, and there are two ancient trees—"

"A stream!" I interrupted, feeling amazingly thirsty. "Well, if nothing's going to eat us, I would really like a drink." My hand moved of its own accord and rested briefly against my stomach. "Then we should probably be getting back." I gave him an apologetic look. "I may be getting tired."

To his credit he didn't say I told you so. He just shook his head and turned back into the forest, motioning for us to follow him.

I clucked at Epi and squeezed lightly with my knees. For an instant I didn't think she would obey me—she felt oddly cold and metallic between my thighs. I ran my fingers through her gleaming mane and down her taut neck, murmuring quiet endearments to her. Then I felt a ripple run through her body and she turned from iron back into horse-flesh. She took a tentative step forward, then another and finally followed ClanFintan's disappearing back away from the path and into the fog-shrouded forest.

Within just a few paces we suddenly ran out of trees, and entered a lovely little clearing, which was oddly free of fog, like it was an oasis of clarity in the middle of the soupy day. My attention was immediately drawn to two massive trees that stood silently in the middle of the cleared area. A ribbon of a stream ran between the giants and off into the forest away from the road. The water looked inviting and cool.

"Let's go get a drink," I said and kneed Epi forward, still surprised by her unusual reticence. Hesitatingly she plodded to the stream and we joined ClanFintan, who was already kneeling and drinking from his cupped hand.

"Let me help you," he said. He moved quickly to Epi's side and put his warm hands on either side of my waist, plucking me neatly off the mare's back and turning me to face him. Smiling, he held me close and let my body slide slowly against his until my feet met the ground. I giggled and kissed the lower part of his chest, where his leather vest was open to reveal his muscular torso (also, where my lips came when I was standing in front of him).

"Get your drink." His voice was rich with emotion. "I look forward to getting you back to the temple. You know, a woman who is with child should take several breaks during the day—breaks where she retires to her bedchamber to *rest*." He caressed the last word, making his meaning clear.

"Will you rub my feet?" I murmured against his chest.

"Among other things." I could hear the smile in his voice.

"It's a deal." I squeezed him hard and planted another wet kiss in the middle of his chest before turning to the stream. As I knelt for my drink, I looked up over my shoulder at my mare. She was standing still, like a silver statue of herself. Her ears were cocked forward. All of her attention was centered on the two massive trees that stood a little way upstream.

"Epi!" I said sharply. Her ears flicked briefly in my direction. "Come get a drink."

She didn't move except to turn her ears (and her attention) back to the trees. I glanced at ClanFintan, and he shrugged his shoulders, obviously as bemused by her behavior as I was. I mirrored his shrug and bent back to the stream.

The water was like liquid ice. Its sweetness reminded me of the refreshing public fountains of Rome. (Yes, I've led students overseas—and yes, they tried to chaperon me properly.) I drank deeply. When I'd had my fill, I settled back on my haunches, and found my gaze shifting to the trees that still held my mare's rapt attention.

They were enormous, obviously ancient. Branches didn't even begin until at least twenty feet up their impressive length. Something seemed odd about them for a moment, and then I realized what it was. They still had their leaves. I blinked and looked around, trying to focus into the fog-covered forest at the trees nearest to the edge of the clearing. Didn't I remember that the other trees had already lost their leaves? Unable to see through the mist, I shifted my attention back to the two giants before me. Pin oaks—with a start the name registered in my mind as I recognized them as indigenous flora of my home state, Oklahoma. Their leaves were shaped in the familiar stilettoed points that I'd grown up raking from our front yard. Only these were still attached to the branches and the vibrant green of new algae. My eyes slid from the heavy canopy of their entwining branches, down to their massive trunks, which were covered with a carpet of thick, lily pad–colored moss. I stood abruptly. The moss seemed to give off a muffled glow, like light shining through satin fabric. It cried to be touched.

And then I felt it—a tickle of emotion, as if a feather had brushed across my consciousness. I concentrated on the trees and the flutter of feeling came again. Realization hit me. It was a feeling akin to what I'd experienced in the presence of the marble column earlier that day. I remembered that Kai had said that because I was born under an earth sign, I was linked to the earth. I felt a smile of wonder spread across my face. Maybe I could "talk" to the trees.

With that thought, I began walking eagerly forward and was interrupted by a sharp squeal from Epi. Surprised, I stopped and turned, almost running into the mare, who was practically walking on my heels.

"Epi!" I stumbled back as she butted me with her head. "What the hell is wrong with you?"

Her only answer was a muffled nicker as she rubbed her head against my chest.

"Jeesh, it's all right. I'm just going to go check out those old trees. Then we'll start back." I glanced over her at my husband, who was watching us with an amused look.

"She's making me crazy," I said. "I'll be glad when tomorrow night's ceremony is over and she's herself again."

"She does seem rather..." He paused, and I was sure he was thinking of and discarding words like *paranoid, hysterical* and *clingy.* He settled on *emotional,* waggling his eyebrows so that we both knew what he really meant.

I winked and smiled my agreement. Rubbing the mare's head, I whispered endearments meant to reassure her. "Hey, sweet girl. It's okay. Everything's fine." She seemed to relax. "I want to get closer to the trees," I confided into her ear. "Kai said I could hear earth stuff, and I'd like to test his theory."

With one last pat I turned and headed purposefully toward the trees. I could hear Epi take a few steps to follow me, but soon she stopped. I glanced back at her to see that she was standing perfectly still. As I watched, a little ripple passed through her body.

"Everything's fine!" I said, waving gaily at the frozen mare, ignoring a twinge of concern at her bizarre behavior. Epi and I were probably sharing hormone surges. No wonder she and I were so skittish. When I turned back to the trees, all thoughts of Epi left my mind.

I was standing within touching distance of the massive oaks, and this close I could clearly feel something emanating from them. I cocked my head, listening intently.

"Rhea?" ClanFintan called questioningly.

"Shh!" I yelled without turning my head, holding up my hand to silence him.

I took another step forward. The ground sucked wetly at my riding boots, and I realized that I was almost standing in the little stream that ran between the two trees. It had narrowed here, so that it was probably only a couple of feet wide, and it tumbled musically over rounded pebbles. Stepping carefully, I straddled the stream and raised my arms, so that one of my hands could rest on the side of each tree.

As I touched the moss-covered bark, a painful jolt traveled the length of my body, like I had just touched a live wire. A blade of fear sliced through me, and I tried to pull my hands away, but they were stuck against the trees as surely as if they had been nailed to the bark. My knees began to sag, and I realized that I was falling forward, and (if the trees loosened their grip) I would tumble headfirst into the little stream. Suddenly it felt like time slowed down to pass frame by frame before my eyes. My head bent, and I saw my rippled reflection in the water. Then my reflection fractured, and I could actually see through the water. I blinked slowly, trying to clear my eyes, and abruptly my vision refocused. I could see into the stream and beyond it to the world on the other side, a world where a movement in the sky caught my attention. A shocked cry escaped my lips as I recognized the narrow metallic cylinder that passed across the distant blue horizon. An airplane. Understanding struck me. Frantically I tried once again to pull my hands from the trees, but instead of freeing me the bark of the trees had become semi-permeable, and my hands were sucked into them, followed by my wrists, elbows…and as

I felt my body fall forward and dissolve into that mirror world I saw an all too familiar skittery darkness, inky with its liquid aura of evil, pulse around me—pressing, searching, attempting to engulf me... I heard the horrified shout that was wrenched from my husband echoed by Epi's piercing neigh of panic.

I opened my mouth to scream, but unconsciousness swallowed me.

PART II

1

My stomach revolted, and I felt myself being rolled onto my side while painful spasms ripped through my body. I heard something odd and whimpering, and I realized it was the sound of my own sobs.

"It's okay, Shannon," a deep, familiar voice spoke soothingly. "You're safe."

I tried to open my eyes, but my vision was so blurred that I snapped them shut again, afraid the spinning would cause me to be even sicker. Slowly, my heaving subsided and I lay still, gulping breaths of the cool, moist air. I realized that the grass beneath my cheek was damp, and I tried once more to open my eyes and focus my vision. Between slit lids I peered blearily around me. I could see the outline of green and gray, but before it could come fully into focus a dark, shadowy shape slid across my field of vision. As the shape caught my attention, a feeling hit me—a feeling that I recognized. It wasn't my hormones or my imagination. Evil *had* been stalking me. It seemed to hover closer, swallowing the shades of green and soft gray and leaving jagged shards of mixed-up color like an exit wound. I tried to open my mouth to scream.

"Shannon! Take it easy," that same voice soothed. "Everything's okay!"

His words seemed to have a negating effect on the colorless shadow. The dark spot dissipated, while shimmering gray ran into the green of forest leaves, tunneling my fading vision. After that I knew no more.

Consciousness flitted across my closed eyelids like lightning that illuminates the night sky but won't leave the clouds. I lay very still, afraid to move, afraid to do anything that would cause my battered body more pain or call back the darkness I had glimpsed. I breathed slowly, trying to still the frantic, hummingbird beating of my heart.

I realized that I was no longer lying on the damp grass. I felt the softness of a well-made mattress beneath me and the thickness of a down comforter that had been pulled up to my neck. I shivered, suddenly feeling a chill that went deep within my body.

There was a rustling of feet moving toward me, then a hand rested briefly on my forehead. I could feel the calluses against my cold skin.

"Don't open your eyes yet. It's easier for your body to reaccustom itself if you keep them closed and rest."

Again, that elusive familiarity in his voice.

"Drink this—it will help." I kept my eyes screwed shut while a strong hand helped raise me into a half-sitting position so that I could sip a warm, sweet mixture. I drank slowly, willing my stomach to stay still. When the mug was empty, I fell back against the pillow, exhausted by the small effort.

"Rest," the voice said. "Everything's okay. You're home."

As enshrouding sleep covered me, I realized that it was ClanFintan who was speaking, only his voice sounded odd. I struggled to stay conscious and understand what it was that was different about him, but my eyes were too heavy. Sleep won the battle.

Coffee...the smell tickled my senses, bringing to mind sleepy Saturday mornings when I used to brew a fresh pot of dark breakfast beans and lace it (liberally) with Irish Cream before retiring back to bed with my steaming mug and a good book.

But Partholon didn't have any coffee.

Memory rushed back with my swift intake of breath. My eyes opened and my vision swam. I blinked and rubbed my eyes, disturbed by the weakness of my muscles as they sluggishly obeyed my orders.

The only light in the cabin came from a low-burning fire within a hearth built in the wall directly across from my bed. I looked around, being careful not to make any sudden movements with my head—scared I would throw my body into another revolt. It appeared to be one large room, which served as a bedroom with a kind of den area partitioned off in front of the fire by two cozily situated rocking chairs which had little whatnot tables standing next to each one. Each table held a modern version of an old-time kerosene lamp, though neither was lit. There was a book opened, facedown, beside the nearest rocker. I could see that there was some kind of loft above my head and another room to my far left divided from the rest of the cabin by a wall. That's where the coffee smell was wafting from—must be the kitchen. The shuffle of tired feet echoed from that vicinity, seeming to come closer. I braced myself.

And ClanFintan walked around the wall.

I must have made some kind of wounded sound, because he jerked, almost spilling the liquid in his mug. Then his handsome face broke into a smile that was ghostly in its familiarity.

"Are you feeling better?" he asked.

I understood now why his voice had seemed so familiar yet at the same time so odd. It was his voice—ClanFintan's voice. But it was devoid of the power of a centaur's lungs and the musical lilt of a Partholonian accent.

"Where am I?" My gravelly voice was flat and emotionless.

Still smiling, he set his mug down on the small table and approached my bed. I couldn't help shrinking back into the pillows. He must have noticed, because he stopped several paces away from the edge of the bed.

"You're home, Shannon."

"And just where the hell do you think *home* is?"

His eyebrows shot up in surprise. "Oklahoma," he said, and his matter-of-fact voice severed my heart from my body.

I could feel the blood draining from my face, and the room abruptly began to spin.

"No!" I whispered, and slammed my eyes closed, willing the room to be still. After taking several deep breaths, I reopened them to see he had moved toward me. "Don't come any closer!" I snapped.

He stopped, holding his hands out in a peaceful offering. "I won't hurt you, Shannon."

"How the hell do you know my name?" My voice shook with the effort to keep my stomach and the room still.

"That's a complex story..." He hesitated.

"I want an answer." I was glad my voice no longer wavered.

He hesitated.

"How do you know my name," I repeated slowly and distinctly, turning the question into a declarative sentence as only an English teacher can do.

"Rhiannon told me," he said with obvious reluctance.

"Rhiannon!" The name came out as a curse. My eyes flitted around the room, expecting her to leap from one of the shadowy corners.

"No! Not here," he said consolingly. "She's back in Partholon where she belongs." He sounded pleased with himself.

I locked my eyes with his and spoke through gritted teeth, "She does *not* belong in Partholon. It is *my* home. He is *my* husband. They are *my* people."

"But—" he looked confused "—I thought everything would be okay if I just re-exchanged the two of you..." His voice trailed off.

Purposefully I sat up straighter and swung my legs over the side of the bed. Looking down at myself, I saw that I was wearing nothing but a man's pajama top, and I scowled up at him.

"Where are my friggin clothes?"

"I—" he stuttered "—they're—"

"Oh, never mind. Just give me some pants and my boots and take me wherever it is you made the switch, and switch us back."

He opened his mouth to answer me, and the ring of a phone interrupted him. Its sound was a bizarre jar to my senses, which had accustomed themselves to Partholon's technology-free lifestyle. It rang again, and he regained movement in his legs, hurrying over to a portable phone that rested in a row of shelves built into the wall beside the fireplace.

"Hello," he said, keeping his eyes on me. Then he blinked and stepped back as if he had received a blast of fire from the receiver.

"Rhiannon!" The name was like a sheet of darkness covering the room.

I felt a chill rush down my spine, and I clenched my teeth together to keep them from chattering.

The man's face looked as drained of color as mine felt. He continued to hold my gaze as he spoke in swift, hard words into the receiver.

"I told you it must end." He paused for a moment then broke in. "I will not listen to your lies again." His voice was ice. "No, I—" He was interrupted. He didn't speak for several breaths, and when he did his voice had taken on the flat affect I had come to recognize in ClanFintan's voice when he was issuing commands in a deadly situation. "Shannon is here."

I could hear the answering shriek all the way across the room. He cringed in response to its volume, and then placed the phone back in its bed with a determined click. He wiped a hand across his eyes, and for the first time I noticed the network of fine lines at the edges of his eyes and the dusting of silver in his thick dark hair.

For a moment I felt my heart go out to this man who looked so much like my beloved husband, then the short, almost military cut of his hair jolted me back to reality. It was because of this man that I had been wrenched away from ClanFintan. He was not a friend.

"I thought you said Rhiannon was back in Partholon."

"I thought she was." He sounded exhausted.

"You'd better start from the beginning. I want to know everything."

His eyes locked with mine again, and he nodded slowly. Then he said, "Would you like some coffee first?"

"I'd like some coffee during." My stomach growled violently, so I added, "And I need some bread or something to settle my stomach."

He nodded again and disappeared around the wall. I resettled myself against the pillows, carefully covering my bare legs. He returned shortly, carrying a tray with a steaming mug of coffee and a nice selection of homemade muffins. He placed the tray over my lap, being careful not to touch me, then he turned away to feed the fire more logs until it flared and crackled. Pulling one of the rockers nearest the bed over to him, he sat facing me, sipping slowly from his own mug. He studied me carefully before he spoke, and when he did begin to speak, his words surprised me.

"It is amazing how much the two of you look alike. More than twins—more than anything I've ever seen before. It's like you literally mirror each other."

"In Partholon some of the people mirror the people from this world." I paused and flicked him a begrudging half smile. "I've felt how disconcerting it can be at first. But don't let it confuse you. Just because we look alike, it doesn't mean we are in the least bit alike inside."

He met my gaze steadily, and I was taken back by the force of his words. "For your sake I hope you're nothing like that—" he hesitated before continuing "—woman."

"I'm nothing like that bitch." I filled in the blank for him. Then it pissed me off that I was bothering to explain myself to him at all. "But what I am or am not is really none of your business. All I want to know is how this happened, and how it can be undone."

"I'm afraid I can only answer part of that for you," he said sadly.

I felt my stomach tense and forced myself to swallow the moist muffin, willing myself not to be sick.

"Just start at the damn beginning and let me sift through this mess," I said through another mouthful of muffin.

"How about I introduce myself first?" he said with the hint of a smile and a soft Oklahoma drawl.

I set my jaw against the familiarity of his expression. "Fine. Whatever. Just talk."

"My name is Clint Freeman." He tipped an imaginary hat. "At your service, ma'am."

Clint Freeman—my mind went round and round the name that sounded so like my husband's.

"Shannon?"

The question in his voice brought me back. "Okay—now I know your name. You already know mine, so get on with your story. How do you know about Rhiannon and me?"

"She told me."

I waited impatiently for him to continue and felt my foot tapping restlessly.

He sighed and rubbed the bridge of his nose. "She showed up here one night in the middle of June."

Here I interrupted. "What month is it now?"

"October—the last day of October."

"So time passes the same," I breathed in relief.

"That makes sense. The worlds are mirror dimensions of one another." His voice was matter-of-fact, like we were discussing Oklahoma's changing weather.

"You certainly seem comfortable with all of this."

"I've seen too much to pretend disbelief." His voice had gone hard.

"Try explaining the 'too much' to me."

He drew a deep breath and continued. "Rhiannon showed up here in the middle of the night, just ahead of a nasty summer thunderstorm."

"Figures," I mumbled. He ignored my comment.

"She appeared at my door like a forest sprite." He shook his head and his voice mirrored his self-disgust. "She looked wild and beautiful. I asked her in, half expecting her to disappear in the light of my lamps." He laughed dryly, like he was making a bad joke. "I wish to hell she had disappeared.

"Of course, I thought she was lost and I asked if I could help her." Suddenly his eyes wouldn't meet mine. "She said she wasn't lost—that she had followed my magic and that she had come for me."

"Your magic?" I asked, and his eyes once more found mine.

"I have a way with the woods," he said slowly.

I raised my eyebrows and waited impatiently for him to finish his explanation.

"I haven't always lived here." He made a gesture that took in more than just this cabin. "Five years ago I lived in Tulsa. I worked and behaved in what I guess society would call a normal manner." He paused, choosing his words carefully. "I always liked camping—always felt most content in the country. Five years ago that feeling of contentment changed, broadened, into more than a feeling." He took a deep breath. "I started to be able to hear the land around me." He smiled a little sheepishly.

"Distinct words, or just a feeling?" I inquired.

He seemed relieved that I hadn't called him insane and he hurried to answer. "Most of the time it's just a feeling." His eyes took on a far-off cast. "It was like the land welcomed me. The farther I was from civilization, the more content I felt. I started spending every free moment camping and hiking. Then I had an accident at work and injured my back, effectively ending my career." He didn't appear too upset at the notion. "So I took my disability pension and retired here."

"Where exactly is here?"

"Southeastern part of Oklahoma." He smiled. "Smack in the middle of Okie nowhere."

"Great," I muttered. "It was after you moved here that you started to hear the land speak to you?" I couldn't keep myself from asking. Besides being honestly curious about this land-speaking stuff, I needed to follow any magical lead I had here in The Real World. Where there was magic, there might just be a way to return to Partholon.

"Yes." His gaze turned far-off again. "The trees whisper—the land rejoices—the wind sings." His eyes found me again. "I realize it sounds overly poetic and schizophrenic, but I can feel it."

"Which is why Rhiannon targeted you."

"Yes," he snarled the word. "She said she was a goddess's incarnation and that she was like the land and the elements—something to be worshipped and adored."

I tried to stop the sarcastic snort that built in my throat. "Let me guess," I said. "She screwed your brains out—literally—and then you believed her."

He hesitated only briefly. "Yes, I believed her. There was something about her that made me *want* to believe her."

"Yeah," I harrumphed. "Her crotch."

He frowned and looked more disappointed than embarrassed or angry. "Maybe, but you should know that you have it, too."

"Oh, please." I rolled my eyes, telegraphing my disbelief.

"You make me feel the same way she did." He didn't say it like he was coming on to me or making excuses; he said it almost like he was apologizing.

"That's crap. There's no hanky-panky bullshit going on between us. I'm a married woman, and I don't even know you."

"It's not about that." He held up his hand to stop my interruption. "Yes, I did sleep with her. Yes, I did want her. But it wasn't just that." Here he faltered, searching for words. "This may sound ridiculous to you." He gave a sharp, dry laugh. "It certainly does to me. But I feel, I don't know, *right* around you, like it's where I belong. With you—both of you."

I opened my mouth to tell him he was full of shit, but the memory of ClanFintan's words suddenly played through my mind. *I was born to love you,* he had insisted. I had come to believe my husband. And the man who sat before me was, unquestionably, my husband's mirror image. Rhiannon and I didn't behave the same; didn't make the same choice, but most of the mirror images I'd met, Suzanna and Alanna, Gene and Carolan, were more alike than different. Already I was getting the distinct impression that this man was disquietingly like my husband.

"All right, well, uh, whatever," I prevaricated, feeling uncomfortable. "If you liked her so much, what woke you up?"

"I didn't, as you put it, wake up at first."

"Translation—she didn't let you out of bed for a while." I knew Rhiannon's M.O.

He had the good grace to look chagrined.

"You could say that. And when she wasn't in bed, she was either out in the forest or on the Internet."

"She's computer literate?"

"Very," he responded dryly.

"So she pretended to be all into the land so that you would stay hooked on her while she obsessed on the Net?"

"Actually, her affinity with the land wasn't a pretense. She seemed to draw something from the forest. She would go hiking alone, didn't want me along, and come back hours later filled with energy."

"Hmm." I filed that away for later. If Rhiannon drew some kind of power from the land around here, maybe I could, too. Maybe it could get me home. "What was she looking for on the Internet?"

"Money—she told me she was into Net trading and she had to keep a check on her stocks, but the property she was after was more than stocks and commodities..." His voice trailed off.

"Well?" I prompted.

"She was after men. Rich, old, single men."

I blinked in surprise. "Did she find one?"

"Yes. Sinclair Montgomery III. Seventy-two, widowed and stuffed with Tulsa oil money. A philanthropist and an honestly nice guy who hadn't had sex since the seventies."

"Sounds like easy pick'ns for Rhiannon." The name vaguely rang a bell. I was pretty sure I'd read it in the I-Have-More-Money-Than-God social page of the *Tulsa World*.

He nodded grimly. "She started an e-mail relationship with him. Said she was a local teacher who would like to begin a career in public speaking."

"Good God, Rhiannon as a public speaker! What the hell was she going to speak about?" The possible topics boggled my mind.

"How to inspire young people to be creative and stay in school."

"I hesitate to ask, but just how was Rhiannon going to *inspire* public school children?"

"I don't think she ever had to actually outline her speaking platform. As far as I could tell, she cast out the local teacher/speaker bait, and he bit, granting her an appointment."

"And a meeting in *person* was all that Rhiannon required to land that old trout." I completed his analogy.

He nodded grimly.

"And you just let her walk out of your bed and into Mr.

Moneybags's bed with your blessing?" If he was anything like ClanFintan there was no way he'd be okay with that.

"Actually, I was so busy hating her *friend*—" he said the word like it tasted bad "—that I didn't realize what was going on until it was done."

"Wait." I shook my head in confusion. "She has a friend here?" My mind rifled through the list of my buds, and I didn't come up with any that would tolerate Rhiannon the Psycho Bitch.

"He called himself Bres, and said he was her follower, if you can believe that."

"Tall, skeletal, stinky-breathed?" I asked dryly.

"Yes!" He said, surprised.

"He *is* her friggin follower. He followed her here. No, scratch that—he came here first, making sure the trip could be completed successfully. She followed him." Along with his inclination to worship dark gods (which makes sense after ClanFintans's explanation). Alanna had told me about Bres's bizarre infatuation with Rhiannon, and how his initial switch with a mirror image from this world had provided Rhiannon with a person to sacrifice so that her trip could be completed safely.

"The bastard would hardly let her out of his sight."

"So Bres kept you in a jealous lather, and you didn't realize she was screwing the old man?"

His jaw tightened, and I wondered for a second if I'd pushed too hard (or at least too sarcastically). Then he blew a deep breath through his pursed lips. "No, he just pissed me off while he lurked around here like a damn cockroach. I didn't know she was screwing the old man because I wouldn't stay in Tulsa with her."

Curiosity whispered in my ear. What happened between Bres and Rhiannon and Clint? Why wouldn't Clint stay in Tulsa with a woman he adored? And just what the hell was it about Rhiannon that had men falling all over their dicks to do her friggin bidding?

I felt the sudden need to pinch (or slap) myself. *Who cares?* My rational mind screamed. I just wanted to get out of here. I was not here to be involved in a mini–Peyton Place.

"Look," I said sharply. "This is very interesting, but all I really want to know is why I am back in Okla-friggin-homa." I held up my hand as he started to speak. "No—here's what I need. Number one—" I ticked the numbers off with my fingers "—why did you jerk me back over here? Number two—how did you jerk me back over here? Number three—how the hell do I get back over there?" I spread my fingers like a baseball ump calling three strikes. (Yes, I appreciated the symbolism.)

"I brought you back here because I wanted to exchange you for Rhiannon and get her out of this world."

"Just because she dumped you for an old rich guy?"

"No, because she is evil. She killed him. And her killing has just started. The only life that has any meaning to her is her own."

I blinked in surprise. "Sinclair's dead?"

"One month after they were married. Heart attack."

"Well, shit. The guy was old and getting ridden like Seabiscuit. He probably died a happy man. Why would you think she murdered him?" (Clint was an Oklahoma guy—he should know every red-blooded bubba dreams of dying in the saddle.)

"She told me she killed him."

Now, *that* got my attention. "What?"

"She told me. Calm as we're speaking here. She said she planned it, chose him because he was old and rich and had no living children to contest the will. First she got him all turned on so that he would be found in an overexcited state." Clint paused, looking uncomfortable with the remembrance. "Then she explained how Bres held him down and she shot a syringe full of air into his jugular vein. She even admitted that she had insisted on rough, biting sex to set up a cover for the needle prick. She said he had a history of heart problems and a written wish for cremation. It couldn't have been easier for her."

"Why did she admit that to you?" I was incredulous. Being a slut was one thing, being a murderess was quite another.

"Rhiannon didn't think I could say no to her. She thought I'd join with her if she said she needed me." His face was an unemotional mask. "She said I could help her harness this world's magic." He stared into my eyes. "Rhiannon thought she could have it all in this world—both magic and technology. She explained it to me—she even let me glimpse that other world for a—"

"Glimpse Partholon!" I yelled.

He nodded slowly.

"How?" I demanded.

"I'm not entirely sure. It was like she hypnotized me, and while I was..." He paused, struggling for words, "Asleep or out, I don't know exactly how to explain my state of consciousness, my soul seemed to lift from my body and was pulled through something that looked like a fiery tunnel." Here he stopped and shuddered at the memory. "At the end of the tunnel I emerged over an amazing building. It was night, but I could clearly see beings that were half man, half horse walking around talking to each other." He shook his head in wonder. "It was fantastic."

"Was the temple made of creamy marble with thick, round walls?" My voice was choked with tears.

"Yes." He nodded. "And it had a gigantic fountain—"

"—That looked like plunging horses," I finished for him.

"Yes, again," he said.

"Epona's Temple." Speaking the words caused a wave of homesickness to wash over me.

"That's what Rhiannon said."

I cleared my throat before asking, "How did your soul get back here?"

"I have no idea. I could have only been there for a few seconds, and then I was pulled through the tunnel and slammed back into my body. I had nothing to do with it. Afterward I felt fine, but Rhiannon was exhausted. She must have slept for sixteen hours without moving."

"And she woke up expecting you to be part of her Let's Rule the World Plan?"

"Actually," he said grimly "she didn't have any delusions about world dominance—she was much too rational for that. She just wanted money. A lot of money. And the power money buys."

"Didn't she have lots of money from the old guy?"

"Yes, but several million dollars wasn't enough for Rhiannon. She had learned her Internet lessons too well."

I must have looked confused because he explained.

"She learned that even several million dollars isn't a fortune by today's standards, and that it won't buy her the power and autonomy she craved. She needed more, so she found it."

"Buried treasure?" I asked only half jokingly.

"Drugs," he answered.

"Drugs? What the hell do you mean?"

"When Rhiannon found out about this world's fascination with illegal drugs, and the profit margin to be made in the drug trade, she said only a fool would pass up the opportunity to get and stay rich by using such an easy method."

"She's dealing drugs?" My mind couldn't quite wrap around the bizarre idea of my mirror image being a female version of Scarface.

"She's dealing drugs," he confirmed. "At first I thought she just didn't realize what she was getting into. I pulled up all sorts of sites that showed the dangers of drug use, what it does to kids, families, communities." His face clouded. "She said it wasn't her concern what the weak did to themselves, and that this world appeared to have too many children anyway. Killing a few would probably be a good idea. Rhiannon believes in the survival of the fittest."

I felt sick and my hand automatically found the small swell of my abdomen, covering it protectively. Clint paused in his recitation but didn't comment on my action.

"I explained to her the jail sentence she could receive for dealing drugs. She laughed and said she simply would not get caught. Then I told her she would have much more to worry about than the police, that if she lived in that part of our world she would be trafficking with thieves and murderers, junkies and liars." He stopped, like he didn't want to go on speaking.

"And that didn't bother her?" I prompted.

"No. She became excited at the prospect. She said that was where I came in, that together we could harness and use an ancient evil to control this modern form of evil." He looked as disgusted as I felt.

"What did she mean by that?" Again, I experienced the same sick sensation I'd had when ClanFintan had told me about Pryderi. Could the ancient evil Rhiannon wanted to use be that terrible three-faced god?

He shook his head. "I'm not sure. I didn't give her a chance to explain. Suddenly it was like scales fell from my eyes and I saw what she really was, an amoral sociopath. I told her to get out and not come back. Then I threw her and her *follower* out of my home."

Neither of us spoke for a moment. My mind was whirring, trying to grasp everything I'd just learned.

"Which brings me to your question number one."

I looked at him, squinting with confusion.

"Why I tried to exchange the two of you," he reminded me. "It's simple—she's evil. She'd already told me all about you, and I decided that the chances of a high school English teacher being a sociopathic goddess who would want to harness and use an ancient evil so she could deal drugs were pretty slim. Besides that, she'd laughed about leaving you over there in some kind of mess with demons."

I gritted my teeth against the treachery and cowardice of Rhiannon leaving her people when she should have been warning and protecting them.

"I thought you would be happy to get out of there. Exchanging the two of you seemed like a good idea," he concluded.

"Okay. After what you've explained I understand your

reasoning, but you need to realize that Partholon is where I want to be—forever. I love the people she betrayed. I worship the Goddess she used. I embrace the husband she rejected."

"I didn't know," he said sadly.

"So we'll move on to questions two and three. How did you get me here, and how do I get back?"

"Well—" he leaned forward, resting his elbows on his legs and steepling his fingers in concentration "—Rhiannon told me about the spell she cast to exchange places with you. She said she used the urn as a focal point. First she got it into this world." He paused and nodded in new understanding at me. "Obviously, Bres brought it when he preceded her here. Once it was in this world, she used it to draw the power to exchange the two of you."

"Makes sense, go on."

"So I decided I needed an object of power from which to work. Something that was in both worlds."

"The trees," I whispered.

"Yes," he smiled self-consciously. "I knew they held unusual power, even in a forest that resonates with energy like this one does."

"How did you know they were in Partholon, too?" I asked.

"They told me," he said simply. "I touched their power and tried to call you to me." He frowned. "At first I didn't think it was going to work. I could get a sense of you, but it was muffled and fragmented, like it wasn't really you hearing my call."

"That's because *I* didn't hear your call, Epi did." I couldn't keep the frustration out of my voice.

"Who is Epi?"

"My horse. Well, scratch that—she's not a pet or anything like that. She's the equine incarnation of our Goddess, Epona. And I guess you could say I belong to her as much as she belongs to me. She was drawn to the pin oak grove, not me." I thought back to her reaction. "But once we got to the grove, she acted strange, like she knew something was wrong."

"That explains why it was so difficult for me to get a lock on you."

"A *lock* on me?"

"I knew how you felt from knowing Rhiannon." He hurried on before I interrupted him again. "Yes, you say you are nothing alike, and I admit that you don't have her hard coldness. But it's like you are parts of the same whole. I don't know how else to describe it."

I gave him a skeptical look.

"Think of it this way. Everyone has an aura—even many scientists accept that."

I nodded.

"While I'm connected to the woods, I can clearly see auras. I can even search for one I know. Your aura and hers are almost identical." He finished simply.

It made me feel sick. "Okay, so you found me because of my aura, which must also be similar to Epi's since you *locked* on and called her, too. Then how did you get me here?"

"I called you through the trees. Rhiannon explained that there are folds between our worlds. She made them sound like louvers in plantation shutters. She said that once you find one of the folds it is possible to slide between the dimensions."

"And the trees cause a fold?"

"I don't know if they cause it, or if the fold caused them, but, yes, there is a dimensional fold between the trees. I went there, concentrated on your aura and the reason I wanted to exchange the two of you. When you touched the trees, you touched this dimension. I grabbed you and pulled."

"You grabbed me through the trees?" No wonder it had felt like I was being pulled into the trees—I was friggin being pulled into the trees!

He nodded apologetically. "I was touching the two trees and concentrating, imagining a sort of slingshot of power that would bring you here and propel Rhiannon there. Suddenly my hands seemed to slide within their bark, and I felt your hands. So I pulled."

"Okay, that's how you got me here. I'm assuming that's how I get back." My stomach fluttered anxiously as I waited for his response.

His silence made me nauseous.

"Clint?" I prompted.

"I don't know."

"Well, we are damn sure going to find out," I said as I swung my legs around and started to stand. Unexpectedly the sound of the ocean rushed in my ears, and the room began to gray dangerously as it tottered precariously on a suddenly tilted axis.

"Whoa!" His deep voice registered through the echoing noise, and I could feel his strong hands steadying me as he guided me back to the bed. "The trees will still be there in the morning."

I looked up to see his image blur, and I snapped my eyelids shut, appalled at my body's weakness. "I just want to go home," I whispered.

"I know you do, Shannon my girl." His voice was kind. "How long were you disabled when you made your first dimensional trip?"

I tried to make my amazingly tired brain concentrate. "At least a couple of days. The memory's pretty hazy." Then I added, "And I'm not your girl."

He ignored my comment. "Keep your eyes closed and sleep. Give yourself time to recover. And don't forget, you have to be strong enough to survive the return trip."

I shuddered involuntarily. Shifting dimensions was horrible. Exhaustion nagged at me, and I realized he was right. And, my mind whispered, now I had more than myself to worry about. For an instant I felt a rush of fear. Maybe I could hurt the baby with too much of this *Star Trek*–like trading of worlds. Then a familiar wave of nausea passed through me, and I felt an ironic sense of relief. As long as I had the urge to puke up my insides, I had to believe my daughter was doing just fine.

I kept my eyes closed, concentrating on relaxing and breathing deeply. I tried not to flinch as a warm hand brushed an escaping curl back from my face.

"Sleep, Shannon," he murmured.

I didn't respond, and I heard him picking up the tea and biscuit tray. Through half-open eyes I watched him disappear back around the kitchen wall, and reemerge with a fresh cup of steaming coffee. He pulled the rocker back so that it was sitting in its original spot, close to the old-time kerosene lamp. He grimaced as he lowered himself gingerly into the chair and lit the lamp. With obvious stiffness he reached for the book that rested facedown on the table. I realized I had watched that same look of pain cross Clan-

Fintan's face after he had been wounded in battle, and I couldn't help but wonder about the injury that had caused him to retire. It obviously still bothered him.

Feeling impossibly heavy, my eyelids fluttered. My last conscious image was that of the cover of the book Clint was reading. It was a collection of essays by an Oklahoma author, Connie Cronley, entitled *Sometimes a Wheel Falls Off*.

Boy, does it ever.

3

At first sleep was a dark, beguiling mist. As I submerged myself within it, a stray Shakespearean quote drifted through my changing consciousness, *O murderous slumber.* Premonition teased my sleep-filled mind, but I couldn't force myself awake, and instead I fell headlong into the arms of DreamLand—a place I usually unabashedly enjoy, even revel in. But from the first moment dream images began to form against my closed lids, I knew this experience would be different from anything I'd known before. Disjointed scenes played against a screen of night. They were ghostly, half-formed apparitions that drifted past my sleeping eyes—part centaur, part demon, part human—nothing that I recognized or could make any sense of.

My sleeping soul shivered and attempted to gain control

of the visions, as I had always been able to in the past, but this time the land that was usually populated with fun and fantasy had changed. It was twisted into a landscape of nightmares.

I knew I was sleeping, and I told myself that I could awake at any time, but this gave me little comfort as the disjointed images merged and solidified, morphing into the grotesquely familiar. Like I was watching a mad picture show at the *Hotel California*, I saw a gore-filled reenactment of the final battle between Partholon and the Fomorians—only this time the scene was minus Epona's intervention and our eventual victory. The corpses of centaurs and humans that I knew had been killed in previous battles were awakened and, zombie-like, they rose only to be slaughtered again.

Some of them only had eyes. Some of them only had fanged mouths. And some of them appeared to have been touched by a divine hand and were unbelievably beautiful. My soul recoiled from all of them.

I did not witness my own death, but I watched as first Alanna, then Carolan, Victoria and Dougal fell under the teeth and claws of the Fomorians. And still the battle raged as over and over again they were resurrected only to be slaughtered anew. Then into my range of vision swept the demon Lord of the Fomorians, Nuada. This time my husband did not vanquish him. I watched helplessly as he ruthlessly disemboweled ClanFintan.

Turning from the body of the centaur, Nuada singled out a lone warrior, one I quickly recognized as the reanimated body of Rhiannon's father, the mirror image of my dad. With a hiss of victory, the winged creature slashed MacCallan's pale throat, almost severing his head.

The scream that had been building within my mind seeped into my dream, and I could hear the echo of my father's name frame the perimeters of the awful nightmare. Suddenly the dark Lord turned and searched the area around him, as if he was looking for someone. His eyes narrowed, and he rose to his full height, wings erect and distended away from his body. Blood and foam spewed from his mouth as if he vomited maggots while he screamed, *"Yes, female! I have heard your call. We will never be free of one another—I will come for you wherever you are!"*

I gulped air and my shriek of terror brought me suddenly awake. Strong arms were shaking me, and a deep voice was thick with worry.

"Shannon—Shannon! Wake up!"

My eyes snapped open, and I looked into Clint's concerned face. My heart lurched at the familiarity of his features. Longing for ClanFintan cut me deeply.

"It's okay. I'm okay." I tried a weak smile as I pulled my arms free from his grasp.

Reluctantly he let me go. "Just a bad dream?" he asked.

"Yes." I nodded. "A nightmare." The word sounded as foreign on my lips as it actually was to my experience.

"Can I get you something? Maybe a drink of water or some tea?" He hovered, obviously reluctant to return to his rocking chair.

"No, I'm fine." His disappointed look made me add, "But thanks. I'm just really tired. I need to go back to sleep."

He glanced at his watch. "You still have several hours until dawn."

"Thanks," I repeated, turning over on my side so that I faced the wall and my back was to him.

I could hear him resettling into his chair, and I wondered briefly if he was going to spend the whole night watching over me. Not that I should care. He could spend his nights any way he'd like—I'd be out of here tomorrow and back with my husband and my people. But worry preyed on my confidence.

I'd never had a nightmare. Ever.

I was in the third grade before I realized that everyone couldn't orchestrate their dreams like I could. DreamLand had always been mine to control, and it was through my dreams that Epona pulled my soul from my sleeping body and allowed me to be her eyes and ears throughout Partholon. But tonight had been different. I hadn't experienced the goddess-induced dream vision known as the Magic Sleep. I was certain of that. The images that had played across my sleeping mind had not actually happened. Not in any dimension. It had been a nightmare—a bad dream—sleeping visions that were as unsubstantial as the booger man or the tooth fairy. Switching back and forth between worlds had probably knocked something loose in my head, and now I'd have bad dreams like everyone else.

That's all it was. Really.

I screwed my eyes shut, trying to forget about the evil I'd thought I'd sensed in Partholon. The same darkness I'd felt when Clint had pulled me through the trees to Oklahoma. The same evil Bres and Rhiannon seemed so interested in. I couldn't do anything about any of that now. I had to sleep. I forced myself to relax.

Thankfully, exhaustion beat out paranoia and worry, and I felt myself drift back into the realm of sleep. I wouldn't think about things like premonitions of evil—things that reminded me all too vividly of my nightmare.

Scarlet O'Hara–ing, I took a cleansing breath and let dreamless sleep claim me. I'd think about it tomorrow....

The incessant chatter of a mockingbird woke me.

"God, what annoying creatures," I grumbled as I rubbed my eyes. (Mockers and their nonstop chirping had been one of the things I hadn't missed about Oklahoma.)

"Good morning, Shannon my girl!" Clint looked rested and refreshed as he pulled a thick cable-knit sweater over his head.

"I'm not your girl," I grumped at him.

He just laughed heartily.

Great. He's a morning person. I filed away another similarity between him and my husband. At least this one was annoying instead of endearing.

I swung my feet over the edge of the bed and stood, careful to keep the thick comforter wrapped around my semi-bare body. "Where's the ladies' room?"

"Through the kitchen." He jerked his head in the direction of the doorway. "There's an extra toothbrush in the cabinet. And I set out some things Rhiannon left." He gave me an appraising look that felt suddenly like he could see through the comforter (which I clutched even more tightly).

"They'll fit. Make yourself at home," he said cheerily.

"Huh," I muttered, heading in that direction.

"I'll put the coffee on and make some eggs."

My stomach lurched rebelliously at the mention of food. But the evidence of morning sickness almost brought a smile to my face. The baby was fine.

"Toast and tea are all I need. And I can make both—there's no need to go to any trouble," I called over my shoulder, slightly disconcerted that he was already making my bed. Was he some kind of neat freak? Without waiting for an answer, I shook my head and walked quickly through the immaculate little kitchen, all at once very aware of the coldness of the wood floors.

The bathroom was surprisingly large and comfortable, complete with a roomy shower, claw-foot tub and, yes, a veritable plethora of toilet paper. I sighed in pleasure.

Modern plumbing *was* one of the things I had missed.

Folded neatly on the washbasin counter were clothes that I could tell were ridiculously expensive even before I touched them. Shaking them open, I fingered the black leather pants; their label read Giorgio Armani. The brown cashmere V-neck sweater was the color of autumn leaves and trimmed with black fur that could only be mink. I guessed Rhiannon had become intimately acquainted with the Tulsa Saks Fifth Avenue. A black lace bra and panty set completed the pricey number. I twirled the wisp of nothing on one finger and shook my head.

"Rhiannon, Rhiannon. Girl, you sure have a thing for thongs." That was one of our many differences. She was obsessed with thongs and bared boobs and being scantily clad. While far from a prude, I was definitely not the exhibitionist she reveled in being. And, please. I liked a nice-fitting panty that wasn't *made* to crawl up your butt. (I mean, truthfully, who doesn't?)

The shower called my name, and I spent way too long beneath the pelting stream. And brushing my teeth (twice) with Crest after flossing was practically a religious experience. Looking through the cabinet beneath the sink, I found a hair dryer and Rhiannon's stash of makeup. Looked like she'd cleaned out the Chanel counter. And in the bottom of the makeup bag was the perfect clip to keep my wild red hair back out of the way.

Pulling on the slim-fitting butter-soft pants, I laughed aloud. In place of the modern zipper was a leather string that laced up the front. She had probably had them specially made. Well, I guess you could take the girl out of Partholon, but not Partholon out of the girl.

The sweater fit like the pants—perfectly. I glanced at myself in the mirror and smiled at my reflection. One thing I couldn't deny about Rhiannon, she certainly knew how to dress us to put our best attributes on display.

Wishing for some socks, I padded quickly out of the warm bathroom and into the brightly lit kitchen. Clint's back was to me, and he was busy stirring something that my quivering stomach told me smelled like scrambled eggs and cheese. I headed to the oak table, where toasted bread was already stacked next to steaming biscuits and a variety of condiments. Nibbling on the corner of a piece of dry toast, I cleared my throat. Clint jumped and turned his head to smile at me over his shoulder. And he froze. The smile slid from his face like the tallow skin of a candle. His expression melted and changed, almost burning me with its sudden intensity. My hand stilled halfway to my mouth as I felt my body responding to that look, because I knew it—intimately. It was my husband's face staring at me with all the heat of his desire.

No! My mind rebelled. He just *looks* like ClanFintan. I pulled my eyes away from him and took a big bite of toast. Through a full mouth I asked, "Do you have any tea?"

I pretended not to notice that his voice was still shadowed with repressed lust. "Yes. I've heated the water."

"Good. I'll take some."

He unfroze and made a rough grab at a pot holder that was hanging on a hook behind the stove, then he carried the teapot over to the table and set it near a mug.

"There's tea over in the pantry." He jerked his hand at the door to the corner pantry and went back to stirring the eggs.

"Thanks," I said between bites.

"Want some eggs?"

"I think I'll stick with toast and maybe some biscuits and jam. My stomach is still doing funny things." I wasn't sure why, but I felt the need to avoid disclosing my pregnancy.

"Suit yourself," he said shortly as he ladled himself a generous helping of eggs.

Upon closer inspection I could see they had bits of ham and mushrooms along with the cheese I had so greasily smelled. I ignored them, ordering my stomach to do the same.

We ate in uncomfortable silence. He didn't look at me. I didn't look at him.

As he poured himself a second cup of coffee, and I spread strawberry jam on a still-warm biscuit, I hazarded a glance at him. He was looking everywhere but at me.

"The biscuits are good," I said sociably.

He grunted a reply.

I sighed. Might as well face the facts and quit playing hide-and-seek. "I guess me looking so much like Rhiannon is kind of a shock, especially when I'm dressed in her clothes."

His eyes slowly found their way back to me. "Shock isn't the word I would use." His tone was hollow.

"Well, you looked shocked."

"Did I, Shannon my girl?" Now he sounded amused. "It wasn't shock that I was feeling."

Uh-oh. I gulped.

Our eyes met and held. His were dark and sincere, and so hauntingly familiar they made my chest hurt. His expression mirrored ClanFintan—he was so very, very much like my love.

But not him, I reminded myself forcefully, taking a loud, unladylike slurp of hot tea.

"Good tea, too!" I smiled brightly, hoping I had a big booger hanging unattractively from my nose.

"Thank you," he said. And then added with a smile, "I think you have something stuck between your teeth."

"I hate when that happens." I laughed and sucked my teeth like an Okie.

He smiled again and shook his head before turning back to his eggs.

The tension broken, I breathed a sigh of relief and we finished our breakfast in much more companionable silence.

After a compulsory scraping of plates and quick cleanup, Clint went to a closet that was built into the space between the kitchen and the bathroom.

"Here..." He handed me a pair of thick socks and sleek-looking English riding boots.

"Thanks." I smiled at him before perching on the end of the bed. "My feet were freezing."

"You should have said something earlier," he said gruffly as he returned to the closet to drag out two thick, down-filled coats.

"It's okay," I pulled the boots on. "The floor surprised me with how cold it is, that's all," I said matter-of-factly, not comfortable with his obvious concern for my welfare.

"It's been unusually cold already this year. Snow's even forecasted for either tonight or tomorrow."

"Jeesh, snow in Oklahoma in November!"

He held the coat out for me and I shrugged my way into it, telling myself that it was ridiculous for me to feel uncomfortable when he was only helping me on with my coat. That's what gentlemen were supposed to do.

But his body seemed so damn close.

"Yes," he breathed. His mouth was near my ear as he repeated, "Snow in November."

Clint's warm breath made me shiver and I stepped quickly away from him, busying myself with zipping the coat.

"I'm ready!" I chirped.

"I forget you're in a hurry." His voice sounded strained and I again noticed the lines around his eyes and the silver in his otherwise dark hair.

A flippant remark died on my lips. I smiled sadly at him. "I'm not her, Clint."

"I don't want you to be her."

I blew air through my nose in frustration. "Well, you don't know me, so what you are attracted to *has* to be just some kind of rebound or memory of friggin Rhiannon."

"I haven't wanted Rhiannon since I realized her true nature."

I didn't know how to respond. Our eyes met. Within his I saw an incredible depth of sadness. God, it was hard to be around him and not care about what he was feeling! I couldn't help but continually notice how like ClanFintan he was, and in more ways than just his appearance. I could tell myself that he was more serious and distant, but all I had to do was think back less than six months and I would remember a handsome centaur who was at first distant and overly serious in response to me, too.

Until I loved him, my mind reminded me. Until I showed him I was not Rhiannon. And Clint didn't need to be shown, he already knew.

I reined in my errant mind.

"I have to go home." Breaking my eyes from his, I turned and walked purposefully to the door.

"I know you do, Shannon." With his long stride he beat me there to hold open the door for me.

I didn't say anything, just gave him a hesitant look, willing him to understand. Then I stepped out into the misty light of a cold Oklahoma morning.

"Brr!" I raised the collar on my coat. "Are you sure it's only the first of November?"

"Just past Samhain night."

"Don't you mean Halloween?" I raised my eyebrows at him patronizingly.

"No, Shannon my girl." He walked past me again, practically leaping down the few steps that led up to the attractive little porch, his sudden agility surprising me after the stiffness with which I'd seen him move the night before.

There was no yard. The forest seemed to begin almost exactly where the house ended. He filled his lungs with damp morning air and turned back to look pointedly at me. "I mean Samhain. I don't have to be from Partholon to understand the changing of the seasons and respect the mysteries of nature."

"I didn't mean anything." I said, chagrined at what a snob I had become (and ignoring the fact that he kept calling me his girl). "I just meant that the name Samhain is archaic here." I followed him down to the forest floor.

"Nothing is archaic that is in tune with this forest," he said gently and motioned toward a barely noticeable path that led off to our right. "This way." He strode away and I scrambled to keep up with him, mumbling under my breath about men and their egos.

"What?" he asked, looking over his shoulder at me.

"Nothing," I said quickly, then added, "How far to the spot with the dimensional bubble?"

He barked a quick laugh at my description. "Bubble—that's a pretty good description of it. Not too far." He ducked his head under a low-hanging limb. "About an hour's brisk walk."

Great. Wonder how far *too* far would be? Jeesh, I hated hiking/camping/roughing it. Suddenly Oklahoma reminded me of Partholon—and not in a nostalgic way.

"Can't we drive?" I asked, pulling what I was sure was a piece of cobweb out of my hair while I checked my wild curls frantically for spiders.

"No way to get a vehicle back here."

"Too bad you don't have a horse," I said wistfully.

"I don't like horses." He sounded defensive.

"What?" I wasn't sure I'd heard him correctly.

"I don't like horses. Never have. I don't ride at all," he said shortly.

My giggles started, and before I could control them they turned into guffaws interlaced with laughing snorts.

"What's so damn funny?"

"Didn't—" I said between giggles "—Rhiannon tell you anything about the people in Partholon?" It was just too damn funny. I mean, please. He didn't like horses and his mirror image was part horse.

"She said she didn't want to be there because she was being forced to mate with someone she didn't love. And there were demonic beings attacking the world. That was it." He sounded curious even though he kept throwing me annoyed looks every time I couldn't swallow my laughter.

"Clint, Rhiannon didn't want to be mated with ClanFintan because he would have cramped her style. She wasn't exactly a one-man woman." Even if that one man was a shapeshifting centaur and High Shaman of his people, I added to myself.

"Yes, I found that out."

The bleak tone of his voice sobered me. It shouldn't be so hard for me to remember that this man had been used and hurt by my mirror. By now I should be getting used to dealing with the consequences of her messes.

"So—what was funny?"

"Uh," I faltered. "Your, um, mirror image in Partholon—let's just say he's quite a horseman." Literally—horse*man*. I had to stifle another episode of giggles. God, I crack myself up.

"That just goes to prove what you've been saying all along about you and Rhiannon. Mirror images can be very different." He looked back over his shoulder and raised one eyebrow at me, using an expression that was so like Clan-Fintan I couldn't help but smile warmly in response.

"Exactly."

He certainly was cute.

Our eyes locked and he stumbled, almost running head-first into a tree. I looked away quickly, pretending not to notice (and practically chewing a bloody hole in the side of my cheek to keep from laughing).

The small trail took an abrupt right turn and headed steeply uphill, causing us to shift our wavering concentration back to what I considered to be the way too strenuous process of hiking.

No wonder there's no such thing as Backpacking Barbie.

The trail continued to snake uphill and Clint set a good pace. I was pleased that I was breathing steadily, not huffing and puffing, and it certainly wasn't a strain for me to keep up with him. Actually, I realized that the farther we went into the forest, the more invigorated I felt. It was like

I was getting my second, third and fourth wind. I grinned at myself, loving the feel of my leg muscles pumping smoothly as I climbed steadily, following Clint's broad back.

I felt so good that I had time to look around. The trees were dense and thick, reminding me of something out of a *National Geographic* snapshot. Oaks and hackberries mixed harmoniously with the evergreen pines and junipers; their arms entwined to block out all but just a glimpse of the slate-colored morning sky. The undergrowth was carpeted with dead leaves, broken branches and prickly tufts of some kind of bramble. It looked like the forest fairies had forgotten to vacuum.

Then I heard the whispering. At first I thought it was the wind through the empty branches. But when I looked up I saw that the branches weren't moving. There was very little breeze, certainly not enough to stir the bare branches noisily.

I passed an especially large tree that I had to literally step around because its thick base almost blocked the path of the trail. My arm brushed against its weathered trunk.

"*Welcome, Beloved.*" The teasing breeze solidified into words within my mind and I jolted to a stop.

"Shannon?" Several yards down the path Clint stopped, too.

"I heard something." I said inanely.

He looked sharply around, listening intently before he replied. "There's no one here."

"No," I said slowly, and pointed to my head. "I heard something in here."

"What did you hear?" His tone was excited as he hurried back down the path to me.

"Something welcomed me." My voice caught. "And called me Beloved." The name my Goddess calls me, I thought, but didn't say out loud.

He looked around us and his eyes came to rest on the huge tree I had just passed. "Maybe it was this ancient one." He stepped to the tree and pulled the glove off his right hand. Resting his open palm against the rough bark, he closed his eyes, his face tight with concentration. Then the lines on his brow smoothed and his lips lifted in a soft smile. He opened his eyes and nodded encouragingly for me to join him.

Remembering the electric zap I'd received last time I'd tried to "listen" to a tree, I froze.

When I didn't move, he reached out and took my hand in his and pressed it firmly against the tree.

I tensed, unconsciously waiting for something horrible to happen. But this time was different. First I felt a pleasant warmth beneath my hand, like it was resting on the skin of a living animal. Then the warmth flowed into my body through my palm, and with it came a wonderful rush of emotion, as if I had just unexpectedly met an old friend.

"Welcome, Beloved of Epona!" This time there was no mistaking them for the wind; the words rang clearly in my mind.

"Oh!" I breathed in awe, raising my other hand to press it, too, firmly against the ancient bark. "You know who I am!"

"Yessss..." The internal voice trailed off in a way that reminded me very much of delighted feminine laughter.

"Oh, Clint!" I stepped closer to the tree, laying my cheek against its rough side. "She knows me." I blinked tears back, unabashedly happy at being hailed as Epona's Beloved again.

"The forest speaks to you." He sounded pleased.

I nodded happily, not wanting to let loose of the tree.

"If they know who I am, surely that means they'll help me get back to Partholon!" I breathed deeply and sent a silent request to the ancient spirit of the tree.

"Then we should get moving." The pleasure was gone from his voice, replaced with grim finality.

I blinked in surprise, feeling an echo of his sorrow within the tree.

Caressing the bark in parting, my mind whispered to the tree that he was not my husband...not my husband...not my husband. I stepped slowly away from the oak.

"You're right." I steeled myself against my emerging feelings for the man who stood so close to me. "I need to be going."

Clint nodded jerkily and turned, abruptly retracing his steps. I fell in again behind him, listening in amazement to the whispers that brushed through my mind.

"Hail, Epona!"

"Well met, Beloved!"

"Blessings upon you!"

"We welcome you, Epona's Beloved!"

I felt submerged in joy at this acceptance and acknowledgment, and took every opportunity I could to brush my fingers caressingly against the trunks and limbs of the trees closest to the path. Each time I touched a tree, especially one of the older, thicker giants, a surge of warmth passed through my fingers and into my body. Very soon I realized that with the surge came energy.

"Hey!" I yelled to Clint's back. "I'm getting some kind of power rush from these trees!"

"I know," he said without turning to look at me or slowing his pace.

I paused long enough to let my hand linger down the spine of another gnarled trunk. Zap! The warmth poured into my body. "Oh, man! It's like I'm friggin Wonder Woman or something." I put my hands to my cold cheeks and felt the lingering heat that had not come from my body. I swear, if I'd untied my hair it would have crackled and stood on end (I mean even more than it usually does).

Suddenly Clint stopped and turned to face me. "Not like a superhero, like a goddess."

"Yes," I said breathlessly as my heart lurched at his words. "Yes," I repeated, "divine. And not divine because of a mistake, divine by choice."

Clint lifted his hand, almost touching my cheek. A raw look of longing crossed his familiar features. It made me ache, but I didn't move toward him. I couldn't. His hand dropped limply back to his side and he broke our gaze. Looking to the right of the path, he pointed.

"It's this way. Follow me."

I nodded enthusiastically, eager to be off the path and even more immersed within the forest. I forced myself to ignore his somber expression and the slump of his broad shoulders.

We hadn't gone more than one hundred paces when we broke free of the trees and underbrush and stood at the edge of a small clearing. I gasped and looked around me in amazement.

"Holy shit! It's exactly like it was in Partholon."

The same clear, tranquil stream gurgled through the glade, its bright waters running into the forest away from us. But my eyes weren't focused on the stream; they were drawn to the two enormous pin oaks that straddled it. As they had in Partholon, their massive branches were filled with verdant leaves, belying the frigid November weather. Their limbs were so entwined that it was impossible to tell where one tree ended and the other began. It was as if time had fused them together. Their thick trunks were covered with luminous moss that glowed and beckoned.

Without a word, Clint and I started walking toward the trees together. I noticed how still the air had become, and the odd absence of birdsong. The closer we got to the trees, the more I could feel them. It was like they radiated a beacon, and I was the magnet it drew. Halting within touching distance, I pulled my attention from the trees and looked at Clint.

"What now?" My voice sounded strained.

"What I did before," he said quietly, as if we were in church, "was to concentrate on pulling the power from the forest into a single ball within me."

I blinked in surprise and he gave me a fleeting smile.

"Yes, I experience the power of this forest, too. Not as much as you do. It doesn't flow freely into me, but I am able to tap into it. Usually I use it to strengthen myself physically."

"You mean like Storm from the X-Men uses the power of wind to fly or something?" I was only half joking. And yes, I know I'm a dork.

"Not exactly." His smile grew. "More like super Tylenol for my stiff back."

No wonder he seemed so agile after he entered the forest. I nodded in understanding and he continued.

"After I pulled what power I could within me, I concentrated on Rhiannon and all the reasons why she should not be in this world. Then I focused on your aura, trying to call you to me. As you already told me, I didn't actually call you, but your horse, to the clearing."

"I could hear the trees calling me once I got here," I said.

"Yes, so I concentrated on slinging Rhiannon there and you here, and when you touched the trees I grabbed you and pulled." He made a yanking motion with his hands. "I have no idea why Rhiannon wasn't affected, but here you are."

"Okay, well..." I rubbed my hands together and stepped determinedly to the trees. "At least this time we don't have to worry about concentrating on Rhiannon. She can stay the hell here. Let's just get me home."

I straddled the stream, just as I remembered doing before I had been yanked here. Resolutely I raised my hands and lay their open palms against the emerald moss. The jolt of warmth I felt zap into my hands thrilled me with its intensity.

Through gritted teeth I said to Clint, "I don't think finding enough power will be a problem. I feel like I could leap friggin tall buildings in a single bound."

"Concentrate on Partholon."

Clint's voice had deepened so that he sounded so much like ClanFintan I looked quickly up at him, almost expecting to see my husband in his place. No, my mind reminded me as I studied his very human features. It's just his mirror; it's not him.

"Go ahead, Shannon my girl." His voice had dropped so low that I had to strain to hear him above the powerful buzzing of the trees. "Go back to him. Go home."

"Thank you," I whispered through unexpected tears before I turned my attention to the trees.

Bowing my head, I pressed my hands more firmly against their mossy sides and stared down into the clear waters of the little stream. It was through them that I had first glimpsed this world again, so it made sense that they held part of the key to Partholon.

I concentrated. Epi came to my mind first, and I let my memory call up the softness of her muzzle as she nuzzled me after whickering a welcome. How her liquid brown eyes seemed to reflect all the best aspects of my soul. And I remembered Alanna, not as a mirror of my friend from this world, but as I had come to love her for herself. Her own unique sweetness and sense of humor, and the way she loved to manage me.

Then I let images of ClanFintan flood my mind. I thought about how he had struggled not to fall in love with me, believing at first that I was Rhiannon, but how he was unable to maintain his unfeeling distance. How he had protected me and loved me. The way he brushed my curls back from my face before he cupped my chin, and the warmth of his body as he bent his lips to mine.

Pushing gently, I tested the tree trunks, hoping to feel them becoming soft under my hands. They were firm and unmoving. I sighed in exasperation and dropped my palms from the trees.

"It's not working." I turned to Clint. "Maybe you have to help. I mean, you got me here, maybe you have to be involved in getting me back." I motioned to the other side of the trees. "Why don't you stand across from me, just like I'm standing on this side. Try thinking about that slingshot thing, like you did right before the trees got soft and you grabbed me through them."

He nodded and stepped around the oak, positioning himself so that he, too, was straddling the stream.

"Are you ready?" I asked.

He nodded again and together we raised our hands until our palms pushed against opposite sides of the trees. We were facing each other, and I looked up to meet the intensity of his gaze. The power of the trees surged between us and I realized that I could feel within them the beating of Clint's heart and the pulsing of his blood. It was as if I was connected to his life force. I blinked rapidly and unexpectedly I could see the aura that silhouetted him. It was jewel blue tinged with faceted shades of amber and gold around the edges. And it was hypnotic.

His voice broke into my mind. It was raw with emotion. "If you want me to think about sending you away from here, you have to stop looking at me like that."

"I'm sorry!" I snapped my eyes shut, forcing his image from my mind.

ClanFintan! I summoned my memories. I remembered his gentleness with me, how he let me accustom myself to the reality of loving a being that was so foreign to everything I'd ever experienced. How I had fallen in love with his integrity and honesty before I knew his heart and soul. I remembered the Change, and its poignant beauty, which caused him to endure such pain before we could make love.

Beneath my palms I felt the skin of the moss quiver. Keeping my head bowed, I opened my eyes and focused on the stream of water beneath me. As I watched, the water shifted and refracted, like a well-oiled window being lifted. I peered through the opening to glimpse the world beyond.

I could see the mirrored clearing. It looked exactly like this one, only it was empty. Without hesitation, I called the power that surged within me and cast it through the water and into Partholon, like a long-distance homing device held on a cord of energy. Again, I felt shivers run through the trees, and I concentrated on the aura I had seen surrounding Clint just moments earlier. I focused on calling its mirror image to me.

I didn't have a sense of time passing, all I knew was that I had to keep all of my being focused on that call. Soon I had to blink quickly to clear the drops of sweat that ran from my forehead and pooled around my eyes. Part of me could feel that my breathing had increased and that my clothes were becoming soaked through, and hung in damp folds against my body.

My arms had begun to shake when I heard a sound that quickly grew in intensity. Almost hypnotized, I gazed through the stream and with a crash of breaking undergrowth ClanFintan stormed into the clearing, his sapphire-blue aura plainly visible—the gold around its edges pulsing wildly.

"*Shannon!*" The power in his voice echoed eerily through the stream.

"Here!" I cried in response.

His centaur body lunged with inhuman speed to the trees. He slid to a halt in the exact place held by Clint in this world.

"How do I help you?" The frustration in his voice was a reflection of my own.

"Concentrate! Put your hands against the trees and think of me."

Immediately he raised his hands so that they lay against the trees. I saw his eyes close and heard the echo of his response. *"My love, I think of nothing else."*

I pushed, and felt my hands slide into moss that now felt like warm jelly. Again I heaved forward and the liquid mass enclosed my arms up to the elbows. I slipped forward even farther and suddenly felt my palms touch another's hands. Those hands were larger and warmer than a human man's.

Through the stream I could see ClanFintan's eyes shoot open and I tried frantically to make my hands obey my order to grab onto his.

Then from somewhere behind him I saw a flutter of activity as a curtain of darkness entered the clearing. At that instant I felt a change within the trees. The power I had been tapping into faltered and sputtered, as if something was draining it away from me.

I turned my head slightly, dividing my attention between ClanFintan and the thing that was now well within the Partholonian clearing. The darkness rippled and oozed from the forest, seeping over the ground like an oil spill. As it got close, I was shrouded by all too familiar feeling. A shudder ran through my body and I identified the source of that familiarity, and as understanding hit me I couldn't believe I hadn't recognized it before now. Evil. The kind of evil that had traveled with the Fomorian army.

The shadow came closer. It had no real form, and was hard to see clearly—like it was a shadow within a shadow.

Through our touching palms, I felt ClanFintan's body shudder.

"*Something is...*" His words echoed through the divide and he raised his head to glance over his shoulder.

And then the dark shape liquefied completely, spilling slickly into the crystal stream. In horror I saw the waters at my feet turn a loathsome, oily black as darkness spewed from one world to another.

"*Shannon! What is happening?*" ClanFintan's voice seemed farther away.

"I don't kn—" My words broke off as the thing swirled past my feet and leeched up on the bank. It drew itself up and solidified into a winged shape that sent my breath rushing from my body in a panicked burst that was one word.

"Nuada!"

"Yessss, female," the creature gurgled from the darkness that was its mouth. "I have answered your call. Now we shall begin our game anew."

"No!" I screamed at him. My concentration shattered. I could no longer feel ClanFintan.

As the trees spit my hands out of their liquid interior, I heard my name torn from my husband's throat in a single savage call. Like a giant had blown its breath over the surface of the stream, the water shifted and the mirror image of Partholon disappeared. I stumbled several steps away from the trees.

The creature moved toward me with a liquid, slithering sound.

"I am pleased you called to me." His voice gurgled with a dark parody of laughter. Then he raised half-formed arms, trying to curl his molten hands into claws.

I stared at the thing in front of me, my mind unable to grasp what I was seeing.

"But you're dead," I said stupidly.

"No longer, female," hissed his wet reply. "We are connected. Do not pretend that you did not use dark power to awaken me and summon me here." He moved closer and I watched in horror as his claws began to solidify. "I have missed you, female, almost as much as I have missed feeling life within me."

"Stay back." Clint's calm voice split the air between us and he stepped protectively in front of me.

Nuada stopped, glaring at the man. "This weak reflection of your mutant mate thinks you belong to him." Pieces of darkness spewed from his lips as he hurled the words at Clint. I could see the creature's aura pulsing around him, with a blackness that was the complete absence of goodness. He pulled himself up to his full height, spreading his pulsing wings. "I shall enjoy killing him."

"No!" I screamed.

Nuada descended upon Clint. A shadow within a shadow, he seemed to melt to the human. I stood frozen in shock; all I could do was watch the creature absorb Clint. But as his claws drove down for a disemboweling blow, Clint's own aura shimmered and the outer gold tinge crackled, shooting sparks where it came in contact with Nuada's darkness.

The creature shrieked and stepped back.

"Human!" Nuada's voice held the sound of death. "I feel your magic, but you have not the strength to stand against me." The creature held his dripping arms to the sky, and it seemed that shadows from the forest disengaged themselves and flew into his hands. His death-colored aura pulsed madly. The creature moved forward again.

This time when he came into contact with Clint's aura, the brilliant golden sparks had faded to the yellow of candlelight. It was enough to make Nuada step back once more, but only just out of reach of the aura. I saw the strain clearly visible on Clint's sweat-covered face, as did the demon.

"Your pathetic strength is waning." Nuada hissed as he moved forward again.

I lunged to Clint's side and grabbed his hand with both of mine, which were still unnaturally warm from their contact with the trees. Concentrating, I hurled all of that warmth into Clint, just as I had hurled it through the stream and into Partholon. At the same moment, Nuada stepped within the walls of the vibrant blue fortress.

Sparks shot like lightning through Nuada's dark body and his scream echoed against the forest edge. Nuada's form seemed to collapse in upon itself as he was flung backward.

"You are mine. Until I posses you, what you love I will destroy, be it in this world or the next." The words hung in the air as the shadowy form dissipated into the forest.

A wave of dizziness sloshed through my head, blurring my sight. My knees buckled. With a groan, I dropped Clint's hand and fell to the cold ground.

"Shannon!" Clint knelt beside me, pulling me into his arms.

"I c-c-can't f-feel my l-legs." My teeth were chattering and I was shaking uncontrollably. I looked up into Clint's pale face and tried to lift my hand to touch his cheek, but my arm wouldn't obey the simple command. I felt oddly detached from my body, like it and I didn't belong together.

"Don't talk," he said. Frantically, he threaded his hands under my armpits and linked them across my chest. Breathing heavily, he heaved backward, dragging me toward the two pin oaks.

My vision tunneled until a thick band of gray framed everything. I heard a strange noise, and realized it was my own breath coming in gasps.

With a grunt, Clint closed the last bit of space between the trees and us. Gently he stepped from behind me, and pulled me into a sitting position so that I was resting my back against one of the mossy trunks.

As if it was happening to someone else, I could feel the heat of the tree against my back, but that warmth didn't seem accessible any longer. The cold in my body was too overwhelming, and my consciousness began to flicker like a candle in a gale.

Through a film of gray I could see Clint drop to his knees, straddling my lap. He reached up and put his palms on either side of my head, pressing them against the side of the tree.

"Help her," he demanded. "She's dying!"

The jolt of warmth that flowed urgently into my body shocked me, and a groan of pain escaped my numbed lips as feeling began to return to my limbs. My arms and legs were being pricked with hundreds of sharp little pins. My expanding chest felt tight as I breathed deeply. I gulped the life-bringing air and realized groggily that I must have quit breathing. With paralyzing fear I thought of my child, and was rewarded with a wonderful rush of nausea. *Oh, Epona, let her be safe.*

The gray mist swirled, and then cleared from my vision.

Clint's face swam into focus. This time my arm obeyed me when I told it to lift, and I reached up, letting my thumb wipe away a tear that slid down the side of his face.

"I'm okay now." My voice was a weak whisper.

"Thank your Goddess," he rasped. I noticed his arms were trembling.

"And you." My hand fell back to my side, and I pressed my back more firmly against the life-giving oak.

Clint rocked back on his heels and moved off my lap to sit beside me, his own back resting against the tree, too. I could feel him watching me, but I didn't turn my head to meet his gaze. Instead, I stared across the clearing, trying to comprehend what had just happened.

At that moment, the slate-colored sky opened and delicate flakes began to fall silently to the ground.

"It's snowing," I said softly.

I could feel Clint's jerk of surprise. "Do you think you can move away from the tree now?"

I nodded weakly, suddenly aware of the chill in the air and the cold dampness of my sweat-soaked clothing. Stiffly Clint pushed himself to his feet. I raised my hands and he pulled me up to stand beside him, putting gloves on us both.

"Can you walk?" he asked.

"Yes." My voice still sounded strange, but at least I was firmly attached to my body again. I was wobbly and light-headed, but I was pretty sure I could walk.

I looked up at the swollen sky. The delicate flakes had been replaced with thicker, thumb-size blobs and the wind had picked up, causing them to fall at a sharp angle. I shivered and drew the damp collar of my coat around my neck.

"We need to get back to the cabin." Clint's tone reflected his worried expression. He linked his arm through mine, and we stepped out of the shelter of the two trees and into the wind-driven snow.

My legs were unsure, and I leaned heavily on Clint's arm. My breath was coming hard as we reached the edge of the clearing and stepped beneath the canopy of the forest. We picked our way slowly through the undergrowth until we found the small path. Not giving me time to pause, Clint pulled me down the path until we came to an especially ancient-looking oak. Then he guided me the few steps off the trail to the massive tree and let me lean numbly against its healing trunk. My eyes closed as I drew within me its warmth and the tendrils of its power.

"Rest, Beloved of Epona," fluttered through my tired mind.

"Ready?" All too soon Clint was prodding me forward.

The journey back to the house took on a surrealistic pattern. I would stumble down the path, holding tightly to Clint's strong arm until I thought I could go no farther, then he would guide me to an ancient tree. I was like a cell phone being partially recharged—my thoughts were broken and scattered.

The ever-present Oklahoma wind continued to increase until snow was forced through the thick ceiling of the forest. Daylight faded and my fragmented thoughts wondered how long we had spent trying to open the door into Partholon. I must have spoken the question aloud because Clint's answer broke the silence.

"Hours." His tone reflected his exhaustion. "It will be dark soon."

I gasped in surprise.

"You can make it, Shannon my girl. We're almost home." He tried to sound reassuring as we continued forward.

Home—the word lingered in the snow-tinted air. Home was what I had just left back in the clearing. The sorrow in ClanFintan's fading voice still echoed in my heart.

I stumbled on a step and lurched back, shaking my head in confusion. Clint's arm went around me and he half carried, half dragged me up the stairs and through the door.

"Sit here. I'll start a fire."

I fell into the rocking chair and watched as he knelt before the fireplace. He tore off his gloves and his shaking hands hurried to strike the match. Our breath was clearly visible in the frigid air of the cabin.

The fire caught easily and was soon crackling with heat. But the warmth couldn't reach me. My teeth chattered and my face felt numb.

Clint paused only long enough to tear off his coat and pull off his wet sweater and shirt before kicking off his boots and pants. He moved quickly to the dresser that stood next to the bed and yanked open one of its drawers. He grabbed a sweatshirt and threw it over his head. With almost the same movement he jerked on a clean pair of jeans. Then he searched through the drawer until he found another sweatshirt and a pair of sweatpants. With his free hand, he grabbed the afghan off the end of the bed. Then he rushed back to my side. By this time I was shivering uncontrollably.

He started fumbling with the zipper of my coat until he had it undone, then he roughly pulled it off and started to yank the cashmere sweater over my head.

"Hey!" I sputtered, but he paid no attention to me. Instead, he pulled off my boots before he boosted me to a standing position where I tottered drunkenly as he stripped me of my leather pants. Methodically he rubbed my body dry with the afghan before dressing me in the sweatshirt and pants.

"Sit while I get us something warm to drink." He pushed me back into the chair, which he then pulled even closer to the fireplace, covered my lap with the afghan and stepped purposefully into the kitchen.

"The man is like a damn tornado," I muttered through lips that I was sure were blue. I could hear him rattling pots and opening and closing the door to the refrigerator. Shifting my weight so that the rocker leaned forward toward the brightly burning fire, I held my hands to its warmth, relieved I was no longer shaking uncontrollably.

Clint returned quickly and shoved a mug of steaming liquid into my hands. I took it and he hurried back to the kitchen.

"Drink it," he threw over his shoulder.

I hugged the mug with my hands and sipped. The hot chocolate was warm and rich, and I felt my body come alive as the drink made its way down my throat and into my empty stomach, which growled menacingly.

Before I could call for him, Clint reappeared, holding a tray laden with hastily put-together sandwiches, another mug and a pan of steaming chocolate. He handed me a sandwich before pulling the other rocker next to mine and helping himself to his own.

I bit into the thick ham and cheese that rested between two slices of homemade sourdough bread. Thankfully, my morning sickness seemed to be (at least for today) limiting itself to the morning, and the sandwich was the best thing I'd ever tasted in my life.

"This is good," I said around the delicious sandwich.

"Just eat." His voice was rough and he was staring into the fire as he ate. Then he must have regretted his tone because his gaze left the fire and softened as it found my face. "It'll make you feel better."

I gulped some more of the hot chocolate and nodded. "I already do."

He smiled his relief and we finished our food in silence.

I had just swallowed the last of the hot chocolate when my yawn started deep within me.

"You need sleep."

A shimmer of fear touched my tired mind. "But what if Nuada comes back?" I could hardly believe I was just now thinking of the possibility.

Clint took my hand and pulled me out of the chair. "Nuada. That's what you called it back in the clearing."

My hand tightened on his. "He was Lord of the creatures we fought against. He's supposed to be dead."

Clint put one finger gently against my lips, effectively shushing me.

"You can explain after you sleep. And I don't think he will come back tonight. He was only partially formed, so his recovery would have to be even slower than ours."

"But what if it's not?" I couldn't help the tremble of fear that went through my body.

"I would know if anything approached this cabin."

"How?" I asked.

"Trust me," he said as he led me to the bed and pulled

back the thick down comforter. I sank into its softness, realizing I would not be able to stay conscious much longer. I curled on my side and Clint covered me before he started to turn back to the chair by the fire. I grabbed his hand, stopping him.

"Is there another bed up there?" I jerked my head toward the loft above us.

"No," he answered quietly. "Just a computer and a desk."

"Then sleep here. You're exhausted, too."

Clint paused and his eyes searched mine. Then he nodded tiredly and went to the other side of the bed. I could feel it sag with his weight. My back was to him, and without a word he put his arm around my waist and pulled me snuggly against his warmth. I knew I shouldn't, but I fell asleep feeling the security of his heartbeat against my body.

5

My dreaming mind felt odd, fuzzy—not like the precursor to the DreamLand I was accustomed to slipping so easily into. My sleeping self cringed, expecting a replay of the nightmares that had visited me the previous night. Instead against my closed eyelids a scene that could have been from my childhood wavered and finally focused.

The brick ranch-style home sat atop a gentle rise in the land. The front door opened to a concrete patio that was surrounded by fragrant butterfly bushes interspersed between homemade brick planters that spilled over with wildly blooming petunias. Half a dozen wrought-iron lawn chairs in various stages of rust were staggered around a huge Oklahoma sandstone rock. An enormous oak stood sentinel in the front yard. My sleeping self smiled as I watched a gentle wind caress the leaves; that front yard never failed to catch a cool breeze.

The screen door opened with a bang and my dad stepped into the scene. He had a horse's halter slung over his shoulder and an ice pick–like tool in his hand. He sat in one of the chairs and leaned forward, spreading the halter out on the rock. Then he began working at it with the tool. His broad shoulders curled and the thick muscles in his football player arms bunched with a strength that belied the gray in his hair.

Even though my conscious mind knew I was dreaming, joy filled my soul. My dad was alive in this world!

"Hon!" The sweet Oklahoma drawl softened my stepmom's voice as she called from the house. "You know you could just go buy a new halter instead of fooling with that old one."

"Nope, nope," Dad mumbled. "This'll be fine."

"Well, how about a cold Coors?"

"That doesn't sound half-bad," he said, a small smile playing across his face.

And the dream scene froze. My sleeping mind instantly tensed as my attention shifted from the freeze-frame of my father to the pastureland that surrounded the yard. And within that frozen dream vision darkness seemed to seep from the edges of the land.

Until I possess you, what you love I will destroy, be it in this world or the next.

Like smooth stones, the words turned over and over in my mind until the dreaming view of my father darkened into nothingness.

My eyes opened abruptly to focus on Clint's back as he bent to add more crackling wood to the cheerily burning fire. I tried to get my breathing under control and still the wild pounding of my heart before he turned around.

As with the dream the previous night, I knew this vision had not been one of my Magic Sleep journeys, which were basically soul-departing trips that my Goddess initiated so that I could witness events that were actually taking place. This had the feel of a dream, with the shadow of a nightmare mixed within its texture. But did the fact that I wasn't actually witnessing events as they happened mean that my Goddess wasn't at work here? Perhaps Epona's powers weren't as clearly defined in this world, especially if my gut feeling was right—Pryderi was somehow at work within this evil. What if Epona was trying to warn me? The rush of emotion that followed that thought was much more refined than simple intuition.

I sat up and Clint turned to look at me, surprised I was awake.

"Nuada is after my dad," I said with grim certainty.

Clint nodded. "I don't doubt that." He paused. "Did he know your father's mirror image in Partholon?"

"Nuada killed him." I spoke quietly. "I watched as it happened."

"Then we will have to warn him." He glanced at the phone.

My laugh was humorless. "I don't think this is something that can be explained over the phone. I need to see him."

"Where does he live?" Clint asked as he went to the window and pushed aside the heavy plaid curtain.

"Just a few miles outside of Broken Arrow, which isn't far from Tulsa."

"I used to live in Tulsa. I know BA," he said over his shoulder. He shook his head as he studied the scene outside the window. "The forest warned me that winter would be long this year, and I knew it had been unusually cold lately, but I wouldn't have believed so much snow so early would be possible."

I rose stiffly from the bed and hobbled to join him. I peered out onto a scene that should have been set in February in Wisconsin, not early November in Oklahoma. The moon's fairy light mingled with the still-falling snow. The treed world outside the door had opened its naked arms to embrace the early snowstorm. Like old men clothed in lopsided furs, the trees and bushes were already covered with a thick layer of white.

"My God! It looks like the friggin frozen tundra." I shivered, doubly glad of the heat of the fire and the thickness of the borrowed clothing.

"Can you travel?" Clint was still staring out at the changed landscape.

"Do you mean walk out of here?" I felt tired deep within my body.

"No, I'm not a total recluse. I have a vehicle. But if we wait much longer I'm afraid the roads will be impassable, and we will have to walk."

I shook off my pervading weariness. "Then let's get out of here." I looked down at Clint's baggy sweatpants that pooled around my ankles. "I don't suppose Rhiannon left any other clothes, did she?"

Clint studied me and shook his head. "Nope." There was a hint of a smile in his voice. "You'll have to wear my clothes until we can get you something else. Isn't there a Wal-Mart in Broken Arrow?"

"A Wal-Mart?" I gave him a sideways glance as I picked up my boots that had been drying in front of the fireplace. "I had no idea you were such a classy guy."

"Just tryin' to help, ma'am." He tipped an imaginary hat at me before he bent to pull on his own boots.

I grumbled under my breath at him. Men.

I didn't realize I was hungry again until Clint mentioned that it would probably be wise to pack some sandwiches to take with us, so I ate hastily while we made food to go and tried not to notice the strange, continuous plopping against the windows of the thick snowflakes carpeting the outside world.

"Ready?" Clint asked as he motioned me to the front door.

I nodded and zipped my coat. Clint opened the door and an icy breeze rushed past us, bringing with it the crisp scent of new fallen snow. We stepped onto the porch.

"Wow!" My breath hung before me like a mini-cloud of fog. "This is amazing."

It was still snowing, and the land had taken on that distinctive silence that snowfall creates, like sound had been swallowed by the whiteness. The wind had let up, so the flakes were drifting almost lazily in a straight downward path—one on top of another on top of another. The scene appeared serene and harmless.

I jumped in surprise as a branch of a tree to my right suddenly cracked under the weight of the thick snow and avalanched to the ground, effectively dispelling my placid snow fantasy.

"We need to go." Clint's voice was grim. "Come on, the Hummer's under the carport on the other side of the cabin."

A Hummer? Good Lord. Disability must be really good to him; those monsters cost a fortune. I didn't have time to comment, though, because I was struggling through the almost knee-deep snow, trying to keep up with Clint's much longer strides as he marched purposefully around the cabin. The moon's waning light was muffled by the thick layer of clouds, so it was hard for me to see the vehicle that sat quietly under the snow-laden carport until we were right up on it, and then I started in surprise. It wasn't one of the new, quasi-military SUVs that were so chic with upper-middle-class aging preppies. Instead, this thing was painted a dull gray-green, and looked like an odd mixture of a Jeep, a truck and a tank. Clint opened a rear door and shoved in the bag filled with our hastily prepared food. Then he moved to the passenger's side and unlocked the door for me. I slid into the cold seat and peered through the darkness at the strange vehicle. Clint turned the ignition key and the thing roared immediately to life.

"What did you call this?" I asked as he slipped the stick shift into reverse and we sliced neatly through the untouched snow.

"It's a Hummer," he said, straightening the wheel, sliding it into first and heading off to his left toward a small break in the trees. "That's a Hum-V. And, no, it's not one of those sissy copies that dealers sell to people with too damn much money. This is an authentic military vehicle." He caressed it into second as we entered the forest.

"It certainly is, uh, square," I said, snapping on my seat belt.

He laughed. "It's not pretty, but it can go just about anywhere a tank can go. And it can get us through this snowstorm."

Clint drove on and I stayed quiet, letting him concentrate on keeping in the middle of the snow-packed path.

After we had traveled for almost half an hour, the snow seemed to be letting up. When I caught glimpses of the sky through the trees, I could see signs of dawn beginning to lighten the otherwise unremitting gray of the clouds.

"Is there really a road out there?" The last few miles the trees had almost brushed against the sides of the Hummer, and Clint had had to slow the vehicle considerably so that we didn't slide off into the midst of them.

"There's what you would call a real road, but it's about thirty miles from the cabin. We'll hook up with it soon enough." He smiled at my shocked expression. "This is just a path that I ground out of the forest over the past five or so years."

"You live thirty miles from a real road?" And I had thought Partholon was rustic! Epona's ancient temple was an opulent, thriving metropolis compared to this wilderness.

"I like being near the heart of the forest," he said cryptically. His tone implied that he didn't want to talk about why. And, sure enough, he abruptly changed the subject.

"That centaur who came into the clearing, he's your husband?" His words sounded clipped.

"Yes. His name is ClanFintan."

"He and I are…" His voice trailed away uncomfortably.

"Mirrors of one another," I finished for him.

He made a sound that was a male grunt for begrudging acknowledgment. Then he was silent. I decided to let him ponder the zillions of questions that must be running through his all-too-human brain.

"He's half horse," he finally said.

"Yes."

"Then how the hell can you be married to him?"

"Easy—we had a ceremony. Exchanged vows. You know, the normal marriage stuff." I deliberately avoided the obvious undercurrent in his questioning. If intimate details were that important to him, he'd have to ask.

He gave me an exasperated look. I blinked innocently back at him.

"Damnit, Shannon! You know what I mean. Rhiannon said she didn't want to marry this guy, but I had no idea it was because he wasn't human. And now here you are, doing your best to get back to that..." He paused, searching for the right word. "Animal!"

I felt the blood rush to my cheeks as my temper exploded to meet his. "I'll have you know, Mr. Freeman, that ClanFintan is decidedly not an animal. He is *more* than a human man—in every way." I spat the words at him. "More noble! More honest! More *everything!* And his being a centaur had nothing to do with why that bitch didn't want to be mated with him. She didn't want him because she got off on letting anyone and everyone crawl between her legs—as she proved by fucking you!"

"You really do love him," he said with disbelief.

"Of course I love him! And Nuada was right about one thing. You're nothing but a weak imitation of him!" I was sorry almost as soon as I'd said the words. Of course, Clint would be shocked at my mating with a creature who was half man, half horse. Shit, *I'd* been more than a little shocked in the beginning. And he had no idea ClanFintan could shapeshift into human form. I realized that my angry reaction was more than a wife standing up for her husband. I sneaked a look at Clint's face, which had frozen into a rocklike expression as he kept his mouth shut and his eyes on the snowy path.

I cared about him. I couldn't help it; he was simply too much like ClanFintan for me *not* to care. I drew in a deep breath. No, I didn't actually love him—yet. But the desire was there, and it was a desire that had more to do with intimacy than just screwing his brains out (although, I admitted to myself, I understood that it certainly hadn't been a hardship for Rhiannon to keep him in her bed). Being with him felt right; falling in love with him would be simple. But it didn't change the facts. He wasn't my husband. He wasn't the man to whom I had promised fidelity. A world away or not, I belonged to someone else. And I would not betray that promise.

"Clint," I said softly. He didn't respond, but I continued. "I'm sorry I said that. It was uncalled for. I know what you're asking, and I really don't blame you for being…well…confused." His face thawed a little and he glanced in my direction. "Would it make more sense if I told you that ClanFintan is a powerful High Shaman, which means he can shapeshift to human form at will?"

"That's possible?" he asked, his surprise overcoming his anger.

"Very," I answered firmly.

"He totally changes his physical form from centaur to human?" he asked again, incredulous.

"Absolutely."

"You could have told me that to begin with."

"I know. I just, well, it's hard that you and he are so much alike," I faltered.

"Are we?" His voice was intense.

"Yes," I breathed the word in a rush.

His eyes met mine and his hand reached out to touch my cheek. For a moment I let my face rest against the warmth of his flesh.

Then the Hummer skidded to the side and Clint grunted as he fought to get it back to the middle of the path.

"Is that the road?" I asked, ignoring the shaking of my hand as I pointed at the charcoal-colored ribbon that glistened in our headlights.

"Yes," he said, and downshifted so we could slow without sliding into the ditch.

"My God! Look at that!" I exclaimed.

Clint stopped the Hummer and we stared. In front of us a small blacktop road stretched to the left and right, but it wasn't covered with snow like the surrounding land; instead, its smooth, untouched surface seemed to have captured the ethereal non-light of the fading moon. It glowed. As we watched, ghostly vapors lifted from its glinting surface like spirits escaping from blacktop graves. They rose to hover around us in gossamer curtains before the snow scattered them and they dissipated into the night.

I suddenly felt incredibly lonely, like I had been abandoned or lost. Without conscious thought, my hand reached for Clint's. He linked his fingers with mine.

"What are they?" I whispered reverently.

"The spirits of forgotten warriors," he answered without hesitation.

"You mean American Indian warriors?"

He nodded. "There is magic and mystery in this land. Some of it was conceived in tears."

"How do you know?"

"They tell me." He shrugged his shoulders at my startled expression, but his attention stayed focused on the ghostly happenings in front of us. "I have an affinity for the spirit world."

I thought about my Shaman husband, and how firmly connected to the spirit world he was—and added another item to the long list of "similarities between ClanFintan and Clint."

"There..." He motioned back to the road. "They're finished for tonight."

Sure enough, the spectral show was over. As I watched, the fat flakes began covering the now-empty blacktop surface.

"What did they want?" My melancholy had disappeared with the spirits, and curiosity was left in its wake.

"Acknowledgment. They wish they weren't forgotten."

I thought of the ceremonies I had been performing over the past six months. Many of them were dedicated to honoring fallen warriors. "I'll remember them," I said automatically. "Partholon's priestesses do not forget heroes."

"Even if they're from another world?"

"I don't think the world is what's important. I think it's the remembering." I probably imagined it, but as I spoke I thought I glimpsed a sudden shimmer pass through the surrounding night.

Clint squeezed my hand. Putting the Hummer in gear he pulled onto the deceptively normal-looking road and turned to the left. We drove on in silence, my thoughts circling around and around Oklahoma's magic, and the man who sat next to me. I could feel the lingering warmth of his touch cooling on my hand.

I sniffled and realized my cheeks were wet. Jeesh—hormones.

"Kleenexes are in the glove box." His deep voice was so gentle it made my throat ache.

"Thanks," I said, grabbing a Kleenex and giving my nose a very unromantic blow.

"Where are we?" I asked, stuffing the damp tissue into my/his sweatpants pocket.

"This blacktop doesn't really have a name. Locals call it Nagi Road."

"Nagi—that's a weird nickname for a country road."

"According to the old-timers around here it means ghost of the dead."

I looked appreciatively at the eerie stretch of road. Sounded appropriate to me.

"Nagi Road eventually runs into old State Road 259. From there the roads get more and more modern until we hit the Muskogee Turnpike, which, as you know, will take us right into Broken Arrow."

"How long will it take?"

"Normally, about three and a half or four hours." He gave the sky a pointed look. "Today I would sit back and relax. I'll be surprised if we get there within eight."

I looked at the snow that was falling quickly and steadily. "*If* we get there."

"We'll get there, Shannon my girl," he reassured me.

I sighed and stared out the window at the bizarre landscape. I had never been this far southeast in Oklahoma, and I was surprised by the wild look of the thickly forested land and the hilly terrain. The snow added to the surreal aspect of the landscape. As the sun rose, giving the morning a weak, pearlized glow, it was easy to believe that Clint and I had been transported to an alien winter world, and were no longer in Oklahoma at all. A thought that, in light of where I'd spent the last six months, didn't seem too damn far-fetched. I was just starting to really worry, when we came to the outskirts of a small town, the name of which was too snow obscured to read. On the right side of the road a huge neon sign proclaimed in bright pink blinking letters that we were passing Concrete World Factory Outlet. I let my face break into a relieved smile at the snow-covered lumps of concrete geese. They probably had seasonally correct little outfits for sale separately. Yes, we were certainly in Oklahoma.

To the left of the 2-lane "highway" was Billy Bob's B-B-Q (really, I'm not making it up). Right next door was Hillview Funeral Parlor. The B-B-Q place looked like it was in better shape than the funeral parlor. I breathed another sigh of relief. This couldn't be anywhere *but* Oklahoma.

It didn't take long to get through the mini-town, (which was, appropriately, flanked by a lovely trailer park whose peeling sign read, Camelot Villa—Units Available). I was considering cracking a *you know you're white trash when*...joke, but I remembered I was an unemployed public schoolteacher with no money, and decided instead that I should probably take note of the location of the trailer parks. That thought depressed me into keeping my mouth shut.

There was no idle chatter as we drove relentlessly into the north. Clint's attention was focused on keeping us on the road, and the changing scenery outside the window held my attention. The whitened land passed by, exchanging the forested wilderness and hills for the gentle roll of pastureland. I knew this part of Oklahoma better because it was spotted with quarter-horse ranches, which I'd visited with my father as we dropped off mares to be bred.

There was very little traffic. Snow tends to freak out the Okie populace. Little wonder they were hiding. This kind of storm was definitely an aberration for Oklahoma. As a matter of fact, the more I studied it, the more I realized that I couldn't remember anything like this deluge of snow.

"How long have you lived in Oklahoma?" I asked Clint.

He divided his attention between the snow-packed, deserted road and me. "My job took me out of state for training and travel some, but except for that, all of my life."

"And how long would that be?"

"Forty-five years."

Hmm—ten years older than me. I smiled smugly—after you reach your mid-thirties it's nice to feel like you're the *younger* one.

"How long have you lived here?" he asked.

"Besides college in Illinois and my six-month foray into another world—" I grinned at him "—all of my life."

He raised his eyebrows questioningly at me.

"That would be twenty-five years." I said mischievously. He crinkled his brow at me, but he was obviously too much of a gentleman to contradict the lapse in my math ability. I smiled and corrected myself, "Did I say twenty-five? I meant *thirty*-five." He returned my smile. "My point in asking wasn't really to find out your age. I was wondering, do you remember there ever being a storm like this before?" I pointed at the fat, Colorado-friendly flakes that continued to fall steadily.

"No. Never."

"Me, neither." I studied the passing scenery. "It's not normal, Clint."

"No, it's not. But the land knew it was coming."

"You said that before. What exactly do you mean?"

"I felt it in the trees. At first it was the same as every year. They gather energy and keep it for the fall and winter, but it didn't take long for me to understand this time there was a distinct difference." He struggled to put it into words. "It was like the forest was closing in on itself—swallowing energy and hoarding it deep within. The animals became scarce. Even the deer, which are usually so thick you can't take a walk without seeing several, were absent. I took my cue from them. I stockpiled supplies and firewood, and thought I'd just wait out whatever ice storm was coming."

I nodded and returned his knowing look. That's usually what happened in Oklahoma. Lots of snow was rare. Blizzards were virtually unheard of, but ice storms, the kind that topple power lines and trees and make driving impossible, they happened about once every 2.5 years, whether we needed them or not (mostly not).

"No, I've never seen anything like this. It'll be a total whiteout by tonight. Shannon, this is not going to be six or eight or ten inches—this snow will cover cars if it doesn't stop."

"Something wrong has happened," I thought aloud.

"Nuada," we said the name together.

"And I would bet Rhiannon isn't totally innocent in this whole situation," Clint said.

"Rhiannon hasn't been totally innocent of anything since she hit puberty," I muttered. Thinking back, I remembered

Nuada saying that I had called to him—and I sure as hell knew I hadn't done any such thing. Taking a deep breath, I said words I fervently wished I didn't have to say. "We need to talk to Rhiannon."

"Unfortunately, I've been thinking the same thing." He sounded resigned.

"Where is she?"

He shook his head. "I don't know. That phone call yesterday was the first I've heard from her in weeks."

"Doesn't she live in Tulsa?" I was pretty sure the Late Mr. Oil Tycoon had left her a fabulous home in which she could nest.

"As far as I know, she only comes to Tulsa periodically." He grimaced. "Usually she contacts me to remind me I should be worshipping her. I know she bought a lakefront condo in Chicago, and she's spent time in New York City and L.A."

"Good God, she's only been here six months!"

"Time is irrelevant to Rhiannon's wishes."

"Well, it's not irrelevant to mine. I want to figure out how to send Nuada back to hell or wherever, and get myself back to Partholon." *Before* I have a baby who belongs in another world. I don't even know if anyone can cross over the divide with me. It had been a difficult enough experience for me—what would it do to an infant? I closed my eyes and sighed, fighting hormone-induced tears of frustration.

"You're still feeling the effects of the crossover." Clint's deep voice was soothing. "Rest for a while. I'll wake you in time for you to give me directions to your father's house."

I could hear the rustling of fabric as he shifted around in his seat.

"Use this as a pillow."

I glanced up at him as he handed me his coat. "Thanks." I squished it into a vaguely pillow-shaped lump and plopped it against the Hummer's door before resting my head on it. The fabric was soft, and it was still warm from his body. Breathing deeply, I inhaled the scent of him—clean, strong man, with a faint residue of some kind of aftershave. In that place between awake and asleep, I recognized the scent. Stetson cologne. The man in the white hat. That figures. I felt my lips curve into a begrudging smile as sleep claimed me completely.

Hugh Jackman and I were flying cross-country through violet-colored puffy clouds. He had his arms wrapped around me and was nibbling on my neck while he described the opulent beachside suite he had reserved for us at the Hyatt in the Cayman Islands…

…And I was sucked out of the dream and through a tunnel of fire. I knew I was no longer physically attached to my body,

but it still felt as if my heart was literally being squeezed within my chest. I couldn't breathe. In a total state of panic, I opened my mouth to scream, and my spirit form exploded through the tunnel. Disorientation and nausea engulfed me. I gulped huge breaths of cool air, wondering how a spirit body could be so close to projectile vomiting. But soon the familiar hovering sensation calmed me and I felt my vertigo fade. A noise below caused my attention to turn downward.

The sight of the enormous temple brought a rush of emotions. Home! Epona's Temple. My body floated gently as I absorbed the wonderfully familiar view. It was late afternoon, and the sky had already begun to be tinted with the delicate watercolors of a Partholonian sunset. The smooth cream-colored walls that surrounded the temple caught the changing light and refracted it with a magical, pearlized glow. Below me I could see that the temple guards were beginning to light the many torches and sconces that kept Epona's Temple illuminated throughout the night.

I recognized several of my nymphets as they moved from courtyard to courtyard, busy arms filled with everything from fine linens to baskets laden with fragrant herbs.

At first the scene looked endearingly normal through my tear-clouded eyes, but as I watched with fond interest, something nagged at my mind. Something was wrong—or at the very least, different. When I saw two of my most youthful maids meet in silent passing, I realized what it was. They weren't talking. No, it was more than that. I drifted closer. It wasn't some bizarre spell of silence that had somehow been cast over the temple. I could hear their little slippered feet pattering on the marble floor. One of the guards (a thick, fur-lined cape only partially obscured his muscular form, I noted appre-

ciatively) spoke a muffled curse as he burnt his hand lighting a torch that was too quick to flame. It wasn't that they couldn't speak. It was that they were choosing not to speak to one another. The atmosphere in the temple was depressed. The air itself felt thick and smothering.

What the hell had happened?

As if my thoughts were directions for my body to follow, my spirit form began to drift toward the center of the temple. I sank through the domed ceiling as the sun dipped beneath the western horizon.

My bathing chamber was unusually dim and had the deserted feel of a house that had stood empty long enough that it was no longer a home. It made me overwhelmingly sad to see the room that had been at the heart of so much happiness and laughter reduced to being an abandoned shell.

A cowl-shrouded figure was meticulously lighting the candles that nestled in the golden skull holders centered within niches in the otherwise smooth walls. Her slender hands shook while she moved from candle to candle. The air of despair that hung about the woman was almost palpable. Her methodical movements were interrupted when the slender stick she was using as a match burned too low. She gasped, dropping the smoldering brand to the marble floor. Moving quickly to extinguish the still-glowing tip, the edge of her hood slid back, revealing the soft curves of Alanna's face.

"Oh, girlfriend," I breathed as I noticed tiny lines around her eyes that had not been there the last time I had seen her. She showed no response to my spirit voice. She sighed deeply, fished down into the pockets of her mantle until she found another lighting brand, then continued mechanically with her duties.

I felt my body rising through the layers of warm, steamy vapor. "No! Let me talk to her!" I pleaded with my Goddess.

Patience, Beloved.

The words drifted through my mind and were gone like the specters I had witnessed rising from the blacktop road. I moved swiftly through the ceiling and began floating purposefully in a northerly direction. I had experienced enough dream excursions to know that my Goddess was in control. She had something she needed me to see. It was best to just sit back and wait for her will to be done. Not that familiarity made it any easier.

I noticed that night had come quickly and totally. This was not the gradual darkening of the land, as I had come to know was typical for Partholon. It was as if, in the absence of the sun, darkness reigned uncontested. For some reason that analogy made me shiver. And my body came to a halt.

Below me the dense forest had parted to expose a clearing, and the flickering glow from a large campfire drew my attention. I began drifting lower. At first I noticed only that this was the same clearing that was mirrored in both of my worlds, but before I could contemplate time travel and what the hell I was doing here, the huge campfire drew my eyes. It was an odd color, not the warm saffron and gold of friendly flames, instead it burned a startling red that looked ready to explode and destroy.

I didn't see him until I had descended to just a few feet above the fire. Then he moved, reaching into a leather pouch at his side to pull forth a handful of something that looked like sand. He flung it into the flames as he spoke the words "mo muirninn" over and over in a guttural voice that sounded strained and rough. ClanFintan's eyes were red-rimmed and fixed as he stood like a bronze statue of himself, staring into the wild scarlet fire. He was close to the blaze; so close that I was amazed that the ends of his thick, dark hair weren't smoldering. His human chest was bare and slick with sweat, likewise the equine part of him was flecked with white foam, like he had been running for days and days.

"ClanFintan!" I gasped his name with all the power of my longing.

His head snapped up and his attention was instantly focused in my direction.

"Rhea, love. Have you finally heard me?" His rough voice grated through the night between us.

"Yes," I yelled, hoping that my Goddess would allow me to communicate with him, if even for just a little while.

Reassure him, Beloved. *The words drifted softly within my mind.*

"I'm here! I'm trying to get home!" As I spoke, I felt the thrill of the sensation that was caused by my ethereal body becoming semivisible. I saw my centaur husband's eyes widen in surprised pleasure. Looking down at my almost solid form I saw, much to my embarrassment, that I was totally naked.

"I see you." His harsh voice had gone liquid and thick with longing.

"Epona doesn't ever seem to clothe me properly." My spirit words drifted hauntingly through the air to my beloved.

"And I thank Epona for it." The intensity in his words said he was talking about much more than my state of undress.

I smiled softly at him and spoke what my Goddess whispered through my mind. "And Epona will make sure I return home."

"When!" His expression was tortured.

"I—I don't know," I faltered.

"You must return," he stated simply. "The absence of Epona's Beloved has taken a great toll upon our world."

"No!" I cried. "I'm not gone forever. Tell the people Epona would not desert them." As I spoke I felt the quiet surety within that said I was speaking the truth.

"When?" he repeated.

"Something has happened in my old world." I took a breath. "Nuada has followed me here."

His eyes narrowed to slits. He was far too wise in the ways of the spirit world to question the fact that our dead enemy had somehow reanimated.

"Your Goddess would not allow that creature to harm you!"

"No! It's not me I'm worried about." I lifted my hands beseechingly. "He's after the people I love. I think I know how to get back to Partholon, but you have to understand that I cannot leave here until I've made sure the people I leave behind will be safe."

A shadow passed over his handsome face, and I felt the tension behind his words as he spoke. "I saw the man in the clearing. The man with my face."

"Yes." I didn't know what else to say.

"He is my mirror image in your world?"

"Yes, he is."

"Then you are protected and safe." His jaw clenched as he ground the words through his teeth.

"Yes," I repeated, feeling disloyal and inept and very, very guilty.

He kept his eyes locked on mine. "Our daughter—she is well?"

I smiled and felt my face relax. "She is still making me good and sick."

"Then she is well." He raised one arm so that his hand was stretched out, reaching over the fire for me. "Come back to me, Shannon."

"I will, love." I felt the sob burn in the back of my throat as my body began to drift up and dematerialize. "Tell Alanna I'm fine. Tell her not to lose hope..." My voice trailed off, evaporating into the night.

The tunnel of flames loomed before me and I braced myself for the return journey, but I couldn't stop the scream that slipped from my terrified soul...

...And I sat straight upright in the passenger's seat of the Hummer.

"Shannon!" Clint was shaking my shoulder. His expression bordered on panic. "My God, Shannon! Are you awake now?"

"I'm...I'm...fine," I fumbled, feeling the horrible disorientation of moving between two worlds.

"First you cried out like someone was trying to strangle you, then you didn't move at all." His face was white. "You hardly breathed."

"It was just the Magic Sleep; the dream vision Epona sends me on sometimes," I said, like I was explaining something as ordinary as how to butter bread. "It's different here—harder. It must be because this isn't Epona's world, even though I'm still her Chosen," I reasoned aloud, feeling a huge sense of relief at more evidence that my Goddess hadn't deserted me.

He paused, as if he was struggling for words. I decided to just sit there and breathe deeply, because my stomach had begun turning itself inside out.

"Damnit, Shannon! Magic Sleep! What—"

"Pull over!" I yelled.

"Wha—"

"PULL THE FUCK OVER! I'M GOING TO—"

I didn't have to finish my declarative sentence. One quick look at my probably green face had clued in Clint. The Hummer swerved delicately as he fishtailed to a stop. I wrenched open the door, and leapt out into the barrage of quarter-sized snowflakes. Two steps from the vehicle I bent over at the waist and began heaving.

Snot—puke mouth—shaking—whimpering—feeling like I was going to die. I hate puking.

"Easy, you're okay." Clint's strong arms braced my body so that I could concentrate on puking up my intestines rather than falling headfirst onto the snowy, puke-spattered roadside. I was very grateful my hair was pulled back. Just thinking about what a horrible mess it would be if it had been free and wild (and puke encrusted) caused me to vomit up what was left of my guts.

"Here..." Clint handed me a bunch of Kleenex when my heaves had subsided.

"Th-thank..." I couldn't get the words out, but I took the tissues anyway and mopped my mouth and blew my nose.

"Don't mention it, Shannon my girl." I could hear the smile in his voice as he guided me back to the open door of the Hummer.

"No!" I pushed against him. "I need some fresh air. I'll stay out here for a while."

"Not long," he said as he propped me against the side of the vehicle, pulling my door closed to stop the snow from falling inside. "It's too cold, and you'll get too wet."

I nodded and concentrated on breathing normally.

"Can you stand by yourself?" he asked. I realized he still had a firm hold on my arms.

"Yes." My voice sounded far away and shaky.

"I'll be right back." He squeezed my arms before letting go and moving to the rear of the vehicle.

This means the baby is fine. The baby is fine. The baby is fine. The words were a litany that played around and around inside my head, beating in time with the pulse that spiked painfully in harmony with my headache.

"Rinse out your mouth then drink this." Clint handed me one of the bottles of water that I remembered packing with the sandwiches. It was still cool and felt smooth and refreshing as it washed the lingering taste of gall from my mouth.

"Better?" he asked.

"Thank you, yes." I managed coherent speech. "I just need to stand here a second."

I sipped the water and we stood. The snow was so heavy it made it seem like we were existing in a little pocket of our own world. Just Clint, the Hummer and me. Everything else was silent whiteness, wet and cold. *Let us be silent that we may hear the whispers of the gods.* Emerson's words flitted through my mind. If only it was that easy.

I looked down and saw that we were standing in snow over our knees, and if there were any other vehicles on the road, we certainly couldn't hear or see them.

"This can't be safe. What if someone hits us?" I blinked snow from my lashes and looked at Clint. He reached up and brushed a blob of snow from my shoulder.

"The turnpike is closed. I haven't seen a car in more than an hour."

"Closed!" I was starting to feel human again. "If it's closed, how did we get this far?"

"This lady has been through desert sandstorms and war, a little snow is nothing to her." He flashed me a teenage-boy smile and gave the squatty vehicle a fond look.

I just shook my head at him. Guys and their cars. Then I remembered my beautiful Mustang and relented, returning his grin.

"You must be recovering." He started brushing the snow off me in earnest. "Let's get out of here." He opened the door and shoved me into the passenger's seat, then waded through the snow to the driver's door, shaking blobs of white wetness off himself before he jumped behind the wheel.

"Want your coat back?" I noticed he was coatless and shaking as he put the Hummer into gear and eased her forward.

"No, I'm fine." He ran his hand through his thick, dark hair. It was wet, and it stayed slicked back after his hand had returned to the wheel.

Just like ClanFintan's. I couldn't help the thought. My centaur husband often combed his thick mass of long, dark waves back and tied them into place with a leather thong. I used to tell him it gave him the rakish look of a Spanish Conquistador, and teased him about the fact that since he was half man, half horse, he could ravish me *and* carry me off with no outside help.

In the slatelike light of the snowy non-day the differences between Clint and ClanFintan seemed to disintegrate. I felt something deep within me begin to tremble.

"Do those dream visions always affect you so violently?"

He barely glanced at me, and I was glad that I had time to compose myself before I answered.

"Not always." I was together enough to know I should prevaricate.

"Where did your Goddess take you?"

"Home," I couldn't keep my voice from sounding shaky. "To Partholon."

"Oh." His light, curious tone changed abruptly. "What did Epona show you?"

"My temple isn't right without me. They're, well, I don't know how to put it without sounding incredibly egotistical." I shrugged my shoulders and decided to just tell the truth. "They need Epona's Beloved."

Clint nodded as if he was trying to understand. Keeping his eyes on the road, he asked, "Did you see—" he hesitated over the name "—ClanFintan?"

"I saw him and I spoke with him." When he didn't respond, I continued. "I told him I would return to him as soon as we took care of the Nuada problem."

"We?" his voice was sharp.

"ClanFintan saw you through the divide, too." I felt a fond smile curl my lips and I added, "He is assuming you will take care no harm comes to me."

"His assumption is correct."

"He appreciates it." I didn't know what else to say. I mean, please. This whole situation was more bizarre than any episode of *Night Gallery* or *The Twilight Zone* had ever been. And that took some damn doing.

"Do you?" Clint's voice shot out.

"Do I what?" My thoughts had been interrupted and I didn't particularly like his tone.

"Do you appreciate the fact that I would die rather than see you harmed?"

Now I understood his tone.

"Yes." My answer was truthful and blunt, but before he could question me further I changed the subject. "Where are we?"

Clint gave me a look that said he was onto my tactics, but he didn't push it. "Around ten minutes from the Broken Arrow exits. Where do I go from there?"

"Dad lives about ten miles east after you take the Kenosha turnoff." I sighed and looked down at my bizarre clothing that was now decidedly puke spattered and damp. "Damn, I hate to show up looking like this."

"I was kidding before, but isn't there a Wal-Mart just off the expressway?"

"Yessss…" I strung the word out, rearranging my thoughts from the mythological world of Partholon to the commercial world of Oklahoma. "Think it would be open in this mess?"

"Wal-Mart?" He laughed. "Nuclear war couldn't close its doors."

"Then go a few exits past Kenosha, and take the 145th street exit." The directions came back to me easily. "There's a Wal-Mart about a mile south of the highway. We can run in, get some clothes and get back on Kenosha. Shoot, we'll be home in time for dinner," I said in my best Okie accent, even though the thought of dinner made me feel green again.

"Your wish is my command." He gave me a playful look. "You are the goddess here."

I gave him a tight smile back. The problem was, I wanted to say, I'm *not* the goddess *here.*

The turnoff to 145th was as deserted as the rest of our journey had been, although the parking lot to the Howard Johnson's Motel that was right off the highway was packed with snow-shrouded cars. Less than a mile away Wal-Mart loomed like a concrete citadel ringed by a fence of fast-food restaurants.

"You're right. This damn place is open for business." I shook my head as I spoke. Wal-Mart was certainly tenacious.

The Hummer crawled easily up the incline that led to the Wal-Mart Super Cathedral, but right away it was obvious that the majority of bubbas who had chosen to do their shopping today were not having our luck with navigating in the snow. An old Ford pickup was fishtailing around the lot, having definitely missed the parking place he had tried to slide (literally) into. (I caught a glimpse of his bumper sticker, which read Armed Okie—it made me feel nostalgic in an inbred kind of way.) An old Impala was spinning its tires uselessly and blocking the front of the store. Of course, a *Super* Wal-Mart has multiple entrances, so no one was panicking. The Oklahoma Southern Baptists would raise their hands and say a "Thank you, Jesus!" about that.

Clint navigated easily around the stuck car and I could see several men hauling tire chains out of the stranded motorist's trunk to help him out. (Needless to say, tire chains are not illegal in Oklahoma, actually it's considered proper winter etiquette—much like shotguns in the window of your pickup truck, except guns are an all-weather accessory.)

"Stay there. I'll come around and get you." I handed Clint his jacket and didn't argue. First of all, I appreciate a gentleman. Secondly, I didn't want to fall on my butt. Obviously, no matter how deep the bizarre snow, it was still Oklahoma snow, which meant that it was packed with a layer of ice. So I just zipped my coat, attempted to smooth back my hair and waited.

The freezing air that hit me carried small, hard snowflakes that stung my face. My breath caught as Clint helped me down.

"It's getting worse," he said grimly as he and I held on to one another and made our way to the neon safety of the store. Then, trying to lighten my mood he added in a conspirator's whisper, "In case you've forgotten, a flexible fashion sense is one of the requirements for experienced Wal-Mart shoppers. You can't swing a dead cat in that store without hitting six or seven fashionably dressed people wearing elastic-waist jeans. Prepare yourself, it's not always a pretty sight."

I laughed and whispered back, "I do seem to remember that prolonged exposure to the school supplies aisles made me want to scream or commit suicide."

"At least you're forewarned." He squeezed my arm and we smiled at each other. I appreciate a guy with a Wal-Mart sense of humor.

Nearing the front of the store, we made a wide loop around the tire-spinning motorist. It looked as if all he was accomplishing was to burn a groove into the snow and polish the sheet of ice under it. I smiled and stifled a giggle as I overheard one of the chain holders yell, "*Sheet*, Gordy, let up on that damn gas some! Yur not goin' nowhare!"

Some poor minimum-wage earner was out front battling the never-ending snow with a shovel and a huge supply of de-ice salt pellets, which translated into ankle-deep slick goop that a surprisingly steady stream of people tracked into the entrance of the store. I was just getting ready to make a smart-ass comment to Clint about the benefits of getting an education so you didn't have to do that kind of shit for a living, when a musical laugh caught my attention. Its familiarity was unmistakable. A couple emerged from the store and I felt my body go still. I know my feet stopped because we had stopped moving forward. Our arms were still linked, so Clint stumbled to a sudden halt beside me, but I didn't have a conscious awareness of standing still.

"Suzanna!" All the joy I felt at the sight of her was reflected in that one word.

Her reaction was like a twisted mirror of my own. Her feet stopped, too. The man at her side, with whom her arm was linked, was pulled to a forced halt, as was the man at my side. But that's where the similarities ended. I knew my face radiated the indescribable pleasure I felt at the sight of her, but her expression immediately clouded over. Her eyes shifted worriedly from her husband to me and back again, as if she had been caught watching an illicit Ping-Pong game.

Without thinking, I rushed forward with the intention of throwing my arms around her, but something about the way she suddenly straightened her body and took a hesitant step back stayed my impulse. Instead, I found myself standing half a step from her with my arms hanging foolishly at my sides.

"Suz…I, uh…" What the hell could I say? *I haven't seen*

you in six months! I missed you! I need to talk to you! I'm married to a centaur, pregnant with his baby and, by the way, I've become Goddess Incarnate in a mirror world… "Suz…um…" No, I couldn't say any of that. Not here. Not now. "It's so great to see you," I blurted ineptly but authentically.

"Really?" Her husband's voice was colder than the crystallizing flakes of snow. "I seem to remember that the last time you saw Suzanna you told her you didn't want to see her ever again." When Suz tried to say something, Gene gave her a hard look and continued, "You called her, let's see if I can remember the exact words—" he scratched his chin in a mocking gesture "—yes, I do recall. You said she was less than a slave to you because she didn't know her place. You told—no, *told* is not the correct word—you commanded her to leave your sight and to never enter your presence again." His eyes narrowed into hateful slits. "And now you say it's *great* to see her?"

Oh, wonderful. Why the hell hadn't I thought about this? Of course Rhiannon had interacted with my friends and family. Of course she had offended and hurt everyone. I mentally shook myself. I'd just spent six months cleaning up her messes in another world, which included convincing Gene's mirror imagine, Carolan, that he didn't need to hate me because I WASN'T FRIGGIN RHIANNON, and I would never hurt Alanna. It was only logical that she had crapped all over this world, too.

"I can explain that, Suz." I ignored Gene's hostile stare and focused on the woman who had been like a sister to me. "I wasn't myself when I said that. Hell—" I attempted a girlfriend smile "—I haven't been *myself*—" I made sure I enunciated the word carefully "—for months." I looked into her eyes, silently begging her to see the differences between Rhiannon and me. "I really can explain. Can we go somewhere for a cup of coffee or something?" I brightened as I remembered. "Isn't there a Panera right down the street?" I knew there was. Suz and I had met there and snarfed down their wonderful pecan rolls many a morning.

I saw her face begin to soften into familiar, loving lines, and she opened her mouth to reply.

"No." Gene's answer beat hers. "We are not meeting you anywhere."

I looked at him—I mean, this time I really looked at him. He had always been a medium-height, ordinary-looking, plump, older guy. Fifteen years older to be exact. He had just turned a rather barrel-chested, high blood–pressured fifty. He was plain—way average-looking, especially when compared to Suz's sparkling cuteness. The only things he had ever had in his court were his intelligence, and the fact that he absolutely adored my best friend. You can forgive a lot for total adoration.

Actually, I realized that I had come to like and respect Carolan much more than Gene. Huh. Carolan was actually a doctor—he healed people. Gene was an academic, a university professor dork. He had a doctorate (two actually), but he wasn't a doctor. Know what I mean? Gene was pudgy; Carolan was lean and wiry, making him look (and act) a decade younger. I hadn't really thought about the differences between them until that moment; I'd just accepted that Carolan was Alanna's love because Gene was Suz's.

Now I watched something ugly take over Gene's face—jealousy, and I knew that even when Carolan had hated "me" because he thought I was Rhiannon, that hatred hadn't been jealous or envious. It had been based solely on the fact that Rhiannon used and hurt Alanna. Carolan was a better guy than Gene, and not just because in Partholon he'd kept himself in better shape and was a gifted doctor, instead of just an overeducated academic nerd. Carolan would never be jealous of my closeness with Alanna—just the opposite. With the clarity that comes with intuition, I realized that the reason I identified Gene's jealousy so quickly was that I had glimpsed it before. Way more than once. Like when I had just "dropped by" Suz's house on a Saturday afternoon to take her out for an impromptu girlfriend lunch. Or when his voice had suddenly turned cold through the cell phone as Suz reminded him that she and I had set aside Thursday evenings for *our* time, and he would have to do without her for a couple hours. And in the way he couldn't quite disguise the sarcasm in his voice when he used to say that Suz and I probably wouldn't mind being joined at the hip. Literally. But until now he'd always managed to charm his way out of any awkwardness. I mean, I guess I'd never considered whether Gene actually liked me, or just tolerated me. He was good to Suz; that was good enough for me. It pissed me off to realize that all this time he must have been camouflaging his jealous dislike, and now Rhiannon the Impostor had given it a viable excuse to be let loose. (Although I was also pleased to note yet another example of mirror images being different—for whateverthehell reason…nature versus nurture…blah…blah.)

"I asked Suzanna, not you." I met his furious gaze calmly. "Since when do you answer for her?" I kept my voice down. I didn't want some kind of ridiculous Jerry Springer episode to call the Wal-Mart shoppers' attention away from falling prices to us. I glanced around, relieved that the passing people were concentrating on not slipping on the ice instead of our little drama.

"Shae..." Suzanna's sweet voice speaking the nickname I hadn't heard in what felt like six years rather than six months made my heart squeeze. "Maybe we can meet later?" she said hesitantly, her eyes sliding nervously between Gene and me.

"I really need to talk to you now, Suz. It's important." I telegraphed her the *it's-an-emergency, girlfriend* look we had been successfully sending to and receiving from each other for years. The look that means Drop Everything, Something's Wrong. A veritable girlfriend SOS.

To my abject horror she simply shrugged her shoulders and avoided my eyes while she said, "I just don't think it's a good idea."

"*You* don't think!" I said through gritted teeth, giving Gene a pointed glance.

"Look, Shannon," Gene sneered, "you need to face it. Your life has changed. You've made it clear that Suzanna doesn't fit in your new lifestyle. You've grown apart. It's not like you two were ever the same kind of people anyway."

I felt like he'd slapped me. Of course Suz and I weren't the same kind of people. That's what made us such great friends. She and I approached situations and life from different perspectives. She was more conservative; she thought things out. I was more outgoing; I tended to jump into things without thinking. We complemented each other. I encouraged her to wear shorter skirts and speak her mind. She prompted me to button one more top button and try to keep my mouth shut (occasionally).

I wanted to shout this in his pompous face. Then I noticed Suzanna's expression. It was begging me not to say anything. Unshed tears brightened her eyes. She looked like a woman who had just had to choose between her best friend and her husband.

Gene's hand tightened over hers where it still held securely to his arm. She put her other hand over his in a gesture that I recognized as one that she made automatically to reassure him. She had chosen, and what else should I have expected? My life had gone in a different direction—one she couldn't follow. What did I want her to do, leave the father of her children for me? No, I didn't want that, not even if I was never able to return to Partholon.

"I understand," I said, trying to make my voice sound normal.

Gene snorted sarcastically.

I ignored him, keeping my eyes locked with Suzanna's. "I'm sorry for the pain these past months have caused you." I wanted to add that it wasn't me who had caused you that pain—that someday I would explain—someday she would understand, but I knew that probably wouldn't happen. Like her, I had shifted my focus. Our lives were irrevocably changed. So instead I just smiled sadly at her and told her the only truth I could. "I'll miss you. I love you."

I saw her mouth tighten, and as Gene hauled her past me, the garish lights of Wal-Mart illuminated the tears that spilled down her cheeks and mixed with the never-ending snow.

As I stumbled forward, the red and blue lights of the Broken Arrow police cruiser pulling up next to the stranded Impala threw bizarre whirling shapes on the snow. Clint's strong arm reached around my shoulder and steadied me. The electric doors whooshed open, but my feet wouldn't take me much farther inside, so they stayed open behind us. The cold air at my back contrasted sharply with the heated air blasting from an air duct above us. I didn't know I was crying until Clint handed me a tissue. I nodded my thanks and wiped my nose.

"She was my best friend," I said stupidly.

"I'm sorry," he said.

A herd of bag-laden shoppers bumped around us, and Clint took my arm, guiding me to the side of the glass entryway. I shook my head violently from side to side.

"I just can't believe she—" And I stopped. She what? She didn't leap forward and gush, *Oh, Shae, I knew all along it wasn't you! I suspected the whole, you've-been-sucked-into-a-mirror-dimension-thing-the-entire-time truth!* Please. How could she have even imagined it?

I breathed deeply, stifling the sniffles that a serious snot cry always caused me to have. I blew my nose and looked up at Clint.

"I guess I should apologize. That was an ugly scene." I smiled sheepishly at him, but he wasn't looking at me. His was looking out the floor-to-ceiling windows that lined either side of the electric doors, and his attention was focused there.

"Clint?" I started to question him, then I felt it—an internal skittering that was teasing and thick and sickening—like I'd walked into a room where a mouse had curled up inside the wall and died, and was just beginning to stink. I spun around so that I faced the row of windows.

The steady snow was like a veil of white beads against

the dim curtain of evening. The light had been fading for the past several hours, and the gray day turned people in the parking lot to ghosts of themselves. The cop was helping in the final stages of attaching the chains to the Impala's tires. With a jolt of surprise, I noticed Suzanna and Gene were standing just a few feet from where we had been talking. Only now they weren't touching each other. Suz's arms were wrapped across herself in a defensive gesture. One of Gene's hands was fisted against his side; with the other he pointed and gestured angrily. Suzanna shook her head decisively, and took a step away from Gene and toward the building. Gene reached out and grabbed her arm. They were drawing the glances of the people who hurried past them.

Then from the corner of my vision I saw a dark fluttering movement, like the wings of a bat against the night sky. My head snapped to the right and I squinted hard, trying to get a clear look at what I thought might be there, all the while hoping fervently I was mistaken.

"There..." Clint pointed to a spot behind the stuck car. At first it just looked like it was a shadow of the car—until I reminded myself that the sun was setting and could not be casting an enormous, ink stain of a shadow.

Then it rippled, gliding forward and under the chain-wrapped spinning wheels of the car. The engine growled.

What happened next was with nauseating swiftness. I started forward, but instead of opening, the doors stayed closed as the fluorescent lights flickered and went out. At the same instant I saw Suzanna shake free of Gene's restraining grip. As she hurried back toward the electric doors, Suz was still looking at Gene, saying something to him over her shoulder, so she didn't see the churning wheels miraculously catch on the surface of the evil-darkened ice. The Impala surged forward and straight into Suzanna. She wasn't thrown into the air by the impact. Instead she fell forward and the car bucked and heaved as it rolled over her.

I tasted bile in the scream that was wrenched from my mouth. My hands were fisted against the glass, pounding futilely on its closed surface. Then the lights blinked once and glared back on. The door whooshed softly open. Clint was at my side as I rushed forward into the throng of people rapidly gathering around the accident site.

"I'm a nurse, let me through!" a solid-looking blond lady ordered, and the ring that had already formed around Suzanna parted quickly. The nurse dropped to her knees and out of my range of sight. I could hear the disjointed clicks and mutters of the officer's radio as he called for an ambulance.

"Stay back! Stay back!" The cop waded into the mélange of people, arms spread wide as he held the crowd at bay. His eyes were focused on the scene in the middle of the ring of onlookers. I pushed my way into the group.

Suzanna lay on her side perfectly still. Her body was facing me; her head should have been pointed in my direction, too. But her neck was twisted back at an impossible angle so that instead of her face, I was looking at the back of her head. I blinked quickly, not really understanding what I was seeing. An ever-widening pool of brilliant scarlet was spreading all around her head and shoulders. Steam was rising from where body-warmed blood met frozen ground.

And somewhere in the midst of the horror before me, I heard the echo of a gurgling laugh as a dark shadow dissipated into the night.

"So much blood," I felt my numbed lips whisper. "Suzanna!" The cry was wrenched from me.

The man who had been kneeling at her side lifted his face. Gene's skin had turned a ghastly shade of gray. His shock-blue lips were pressed into a thin line.

"You did this," he hissed.

"We have to go." Clint's voice was as strong as the arm that encircled my shoulders.

"I can't leave her," I sobbed.

"You can't help her, Shannon. She's dead."

Those words, *she's dead,* felt like a physical blow to my body.

"Back off, folks! Back off!" The one uniform had been joined by several more.

"Oh, Jesus Christ!" An agonized shout came from the man I recognized as the driver of the Impala. He staggered through the group surrounding Suzanna's body.

"Sir! Please step over here!" One of the cops pulled him away.

"Oh, God! The car wouldn't stop!" The man was sobbing uncontrollably. "I buried my foot in the brake, but nothing happened. I swear it!"

"We leave *now,* Shannon." Clint said with steely determination.

I felt a sense of detachment that I recognized as the beginning stages of shock, and I didn't stop Clint from leading me away.

"She did it!" Gene's voice was filled with loathing. "She caused this!" he yelled at my departing back.

I craned my head to look over Clint's shoulder. Gene was standing beside Suzanna. His clothes were blood-spattered.

Foam flecked his chin and mouth, and he pointed hysterically in my direction.

"Sir!" The same officer who had handed the driver over to his partner stepped quickly to Gene's side, touching his arm and visibly trying to calm him. "I saw the whole thing. I wasn't even two feet away from her. It was an accident. No one…" His voice faded as we got farther away.

"Don't stop." Clint spoke in my ear. "Just breathe and walk. Keep moving forward. That's good, Shannon my girl, that's good." Clint kept up a soft murmur in my ear.

It wasn't until he lifted me into the passenger's side of the Hummer, snapped my seat belt into place and stepped back that I noticed his sapphire aura was shimmering vividly all around him.

The Hummer crawled over the ice-slick snow with the same serene confidence it had shown all day. Clint turned the heater on high and, once again, shrugged out of his coat.

"Wrap this around you." His eyes were dark and worried.

"Wh-why c-couldn't we have stayed?" I realized with a detached observation that tears were leaking steadily from my eyes and I was shaking violently. "She may have needed me."

"She was beyond needing any of us, Shannon, but that thing was still there." He kept looking over at me, dividing his attention between the icy streets and me. "What would have happened if it had attacked us again? We have no forest here from which to draw power." He ended flatly. "More people would have died."

"You turned blue again," I said absently.

"Blue?" He looked at me as if he was sure I was totally mad.

"Your aura. It's blue with gold around the edges. I can't usually see it, but it was visible while you were leading me to the Hummer." The more I talked the more normal my voice sounded.

He flashed me a surprised look. "I could sense that thing coming close to us, and my aura must have reacted defensively. But it didn't feel like we were Nuada's target. Not this time."

"Until I posses you, what you love I will destroy, be it in this world or the next." I whispered the words through lips that felt numb. "Nuada wasn't after me," I said with surety. "He was after Suzanna because somehow he knows I love her." I looked at Clint and suddenly everything around me came into stark focus. Understanding is sometimes a frightening thing. "That means it's not just Dad he's after. No one I care about is safe until he is destroyed." Before he could reply, I pointed a shaking finger and directed, "Take a right here on Kenosha Street.

Clint pulled onto Kenosha, and I could see the eerie flashing lights of the ambulance turning into the Wal-Mart parking lot.

"Are you sure she was dead?"

"You know she was, Shannon." Clint's voice gentled and he took his hand off the gearshift long enough to let it rest reassuringly on my knee. "No one could survive that kind of head injury."

My fault. It was my fault. I shuddered and drew the coat more closely around my body as a tide of nausea beat against my throat. Resting my forehead against the cool window, I closed my eyes and concentrated on not puking. I couldn't think about Suzanna now. Couldn't remember how we could talk to each other for hours on end, forgetting time and the outside world. How she could understand whether I was happy or sad just by the way my voice sounded on the phone. I wouldn't remember how, years ago, her oldest daughter had been one of my favorite students and she had decided, "You and my mom need to be best friends." Then she had proceeded to "fix us up." Literally. She made sure her mom and I met and became friends, much to the delight of both of us.

And now she was gone. Her three beautiful daughters were motherless. Because of me.

"Shannon!" Clint's voice interrupted my broken sobs. "Stop it. You'll make yourself sick again."

I wanted to draw myself up and spit back at him that he had no damn right to order me around, but I only had the energy to sit there with my forehead against the cold glass.

"Tell me where the hell we're going."

I turned my head and blinked at him, wiping my eyes on a piece of his coat.

"Directions, Shannon…" His voice was firm. "How do I get to your father's house?" He leaned forward and popped the glove box, pulling out several tissues and tossing them at me. "Don't wipe your nose on my coat."

Shit! I'd just lost my best friend and he was worried about his nappy coat? To hell with Mr. Obsessive-Compulsive. I blew my nose and straightened my spine. Peering around, I tried to get my bearings. We were on the outskirts of town, and the streets were totally deserted. Actually I was a little surprised to see the streetlights were still illuminating the steady stream of falling snow. Usually during winter storms electric power was the first thing to go.

We were heading up a gentle incline. To our right I saw the white fencing and well-manicured shrubs that framed the classic elegance of Forest Ridge Country Club. Complete with a spectacular golf course and an excellent clubhouse restaurant.

"Keep going straight." My voice sounded wounded and hiccupy. "When this four-lane narrows to a two-lane, turn right. That will be Oak Grove Road."

"You'll have to let me know when to turn. I can't tell road from ditch—there's no way I can see when this changes from four to two lanes."

I nodded at him and rubbed my eyes, concentrating on the snow-masked scenery. Country neighborhoods where I had played as a child, passed by. Houses gradually became farther and farther apart.

"Slow down, we're almost there." He downshifted. "There, see that squat-looking white concrete building?" I pointed. "Turn there." The Hummer crawled to the right. As we took the turn the streetlight fluttered and went dead, as did all the lights in the ranch houses surrounding us.

"Oh, God!" I felt myself begin to tremble again. Funny—I hadn't realized till then that I'd stopped shaking. "Is it Nuada again?"

Clint shook his head. "No. Breathe and think, Shannon. Do you feel his presence?"

Instead of getting pissed at the shortness of his words, I closed my eyes and centered my thoughts while I breathed deeply. Did I feel the premonition of evil that was always present with Nuada? No. I sighed in relief.

"I don't feel him."

"It's just the storm. That's why the lights are out. I'm surprised they've stayed on this long." I could hear the strain in his voice as he concentrated on staying in the middle of the undefined road. I looked closer at him and realized he was sitting at an odd angle, with his broad shoulders kind of cocked awkwardly to the side like his back was bothering him. I reminded myself that he had been driving through this mess for more than eight hours; he must be exhausted.

"It's not far from here. Just over this little rise in the road there's a stop sign." We came to it. Clint didn't stop.

"It's safe to say there's no other traffic tonight." He managed a slight grin in my direction.

"Okay—now start looking to your right. Do you see where that line of junipers break?" Clint slowed almost to a halt. "There's a little side road there, to the right. Turn onto it." Clint followed my directions and the Hummer plowed through the drifts like a tank. "Just keep following the tree line up this hill. Dad's place is there on the right." I pointed at the lane that divided two lush pastures at the top of the little hill. "Thank God they left the gate open." I sighed in relief.

Clint turned into the lane. It was obvious Dad had attempted to keep the lane plowed for at least part of the day. I smiled to myself at the mental image of Dad all wrapped up in his thick, scraggly parka, hunting cap slung low on his head (the kind with the fur-lined hanging-down earpieces that looked especially nerdy), mumbling to himself as he fought to attach the box blade to his old John Deere.

Unlike the dark neighboring houses, here one light was burning over the front door. Clint shot me a questioning look.

"Dad has had solar power for about a zillion years. I think he installed it as some kind of tax scam in the mid 70s. No one was more surprised than him that it has proven to be an excellent investment." I shook my head fondly while I remembered. "What time is it?"

"Just past eight."

"Park anywhere behind the two trucks." As usual, my parents hadn't pulled their trucks into the garage. They didn't use the garage as a shelter for vehicles, instead, they used it as a general tool storehouse, wood workshop, machine repair shop, etc. I've always thought of it as their shit catcher. (My Mustang, on the other hand, had been an "inside" car. She lived in the garage and was only allowed outside at night with adult supervision.)

"Stay here. I'll come around and get you."

I watched as Clint moved stiffly out of the driver's seat. He straightened slowly, with one hand pressed against the small of his back. Carefully he made his way over to my side and opened my door.

"Is your back bothering you?"

"Don't worry about it—it gets like this."

I wanted to ask him like what, but he brusquely motioned for me to join him.

I felt shaky as I climbed from the Hummer. Clint took my arm and helped me plow through the snow to the front door, where we stood in a small pool of light.

"Uh-hum," I cleared my throat nervously. I didn't know how to proceed. Usually, I'd just holler, *Dad! Hey! It's me!* And let myself in. But now I was suddenly unsure of my reception. What if Rhiannon had alienated my parents, too? What if Dad didn't want to see me? I looked down at myself, realizing that I was still puke spattered and totally bedraggled.

"You okay, Shannon my girl?" Clint asked, pushing a loose curl back from my face.

"I'm not sure—" Before I could finish my answer the front doorknob jiggled. The thick inside door swung open and I was left to squint through the screen door at the hulking shape standing inside.

"Shannon?"

"Yeah, it's me, Dad. I have a friend with me. Can we come in?" My voice sounded like I was six years old again.

"Yep, yep." Dad unlatched the screen door. "Worse storm I can remember. Damn near makes me think I'm back in Illinois!"

We stepped into the little foyer. There was a large oil lamp burning dully on the whatnot table near the door. Dad reached over and adjusted the wick so that the flame danced and we were suddenly illuminated in a flickering of soft yellow. Dad was wearing sweatpants and a sweatshirt that had the University of Illinois logo emblazoned in orange on navy (once an Illini, always an Illini). His feet were covered in thick socks that were pulled loose and floppy at the toes. His hair was mussed and he had his reading glasses on. He looked wonderful and solid and safe. I wanted to hurl myself into his arms and cry like a baby.

Instead, I shuffled my feet nervously, grasping at anything to say. "Um, why didn't the dogs bark?" Dad raises dogs that are an imposing mixture of Irish wolfhound and greyhound. He doesn't race them—he just enjoys them. And he really likes it that they keep the coyote population on his land at a decided minimum. There are usually half a dozen sleek, multicolored dogs maniacally greeting any and all visitors. (Note to self: remember those tails are like whips—beware.)

"Closed 'em up in the barn. Too damn cold and nasty out. I turned the heat lamps on, gave them a big bucket of food and shut them in with the horses." He chuckled. "Those puppers probably think they've died and gone to doggie heaven."

"Oh, Dad, I've missed you so much!" I stood on tiptoe and hugged him hard. He gave me a quick kiss on the cheek.

"Well, you're home now."

I smiled up at him through tears of relief, thanking my Goddess that whatever else Rhiannon had done, she had not ruined my relationship with Dad. His eyes strayed curiously to Clint, who immediately held out his hand.

"Mr. Parker, it's a pleasure to meet you—"

"Dad, this is my friend, Clint Freeman." I broke in, blushing furiously at forgetting my manners. "Clint, my father, Richard Parker."

They shook hands and Dad pointed into the living room. "Come on in—make yourselves to home. Shannon, why don't you get Clint and yourself something to drink. You know where everything is."

We followed Dad into the living room, which was separated from the kitchen by an island that held the grill and lots of kitchen cabinets. Dad motioned Clint to the couch and he took his usual easy chair that sat next to a table laden with books and racehorse magazines. I retreated to the kitchen.

"What can I get you, Clint? Coffee, tea or something stronger?" I asked as I searched for mugs.

"I'll take coffee, if it's not too much trouble."

"Already have some made," Dad spoke up. "Hope you like it strong," he said to Clint.

"I do." Clint smiled.

"Bugs, I believe I have some single malt in that cupboard that you haven't touched in more than six months, in case your taste has turned back to it."

Hearing him use my nickname made tears rush to my eyes, and I had a hard time focusing on pouring Clint's coffee—until I processed the rest of what he had said. I love single-malt scotch. I have since my first trip to Scotland more than a decade ago. But I had learned during my time in Partholon that Rhiannon loathed scotch. She thought it was common. Dad's comment was a tangible reminder that she had been here; she had been poking through and intruding upon yet another aspect of my life. It made me feel pissed off and violated.

I nuked some warm water for my tea and carried both mugs into the living room.

"Do you need anything else, Dad?"

"Nope. I'm still working on my Baileys and coffee." He looked curiously at me and added, "You know I usually don't drink coffee so late, but something told me I should stay awake tonight."

I sat on the couch next to Clint, and tugged fretfully at my tea bag.

"Still don't have a taste for your scotch, huh? I think you drank all of that expensive red wine you brought over that time..." His voice trailed off like he didn't want to complete the memory.

"No! I mean, yes!" I shook my head, trying to think

clearly. "What I mean is, I still love scotch. I just think hot tea is a wiser choice tonight." And, I added silently, for the next seven months or so.

We sipped our drinks quietly. I didn't know where to begin, but just being in the familiar room made me feel better, stronger, more able to cope with the horrors of the day.

I blinked and said abruptly, "Where's Mama Parker?" My stepmom's absence was suddenly keenly felt. She should have been bustling around, insisting on fixing us something to eat, fussing about getting me out of these dirty, wet clothes. In general, doing mom things that always made me feel loved. I was ashamed I hadn't questioned where she was immediately.

"Mama Parker's been visiting her sister in Phoenix."

"Without you?" Hard to believe. They've been married for a zillion years, but they still did everything together. It's sweet but disgusting.

"She's had the visit planned for months. I meant to go with her, but one of those idiot yearlings thought he should run through a fence and try and take a leg off, so I stayed to doctor the knot-headed moron."

I nodded my head in agreement at the familiar litany of horse complaints. There were few things Dad thought stupider than racehorses—and there were few things he loved more.

I knew I should launch into the reason for my visit, but the comfortable conversation made me realize how much I ached for normalcy, even if it was just an illusion and temporary.

"So, how's school?" Until I was swept into the life of High Priestess in another dimension, I had been very happy teaching English at Broken Arrow High School, which just happened to be the same school at which my father had been a teaching/coaching legend for almost three decades. I had loved teaching. Teenagers supplied me with endless comedic fodder. Really. Where else but in the public schools could you find a job that allows you to be onstage every day in front of more than one hundred semi-humanoids (teenagers), where you could come to work several times a year (during Spirit Weeks) dressed in a variety of costumes—everything from "Pajama Day" to "Your Favorite Superhero Day," where the more embarrassing you look and act the "cooler" you are, and get paid for it? (Well, in Oklahoma we *kind* of get paid for it.) I'm telling you, only in the public schools.

Oh… One thing Dad and I have always been in total agreement about is that teenagers are one of the few creatures that have less sense than racehorses. I watched the slow grin spread over his face.

"Little morons—they get squirrlier every year." He chuckled. "And this year we hired the most god-awful pansy-assed new vice principal from one of those touchy-feely middle schools. Silly bastard wouldn't know discipline if it came up and bit him. All he does is move furniture, screw with the thermostat in the teachers' lounge and sneak around the halls trying to catch us leaving our classrooms unsupervised when we go get a goddamn cup of coffee. I swear he squats to pee." He shook his head and gave me a long-suffering look. "Damn good thing you got out of it when you did."

At his mention of my change in career, the warmth I'd been feeling from the familiar talk chilled. I studied my tea miserably.

"You look bad, Bugs." Dad's voice tried for a joking tone, but the lines that creased his forehead deepened as he spoke. "You want to tell me what's going on?"

My eyes shot up to his. I never could hide much from him—actually I've never tried. Even as a teenager I told him everything. I blinked as a sudden thought washed over me. Maybe Rhiannon hadn't been able to hide her true nature from him, either. Maybe he'd *known* Rhiannon hadn't been me.

I took a deep breath and squared my shoulders.

"I don't know how to begin. It's complicated."

"Life's complicated," he said simply. "Just start at the beginning—we'll work it from there."

"Dad, I haven't been me for the past six months."

Dad nodded his head and agreed. "Yep, yep. You were damn rude to Mama Parker. Good thing she loves you so much. Glad you're back to normal now and—"

I held up my hand to stop him.

"No, I don't mean I haven't been *acting* like myself. I mean I haven't *been* me—*literally*."

Whatever comment he was getting ready to make died on his lips as he studied my face.

"Explain what you mean, Shannon Christine."

His use of my middle name told me he was taking me seriously.

"Do you remember that six months ago I had an accident?"

"A car accident—of course I remember. You were out of it for days. Worried us practically to death. I knew you were going to wrap that damn Mustang around something some day. Too fast..." he muttered and shook his head in disgust, ready to rekindle an old argument.

"It wasn't a normal accident, Dad. And I didn't wrap it around anything," I added, exasperated. "I bought a pot at an estate auction. It was an old burial urn. On it was a picture of the High Priestess Goddess Incarnate for Epona."

"Celtic horse goddess." He nodded. (Dad's a well-read man, as the mounds of books all over the living room can testify to.)

"The goddess was me—or more accurately, my mirror image," I paused to be sure he was getting all of this, "from another world in another dimension. A world where mythology exists instead of technology, and where some of the people there mirror the people here."

"Shannon, this is a silly-assed thing to joke around about."

"I'm not joking!" I looked at Clint who, until now, had remained silent. "Tell him," I prompted.

"Sir—" Clint's steady voice seemed to lend sanity to mine "—hear her out. She's telling you the truth, and she can prove it."

My eyes narrowed briefly and I shot him a *what-the-hell-are-you-talking-about* look. Prove it? Clint just nodded encouragement.

I cleared my throat and turned back to Dad. "The pot caused my accident, and more than that. It caused me to be pulled into the other world and exchanged for my mirror image, the Goddess Epona's Incarnate."

His eyes widened, but he didn't interrupt.

"So the bitch that has been screwing with my life and my family and my friends for the past six months hasn't been me!" I finished in a rush.

"You're saying you have physically not been in this world?"

I nodded.

"And the woman who quit your job, married then buried a millionaire and has been jetting all over the US of A isn't actually you?"

"That's what I'm saying."

"Shannon..." He started shaking his head. "Do you have any idea how flat out crazy that sounds?"

"Hell yes!" I stifled the impulse to scream and continued in a more normal voice. "I'm the one living it, and it sounds ridiculous to me." I closed my eyes and rubbed my temples as nausea growled in my stomach and a headache pounded with each heartbeat. He wasn't going to believe me.

Then Clint's strong hand was kneading the knotted muscles of my neck. "Mr. Parker—" he spoke with the calm voice of reason "—it's late and Shannon has been through a lot today. Maybe it would be best if we slept on this and finished explaining in the morning."

"You do look like hell, girl," Dad said to me.

I opened my eyes. "Dad, Suzanna's dead."

He jolted in surprise. "Little Suzanna! My God, how did that happen?"

Clint broke in. "That's only part of the story, Mr. Parker. Right now it's enough that you know that it just happened tonight, and Shannon had to watch her die." His voice had taken on a hard protective edge that surprised me.

I watched my dad's eyes narrow speculatively at the man sitting beside me. "All right then, son. Let's get our girl to bed." Dad walked over to the couch and took my hand from my forehead, pulling me to my feet. He hugged me, patting my back. Then he sniffed at me. "Good lord, Bugs, you smell terrible."

"I know," I said miserably.

Still holding my hand, he pulled me toward the hall that led to the bedrooms, grabbing the oil lamp from its resting place in the foyer. The first room to the left was the guest room. Dad opened the door and walked into the room, fumbling in the bedside table's top drawer for matches to light the thick, vanilla-scented candles that decorated the dresser, then he turned and looked pointedly at Clint.

"This is Shannon's room. I'll bunk you up in the daybed in the office. That all right with you?"

"Yes, sir." Clint held his gaze.

Dad nodded and grunted before turning back to me. "I think there are some old nightshirts and other things of yours in the dresser there, and I imagine there's enough hot water for you to take a quick shower." He wrinkled his nose at me. "You need it. We'll get all this straightened out in the morning."

I stepped gratefully into his embrace and whispered, "I love you, Dad," against his chest.

"I love you, too, old Bugsy." Then he turned and pushed Clint out of the doorway. "Come with me, son," he said before firmly closing my door.

Dad's typical protectiveness made me smile as I rummaged through the top drawer of the dresser. Sure enough, I found a couple pairs of my old jeans, and a well-worn sweatshirt, as well as one of my favorite old nightshirts, the one that had a picture of Santa pooping down a chimney. The caption read *How to tell if you've* really *been bad.* It had been a Christmas gift from a student.

"Oh, what a beautiful sight!" I sighed happily as I also found a pair of my panties—soft violet silk from Victoria's

Secret—*with* a butt. "Damn, I'll be glad to get out of these thongs!" It's amazing how little it takes to make me happy when I'm stressed.

Dad was right. There was just enough hot water for a quick but complete shower. The water acted as a tranquilizer, and I barely pulled the nightshirt over my head and stumbled back to my room before my eyes began to blur and close. I blew out the candles and crawled under the quilt my grandma had made decades ago. Reaching down to the foot of the bed, I unfolded the goose down comforter and pulled it snuggly around my shoulders. I breathed in deeply. The sweet scent of vanilla mingled with the unique smell of the clean, well-used old quilt; it was the scent of memories, reminding me drowsily of my childhood as I surrendered to the feeling of security and let sleep claim me.

I know for most people it's hard to tell such things as they sleep, but my sleep has always been mine to manipulate, and I knew I slept deeply and dreamlessly for hours, so my unconscious body felt rested and refreshed when my spirit drifted into DreamLand.

I was reclining on gigantic down-filled pillows that floated on violet-colored cumulus clouds. Fat black-and-white cats were lounging around me, purring contentedly. Jamie Fraser (of Diana Gabaldon's Outlander books) was explaining to me (in his sexy Scottish brogue) that he was dumping Claire and that I was now his true love. Hugh Jackman (in his Wolverine persona) was frowning in displeasure at Jamie, but he said he wouldn't duel for my affections until he had finished giving me a proper foot rub. I opened my mouth to tell the boys to be good and not fight over little ol' me…

…And I found myself sucked out of my body and through

the roof of my parents' ranch house. Hovering in the snowy sky was a bizarre experience. It was like the white crystals were inside me and around me all at the same time.

"Ugh! Feeling sick again!" I said to the night.

Breathe, Beloved. I noticed the voice in my head was stronger and clearer than it had been since I had been forced into this world.

"You sound like Clint," I said aloud. The Goddess didn't answer, so I did as she instructed, inhaling the crisp, icy air deeply. Almost immediately my vertigo faded. It was disconcerting to realize that I was becoming not just experienced in the Magic Sleep of spirit travel, but comfortable with it.

I gazed around me, amazed at the change in the land below. It looked like a scene from a Colorado winter postcard. Dad's pastures had been transformed from the green of Oklahoma pin oaks and junipers, to the enchanting white of a snow-bathed wilderness.

"It's beautiful," I whispered.

I looked back toward the barn. A warm light glowed from behind the shuttered windows and the snow piled in graceful, curving mounds around the base of the barn. Surprised, I noticed that the mounds actually came up several feet against the red and white of the barn's siding.

"There must be almost three feet of snow down there."

It is not natural, Beloved. The Goddess's voice rang in my mind.

"I know!" I spoke aloud to the listening night. "It never snows like this in Oklahoma."

It is because what is unnatural has entered this world. True evil is at work here.

The Goddess's words drove crystallized shards of fear into my body.

"Nuada." The name was a curse on my lips.

You must stop him.

"Me!" I yelped. "I don't know how to stop him!"

You must, Beloved. You are the only one who can.

"How? The only reason I was able to figure out what to do in Partholon was that I was surrounded by a world of people who understood magic. They helped me. And you helped me!"

You trust yourself so little, my Beloved one. *I was alarmed to hear the divine voice in my mind beginning to fade.* Rely on what is within.

"No! Don't go!" I felt panicky. "I don't know what to do!"

The ancient ones will guide you...as will the Shaman in this world...

"Epona!" I yelled the Goddess's name. "What ancient ones? What Shaman?"

Remember—*the voice was so faint I had to strain within to hear her last words*—You are the Chosen of a Goddess...

And, like mist, she was gone.

7

I gulped in air and sat straight up.

"Shit!" I swung my feet around and almost leaped out of bed. "You'd think coming back to Oklahoma would be a normal experience. Oklahoma used to be entirely normal…mundane…boring even. Damn, I could use some good ol' fashioned Okie boredom," I muttered at my dim reflection in the mirror above the dresser. Pawing through the top drawer, I snatched at a pair of old jeans, the homey sweatshirt, followed by a thick pair of workout socks. "But, no! Instead you're pregnant, scared, in the middle of a blizzard, being chased by some big-ass booger monster," I kept talking to myself. "And starving."

I shut up as I opened the door and tiptoed to the kitchen. Goddess knows I wasn't going to be able to go back to sleep, and all of a sudden scrambled eggs, toast and bacon sounded incredibly yummy. At least I knew my way around.

I felt through the drawer we called the gobble drawer—I knew it held a little bit of everything, which should include matches to light the oil lamp that always sat on the kitchen table.

"There you are," I whispered as my hand closed around the familiar box shape.

"You could have saved yourself some trouble. I think your dad left matches over here by the lamp." Clint's voice scared me so badly I almost peed my pants.

"Damnit, Clint! What the hell are you doing sitting out here in the dark?" Before he could answer, I struck the match. He was lifting a mug to his lips as the golden spark illuminated his face. "And why didn't you say something? You scared the shit out of me."

"You looked like you were on some kind of mission. I thought I'd just sit here and stay out of your way."

"Huh," I grunted at him and lit the lamp, adjusting the wick so that the edges of the kitchen played in a trembling light. I turned my back on him and started pulling eggs and such out of the refrigerator. "Why are you awake?"

"Why are *you* awake?" he countered. "After what you've been through the last couple of days I would have thought you'd be due for a good long sleep."

"I slept," I evaded, searching through the cabinets for the right pots and pans.

"You had another one of those dream things?" His voice was gentle.

"Yes," I said without turning.

"You saw ClanFintan again?"

"No." I checked the gas flame and spread out plenty of bacon in the iron skillet. "This time I just floated around and had a brief conversation with Epona." I glanced over my shoulder at him. "I'm making eggs and bacon for everyone. Don't tell me you're not hungry."

"I would love for you to feed me." His eyes met mine and their brightness hinted at a double meaning. I looked away quickly.

"What did your Goddess say?"

"Oh—" I flippantly cracked eggs into a bowl "—let's see—evil is loose—Nuada must be stopped—the ancients will help—the Shaman will help—trust myself." I whisked the eggs maniacally. "Only I usually prefer to avoid evil. I don't know how to stop Nuada. I don't know any ancients or a Shaman. And the one thing I do firmly trust about myself is that I am way out of my league here." I realized I was fighting tears, which only pissed me off more. The morning sickness may have let up, but the hormones were certainly still in full swing. Wonderful.

Clint's hands closed over mine so that my psychotic whisking stilled. He rested his chin on the top of my head and pulled me back against him.

"I'm here. Your dad's here. Between the three of us we'll figure this thing out." He guided the bowl back to the countertop and turned me around to face him. He put one hand on my shoulder; with the other he lifted my chin so that my eyes met his. "You are the Chosen of a Goddess. Don't forget that."

"That's what Epona reminded me of, too."

"Well, if you won't listen to the Goddess, will you listen to me?" His dark eyes smiled down at me. "After all, I am the mirror of your husband," he said playfully, unknowingly mimicking ClanFintan's tone so accurately that I felt my heart leap in response.

"Yes, you are," I whispered tremulously.

He read the yearning in my face, and his teasing instantly sobered. I was close enough to him to feel his breath catch, and the hand that he had placed on my shoulder tightened. Then the fingers that were resting under my chin moved, gently tracing the curve of my cheek down the side of my neck. They threaded their way around until he was lightly caressing the back of my neck. A chill of response fluttered through me.

"Shannon my girl," he spoke the endearment in a hoarse whisper as he bent to touch his lips to mine. The kiss was fleeting and deceptively chaste. He pulled his head back so that he could look into my eyes.

"Let me kiss you, Shannon."

"You just did." My voice sounded breathless.

"That wasn't a kiss, love." His half smile was full of promise. "Let me kiss you, Shannon," he repeated softly.

I wanted him to kiss me. I needed his mouth against mine. His wonderfully familiar lips curled into a brief, full smile when I silently nodded my permission.

Then his arms were sliding around my body and I felt myself following old pathways as my hands crept up around his broad shoulders. Our bodies pressed together as our lips met. I could feel the restrained passion in the tautness of his body as he took his time tasting my mouth. I let my tongue meet his.

I have always loved the wonderful mixture of clean lines, muscular hardness and surprisingly smooth, soft places that blend together to form the body of a man. I ran one hand down his arm, delighting in the strength I felt there and marveling at the way I could make this strong man tremble just by taking his tongue within my mouth.

Exactly like ClanFintan. The dreamy thought was a fist in my stomach.

I pulled abruptly back and out of his arms. Shakily I ran a hand over my eyes and pushed my hair out of the way.

"I'm..." I faltered as both of us struggled to regain control over our breathing. "I'm sorry. I don't want..." But the words died in my mouth. "No, that's not true. I do want. I want your hands on me; I want your lips against mine. You are just so much like him I can't help but want that." I looked at him beseechingly. "But I'm married. And not to you."

"You're married in another world, Shannon, not in this one."

"Would it matter to you?" I shot back at him. "If I belonged to you, would you mind me sleeping with *him*—be it in another world or not?"

His silence was all the answer I needed.

"I didn't think so. The facts don't change. Be it here or there, I'm still married to another man."

"What the hell are you talking about, Shannon?" my dad's voice broke in.

Clint and I both jumped guiltily.

"Um..." I was having a hard time meeting his eyes. "Good morning, Dad."

"You better turn that bacon," he said as he walked over to the kitchen table and sat in a chair across from Clint. "And you can pour me some coffee, too."

I did as he asked.

"Thanks, Bugs." He sipped his coffee while I poured the scrambled eggs into the waiting skillet. When he spoke, his voice was thoughtful. "I can't say I understand or even really believe what you started to tell me last night. But I do know you well enough to know that *you* believe it. And you've never been a flighty girl, so there must be some truth to what you're saying. I'm willing to hear it with an open mind." He sipped his coffee again and glanced at Clint. "But first I want to know who the hell you're married to, and why this man's here with you instead of your husband." His expression said that dads are not very keen on the whole you're-committing-adultery-with-my-baby thing.

I stirred the eggs and spoke matter-of-factly over my shoulder. "I'm married to a High Shaman and warrior, who is also leader of his people. His name is ClanFintan. He's not here with me because he exists in another world."

To his credit Dad didn't miss a beat. "You said you were only there since your accident. That's been six months. Doesn't seem enough time to meet and marry someone."

"It was an arranged marriage. I woke in Partholon after the accident to find myself betrothed to him. It was one of the things Rhiannon was running away from."

"Rhiannon?"

"That's her name, Dad. The woman who has been masquerading as me." I drained the bacon on some folded paper towels and pulled three plates out of the cabinet nearest the sink. "Breakfast is ready. Y'all can help yourselves," I drawled. An Oklahoma accent is always useful when bossing around Okie men.

Dad and Clint responded true to form (like I was a drill sergeant calling them to chow), and soon the three of us were seated in a circle around the small kitchen table. I was pleased that my stomach was staying still and seemed to be able to enjoy a real meal for a change.

Between bites Dad kept up the questioning. "Sounds like you stepped into a mess if this Rhiannon woman ran to another world to get out of marrying the guy."

"It wasn't just that," Clint spoke up. "Rhiannon left a world that needed her not because she was being forced into a marriage. She left it because she was a selfish coward and she lusted after the type of power she glimpsed in this world."

Dad chewed, and studied Clint speculatively. "Where do you fit into all of this?"

"I brought Shannon back to this world," Clint said simply.

"You?" Dad's eyes widened in surprise. "Why?"

Before Clint could answer, I said, "To understand that, you need to understand Rhiannon, which means you need to know the whole story."

"I'm listening."

I smiled my appreciation of his open mind, and launched into my story. Dad listened closely without interrupting, except for several questions about centaurs and shapeshifting. The idea of the human/horse merger appeared to fascinate him. Clint listened attentively, too. I realized that, although I had explained bits and pieces of what had happened in Partholon to Clint, he had never heard the entire story except from Rhiannon's manipulative perspective.

"...So ClanFintan and the warriors had returned from

Guardian Castle, and it was just days away from the Samhain celebration when Epi would be mated with a stallion to ensure fertility of the land. She was restless, so ClanFintan and I took her out, thinking it would help her to settle down. Instead, she led us to an ancient grove." Here I paused and glanced at Clint. He continued for me.

"I was causing the mare's restlessness. I had found the mirror of the Partholonian grove, through which there was an opening between worlds. I realized Rhiannon's evil nature, and I was trying to call Shannon here, and expel Rhiannon from here to there." He gave me a sober look. "I thought I would be rescuing her from a world that Rhiannon had described as horrible. But actually I was pulling her away from a husband she loved, and people who needed her. To add insult to injury, I didn't even get rid of Rhiannon."

"What?" Dad rediscovered his voice. "Rhiannon is still here?"

"Well, I don't think she's in Oklahoma, but she is most certainly in this world," Clint said. "I'm not sure why I was only able to bring Shannon here without expelling Rhiannon."

"Best guess?" Dad asked.

"I underestimated Rhiannon, which won't happen again."

"And that's not all, Dad." His gaze shifted once more to my face. "Remember the ancient evil I told you about that corrupted Guardian Castle? I think it's working again. Somehow Nuada's spirit or essence or—oh, hell, I don't know what to call it—he's alive. And he's here. He caused Suzanna's death last night."

"Explain that, Shannon."

"Nuada was there last night. He made a car propel itself into Suz." My voice cracked on her name. "It looked like an accident, but Clint and I felt his presence, and we know he did something to the car. And, Dad, I think he may be coming here next."

"Here? Why?"

"He's obsessed with me. He thinks I called him back from the dead. Of course I didn't—I don't want anything to do with him, even if I did know how to call up the dead, which I sure as hell don't. I think whatever resurrected him has something to do with the dark god from Partholon. But when I rejected him he swore that he would kill my loved ones in this world, as he had in the other."

"You already saw him kill my mirror image in Partholon."

I nodded, swallowing back tears. "And Epona has warned me that it is because Nuada has been released here that this unnatural weather is happening. The Goddess says he must be stopped..." I hesitated and added quietly, "Before I can go back."

"Go back?" Dad's spine straightened in surprise. "I realize you became attached to some of those people, but this is your home, Shannon. This is where you belong. We'll figure out a way to send Rhiannon back there and she can take care of her own responsibilities."

I couldn't help but smile. Same Dad—same teacher logic.

"Dad, I have to go back, and not just because they need me." My eyes pleaded with him to understand. "I love ClanFintan."

"Huh," Dad scoffed. "You said Clint here is his mirror image. Right?"

I nodded. Dad looked at Clint.

"Well, a blind fool could tell that he loves you. Isn't that the case, son?" he asked Clint.

"That's the case, sir." Clint didn't hesitate.

"And the way you were locking lips in the kitchen not too long ago tells me that you have feelings for him, too. Don't you?" Dad's square gaze met mine.

"That's beside the point, Dad." I blushed.

"Doesn't seem like it to me." He motioned to Clint. "Or to him. Seems like we need to kill that damn Nuada creature once and for all, send Rhiannon and whatever evil is hanging around back to Partholon, and you need to stay your butt here."

"I'm pregnant, Dad."

"Huh?"

"What?"

Both men spoke together. I sighed.

"I'm pregnant with ClanFintan's baby. I have to go back."

"Damnit, Shannon!" Clint yelled as he pushed up from his chair. I noticed he grimaced as if he'd stood too fast, and I wondered again what was going on with his back. He stalked a couple of steps away, looking like he wanted to hit something.

"You're sure you're pregnant, Bugs?" Dad's voice was rough.

"Absolutely, Dad."

"With the centaur's baby?" He sounded as if the concept confused him.

"With the centaur's baby," I acknowledged.

Dad glanced at my stomach. "Are you going to have room for all that in there?"

"ClanFintan assures me I will give birth to a human

child. But," I added with a teasing smile, "he says the baby will be one hell of an equestrian."

Dad's full-bellied laugh lightened the mood of the kitchen. "Is that what he said?"

"That and he was born to love me."

"You have to go back, Bugs. A child needs its father." His voice sounded sure, but his eyes were filled with sadness.

"Her father," I corrected him.

"Her?"

"Epona's Chosen is always gifted with a daughter as her firstborn," I explained to him.

"Your Goddess and I agree on one thing."

I raised my brows at him. "What's that?"

His work-roughened hand covered mine. "That daughters are a gift from the gods." We both blinked tears from our eyes. Then he squeezed my hand and stood, nodding his head in Clint's direction. "I have chores to do. I'll leave you two alone for a little while, but I could use some help carrying feed—so don't be too long about it." He turned and met Clint's troubled eyes. "This changes things, son."

"I know, sir," Clint said.

Dad nodded, and then walked briskly to the kitchen door, which led to the utility room and garage. Then he stopped abruptly and turned around to face Clint.

"Now I know why your face seems so damn familiar." He shook his head like he couldn't believe it'd taken him so long to figure out two plus two. "You're that colonel from the Air Guard fighter unit in Tulsa, the one whose F–16 went bad right over the city and you stayed with it long enough to get the damn thing to crash right in the middle of the Arkansas River. The story was plastered all over the media." Dad glanced at me. "You remember, Shannon? Happened about five years back."

All I could do was nod and blink like an idiot. I did remember, but I hadn't recognized him from the media blitz.

Dad lifted his brows at Clint. "They said you stayed with it too long so that you could be sure it wouldn't crash downtown. Ejected too low." Here he paused, looking up at the ceiling as if the newspaper article was plastered there. "Broke your back, if I remember correctly."

"You remember correctly," Clint said quietly.

"They said you were a hero."

"Just doing my job."

Dad nodded in respectful acknowledgment.

"There's knee boots and coats in the closet out here, see that you're properly covered before you come to the barn. Don't want my granddaughter to catch cold." He closed the door securely, leaving me alone with Clint.

I looked at Clint and finally saw him with real clarity. He was a self-sacrificing F–16 pilot, a hero and a warrior. He could talk to the spirits of the trees and he had an aura that glowed like sapphires with a halo of gold dust, which made him a Shaman. A chill rippled through me. He was truly ClanFintan's equal.

I thought it best that I make myself oh-so-busy cleaning up the dishes.

"So that's why your back hurts," I said as I systematically cleared the dishes.

"Yes."

"And living in the middle of the forest helps?" I asked as I filled up the sink with soapy water. (My parents have always refused to get a dishwasher. They say it's against the laws of nature. Whatever the hell that means.)

"It's the only way I can really be mobile," he said hesitatingly, like he hated talking about it. "The longer I'm away from the heart of the forest, the worse it gets. That's why I couldn't stay in Tulsa with Rhiannon when she came here. And that's also why I didn't realize what she was doing until much later."

"Are you okay right now, or do you need to go back today?" I couldn't keep the wistful sound out of my voice.

"I can tolerate it for a few days, and your dad's land is still forested enough that it gives me some relief. It's in the city that I get most quickly drained."

"Well, let me know, I…I don't," I stuttered, "I don't want to, well, to be the cause of—"

He cut me off, sounding more sad than angry. "You could have told me about the baby."

I shrugged my shoulders, soaping up a dish. "It really doesn't make any difference. I would still want to go back, even if I wasn't pregnant. It just makes it easier for Dad to understand."

"It makes it easier for me to understand, too." Clint spoke slowly. "But I want you to realize something."

I wiped my hands on the dish towel and looked up at him.

"I still want you to stay." He held up his hand as I started to speak. "No, let me finish. If you can't get back, or if for some reason you decide not to, for whatever reason, you need to know that I would love you and want you." He didn't move closer to me, but his eyes warmed and he reached out and took my hand in his. "You and your daughter."

"Thank you, Clint. I will remember."

He lifted my hand and turned it palm up before he kissed it on the pulse point of my wrist. Reluctantly, I pulled it from his warm grasp.

"Let's get these dishes in the sink so we can go help Dad."

"I'm yours to command, ma'am." His liquid voice said he wanted me to read volumes into those words, which I struggled not to do, as we stood hip to hip cleaning up the breakfast mess. His hands touched mine more often than necessary. His arm was warm and near.

He was making me crazy, but I was having a hard time summoning up the desire to tell him to stop. It felt too good to have him close.

"Done!" Finally. I wiped my hands on the dish towel and offered it to him.

"We make a good team..." He paused for effect. "In the kitchen."

"Yeah, I'm sure we'll go down in the Dishwashers Hall of Fame." I said sarcastically. "Let's go help Dad." Without waiting for him to find an excuse to kiss any other part of my anatomy, I led the way through the kitchen door to the utility room.

The utility room was built as a go-between from the house to the garage, and it was usually a controlled mess. Shelves filled with homemade canned goods lined two walls, the washer and dryer and an enormous coat closet lined the others. Clint and I struggled our way into old work coats, hats, gloves, scarves, and then pulled on knee-high rubber boots with thick-soled treads.

The zipper of my coat was catching and I cursed at it under my breath.

"Here..." There was a smile in Clint's voice. "I'll get that."

His fingers took over from mine, and he ran the zipper down a few inches then tugged it quickly up, securing it snuggly under my chin. Then he tapped the top of my oversize work hat that looked vaguely Russian (but covered my ears and had enough room for all of my wild hair).

"You look like a little girl." And before I could say anything he bent and kissed me softly, first on the tip of my nose, then on my lips. Then he took me by the shoulders and turned me to the door that led to the garage. Opening it, he gave me a little push through.

"I know the way!" I grumped at him.

"Then lead on, my Lady," he said in a voice that sounded so much like ClanFintan that I felt a responding flutter in my stomach that had nothing to do with the baby growing there.

"I'm leading, I'm leading," I snapped, trying to ignore the feelings this man was evoking more and more frequently within me.

We shuffled our way through the mess in the garage that was definitely uncontrolled, opened the side door and stepped out into a world gone white.

The snow was still falling. This morning it was a soft-looking, crystallized snow, which slanted its way to join the glistening mounds that already covered everything.

"It looks like someone has opened an enormous box of white glitter, then set up a huge fan to blow it all over," I said.

Clint shook his head. "It sure looks like something's been opened up—something not right."

I shivered and pulled the collar of my coat up around my neck.

The Oklahoma wind howled, which was the only thing that was familiar about the weather.

"*'Perhaps the wind wails so in winter for the summer's dead; and all sad sounds are nature's funeral cries for what has been and is not.'*" I whispered the obscure quote, struggling to remember which dead Englishman had written it.

"What?" Clint asked.

"Nothing." I forced my thoughts into line. I was just creeping myself out, and there was no point to that. I gestured to the left of us, where Dad's tracks led from the house to the snow-obscured barn. "That way."

"Hold on. Your dad would stake me out to freeze if I let you fall and hurt yourself." He offered me his arm, which I latched onto gratefully.

"He wouldn't stake you out," I panted as we forced our way through the hard top layer of snow that was almost thigh deep. "He'd just shoot you."

"Well, that's a comfort."

The barn door was pulled back, and as we got within hearing range of it a multitude of slender, wire-haired bodies burst out of the warm interior. The hounds leaped toward us, splayfooted, trying to stay upright atop the icy surface of the snow. Every few steps one paw would break through the brittle crust and the dog would have to struggle its way out of snow that threatened to envelope it.

"Watch their tails," I said to Clint before the group reached us. "They're like friggin whips, especially if they're a little wet."

Clint laughed at me.

"You think I'm kidding? Try being out here in shorts and having this horde race around you wagging and whining. Those tails leave welts." Then I yelled to the interior of the barn, "Jeesh, Dad, didn't you just have three dogs six months ago?" I reached out and patted the nearest pointy muzzle, which set off an explosion of doggy happiness as they all tried to wriggle and whine their way into some personal attention. "I count five dogs out here—I think."

"Yep." Dad appeared in the doorway with a white grain bucket in his hand. "Mama Parker fell in love with that little brown pup a couple months ago while we were in Kansas. Said the pupper begged to come home with her, so here she is. We call her Fawnie Anne."

"That makes four. I'm still counting five."

"Couldn't get just one," he said like they were furred potato chips. "That silver pup came with her. Mama Parker named him Murphy, after the war hero."

Clint and I broke through the snow and the dogs and entered the barn. The wonderful alfalfa smell enveloped me and I breathed deeply of the sweet scent of hay mingled with horse. The barn was large and well built. Along one side were eight stalls, filled with a mixture of mares, yearlings and a couple of slick-looking horses that could only be Dad's current racing stock. The other side of the barn was piled to the ceiling with hay. Next to the hay a tack room beckoned with the smell of grain and well-used leather.

"Where are the rest of the horses?" I asked, peering into the first stall and rubbing the velvet muzzle that was thrust toward me.

"Back pasture. They'll be fine if they stay together under

the shelter. Have enough hay to last for a couple days." He gestured to the levered faucet that jutted up from the barn floor. "Bugs, you can top off their water buckets. Clint, fill up those hay nets hanging in the stalls while I get this grain measured out." He stopped and looked at Clint. "If your back can stand it."

"My back's always willing to work in country air," Clint assured him.

"Good. And dogs, get!" He gave the pups within reach several resounding thumps with the bucket in his hand. "Go on out there and stretch your legs! You're too damn much in the way in here."

All of us did as we were told.

The barn was filled with the companionable sounds of people doing chores, talking to horses, and the mewing of a stray cat here and there that jumped in, ready for attention now that the dogs had been temporarily banished from what was usually the cat domain. The mares were good-looking quarter horses, all well built and good-natured. The two yearlings were gangly and big-headed, reminding me of fifteen-year-old boys (minus the zits and goofy smiles). I pushed through the door to one of the colt's stalls, checking on the half-filled water bucket. This colt had a neatly wrapped bandage that covered most of his right foreleg.

"Whoa," I said, feeling down the length of the limb. "Leg feels good, Dad," I called. "Not warm at all."

"Yep, he's doing well." Dad's head appeared over the half door to the stall. "You can help me change the dressing tonight."

I had just nodded at Dad when I noticed an odd sound.

It was a bizarre cross between a howl and a whine. It sounded panic stricken, and like no dog noise I had ever heard.

"What the hell?" Dad asked aloud to himself as he started toward the barn door.

"Clint!" I yelled, but he had already heard it. He threw down his bale, and started to move to me. We were only a step behind Dad when he reached the door.

Oddly enough, in the time we had been working in the barn, the wind had completely stopped, but the snow had picked up. Thick flakes obscured all but a veil of morning light. Looking around, I was reminded again of Colorado and a weekend I'd been trapped at a lovely lodge in Manateau Springs because of a snowstorm much like what was now carpeting Oklahoma. Amazing.

We stood there trying to locate the direction from which the noise was coming.

"Those two new pups have probably gotten themselves caught somewhere in the snow, and they don't have enough sense to get out."

Dad's piercing whistle split the air.

"Fawn! Murphy! Come here, pups!" He whistled again.

Suddenly from around the east corner of the barn flew a tangle of hounds. They ran to Dad, shivering and whining. They couldn't get close enough to him.

"What's wrong with you knot-heads?" he asked affectionately as he stroked heads and tickled ears.

"Dad, the dogs are terrified," I said, then added, "And you're missing two of them."

"Those two pups. Thought so—they're just stuck in the snow. Sounds like the howling is coming from over there by the pond. I'll go out and pull their silly asses from the snowbank they've tangled with." Dad started out into the pasture, but Clint's voice stopped him.

"Wait." His tone set the hair on the back of my neck on end. "Something's out there."

"Speak clearly, son," Dad ordered.

Instead of answering him, Clint looked at me. "Do you feel it?"

The moment he said it, I realized I did feel it. It hadn't been Clint's voice that had roused my neck hairs.

"I feel it," I said with difficulty around a mouth that was fear dried.

"Is it that creature?" Dad asked.

"Yes, it feels like Nuada," I told him.

The frantic howling intensified. Now the direction was clear. It was coming from the pasture just east of the barn where a large pond held plenty of drinking water for the horses, and lots of fish for any neighbor who had a mind to cast a line.

"Well, the damn thing is doing something to my dogs, and that pisses me off. Shannon, the rifle's in the tack room where it's always been. And it's loaded, so be careful."

"We stay together," I heard Clint telling Dad.

"Then you better be damn sure Shannon stays safe," Dad said shortly.

"Sir," Clint countered, "Shannon has more power inside her than that gun has inside it."

I handed Dad the rifle as he mumbled a nonresponse to Clint. The three of us plowed through the snow around the side of the barn, Dad first, Clint next, then me. We followed the fence line until we came to a chained gate. Dad unhooked the lock and the two men heaved together against the drifted snow until there was enough space for each of us to slip through.

An abandoned horse feeder loomed in front of us. It looked eerie with its open arms filled with white powdery snow, like it was a moon vehicle that had escaped the pages of a Bradbury novel. In the distance, probably twenty yards behind the feeder, we could barely make out the smooth outline of the snow-covered pond.

The terrible howling was definitely coming from the pond.

Even though Dad was breaking through the new snow crust himself, and was more than twenty years older than us, he was pulling away from Clint and me as he rushed to cut the distance between himself and the pups. Every few seconds he'd give another whistle and call out to them.

"Fawn! Murf! Here pups!"

Then my foot caught on the edge of a buried rock and I fell face-first into the snow. I barely had time to blink and Clint was at my side. He pulled me to my feet and brushed snow from my face.

"You okay?"

I nodded, looking over his shoulder at Dad. He had come to a halt at what must be the western edge of the pond. I remembered it as the only side of the pond where the bank was not steep and crowded with trees and brush. It's where the horses drank and where we waded in to escape the blazing Oklahoma summer. Dad was staring out at the smooth expanse of white. The pristine surface was only interrupted by two rows of tracks that began on the north edge of its surface. I followed those tracks, and my eyes widened in horror as I saw that they led straight to the middle of the pond, where the two pups were floundering within a dark circle of water. Their heads were barely visible as they struggled to stay afloat. Every few seconds a panicked howl would break from one of them. I watched as the silver male threw a paw up and tried valiantly to heave himself out, but he could find no hold and he plunged back into the freezing water. The jagged ice that framed them was spattered red with blood from their desperate pawing.

"Oh, Clint. It's awful."

Then my attention was pulled from the struggling dogs as I saw a figure moving out onto the surface of the ice-covered water. It was Dad. He had dropped to his belly, and he was crawling crablike toward the break in the pond.

"Dad!" I screamed. Clint and I plunged ahead again.

"Stay back!" Dad ordered, but he kept inching forward.

"Stop, Dad! It'll break and you'll fall in, too!" I felt a sob build in my throat.

Dad didn't answer, he just kept moving forward. I could hear him speaking in a soothing tone to the pups, who responded by reducing their terrified howls to fearful whines.

Then I felt the color drain from my face as I watched the water ripple and move with a dark life of its own. First it lapped eagerly around the tan pup, closing over its head with an oily sound. The water surged briefly, but the brown head didn't resurface.

"Fawn!" I heard Dad yell.

Then the inky wetness began to lap thickly around the stronger silver pup.

"It's Nuada. He's out there." Clint's voice sounded calm.

I pulled my eyes from the macabre scene before me. Clint was outlined in his aura's metallic glow of sapphire. "Get to the tree line that rings the pond, Shannon." He pointed to a huge, snow-encrusted willow whose branches hung out over the pond's frozen surface like the white hair of a resting giant. "Be sure you're touching the tree—and be ready."

I didn't ask ready for what—I took off, sloughing my way through the entrapping snow. I couldn't waste energy watching what was happening on the pond. I kept my focus on the enormous old willow and pumped my arms, frantically trying to hurl myself to it more quickly.

"Murphy! No!" I heard Dad's shout when I was almost to the tree.

Then a hideous cracking sliced the air. I stumbled and fell through the curtain of branches, and caught myself against the rough bark of the willow's trunk. I turned in time to see the ice beneath my dad's outstretched body split by a dark, watery fist. Then he was submerged in the freezing water.

"Dad!" My scream echoed with a hallow sound in the unnatural quiet that had fallen over the pasture.

I watched helplessly as he struggled against the weight of the water and his clothes. One of his fists shot out, slamming down on the thick ice that ringed him, while he tried to punch a hole and grab on to something firm. But his hand sliced sideways and a line of blood spurted from his palm.

And the oily water lapped around his neck.

"Shannon!" Clint yelled. He had positioned himself at the edge of the bank, which was down an incline and directly in front of me. He stood sideways, with his arms stretched away from his body, like Christ on the cross. One of his outstretched hands pointed at me, the other pointed at my father. "Reach into the tree. Use its power to send your energy to me, just like you did in the grove when our hands were touching."

I took a step backward so that all of my body was pressed against the old willow.

Welcome, Beloved of the Goddess.

The ancient voice sounded softly in my head.

"Oh, help me!" I sobbed.

We are here for you, Chosen, but you must have the courage to call forth our power.

We? What was it saying? I looked back at it and noticed that its branches were entwined with the tree closest to it. And that tree's branches touched the next tree over. All around the pond there was a living chain of willows, a superhighway for squirrels, broken only at the shoreline where the horses came to drink.

"Now! Shannon!" Clint's voice was raw with desperation.

I snapped my eyes shut. Don't think about Dad. Don't think about Nuada's evil. Don't think about what's happening out there. Just think about the warmth, and what it was like to channel it in the grove. Suddenly I felt heat pulsing against the length of my back. Squeezing my eyes shut even more tightly, I concentrated on Clint, much as I had concentrated on finding ClanFintan through the louvers of the dimensional divide. Against my closed lids I could see the pulsing of his spectacular aura, and with that foremost in my mind I took the heat building within me and hurled its power from my fingertips like I was throwing an imaginary ball of flame.

"Yes, Shannon! That's my girl!" Clint's voice sounded amplified.

I took a deep breath, relaxing into the sense of limitless energy behind me.

"I am the Chosen of a Goddess."

My whisper was picked up in the branches of the willow, which began a rustling that had nothing to do with the absent wind. It shimmered from one tree to another, like the greeting of a missing friend rediscovered. I could feel the energy building with that joyous whisper and I focused it, imagining I was holding it like a bright ball within my fingertips. Then in one quick motion, I flung the ball away from me to where I sensed Clint's aura.

I opened my eyes. A shaft of pure, silvery white light shot from my hands. It was a color I recognized instantly because I had seen it many times reflected in the shining mane of Epi. The shaft of light streaked the distance between Clint and me, which I now saw was much greater than when I'd first closed my eyes, because he was steadfastly making his way to the hole in the ice in which my dad was still struggling. The ice directly under Clint's feet had taken on an unearthly luminescence that was spreading with each of his steps. The glow that surrounded Clint made the darkness that encircled the gash in the ice even more obscene and obvious.

An oily wave crawled over Dad's head, and with a sucking sound he was pulled under the surface.

Clint reacted with blurring speed. "More, Shannon!" He leaped forward as he yelled.

I felt a sickening tug within me like my soul was being emptied. My teeth ground together and I pushed myself harder into the solid bark of the tree.

"I am the Chosen of a Goddess, and I call forth your power!" This time it wasn't a whisper but a shout that burst from my lips. The answer was swift in coming, and a column of brilliance cascaded from my hands, wrapping around Clint so that his sapphire aura blazed with a light that caused me to blink away tears.

Dad's bloody hand was the only thing above the water. Clint grabbed it, and blue fire sparked down the length of his arm to the slick water, igniting it in an ethereal flame. An agonized shriek sounded from the bowels of the pond, and Dad's body was suddenly vomited from its dark surface. Clint's blue aura spread to encompass Dad's still body.

I wanted to run down the sloping bank and help Clint drag Dad to firm ground, but Clint must have felt a wavering in my channeled power because he yelled up to me, "Stay there! Keep feeding me more power. I'll take care of your dad."

I obeyed, struggling to stay focused on being a conduit for the ancient energy, but instead of pulling Dad to safety, Clint crawled closer to the gaping hole in the ice. I wanted to scream at him to stop, but an intuitive tremor within me stilled my words. Silently, I watched Clint stretch out his hand until it was only a foot above the surface of the deadly water. He bowed his head and withdrew within himself. Then, with a sound like a thunderclap, sparkling blue shot from his open palm, filling the break in the ice and covering the evil blackness totally like the vacuum-sealed lid of a canning jar.

From under the ice rose another shriek, and the gurgling words *"It is not over, female."*

Clint's blue aura had faded to a barely visible sky-colored

outline, and he crawled back to Dad's body, rolling him over on his stomach while he began CPR for a drowning victim.

Dad hadn't been under very long, I kept telling myself as Clint worked on his still form. My vision blurred and I wiped unnoticed tears from my eyes. It seemed that a long time passed, but it was probably only minutes or seconds, and Dad coughed then vomited mouthfuls of pond water. As soon as he was breathing on his own, Clint rolled him over onto his back. In one smooth motion he lifted him into a fireman's carry. Clint staggered off the frozen pond, laboring under the considerable weight of my dad's limp body.

"He needs a doctor, Shannon. Come on!" Clint's voice sounded strained.

Quickly, I stroked the side of the willow. "Thank you for my father's life."

You are well and truly welcome, Epona's Beloved. The answer was a gentle farewell echo in my mind as I stumbled and half fell my way to Clint's side.

Without hesitation I grabbed Clint's free hand, willing strength and warmth into him. My palm burned as energy passed between the two of us.

"No," he gasped. His pallid face was set in deep lines of pain. "Save it for him. I'll be fine."

Reluctantly, I dropped his hand and we struggled our way back to the barn.

The three remaining dogs were silent and withdrawn as we entered the barn. A groan of pain escaped from Clint's rigid lips as he lay Dad gently in a pile of hay near the door.

"Give me your scarf."

I yanked it off and handed it to him. He wrapped it tightly around Dad's still-bleeding hand.

"Get a blanket from the tack room," Clint ordered. I sprinted off while he checked Dad's pulse.

By the time I came back with several horse blankets clutched in my arms, Clint had Dad's coat and sweater stripped off.

"Cover him and talk to him while I bring the Hummer here." Before he turned to go, he said, "Now is the time to share the tree's healing power."

I nodded and began wrapping blankets securely around Dad. I was horrified by the blue-gray color of his skin and his stillness. I took his uninjured hand in mine. Quickly centering myself, I focused all the warmth from the willows I had stored within me into that hand. I felt the familiar burning tingle through my palm.

"Dad, can you hear me?" I took an edge of one of the blankets and rubbed at his water-soaked hair. The ends were brittle and frozen. Please be okay. Please be okay. "Dad, you have to wake up now." I poured all the heat I could from my body into his.

His eyes flickered and opened, but they had an odd, glassy look.

"Dad!"

"Bugs?" His voice was gravelly and faint, like he had a terrible case of laryngitis.

"It's me. You're okay."

He blinked and looked around like he didn't know where he was, then the light of remembrance returned to his eyes.

"The pups?" he rasped.

I shook my head. "There was nothing you could do."

"Mama Parker's going to be upset."

I wanted to say that she'd be much more upset if he'd

gotten himself killed, but I decided that this was one of the times I should keep my mouth shut.

His eyes were closed again, and I squeezed his hand frantically, worried that he'd fade away. But he squeezed back and I resumed breathing.

"I believe you now." I almost missed his hoarse whisper. "About Partholon. I believe you."

The Hummer roared up. Clint moved quickly but stiffly back to Dad's side. Dad looked up at him.

"Ready, big guy?" Clint asked.

"Just give me a minute. I can walk," Dad whispered.

"Maybe another time." Clint chuckled, and then heaved him back over his shoulder, staggering the few feet to the vehicle, where he deposited Dad in the back seat. I saw the grimace of pain flash over Clint's face as he tried to straighten, but he was all calm authority when he spoke.

"Shannon, get in the back with him. Keep channeling into him all the power you can spare." He smiled grimly at me. "Just be sure you don't drain yourself like you did in the grove. There's not much opportunity for you to recharge right now."

"What about you?" I asked as I climbed into the back seat next to Dad.

"We'll worry about me later." I was alarmed by the stiff, crooked way he sat behind the wheel. "Hold on, this will be a fast, slippery trip." Clint gunned the engine, turned in a tight circle and shot toward the lane.

My respect for military vehicles, and military men, grew with each second.

"Check that hand," Clint said, glancing in the rearview mirror.

It was his right hand that had been cut, and Dad was holding it cradled against his chest. I was sitting to his right, and I leaned close to him.

"Let me see it, Dad."

He grunted painfully, but he let me have his hand. It had soaked through the scarf and was leaking red streaks on the horse blankets.

"Still bleeding," I told Clint.

"Here—" he unwound the scarf from his neck "—wrap this around the wound and keep pressure on it. It's cut pretty bad."

"Sorry, this is going to hurt," I said to Dad. Then I wrapped the blood-drenched hand with Clint's scarf, tied it and pressed firmly, focusing more warmth from me to him. Dad closed his eyes.

"Shit!" The word whistled through his gritted teeth. "It was better when I couldn't feel it."

"At least your voice sounds better."

"Yeah, just in time for me to cuss a blue streak." Dad's teeth were beginning to chatter, which I took for a good sign. His eyes locked with mine. "That Goddamnable thing was down there. It was part of the pond."

"I know. He's not fully formed here, not like he was in Partholon. His body is more liquid and darkness than solid mass."

"It's evil. I could feel it."

I just nodded and kept focusing on channeling power into my father.

Suddenly Dad tried to sit straight up, and I had to scramble to get him to be still.

"That thing's still there with the rest of my animals!"

"Sir," Clint spoke quickly. "I've trapped it, at least for a while. And I don't think Nuada would think to attack an animal unless it was directly tied to a human—like the way he lured you out to the pond through your pups, or the way Shannon described him attacking her mare in Partholon. We're gone now, so there's no reason for him to focus on your animals."

Dad relaxed a little.

"He's single-minded." I agreed with Clint. "And right now he's fixated on anyone I love. He wasn't after the pups. He just used them to get to you."

Dad nodded. "Makes sense—if any of this makes sense." He looked at me. "How could that thing believe you called it here?" Dad's voice broke between his chattering teeth.

"I don't know, I'd never—" A sudden thought made me pause. "Unless Nuada was being called here, but not by me."

Clint met my eyes in the rearview mirror, and he nodded in grim agreement.

"Rhiannon called him," I said.

"Why would she or anyone do that?" I was pleased that Dad sounded more pissed than wounded and weak.

"She's into some bad stuff, Dad." An idea was forming within my mind. Again, I caught Clint's gaze in the mirror. "Bres was definitely into dark powers and such. Alanna knew that. And ClanFintan told me about that awful evil god, and how the people at Guardian Castle had started worshipping him. Maybe Rhiannon opened herself up to that evil without really understanding the consequences. She might not have meant to, but whatever she's been doing has called Nuada here from the dead. You said she kept trying to get you to help her, right?"

"That's right." Clint nodded. "She went on and on about how together we could harness the power of the forest."

It made sense. "It's like the power from the trees is amplified if I channel it through you. I didn't understand that until we blundered into it, but Rhiannon has had considerably more experience with magic. She'd know about you the moment she met you—" I thought about his sapphire aura "—or even before. But when you wouldn't let her use you, she needed to find someone who would."

"Or *something,*" Clint added.

The Hummer bounced over a dip in the road and a grunt of pain escaped Dad's pursed lips. The grunt turned into the words "How could anyone believe they could control evil?"

"Rhiannon is used to being in charge of a world, and everything in it. There's nothing she doesn't believe she can control." As soon as I said it I knew it was true. I felt it like it was part of my own being, and I wondered—not for the first time—if I would have been as dark and twisted as Rhiannon if I had been raised differently. Was that capability within me? I didn't like to think so.

"Isn't the Broken Arrow hospital just down the street off Elm?"

Clint's question made me sit up and look around us, and a wave of dizziness butterflied through my body.

"Yeah," I said weakly. "It's between 91st and 101st Streets."

Clint made the turn and I caught him studying me in the mirror.

"Keep your eyes on the road, Colonel." I tried to sound perky. Instead, I slurred my words like I was drunk.

"How are you feeling, Mr. Parker?" Clint asked quickly.

"Better, son. Better." And I had to admit that he did sound more like his old self.

"Let go of his hand, Shannon," Clint ordered.

"What?" I'd heard the words, but I was having trouble understanding their meaning.

"Sir, you need to take her hand from yours. She's used all of the willow's stored power, and now she's sharing her own with you. It's not good for her, or for her baby."

That set off alarm bells in my mind, but I couldn't seem to make my hand respond. Thankfully, Dad wasn't likewise affected.

"Here, now, Bugsy old girl. Let go. I'll be just fine. Let's look after that granddaughter of mine." He pried his hand from mine and patted me roughly. I tried to smile at him, but my face wouldn't mind me.

"Shannon my girl? You still with us?" Clint's eyes kept sending worried glances back to me through the mirror.

I tried to say yes, there's nothing to worry about, I'm suddenly just really, really tired, but my voice wouldn't cooperate. I did manage something that sounded like *mumph.*

Dad touched my forehead with his good hand, cussing at the pain the movement caused in his other hand.

"What the hell's wrong with her?" he yelled at Clint. "She's cold as ice. She was fine just a minute ago."

"Here's the hospital," Clint said as he skidded the Hummer into the side road marked Emergency Room Entrance Only. He was out of the vehicle, opening the door for Dad, and pulling him toward the entrance ramp in what felt like seconds.

"Get Shannon help first!" I could hear Dad arguing weakly with Clint.

"The help she needs can't be found within walls."

The two of them disappeared with a swoosh of the electric doors. I let my head fall against the leather seat back. It felt good to just sit there. I took a deep breath and wondered why my chest felt so tight. Maybe I should just go to sleep. I probably needed to rest….

9

"Shannon! Damnit! Wake the hell up!"

The sound of Clint's panicked yelling brought my eyelids open. Then he was grabbing me out of the back of the Hummer and carrying me in his arms like I was an overgrown baby. He waded determinedly through the snow-covered parking lot behind the emergency room.

I wanted to tell him to put me down, that all of this carrying around of folks couldn't be good for his back, but my voice didn't seem to be obeying me. Instead I lay my head on his warm shoulder and closed my eyes.

"Shannon!" He shook me roughly. "Don't you pass out on me!"

I tried to glare at him. I really just friggin wanted to sleep. Wouldn't anyone let me get some damn rest?

Then I was plopped on top of an ice-crusted drift. Clint shoved my back hard against something very rough. One of his hands pressed my shoulder, holding me firmly against what I now realized was a tree. With his teeth he pulled the glove off his other hand and pressed his palm against the bark.

"Please help her!" he whispered urgently.

Epona's Beloved! The voice that popped into my head sounded young and excited. Instantly my back began to tingle, then warmth shot from the bark into my body.

"Huh!" I gasped aloud as the power flowed into me.

Forgive me, Beloved of the Goddess. I shall be more careful. The jolt of power slowed to a steady, bearable stream of warmth.

I closed my eyes, this time not because I was losing consciousness, but because I was savoring the return of feeling to my body. I told myself I didn't even mind the painful tingling in my hands and legs. Then my eyes opened and I barely had time to shout a warning to Clint and let him jump back out of the way before I was bending sideways and projectile vomiting my once-yummy breakfast all over the pristine snow. When I was done I wiped my mouth on my sleeve and scooted around the tree away from the steaming pile of puke. I looked up at Clint, who was leaning heavily against the side of the tree.

"At least this time I didn't quit breathing," I said softly, glad my voice was returning.

"I told you to stop before you drained yourself." He tried to sound pissed, but the hand that pushed a stray curl back from my face then traced the line of my cheek was gentle.

"It's hard for me to tell when enough is enough." I smiled

and pressed myself more firmly against the warm bark. "It sneaks up on me, and by the time I realize what's going on, well, um, I'm..."

"Almost dead?" he finished sardonically.

"No, almost unconscious."

He blew out through his nose in a gesture that was so like ClanFintan that I had to laugh.

"What's funny?"

"You." I started to push myself to my feet, slipped on the slick, snowy surface, and Clint's arms steadied me. I looked into his familiar face. "I was just thinking that you'd make a pretty damn good centaur."

His arms tightened around me and I allowed myself the luxury of resting my head against his chest.

"I don't like horses, Shannon my girl."

"Centaurs aren't horses," I countered.

"They're close enough."

"ClanFintan would be annoyed to hear you say that."

"Tell him to come here and take it up with me." I could hear the smile in his voice.

"He may just do that."

"Good. We know how to handle horses here in Oklahoma. I'll bet he'd make one heck of a barrel pony."

I laughed and pushed him away. "You're awful." I looked up at the tree against which we had been resting and realized it was a small Bradford pear. It couldn't have been more than five years old. Amazed, I pulled off both gloves and laid my palms, and then my forehead, against the grainy bark. "Thank you, little one, for your gift."

Oh! Beloved! You are most welcome! The small voice bounced around inside my head.

I winced, but I adored the exuberant, childlike intensity of the young tree. "May the Goddess bless you and make you grow tall and strong." I caressed the bark in parting. I swear I felt the tree quiver like a happy puppy beneath my hands.

"Let's go check on Dad." I looped arms with Clint, and we started back to the emergency room. "Hey, it's quit snowing."

"It stopped as soon as I trapped Nuada in the pond." He studied the sky before saying, "It won't last, though. Look at those clouds, they're filled with snow. Can't even see the sun."

I almost tripped over an especially high snowdrift.

"Careful, there." Clint righted me, and I saw him grimace at the pain in his back.

"Shouldn't you rest against the tree for a while yourself? Your back can't be doing very well, what with carrying me and my family all over Oklahoma."

"It doesn't work like that for me," he said, obviously uncomfortable with the topic. "I'll be fine when I'm surrounded by the forest again. Until then, this is about as good as it gets."

I was willing to bet it would get a lot worse if he didn't get back to his forest, but the closed look in his face kept me from questioning him further.

Fluorescent lights and warmth rushed out in welcome as we entered the sterility of the hospital. A clean, medicinal smell enveloped us. It brought back my college years, and reminded me of long nights when I had worked as a unit secretary for a large hospital just off campus near the University of Illinois. My nose wrinkled—that hospital smell just never changes.

"May I help you?" A plump nurse slid the glass window open and smiled efficiently at us.

"Yes, I'm Richard Parker's daughter."

"'Course," she said with a warm windowside manner and a long, sweet Okie drawl. "I'll check on him for ya. I believe the doc's with him right now."

"I'd like to see him, please."

"Let me just make sure he can have visitors." She glanced at Clint.

"Oh, this is my husband."

She nodded and gave Clint an appreciative look. "Have a seat in the waiting area, and I'll be back in just a minute."

We sat. I could feel Clint's dark eyes on me.

"Husband?"

"Don't start," I said. "I'd elbow you in the side, but I don't want to hurt your friggin back."

He chuckled.

"Mr. and Mrs., um..." The nurse struggled for a name.

"Freeman," Clint spoke up proudly, helping me to my feet and putting a possessive arm around my shoulders. "Mr. and Mrs. Freeman—that's us."

"Y'all may see your daddy now, but only for just a sec. The surgeon's been called in and it looks like she'll have to perform reconstructive surgery on that hand, so we'll need to get busy cleaning and prepping it." She chattered and we followed her back to the U-shaped emergency department. "But he'll be just fine. Doctor wants to keep him here a couple days after the surgery for observation, though. Hypothermia can be dangerous, and he does have a nasty bump on his head."

"Good thing his head is so thick," I whispered to Clint.

"Like father like daughter," he whispered back.

She motioned us into Room 4, where Dad was reclining half horizontally in a bed that his bulk made look small. Tubes were running from an IV that was attached to his left arm. His right hand was lying palm up on a raised stand with a little protruding arm, which sat next to his bed. The hand rested on a pile of blue cloth, and was still slowly seeping scarlet. I only glanced at it, and swallowed hard. It was split wide open and looked disquietingly like a gross baked potato. My eyes studied his face instead. He did have a horrible-looking welt on the left side of his forehead that had already begun to turn several brilliant shades of red and purple. I was shocked to see how pale he looked against the bleached pillows.

A male nurse was rummaging through some jars and drawers in a cabinet at the far side of the room. He nodded to us politely.

"How're ya doing, Dad?" I disengaged myself from Clint's arm and took Dad's uninjured hand, being careful not to mess with any of the tubes.

"Fine, fine." He sounded his usual gruff self. "These idiots keep trying to give me morphine, and I keep telling them that I act goofy on that stuff." He raised his voice, motioning toward the back of the male nurse. "Shoot, I played ball against Notre Dame in '60 with a broken arm. Beat the hell outta them. Just put some damn butterfly stitches in it and let me go home."

The nurse turned around and glared at Dad. He had an evil-looking syringe in one hand. The other was planted delicately on his hip. His voice was pleasingly soft, but his tone said he was tired of Dad's heroics. "See here, Mr. Thing,

I understand you're a handsome, muscular tough guy, but your playing-football-with-a-broken-arm days were FORTY-PLUS YEARS AGO." He made a very *In Living Color* snap with his free hand. Sounded like this argument had been going on for some time.

Dad opened his mouth and I jumped in, hopefully saving the scene from deteriorating into a tasteless brawl. "Dad, would you please take the shot? I don't think I can stand to see you in any more pain." I leaned close to him and whispered, "Don't make me call Mama Parker. You know what she'd say." We both knew I'd threatened to bring in the big guns, and he threw me a fearful look.

"No need to bother her." He squeezed my hand, and then growled to the nurse. "Go ahead, give me that damn shot. But just this once."

"Well, thank you, Your Majesty." He rolled his eyes, gave me an exasperated girlfriend look and thoroughly injected Dad.

I figured it was good for him. (Dad, not the nurse.)

The surgeon, Dr. Athena Mason, chose that moment to appear. She was a professional-looking, attractive, middle-aged woman whose voice and manner immediately instilled confidence. She seemed to be one of those rare doctors who actually treated her patients as if they had functioning brains as well as bodies. Plus, I thought her first name was cool.

Dr. Mason already had Dad's chart, and after exchanging pleasantries with Clint and me she took her stance next to the mangled hand. After a nod from Dad, she told me the situation.

"Your father's hand has severe nerve damage. With surgery, I can probably bring its function back to eighty percent. Without surgery, he will not be able to maintain a grip on objects, nor will he have feeling below his wrist. He and I have concurred that surgery is the best choice of treatment."

"Will he be okay?" I felt a little light-headed.

"Yes." She gave me a reassuring smile. "I'm ready to take him immediately into surgery. If you and your husband will wait outside, we will prep your father. I'll have you called back in before we take him up."

I gave Dad a quick kiss and allowed Clint to usher me from the room and back to the E.R. waiting area.

"I can't tell you how much I hate hospitals," I muttered to Clint after we had resettled ourselves into the almost comfortable chairs.

Clint leaned over and spoke into my ear. "You're telling a man who spent the better part of a year in a hospital ward? The smell alone makes my skin crawl."

"There's coffee and snacks around the corner in the break room," the healthy-looking nurse advised us through the half-open window.

We nodded our thanks like marionettes.

"Want something? I think I'd better get some coffee—seems like it might be a long day," Clint said as he pulled himself awkwardly to a standing position.

I watched his expression war with his pain. It was obvious he was trying to mask it, and it made me feel horrible that I was the reason behind that pain.

"Clint," I spoke with low intensity, trying to make him believe my words. "You don't have to stay. Go on back to the forest. Dad will be fine. When he's out of surgery I'll see he's settled and then I'll..." Here I faltered, wondering what the hell I was going to do next. "I'll, um, I'll borrow one of Dad's trucks and drive down to your place. Then you and I can plan what we'll do next from there."

"Don't patronize me." Clint's eyes had gone flat.

"I'm not patronizing you!" I shouted, then immediately lowered my voice at the curious look from the nurse. "I just hate being the cause of your pain."

"You are not the cause of it, Rhiannon is."

"You know what I mean," I said, exasperated.

"Yes, I know what you mean." He sat next to me, but his body was ramrod stiff—he wouldn't touch me. "What you mean is that I'm not involved enough with you or your family for you to allow me to stay here with you. I know you don't believe I love you like he does, but I thought that my actions have proven to you that I belong with you for as long as you are here and as long as you need me."

I didn't know what to say. If I acknowledged what he was saying wouldn't I simply be causing him more pain?

"Even ClanFintan told you that I belong at your side." He stood again, this time without letting me see the effort it cost him. "I'm getting some coffee. Can I bring you anything?" His eyes bored into mine, daring me to challenge him.

And I couldn't. I knew that what he said was true. He did belong with me. He was the only person besides my father who I could trust. And he was the only person who understood what we were up against.

"Some hot tea would be nice," I said inanely.

He grunted and turned away.

"Green tea, please, if they have it, and I don't take sugar," I said to his back.

He just nodded and kept walking, holding himself stiffly, like everything from his waist up hurt to bend.

I sat and brooded. Well, I didn't mean that I didn't think he deserved to be here. And I didn't mean that I didn't like him. Okay—*love* him. I just thought that maybe it would be best if he…

…He what? Waited in the middle of Bumfuck Nowhere, Oklahoma, until it was "nice and safe" to reappear? Mr. Hero Fighter Pilot? Oh, please. Error in judgment was an understatement.

"They didn't have any green tea." Clint roughly handed me a foam cup that had the end of a Lipton tea bag dangling off the side of it. He sat next to me and blew on his coffee. We didn't speak.

"Doctor says y'all can come back now." The nurse's twang echoed through the empty room.

"Thanks." I smiled at her, pleased that someone was still speaking to me.

A nurse in surgical scrubs was pushing Dad's movable litter into the hall. She paused.

"The doctor is waiting."

I nodded at her and kissed Dad on the forehead. He had about a bazillion tubes stuck into various places. His bad hand was tented and out of sight like a small dead body. The analogy grossed me out. I gave him my best perky smile.

"We'll be right here, Dad. Don't worry about anything."

"Hey, Bugsy. This morphine is making me silly as shit." His words were adorably slurred. "I think I was flirting with that girly nurse." Then my father actually giggled.

I laughed and gave him a kiss on the cheek. "Now I know why you didn't want any morphine."

"Damn straight," he said. His fragmented attention found Clint. "Take care of our girl, son."

"Yes, sir."

"Oh, and you don't have to worry about Mama Parker." Dad said. "I called her. Her brother-in-law's putting chains on their old Buick. She'll be here before these jailers let me go."

"She's gonna be mad at you," I laughed.

"I know." He grinned drunkenly.

"Time to go, Mr. Parker." The nurse continued pushing the gurney down the hall.

"I love you, Dad."

"I love you, too, ol' Bugsy."

The elevators that led to the surgery unit closed silently. Clint followed me as I walked dejectedly back to the waiting room. I glanced at the clock and was amazed to see it was well past noon.

The E.R. nurse was back at her station. "Doc said your daddy'd probably be in surgery a couple hours."

I nodded thanks to her.

"I think I'm hungry," I said to Clint, testing the waters

"It would probably do you good to eat." His voice was neutral. Not pissed and not unpissed.

"But I don't want any hospital food." I wrinkled my nose.

At this the nurse pricked her ears. "If y'all have something that can drive on that mess outside, the Arby's down the street is open." She giggled. "A whole shift got stuck there when the weather turned, and they're just cooking their little brains out." She shrugged her shoulders. "Nurses don't like hospital food, either."

"Arby's sounds good. Thanks," Clint said to her.

"Do you want us to bring you back anything?" I asked.

"Oh, no. We've already been." She slid the window shut, waved us out the door and returned to her very steamy-looking romance novel. (Wonder if she'd let me borrow it if Clint kept refusing to talk to me.)

The afternoon was cold and slate colored, but it still hadn't started snowing again. I took Clint's hand as we stepped out into winter. The Hummer was parked in one of the Emergency Room Patient Parking Only slots. Its engine turned over and growled like a sports car.

"The Arby's is on the corner of the next intersection just south of here." I pointed and Clint nodded, carefully pulling out onto the nearly deserted street that ran in front of the hospital.

The silence grew.

"I'm hungry," I said.

"You already said that."

"Oh."

The big Arby's hat sign came into view. "There it is."

"My vision is just fine," Clint said sarcastically as he pulled into the parking lot.

I waited for him to turn the engine off. Then I confronted him. "Look, you don't have to be such an ass." His lips narrowed but he didn't say anything, so I continued, "I never said I didn't want you here. I never said I didn't think you had a right to be here. I'm just worried about your damn back, and I don't want anything to happen to you." I paused and looked away from him. "I almost lost one man I love today. I don't want to take the chance of losing another."

I felt the heat of his hand as he brushed a curl back from

the side of my face. I tilted my head in his direction and he laid his palm against my cheek.

"You won't lose me, Shannon my girl." His deep voice made me feel warm and liquid inside.

I turned my body toward him and his arm went around me while my head rested on his shoulder. He kissed the top of my head.

"Will you feed me now?"

Clint squeezed my shoulders and kissed me again before letting me go. "Come on. I'll feed both of you."

"There's nothing quite like a Giant Arby's sandwich with extra horsey sauce, large curly fries and a Diet Pepsi." (It's a well-established fact that a Diet Pepsi cancels out a large curly fries.)

Back in the E.R. waiting room I smacked my lips contentedly and sucked on the straw, trying to get the last little speck of liquid. "Now that I don't feel sick all the time, food is tasting yummy."

Clint watched me with fond amusement. "Woman, you can eat!" He purposefully played out his Okie twang.

I patted my tummy. "Yes, we can."

"Feel better now?"

"Amazingly." I grinned at him.

"Ready to talk about our plan?"

"We have a plan?" I asked, surprised.

"If we don't, we should."

"Well, I know what I *don't* want to do," I said, suddenly serious.

"That's as good a place to start as any. Let's take out what we won't do and build from there." He sounded very Military Man In Charge. Thank Goddess one of us knew what we were doing. I think.

I lowered my voice. "I'm not going back out to Dad's place." I shivered. "I couldn't stand to be around that pond."

"I agree. It wouldn't be safe, even with the trees to aid you. They're powerful, yes, but there's a difference between their power and that of the grove—and you're going to need true power from the ancients in the heart of the forest to kill Nuada."

"If he can be killed. I mean, shit, he's already supposed to be dead."

"Then he needs to be sent back to the darkness where he belongs."

He spoke with a confidence I wish I felt. And I couldn't help but wonder where the dark god Pryderi fit into all of this. Fighting a resurrected Nuada was horrible enough. Fighting an ancient god would be…

"It hasn't started snowing again, yet." Thankfully, he interrupted my morbid thoughts. "But the way it looks, it could begin again at any time. Which probably means Nuada will not be trapped for very long."

"We need to find friggin Rhiannon," I said, not for the first time, "and make her tell us what the hell's going on."

"You mean what the hell she's done," Clint corrected.

I nodded grimly. "Didn't she leave you with any phone numbers or any way to reach her?"

"She tried." His jaw was set as he remembered. "I wouldn't take them. I didn't want anything to do with her. It was like every place she touched in my life she left a dirty stain. I needed to be clean of her."

"That's it!" I yelped. "Why didn't I think of it before?" Clint was looking at me with his forehead wrinkled in confusion, but as I continued to explain, his expression cleared and changed to an understanding grin. "We don't need a friggin phone to call Rhiannon the Great! She's bound to me. Remember you said she and I have the same auras? Knowing that, you could probably call her by yourself, or at least with the help of the ancient grove, but imagine what kind of message the two of us plus the grove could send together."

"It'd definitely be something she couldn't ignore." His grin mirrored mine.

"And if she does manage to ignore our first *invitation*, well, we'll just keep *inviting* and *inviting* and *inviting*."

Clint whistled low. "She'll be madder than a wet cat."

"Don't insult cats—I like them. I was thinking more like a pissed-off cobra."

"She'll see it as a challenge."

"Good—that's what it is." The confidence was back in my voice. I may not know how to vanquish Nuada or a dark god, but Rhiannon was something I knew I could handle. She was me—a selfish, bitchy, hateful version of me. And I'd been successfully vanquishing that side of me all my life. I thought about what my ex-husband would say about that and cringed. Well, I'd been vanquishing that side of me *most* of the time.

I looked up at the clock. More time had ticked away—it was now past 5:00 p.m. Peeking outside, I could see the slate-colored sky had turned a deeper coal. Night again. The thought of the long drive back to the forest made me sigh in weariness.

"Not tonight." Clint read my thoughts. "We'll wait till morning. Make sure your dad's settled in and your stepmom's on her way here. And we'll travel during the day."

"Mr. and Mrs. Freeman." The sound of Dr. Mason's voice made me jump, and my heart beat wildly, but the satisfied look on her face as she approached us allowed me to relax. "Your father came through the surgery just fine. There was more damage than I had originally thought, which is why the surgery lasted longer than I expected."

"But he'll be able to use his hand?"

"It'll take several months of rehab, but yes, he should be able to return to training his racehorses and baling his hay."

Dad must have been doing some talking. "May I see him?"

"We have him pretty drugged up, and he's exhausted from the hypothermia, so he's sleeping right now." The doctor dug through one of her pockets and handed me a slip of paper. "Your father made me promise to give this number to you. He said you were to call his neighbor so that his animals could get fed. And he wanted me to tell you that he didn't want you or your husband to go out to his place. He seemed very concerned about you having some kind of accident if you drove back there."

I took the paper. "Thank you, Doctor. Would you please have the nurses reassure Dad that Clint and I are not going out to his place? We'll stay in town. I'll call, and leave the number of the hotel with the nurses' station."

"Excellent. He should be up and around in the morning." She gave us a polite dismissive nod. "And drive carefully."

"Thank you, Doctor," Clint said and took the number from me. "There's a phone in the snack room. I'll call the neighbor..."

"He probably means Max Smith," I supplied the name.

"...Smith, and tell him what's happened." We shared a look. "I'll tell him an edited version of what's happened."

"I'll be here when you get back." He nodded and I allowed myself a lingering glance at the strong line of his retreating body. Broad shoulders—tapered waist—tight ass—long, strong legs.

He glanced over his shoulder and caught me looking. "Did you want something, Shannon my girl?" he asked with a smile playing in his voice.

"Nope, uh, I was just, uh, thinking," I stammered, blushed and turned away. His laugh trailed down the hall.

"He is one damn fine-lookin' man," the nurse said with a sigh.

"Yeah," I muttered, returning to sucking on my straw. And, no, I wasn't going to think about sucking on anything else. Really. I mean it. Really.

At least that's what I kept telling myself.

Clint was back almost before I could quit grumbling. He charmed the nurse into giving him the direct line to the Surgical Intensive Care Unit, pulled me out of the chair by my elbow, and before I had time to get cold, he had me stuffed into the passenger's side of the Hummer and we were rolling.

"Which way to the nearest hotel?" he asked as he adjusted the vehicle's heater.

"I don't suppose you know anything about what happened to my condo?" If Rhiannon hadn't sold it, or let it get repossessed, or whatever, we could stay there. I always kept a key hidden outside, so getting in shouldn't be a problem. My wistful thoughts said it would be easiest to stay the night in my own place.

"Uh, that was one of the first things she had her oilman take care of." He gave me an apologetic look. "If I remember correctly, he sold it very quickly."

"That bitch," I breathed. But it figured. Why would she stay in my cute but modest condo when she had world domination and random acts of evil to commit whilst a millionaire lapped from her hand? "Go north down Elm. Right before you come to the highway, there should be a couple of hotels."

Clint nodded and the Hummer slid out onto the frozen street. I stayed quiet and let him concentrate on the short drive. Again, the streets were deserted. It was almost dark, and the streetlights cast weird, ghostly halos of color around them.

"Nuclear winter," I whispered.

"What?"

"It reminds me of a scene from *The Day After,* that miniseries about the aftermath of nuclear war that was on TV in the eighties."

"I remember it. Damn grim movie." He reached over and patted my knee. "Are you okay?"

I shook myself. "I guess I'm just tired."

"Need another Arby's?" He smiled at me.

"Maybe later." I smiled back, trying to ignore the somber mood that had suddenly settled over me. "Now I think I just need some sleep."

"*That* I can help you with." He motioned to the buildings ahead. "Looks like there's a Canterbury Inn and a Luxury Inn. Which is your favorite?"

I studied the two hotels that sat next to each other. "Looks like it'll have to be the Luxury Inn." The Canterbury had a red neon sign that read No Vacancies.

"Luxury it is." Clint downshifted and the Hummer crawled up the incline to the front of the small hotel. "Damn, looks like this parking lot is packed. Wait here—I'll go see what's available."

He returned much too quickly. "All full. Where else?"

"If I remember correctly, they were just opening a new Best Western a mile east of here. Let's try there." Actually, I remembered the Best Western because it had been built behind a lovely little liquor store, BA Wine and Spirits. I drove past it frequently as it was being constructed. I sighed nostalgically, remembering the fun of browsing their well-stocked wine racks for a new, tempting red, especially on Ten Percent Off Tuesdays.

"Why the sigh?"

"I was just thinking about a very cool liquor store not far from the Best Western, and remembering my hunt for the perfect bottle of red wine."

He laughed. "Shannon my girl, I don't think your daughter can appreciate red wine." He paused. "Yet."

"Definitely not—and I won't appreciate it for another—" I counted quickly "—seven months or so."

"A spring baby?"

That did make me smile, and I felt my dark mood lift. My hand rested lightly on my stomach. "A spring baby."

The Kenosha Street Best Western had that sparkling look of a newly built hotel, especially as it was illuminated by a row of blazing lights. It sat behind the Reasor's Grocery Plaza (which included "my" liquor store, as well as a Quick Trip, a Blockbuster Video and various other typical little yuppie shops). It was ringed by the dark shapes of snow-packed trees and had a frontage of what I remember as azalea bushes, but now they looked like another blob of light shadow covered in a white canvas of snow. The parking lot looked too full.

"I really don't want to drive all the way to Tulsa to find a hotel." I grumped.

"Let me check it out."

I watched Clint slip and slide to the entrance and disappear within the shiny doors. This time it took longer, and when he returned he was smiling and flashing a room card key.

"They had one left!"

He parked quickly and helped me navigate the slippery parking lot. Our room was on the third floor. The card slid neatly in the groove and the door light blinked green. The room had that new smell that was a mixture of clean carpet and fresh wood. It was decorated semitastefully in a blue, beige and gold paisley/floral wallpaper print. The bed was covered with a thick spread that looked soft and inviting.

It had a single king-size bed.

I realized we were both still standing awkwardly in the entryway just inside the door, so I strode briskly to the window that was heavily veiled by the typical plastic-backed hotel drapes. Drawing them aside, I checked out the view.

Our room faced the rear of the hotel, and all I could see was the backside of the ring of snow-covered trees. Beyond that I knew there was a highway, but it was impossible to see that far with no headlights illuminating the darkness.

I felt a familiar prod within me that signaled an idea that had its roots in Epona. And, sure enough, a thought popped unbidden into my head, which made me temporarily forget about the single big bed and our sleeping arrangements.

"Hey, why don't we start calling her now?" I turned to find Clint near my shoulder.

"Rhiannon?"

"Of course. Look, this place is ringed with trees." I motioned to the scene outside the window. "They're not old, but look how they're positioned. It's kind of like the willows that frame Dad's pond. I drew power from all of them because they were so close together. I may be able to do that here, too." I thought about how Clint's presence seemed to amplify my ability to draw from the trees. "Especially if you help me."

"I think you're too tired to do that. You've depleted yourself today."

He had a point, but I didn't want to dwell on it. I knew from experience that sometimes Epona placed me in situations that were difficult, even dangerous, but my Goddess always had her reasons. And I trusted her.

"I'll be careful. We're not doing what we did before. I won't be draining myself. We'll just be casting out a lure. Let's see if she bites." I smiled confidently at him.

"I don't like it, Shannon." He sounded worried.

"I could do it without you." His jaw started to tighten in what I was beginning to recognize as a prelude to his being pissed. "But I don't want to do it without you." I took his hand. "Please help me."

"All right," he said grudgingly. "But let's make it quick. If we don't find her right away promise me that we'll stop and wait until we get back to the grove to try again."

"I promise." I squeezed his hand and started pulling him to the door. But I knew keeping that promise wouldn't be difficult. Epona was behind this idea, and with the Goddess backing us, success wouldn't be something we'd have to wait around for.

We made our way quietly out the back of the building. The snow here stretched before us untouched. Its surface glistened with an almost magical glow. The wind had died, so silence lay heavy on the night. It wasn't snowing, but the air felt ponderous and it smelled of impending snow.

Clint motioned silently to the tallest of the trees, which was off to the right of us, directly in the middle of the line of snowy shadows. We plowed slowly through the drifts, trying to be as quiet as possible, even though the windows to the rooms that faced us were drawn and dark, with only an occasional blue TV light glinting from between the drapes. When we got to the tree line I was surprised that they seemed so much larger up close.

"They're bigger than they looked from our room," I whispered to Clint.

"Bradford pears again," he observed.

"Good. I liked that little Bradford pear outside the hospital."

"Okay then." He pulled off his gloves and I followed suit.

"Let's do this like we did in the grove." He placed the palms of his hands against the gritty bark and motioned for me to mirror his actions on the opposite side of the tree. "Concentrate on Rhiannon and her aura." He bowed his head and I could see the sapphire of his beautiful aura begin to glow softly.

"Hey," I whispered. "I don't know what the hell my/her aura looks like."

His head came up and I heard the smile in his voice. "It's silver, like someone melted a full moon into a pot of liquid mercury. And the outline is tinged the deep purple of ripe plums."

"That was very poetic, Clint," I quipped, trying to cover how breathless his description had left me.

"Just describing what I see, Shannon my girl," he replied softly, which did nothing to still the fluttering of my heart.

"Just concentrate, Mr. Fighter Pilot," I muttered, and closed my eyes.

"Yes, ma'am." His laugh floated around the silent trees.

I placed my palms against the young tree. Almost immediately the bark beneath my hands quivered and I felt a surge of warmth.

Epona's Beloved!

"Hello, young one." My lips lifted in a smile, but I kept my eyes closed. "I need to ask for your help."

I am here to aid you, Beloved of the Goddess!

I cringed at the intensity of the tree's reply.

Is this more pleasing, Goddess?

I sighed in relief as the volume of the young one's reply was turned down a notch. "Yes, much better, thank you."

The tree trembled beneath my hands like an exuberant child. "And I'll need the help of your sisters surrounding you."

We are here, Beloved.

Their reply was like the echo of a secret.

Okay. Here we go.

First I pictured Clint and his magnificent jewel-blue aura with its rich outline of gold. I thought of the strength I had felt within that aura, the strength I knew was within him. I thought of his goodness and his loyalty. Against my closed lids I could see the pulsing of his aura, and how it wavered toward me, waiting for me to tap into it and use it, which I suddenly understood how to do. I drew in a deep breath, and with that breath I accepted him, pulling his strength within me. Clint's aura filled me until my skin pulsed and tingled. I wanted to open my eyes and shout with joy. Instead, I shifted my focus from within myself to the small tree. I could clearly feel the green, vibrant power inside the Bradford pear. My focus traveled up her trunk and out to the very top branches, where I gathered myself.

"Help me, sisters..." My voice sounded eerie. It didn't come from my lips, but it rang hauntingly from the uppermost limbs of the tree. At once the green strength of the tree was amplified tenfold as I tapped into the essence of the young grove.

Collecting my focus, I thought about Clint's description of my aura and visualized it glistening sliver. The silver of a full moon... The silver of an ethereal mare... Gathering Clint's strength, I mixed it with the green warmth of trees, and hurled a thick line out into the night, searching for its mirror image.

Keeping my eyes tightly closed, I followed that probe. It

shot straight up and headed north into the blackness of the cold night. This journey was different than the Magic Sleep. I could feel where the probe was heading, but it wasn't like I was a part of it. It was more like I was looking through an incredibly long telescope. My vision was limited, but I could sense direction and see the cloudy, starless night flashing past.

Suddenly the almost painfully bright lights of a city skyline illuminated the night sky, and the probe of power arched straight though the glassy skin of an impossibly tall skyscraper. The line of power melted through the ceiling of an opulent room, lit only by dozens of golden candelabra. I pulled more power from the trees and felt my breath catch as the probe turned toward a female figure who reclined gracefully on a richly upholstered divan. Next to her sat a hawkish-looking, gray-haired man who was vaguely familiar. But my attention didn't stay with him. It was the woman to whom I was drawn. Her back was to my probe. Her golden-red hair curled past her shoulders with a familiar wildness. The probe crept closer and the woman's aura began to glow pearlized silver, framed by a ring of plumlike purple.

Rhiannon's breath hissed from between bared teeth as she stood, and in a fluid motion whirled around so that she faced the probe. She was wearing a silk dress, the color of the golden candelabra. It wrapped seductively around her body, leaving very little to the imagination.

Holy shit, it was me. For a moment my concentration faltered and I felt my hold on the probe waver.

Get it together, Shannon! I pulled more energy from the trees and held on, forcing myself to ignore how disquieting it was to look at this version of myself.

The man at her side started to speak, but she spat a single word at him, "Silence!" All of her attention was focused on the shaft of power, which pulsed for her eyes only.

"Is that you, usurper? What is the meaning of this intrusion?"

My voice—she has my voice. Again my concentration faltered.

And she laughed. "Too difficult for you? Yes, it must be disturbing to see what can be done with knowledge and power, and not have the ability to do it yourself." Her arms spread wide to take in the richness of the room; her voice was taunting. She sounded like me when I was at my most sarcastic.

And that single thought broke the spell.

It was just me—just an indulged, selfish, immoral version of myself.

I smiled and felt power flow through me. I knew exactly what to say to her.

"Actually, I just thought it would be polite to thank you for the gift you left me." My voice floated around her like I was a tangible presence in the room. I saw the man blink in amazement. Rhiannon's green eyes narrowed.

"I left you nothing of any use in either world, you fool."

"Really?" I sounded amazed. "I have found many uses—" I purred the word "—for Clint. Almost as many as he has found for me."

"You lie!" she shrieked.

(Note to self: don't shriek when you get mad. It's really not attractive.)

"Come see for yourself. Obviously he chose me over you…" I reached out and yanked the probe back, but left the ghost of my sarcastic laughter to linger like smoke.

...And suddenly I was back in Broken Arrow, realizing how cold my feet were. I looked around the tree and caught Clint's questioning look.

"Bingo!" I said. Then I patted the skin of the tree. "Thank you, little one." I reached into the trunk and through the branches, projecting my voice like the young pear was a microphone. "And thank you, sisters."

We will always serve the Goddess! they chimed back.

I pulled on my gloves and grabbed Clint's hand. "Let's get back inside before someone sees us and calls the loony bin. I can hear it now—yes, Officer, they were talking to the trees! It's not like this is Seattle. Okies don't talk to trees, they shoot deer from them. Here they'd put us away forever."

Clint chuckled and led me back to the room, holding his questions till then.

"What did you say that made her so angry?" he asked after he secured the bolt on the door.

"Do you mind if we talk after I take a shower? I can't believe how cold I suddenly am." I was shivering. It felt like my lips were blue.

Clint's questioning immediately changed to nursemaiding.

"I told you not to overextend yourself." He pushed me toward the small bathroom. "I'll call and get some extra blankets."

I just nodded and shut the door, glad he was keeping himself busy. Studying my reflection in the glass above the sink I was shocked at how horrible I looked, especially when I compared what I was seeing now to what Rhiannon had looked like just minutes before. Where she had been healthy and tanned I was red-eyed and sallow. And, I was surprised to note, my cheekbones stood out prominently. I'd obviously lost weight.

"Good Lord, don't tell me you look *thin,*" I accused my reflection. Not that I was fat before, but I have never been considered thin. Think Sophia Loren, Anne-Margret, Raquel Welch. Okay, if you're young think J.Lo or Catherine Zeta-Jones (only more breasts and less butt).

I pulled off my clothes and continued studying myself. Sure enough, except for a cute little pooch of a tummy, I looked thin. My ribs were sticking out! I've never considered thin women particularly attractive. I mean, really. How can you look like a woman if you're shaped like a little boy? It was tragic, and I had a sudden desire to wolf down a box of HoHos. Conversely, my breasts, which had always been full and well shaped, were definitely fuller and shapeller. And I did like the little pooch of a tummy. I patted it wonderingly.

"What are you thinking in there, little girl?" I whispered.

Clint's loud knock scared me so badly I almost peed on myself.

"Shannon? You okay? I don't hear any water running."

"That's because I haven't started the shower yet." I tried to keep my voice sweet, remembering how shrewish Rhiannon had sounded when she yelled, but I'm pretty sure the sentence ended in a snarl. Clint didn't seem to notice.

"I got those extra blankets and I scared up some hot tea and a few necessities in the lobby. Also talked them out of a couple of nice terry-cloth robes. Here ya go." My eyes widened in horror as the knob on the bathroom door started turning. I yanked a towel off the rack and held it in front of me as Clint's head popped into the room.

"Jeesh! You could knock."

"Oh, uh, sorry." He blinked in surprise at the state of my undress. I swear, guys really are morons. "Here—" He thrust a thick white robe and a brown paper bag into my hands. Then he slammed the door like I was a demon from hell.

Shit, did I look that bad?

Apparently so.

I turned the water on and let it get nice and hot while I rooted through the bag. Toothpaste, two toothbrushes, some cheap disposable razors, a comb and a brush and a jar of multivitamins. I smiled at the jar before opening it and taking one.

I probably spent too much time standing in the hot stream of water, but my body felt chilled, like it needed to reabsorb warmth. I used the hotel soap, shampoo and conditioner, luxuriating in the wet heat. The thick white towels felt almost as good as the terry-cloth robe. I left my wet hair wrapped up turban style, grabbed the brush and walked out of the bathroom in a gush of steamy air.

Clint was watching the Weather Channel, and he jumped when I reappeared.

"Hope there's some hot water left for you," I said pleasantly, ignoring how skittish he was acting.

"Urmph," he said, and retreated into the bathroom.

I rolled my eyes and shook my head at the closed door. Men.

Propping the pillows up behind me, I burrowed under the extra blankets. They were those ultrasoft blankets that made me want to rub my face against them. I sighed in relief. It felt wonderful to be warm.

The channel changer was lying within the indention Clint's body had left next to me in the bed. Might as well channel surf while I was still in this world, and the Weather Channel certainly wasn't my idea of stimulating entertainment (nor, by the way, was MTV or any sports channel—unless they were showing figure skating).

The last fifteen minutes of a *Will and Grace* rerun made me laugh, and then I was thrilled to find that on TBS one of my favorite John Wayne movies, *The Angel and the Badman*, had just started. I snuggled down to enjoy.

The Duke was getting into some serious wooing of his little Quaker farm girl, when Clint finished in the bathroom. I glanced up at him. The robe made his shoulders look even broader. His dark hair was towel dried and adorably tousled. He wasn't looking at me, though. His attention was on the TV (typical guy).

"Old John Wayne movie?" he asked.

"Yep."

He squinted. "Don't think I've seen this one."

"You're kidding! It's one of my favorites." I patted the spot next to me. "It just started, I'll fill you in." Then I hesitated. "You *do* like John Wayne, don't you?"

"I'm getting by your tone that there's only one answer to that question."

"Only one correct answer."

"Shannon my girl, John Wayne is an American icon," he said, placing his hand reverently over his heart, like he was going to recite the Pledge of Allegiance.

"Correct answer, Colonel Freeman. Have a seat."

I quickly explained the plot to him, glad that he had quit acting like I was Medusa (or, for that matter, Medea). And

I am always relaxed and agreeable when watching My Hero, unless it's one of the few movies in which he dies. Then I'm weepy and tend to drink too much. Good thing *The Cowboys* wasn't on—that one makes me cry so hard I snot on myself. No telling what watching it sober and pregnant would do to me.

Unfortunately, my eyelids didn't seem to understand they needed to cooperate and stay open. I vaguely remember them fluttering as the Duke helped his Quaker friends raise the barn, then Clint's deep voice said, "Just sleep, Shannon. I'll buy you the video and you can watch it later." My lips curled up and I wanted to laugh and remind him that there are no DVDs in Partholon, but I gave up the fight against sleep and drifted down into the warmth of unconsciousness.

Hugh Jackman and I were sprawled in the back of a buggy (much like the one John Wayne and his ladylove had driven off in during the closing scene of The Angel and the Badman*). We lay on a delightfully fragrant bed of lavender. My head was in Wolverine's lap, and he was gently (but firmly) combing through my red tangles with his metallic-claw thingies while he explained to me that he never found women even vaguely interesting unless they were over thirty-five. I peeked through the buggy slats and saw that a human-headed donkey was drawing the carriage. I whistled and the ass turned to look back at the sound, which is when I realized it was my ex-husband's head. I was still laughing when I opened my eyes and found my spirit body hovering above the Best Western.*

"Sometimes I crack myself up," I guffawed, glancing around

at the expanse of sleeping whiteness below me. I was glad I didn't feel the actual cold of the night except as a faint echo against the outline of where my body should be. The instant I began to move determinedly forward, the sky opened and kept the promise it had been threatening all day. Thick flakes drifted lazily to the already snow-laden world below.

Unfortunately, I thought I knew in what direction we were heading.

"Oh, Goddess, no! Please don't take me back there." I could feel my spirit quaking. I knew Epona would protect me, but I dreaded facing that creature's evil twice in one day.

Patience, Beloved. *She whispered comfort within my mind.*

"But I know he's free, it's snowing again. Do I have to actually see him?"

You need not see Nuada, My Chosen One, but you shall witness what has freed him.

Now, that *intrigued me. I felt a new determination as my spirit moved forward, picking up impossible speed as if I was being hurled from a slingshot. Soon a familiar skyline glittered like a fairy kingdom against the night. Chicago—here, too, it was snowing. Instead of stopping at the skyscraper I recognized from my earlier trip, my spirit changed course and floated silently past the section of downtown known worldwide as the Magnificent Mile. It looked like I was going to end up over Lake Michigan—I could see the lights of Navy Pier glittering off the water, then I abruptly turned right. Soon modern marvels gave way to soft lights and trees.*

"Grant Park." I smiled, remembering a wonderful trip I had made to Chicago one spring with a group of college friends. Chicago can be especially beautiful in late spring, provided the wind isn't blowing at its usual gale force, whipping freezing air

off Lake Michigan. That particular trip to the City of Big Shoulders had the mild, sweet weather of an exceptionally lovely spring, and my group had spent hours exploring the city, mostly by foot (because we were attempting to walk off the copious amount of food and alcohol we kept ingesting).

I had never seen Grant Park at night, and as I descended slowly through the skeletal canopy of winter trees, I was amazed at how untamed it looked. It didn't seem possible that the heart of Chicago was only moments away. The park was dark and silent. Unnaturally silent.

"Come!" The word split the stillness like the crack of a whip, startling me with its unexpected command.

I recognized the voice immediately and mentally squared my shoulders. I was hovering about twenty feet above the ground. My body had quit moving, but at the sound of the voice I started forward again, drifting toward the flickering of a lone light. I broke through a stand of stately oaks, in the middle of which was a small clearing. Within the clearing was an old-fashioned campfire, wherein a tongue of flame flickered.

A circle had been drawn around the fire with something that had melted the snow.

Salt, I thought with surety, and then wondered how I had known.

Listen within, Chosen.

The fire wasn't large, and there was something odd about it. At first I couldn't figure it out. Then I realized the flame was flickering wildly, as if a brisk wind was blowing. But there was no wind. The snow was falling in a straight line from the sky.

She stepped out of the shadows and entered the circle. Rhiannon wore a full-length fox-fur coat. In the firelight the red-gold sheen of the fur mirrored her hair, which seemed to crackle and glow with a life of its own. Suddenly Rhiannon lifted her arms and flung off the coat.

She was butt-assed naked. Shit, she didn't even have on any shoes.

I gasped in surprise, but quickly stifled the sound. Intuitively I knew Epona did not want my presence betrayed this time. But I needn't have worried—it was obvious that Rhiannon's attention was elsewhere. She was oblivious to me.

Slowly, she started to dance, always being careful to stay within the circle. Her body undulated seductively, and I recognized the sensuous style of dance I had seen before when the Muse, Terpsichore, had performed at my marriage ceremony to ClanFintan. Well, Rhiannon was most definitely performing a mating dance, designed to produce a very specific reaction in those watching. But no one was there. Except for me, Rhiannon was alone.

Her tempo increased and her hands roamed suggestively down her body.

"Come!" she repeated the command.

I metaphorically crossed my arms and tapped my foot in irritation, thoroughly pissed that I didn't know how to dance like that. I'd always known my college education had been lacking something—at least now I knew what the hell it was.

Then a second figure entered the circle and I grimaced in disgust. It was Bres. He, too, was naked, and quite obviously found Rhiannon's dance more than a little appealing. His thick penis jutted away from his emaciated body in a tremendous erection. I remembered the smell of his nasty breath and shuddered, wishing I wasn't witnessing this bizarre little mating ritual.

At his appearance the trees that ringed the small clearing rustled, like their limbs momentarily shivered. Oaks surrounded us, and their size told me that they must have been old—certainly older than the little Bradford pears that had been so helpful to me earlier. Yet, except for that brief, uncomfortable movement of their branches, the clearing remained silent. Rhiannon was obviously performing some kind of magic, but she was doing it without the trees. They were not speaking to her.

Rhiannon undulated her way to where Bres was standing. He held something in his hand and I saw the firelight glint wickedly off the blade of a dagger.

What the hell?

Rhiannon took the knife and dropped fluidly to her knees in front of Bres. She grasped his hard shaft, and in one swift motion she drew the blade of the knife down the length of his penis, neatly slicing the taut, blood-filled flesh.

I flinched in horror, but Bres didn't move except to quiver in anticipation and moan low in his throat. His eyes were pressed firmly closed.

A crimson line had sprouted where the thin blade had cut, and blood was dripping steadily onto the white of the snow-covered ground. There seemed to be a stirring in the shadows at the edge of the circle, and my attention was pulled there. All around the outside of the melted snow, darkness within darkness moved. It reminded me of the scene from the movie, Ghost *(with Demi Moore and Patrick I'm-So-Yummy Swayze), when demons grabbed an evil soul and pulled it to hell. I had a feeling the analogy was appropriate.*

"Come!" This time her command was a sexual purr. "Using the knowledge of ancient darkness, I awakened you. I called you forth from death. Now with this Servant of Pryderi's pain and pleasure, his blood and seed, I command you, Nuada. I order you to the place of power!"

My stomach lurched in nausea as Rhiannon lowered her mouth to the scarlet penis and began sucking rhythmically.

Enough of this perversion. *The Goddess's voice speared my mind and I was lifted swiftly from that tainted glade.*

I sat straight up in bed. The TV was muted, and the blue shapes of the Weather Channel cast odd shadows over the mound that lay next to me.

"Rhiannon's calling Nuada to her." I threw the blankets back and stomped into the bathroom, filling a glass with cold water. "And she's definitely using dark powers to do it."

"What's going on, Shannon?" Clint ran a hand through his bed-head, blinking sleep from his eyes.

"I watched it." I didn't hide the disgust in my voice. "She's calling him. Somehow through Bres she's using Pryderi's power. She friggin brought Nuada here." I paced in front of the bed. "No wonder he's obsessed with me. He thinks *I'm* the one who wants him. *Yeesh.* There is one thing we can be pretty damn sure of, after the spell, or whatever, I watched her cast tonight. He won't be hanging around here messing with Dad." I drank the rest of the water, liking the way its coldness cleared my mouth. It was almost as if I could taste…

"Oh, God, I'm going to be—" At least this time I made it to the toilet in time.

Clint handed me a damp washcloth and I heard him refilling the glass with water. He flushed the toilet and helped me stand up.

"Here, rinse your mouth out with this." I did as he told me to do. "After you brush your teeth you can use this."

He unwrapped the plastic seal around the top of the complementary minisize mouthwash and opened it for me.

"Thanks," I said after I'd spit.

I felt tense and preoccupied as he steered me back to the bed and covered me gently with the soft blankets. Then he sat on my side of the bed, facing me. But instead of sitting up close to me, he scooted down to the foot of the bed.

"Here, give me your feet."

"What?"

"Your feet," he repeated. When I sat there and stared stupidly at him, he sighed and pulled the blankets aside to expose my bare feet. Matter-of-factly he took one of them and began rubbing my instep with sure, firm strokes.

I blinked in confusion at him (as my body melted from the feet up).

"It'll make you relax," he said simply.

I started to ask how the hell he knew that, but he beat me to a question.

"Could you tell where she was?"

Oh, yeah. Back to Rhiannon the Pervert.

"Chicago—she was in Grant Park. Bres was with her." I made a face like I'd just licked a lemon. "You would not friggin believe what she did."

"Yes, I would." His voice was flat, and I wondered just exactly what all he had experienced with Rhiannon. And I decided that I most definitely didn't want to know—ever.

A sudden thought struck me. "At first it sounded like she was calling Nuada to her there, but at the end she said she was calling him to—" I struggled to remember her exact words "—to the place of power, I think that's what she said."

"The grove." Clint sounded sure. "She thinks that's

where we are. She knows I don't like to leave the forest, and you made it clear that you and I are together."

I nodded in agreement, trying to ignore the double meaning of his words, which was damn hard to do while he was rubbing my feet and looking at me with those amazing eyes. So I pulled my feet out of his intimate grasp, and forced my gaze from his.

"Thanks, I'm all relaxed now." I forced a yawn. "We better go back to sleep, we have a long, snowy trip tomorrow." I curled up on my side and closed my eyes.

He didn't move or say anything at first. Then I could feel him stand. He retucked the blanket securely around my feet and turned off the TV. In the darkness the bed sagged under his weight.

"Good night, Shannon my girl."

"Good night," I whispered.

The eight o'clock wake-up call could have been more annoying, but I'm not sure how. I looked blearily around, pushing my hair back from my face. I hadn't brushed it out the night before, and it was in full revolt. Already dressed, Clint walked briskly from the bathroom and handed me a steaming cup of tea.

"Thanks," I mumbled, trying not to breathe my horrible morning breath on him. I sipped the tea and studied him as he clicked on the TV. The Weather Channel said it was snowing again. Big surprise.

Clint lowered himself stiffly into the only chair in the room.

"Have you been up long?" I thought small talk would be good.

"A while." Which in Okie talk could mean anywhere from four hours to four weeks.

I wanted to ask how his back was, but this morning his face looked set and closed off. He had definitely retreated into his cave. I felt a little pang, missing that closeness we had been sharing.

No—I scolded myself—his withdrawal is a good thing. I'll be leaving soon, and Clint needs to quit thinking he's in love with me. (And I with him, my errant mind whispered.)

"I'll be ready in just a second," I chirped, trying to sound perky and businesslike as I climbed out of bed and raced to the bathroom.

"Feel up to breakfast?" Clint asked. We were driving silently to the hospital. The snow was steady but light. There was some traffic out and about, mostly old trucks. We passed one snowplow.

I silently communed with my stomach and it growled very un-silently.

"Sounds like a yes to me," Clint said, trying (unsuccessfully) not to smile.

Clearly my ladylikeness was continuing to impress him. "How about Brams? There's one not far from the hospital. They make the best biscuits and gravy in the known universe." People (mostly Yankees) who don't know about Brams have no idea what they're missing—homemade ice cream, farm-fresh milk, eggs, bacon, etc. and amazing breakfast. All that and a drive-through!

"Sounds good."

I gracefully wolfed down my biscuits and gravy (and a large ice milk) as Clint drove with one hand while he stuffed a ham, egg and cheese biscuit into his face (homemade biscuits, too) with his other. Yum.

Someone had plowed a little area of the hospital parking lot. It looked like more people were venturing out. Oklahomans aren't very good snow drivers. Okay, honestly, they're really awful snow drivers. They just don't have enough experience with it. Billy Jo Bob thinks if he guns his Ford pickup enough, that there snow will just get the hell right outta his way. He's usually wrong, which is probably why hospital business seemed to be booming this morning.

We made our way to the SICU floor in time to see a pretty blond nurse clearing away Dad's breakfast dishes. He was propped up in bed with his hand lying stiffly off to the side. When he saw us, his face broke into a big grin. He was still looking a little glassy-eyed, but his color was better.

"What's going on, you two?" Dad's voice boomed.

"Not much, Dad. Thought we better check on you and make sure you're not being too big a bother to the nurses." I smiled and kissed him, pleased he was sounding like himself.

"Well, they're still giving me some medicine that makes me feel squirrelly, but besides that I'm just fine."

"Hope you haven't been coming on to any more guys," I teased.

"Nope, nope—not that damn squirrelly."

The nurse came in to check his IV. She nodded professionally to us.

"Has the doctor been through to see my dad yet?" I asked her.

"Yes, she made rounds earlier this morning." She puttered around Dad's bed, checking the dressing on his hand.

"Doc said I could go home in a couple of days." Dad looked at me carefully as he spoke.

"That's right…" The nurse patted his shoulder. "You're healing very well. I'll be right back to give you your medicine." She left in a flurry of efficiency.

"I hear it's snowing again." Dad lowered his voice.

"Yes," I sat at the edge of his bed, speaking softly. Clint stood next to my shoulder.

"Nuada is no longer trapped, but—" Clint rushed on when Dad opened his mouth to speak "—we believe he's no threat to you anymore."

"Why not?" Dad's voice was no nonsense.

"Rhiannon called him away," I explained. Dad's eyebrows shot up in surprise. "I saw her. Well, actually I contacted her, and she seems very interested in, uh, meeting with me." I glanced at Clint, silently telegraphing him to go with my edited version. "So, Clint and I are going to meet her back at his place. I think between us we can get rid of Nuada." I mentally crossed my fingers, hoping Dad was under the influence enough that he wouldn't recognize my lie.

"And get you back to Partholon?" he asked quietly.

"I think so. At least that's what I'm planning."

The nurse bustled in with a loaded syringe in her hand. She stuck it in the IV line that ran to Dad's good arm. "This will help that pain," she said to Dad. Then shifted her attention to Clint and me. "He's still very tired."

I nodded. "We won't be long—I know he needs his rest."

Placated, she left the room.

"Bugsy." Our heads were together so that our bizarre conversation couldn't be overheard. "I want you to be careful. That creature is nothing to mess around with."

"I know, Dad. I'll be fine. I'm pretty sure I know how to get rid of Nuada." Clint and Dad were looking expectantly at me. I swallowed. "It has something to do with the trees," I whispered conspiratorially.

Dad nodded appreciatively. "Yep, yep. Those willows helped you last time."

"How'd you know that, Dad? Weren't you unconscious?" I felt a jolt of surprise. Hadn't he been?

"Felt it—I could feel them helping you." He jerked his head in Clint's direction. "And Clint, too."

I nodded, hoping he wouldn't ask for any more details.

"I'll miss you, Bugsy old girl." He took my hand. "I know you have to go back, but I'll hate like hell not knowing my granddaughter." Then his face brightened. "Hey! Why can't you use some of that dream power goddess stuff to visit once in a while?" His words were slurring and his eyelids were fluttering.

"I'll do that, Dad," I said, kissing his forehead softly. The thought flitted through my mind that if Dad was able to feel the power of the trees, even when he was unconscious and near death, maybe I could somehow reach him from Partholon.

"Talked to Mama Parker this mornin'. She's on her way here."

"That's good—you need a keeper." I smiled through my tears.

"Yep—I wouldn't trade Mama Parker for a goat. Not even two goats." His eyes closed.

"Goodbye, Dad. I love you," I whispered, wiping tears from my eyes. I kissed him again and turned away.

"Son!" Dad came abruptly awake.

"Sir?" Clint leaned over his bed.

"I expect you to keep our girl safe while she's still here."

"You have my word on it, sir," Clint said solemnly.

"Good…" The word trailed off into a soft snore.

Clint followed me out of the room.

"Where's a ladies' room?" I was blubbering like a baby as I flagged down a passing nurse.

"There's one right outside the waiting room over there, honey," she said, patting my shoulder and giving me a kind look.

"I'm going to go blow my nose, wash my face and try to stop bawling," I hiccupped to Clint.

"I'll be in the waiting room."

One thing I can say for them, hospital restrooms are certainly clean, even if the toilet paper is rough on the nose. I splashed water on my face, hating the red, puffy way my nose and eyes looked.

"Maybe Dad was right," I said to my reflection while I sniffled back more tears. "Maybe I can use the Goddess's power to visit." Speaking the words aloud enabled me to eke out a smile. "So this isn't really goodbye. I'll just figure out a way to come back and see him—even if it's just through the Magic Sleep." I knew I was Scarlett O'Hara–ing the situation, but if I didn't spend time thinking about it *tomorrow,* I'd be a blubbering, pregnant wreck *today.* And I was pretty sure that would leave me in no shape to deal with Rhiannon, let alone Nuada. I blew my nose again and squared my shoulders.

Clint was sitting in front of a TV that was tuned to a local news station. Seems it was snowing—again. I could hear the weatherman taking a lot of abuse from the newscasters.

"Better?" He stood up and gave me a concerned look.

I nodded. "Sorry about that, I—" And something flashed onto the television screen that tugged at my attention. I tilted my head so I could see around Clint to the TV.

The perky blond newswoman's smile was twisted sardonically. Over her left shoulder was the Playboy bunny logo, and underneath it huge, black letters read: **BROKEN ARROW TEACHER TURNS FROM TEACHING TO TANTALIZING.**

"Ohmygod," I breathed, my attention focused on the screen like it was a car wreck.

"Now some local news that's much hotter than the weather. The publicist for former Broken Arrow High School English teacher Shannon Parker has announced just this morning that the thirty-five-year-old has been asked to pose nude for Playboy *magazine. And it's already creating quite a stir—seems the ex-teacher, who currently resides in Chicago, is insisting the photo shoot take place back in her home state of Oklahoma."*

Her cohost made some glib remark and they changed to sports. I felt dizzy and sat heavily into the nearest chair.

"You're not going to lose it again, are you?" Clint was peering at me with a guarded looked on his face—like he wasn't sure if fight or flight would be his best choice.

"Hugh Hefner!"

"Come again?" Clint sounded as if he thought I'd lost my mind.

"That's who the hawk-looking guy was who was with Rhiannon when I saw her through the probe." I shook my head. "Posing in the friggin nude for friggin *Playboy!* Dad is going to shit." I covered my face with my hands and slumped down in the chair.

"He'll know it's not you."

"Yeah, but that won't make a damn bit of difference, no one else will know." Suddenly I sat straight up and uncovered my face. "She's coming to the forest. She wants to get you away from me, and she thinks a sexy *Playboy* shoot in your backyard will do it. And she's calling Nuada there as some kind of backup plan." It all came together. "The bitch wants to bump me off. She's probably going to try to feed me to Nuada like I'm a real big kitty treat."

"She's at her most powerful within the forest," Clint added.

"So am I," I said determinedly. "And I have three things she doesn't have."

Clint gave me a questioning look.

"One—experience. I've been involved in killing Nuada once. All she's done is taunt him awake with sex and evil. Two—the forest acknowledges me as Epona's Chosen. And three—" I smiled at him "—I have you. Your power amplifies mine, and she has no clue how much. Actually, I have a very strong feeling that she has completely underestimated me, which is really good for us and really bad for her." I stood up and grabbed Clint's hand. "Let's go. I'm sick of tiptoeing around in her shadow."

PART III

1

The ride back to the forest was long and exhausting. We left Broken Arrow at a little after 9:00 a.m., stopped in some nameless town about six hours later to refuel the Hummer and ourselves (we found an open Sonic Drive-In. I felt up to a foot-long chili-cheese dog and tots. Don't ever say I'm not a brave woman). Four hours later as the sun was setting, Clint finally braked to pull off the blacktop road and onto the snow-obscured path that led to his cabin.

"Nagi Road," I whispered as I studied the innocent-looking stretch of road outside the window. "Ghosts of the dead." I would have known that road anywhere, even if my eyes were closed. It had a feeling to it—a sad, lonely feeling. I lifted my hand and pressed it against the window. "I will remember," I murmured to the spirits that seemed to hover invisibly over the snow-covered road.

Yes, it was still snowing. Not hard, but enough to let us know it still meant business.

"Talking to ghosts?" Clint asked softly.

"Definitely," I responded quickly, making a mental note to be sure my handmaidens poured libations in remembrance of the Indian warriors at the next festival of the full moon.

"Shit! It's freezing." My breath drifted around me in the frigid air as I got out of the Hummer and ran for the cabin. I kicked off my boots inside the door and followed Clint over to the fireplace.

"Just takes a second for this place to heat up." He smiled at me over his shoulder. "Have a seat—keep your coat on for a little while. You'll be surprised how quickly you'll get warm."

I nodded and did as I was told. The trip down had served to thaw Clint's withdrawal. He and I hadn't exactly chatted like old friends, but he was definitely out of his cave again. I knew it was selfish, but I preferred him this way—charming and attentive (who wouldn't?). And, of course, as we had gotten closer and closer to his home, he had begun to relax. That stiff way of holding himself, like he would break in half if he bent too quickly, had almost disappeared.

"There—" he finished feeding dry logs to the starter twigs "—that should do it." He busied himself lighting the old-fashioned kerosene lanterns that stood on the sturdy end tables.

"Do you think she's here yet?" I asked.

He sat in the rocking chair that faced me. "Well, I don't think so, but I know one way we can find out." He nodded toward the door.

"You want to go look for her? Oh, please, no, not the grove. I'm just too damn tired."

"I think there's an easier way. The trees might let me know if she was somewhere within the forest, but I'd be willing to bet a good load of firewood that they definitely would tell you."

I perked up. "Huh. I'll bet you're right." I thought back to the twisted scene I had witnessed the night before. "Clint, I don't think the trees like Rhiannon very much. I mean, not only do they call me Epona's Beloved, and not Epona's *other* Beloved, but I didn't sense that they were helping her at all in her nasty little ritual. Do you think that's really possible?"

"Before I knew you I would not have thought it possible. But she's not like you are with the trees. It seems she pulls power from somewhere—I mean somewhere in the land—but I know the trees don't speak to her. And I know they didn't welcome her like they did you."

"They were definitely silent in the grove in Chicago," I added.

"You're the Goddess's Chosen, Shannon my girl. She's not," he said simply.

"Then let's go see if the trees will rat her out." I grinned and headed for the door.

As he had last time we had walked in the forest, Clint led the way. The other trip we had taken to the heart of the forest seemed like an eternity ago, but it had only been days. It's so odd, the way time flows.

The forest was cold and beautiful. It looked formal dressed all in pristine white. Flakes floated gracefully around us as we plowed our way forward. It wasn't full dark yet, so the clouds still reflected soft gray tinted with just a touch of the mauve the departing day leaves behind like a discarded scarf drifting down the sky.

I studied Clint's back. He walked strong and straight; all signs of the pained cripple had vanished.

We hadn't gone too far when he stopped abruptly and I almost crashed into him.

"Over there." He pointed off to the right of the trail and linked arms with me to help me navigate the rougher ground. "The trees aren't as old as the ancient pin oaks in the glade, but I don't think we need to go all the way there to get help."

The moment we stepped off the path I heard the whisperings.

Welcome, Beloved!

The Chosen One has returned!

"No, we don't have to travel any farther to get help," I assured him, and I reached out, letting my free hand brush trunks, basking in the warmth of their acceptance.

An enormous pine loomed in front of us. Its long-needled branches, which began well above my head, were clumped in glistening white. The sharp odor of pine washed over me, calling alive Christmas-morning memories.

"Hello, old one," I said, pulling my glove off and pressing my palm against the sticky bark.

I hear you, Epona's Beloved.

The voice in my head was rich and masculine.

"Will you aid me?" I asked.

You have only to ask, Chosen One.

I nodded at Clint. "He'll help."

"I never doubted it," he said, brushing an errant strand of hair from my face.

Oh, Goddess, he looked strong and handsome.

Tearing my eyes from his I refocused on the tree. "Is there another like me in the forest?"

There is no other like you, Beloved of the Goddess.

I sighed in frustration. How the hell do I communicate with a tree about Rhiannon? Then something the Goddess said flashed into my mind. Just before she had plucked me out of the grove in Chicago, she had said, *Enough of this perversion.*

"Not like me then. Someone who has my appearance, but who perverts Epona's will and consorts with evil. Have you seen her?"

Not for some sunrises.

"So she's not here now?" I asked quickly.

She is not.

"Thank you, old one." I turned to Clint. "She's not here yet."

Evil comes, Chosen One.

"What?" I felt a chill run through me that had nothing to do with the weather. "You mean her?"

I feel another—an evil that has passed through here before. It returns.

"Now?" I squeaked. "Is it here now?"

Not yet, but soon. Not many more sunrises. It comes.

"Will you tell me when it gets here?"

You need only ask, Beloved of Epona.

"Thank you," I repeated. I took Clint's arm. "Let's go

back. I'm freezing." We stumbled to the path and began walking quickly to the cabin.

"Nuada?" Clint asked.

"Of course. The tree says he's on his way back here. Not here yet, mind you, just on his way." I tried to let go of Clint's arm and he grabbed my hand so that I kept walking beside him. "It really freaks me out to think that he's so damn evil that the trees can feel him when he's not even here." I shivered. "And Rhiannon resurrected him." I glanced up at Clint. "What the hell's wrong with her?"

He shrugged his shoulders.

"Really," I persisted. "It doesn't make any sense to me. You say she's so like me physically, and our auras are the same. But it's like she's rotten inside. I just wonder why."

"Maybe she got all the evil and you got all the good."

"Oh, please. That theory might fly if I was a saint, but I'm not. I've done my share of shitty things. I have my share of mean, nasty thoughts. I'm certainly no saint."

"So, you're normal. Most people have some bad in them."

"You're right," I had a sudden thought. "And maybe she has some good in her."

Clint raised his eyebrows and looked down at me like I was nuts.

"Well, maybe she does!" I repeated as we entered the cozy cabin.

"You'll pardon me if I don't adhere to your theory. I've spent more time with her than you have," Clint said simply, as he led us back to the cabin.

I was still deep in thought as I kicked off my boots and hung up my coat.

"Shannon—I asked if you're hungry," Clint repeated, sounding exasperated.

"Oh, sorry. Yeah, I guess I am, kinda."

"Why don't you look through the middle drawer of my dresser for something more comfortable than those jeans to wear to bed, and I'll fix us a couple of hot ham-and-cheese sandwiches."

"Sounds like a plan," I called to his back.

I could hear the homey sounds of cooking as I pawed through his drawer. My hands sank into the well-washed thickness of a sweatshirt. Holding it up, I could barely make out the round logo on the front. It was a top-hatted beaver who was displaying playing cards in one hand and a white-tipped cane in the other. He looked like a furry, buck-toothed mini-gambler. Around the insignia were the words Beaver Air 125th Fighter Squadron. On the back there was a black-and-white picture of an F–16, the outline of the state of Oklahoma and another gambling beaver, with the words BEAVER AIR emblazoned over it, and Oklahoma Air Guard 138th Fighter Group Tulsa Oklahoma in bold letters under it.

Flying beavers. Jeesh. Men—I shook my head. But I couldn't help the smile that curved my lips.

I listened to make sure he was still keeping busy in the kitchen before I pulled off my jeans, bra and shirt, and replaced them with Clint's incredibly soft sweatshirt, which came down almost to my knees. I pulled the way-too-long sleeves up while I padded on sock feet into the kitchen.

"Yum—sure smells good." The frying ham sizzled in the cast-iron skillet. "Can I do something to help?"

He glanced at me, smiling at the oversize sweatshirt. "I see you discovered my favorite."

"Oh…" I fidgeted. "I didn't mean to wear your favorite. I can find anoth—"

"Shh," he hushed me. "I like you in it." Before I was through blushing, he added, "Yes, there is something you can do. Make us a couple of salads. You'll find the stuff in the veggie drawer."

We worked in companionable silence. Soon we were gnawing contentedly on thick ham-and-cheese sandwiches and crisp salads.

"So, do you really have a plan to get rid of Nuada that has something to do with the trees, or was that just a line you were feeding your dad?" Clint asked through a bite of salad.

"It was total bullshit. I don't have a clue how to kill him. Oh, by the way, thanks for not blowing my story about Rhiannon helping us. Dad needs to concentrate on getting well, not on worrying about me."

He gave me a mock salute. "You're the Chosen One—I'm just one of your adoring minions."

I ignored his comment but added, "And a damn fine cook."

"Why, thanks, Shannon my girl." With a flourish he started cleaning up the dishes.

"Let me help," I said through a very unladylike yawn.

"No, you don't know where anything goes. I can do it quicker myself. Just go lie down. You and your daughter need rest." He shooed me out of the kitchen.

Actually, I was grateful. Even though the clock on the fireplace mantel said it was barely 8:00 p.m., I felt like it was past midnight. My body was craving sleep. Clint's tall bed was mounded with comforters and I snuggled underneath them. Warm and contented, I curled on my side, staring sleepily into the crackling fire. The familiar weight of my lids felt comforting and I allowed myself to drift off into seductive sleep.

* * *

Sean Connery and I were floating on a giant raft that was shaped like a huge heart. We were somewhere in the Caribbean, and the water was a lovely clear turquoise. I was sipping a giant margarita and wearing…well…nothing but a smile and a tan (obviously I'm not pregnant in DreamLand). Sean was pouring coconut-flavored oil all over the back of me and whispering in his sexy Scottish accent how he was going to enjoy licking it off…

…And I was suddenly suspended over Clint's cabin.

"I don't suppose you could've waited till Sean had finished what he had started?" I sighed. DreamLand just hadn't been the same since my Goddess had taken over.

The Goddess ignored my quip and whispered within my mind. Beloved, it is time for you to see why events have come into being.

"What events?" I was intrigued.

Rhiannon's fall. *The Goddess's voice was heavy with sadness.*

"You're right. I do want to know." After all, in many ways Rhiannon seemed a part of me. I felt compelled to understand how she had become so twisted.

It will be a difficult journey, Beloved. We must travel through the layers of time, and we may stay only briefly. Do not speak. Touch nothing. You may only observe the past, not interact with it.

"Kind of like Scrooge's trip with the Ghost of Christmas Past?" I guessed.

I thought I felt the tinkling of my Goddess's laughter for a moment, then the words, Ready yourself, my Chosen One. Remember that I am with you.

That sounded ominous, but before I could become too afraid I started floating up into the dark, starless sky. I went higher and higher, through the thick layer of snow-filled clouds until I popped out into the cold, silent night sky. More stars than I had ever before seen, even in Partholon, surrounded me. It looked like a goddess had broken a diamond-stranded necklace, and scattered the faceted beads across a blanket of black velvet. Then in front of me the sky rippled and opened. I just had time to peer into the shaft of darkness when I felt my soul ripped from its place in the night and thrown down that tunnel of colorless, churning black.

Instantly it was cold. Normally, I can't actually feel my body when I am on a Magic Sleep journey, but in this shaft of timelessness I was only too aware of myself. Every nerve screamed at the frigid nothingness. I felt a thousand tiny frozen needles piercing my body. My soul quaked in terror and I tried to wrench open my mouth to scream, but the blackness of the tunnel absorbed all sound, and I was left to suffer in silent agony.

I burst out into the calm of another night's sky.

I floated over the distinctive pearlized marble of Epona's Temple. The fragrant air of a warm spring night wrapped my trembling soul in loving arms. I felt my terror abate, and I breathed deeply, instantly reassured and relaxed. A wealth of richly blooming lilacs surrounded the enormous mineral spring fountain that gushed heated water up into the night. I sighed in pleasure as I took in the beautifully familiar scene beneath me.

Then I blinked in confusion.

I didn't remember any lilac bushes anywhere by the plunging horse fountain. I studied the creamy walls of the temple.

Stands of blooming ornamental trees surrounded by carpets of flowers dotted the area that spread outside the temple gates.

Those weren't there before.

The final shock was the long, waving strands of flowering ivy that dripped thick fingers of fragrant red and yellow blossoms from the balustraded walls of the temple.

None of this had been there when the temple had been mine. My temple was a beautiful place, yes, but it wasn't a palace dedicated solely to the worship of beauty, it was a warrior's temple. As such, it had to be kept in a state of readiness for war. This temple looked dressed for a party.

The One who was my Chosen before Rhiannon had grown quite old.

The Goddess's voice was still in my head, but this time her presence seemed more tangible than ever before. A movement in the sky beside me caused me to turn my attention from the odd scene below. My breath caught as I saw the glistening outline of my Goddess. Epona's body wavered once and then became visible. She was magnificent. A thick mane of blond hair, the color of ripe wheat, swirled around her, partially obscuring her face. She wore a linen drape that glowed with the same marbleized pearl as the walls of her temple beneath us. It floated around her like gauze, clinging sensually to her graceful curves.

I was wordlessly studying her when she turned to me.

"Oh! Goddess…" My voice trailed off and my head bowed in wordless supplication. I had never seen anything like her. She was beauty sculpted from time immemorial. She was what artists had been trying to re-create for age upon age. To be so tangibly in her presence left me speechless.

With a smile that radiated love and understanding, she

passed a hand over her face and her image was obscured so that I was now looking into a glistening mist that had her form.

The One who was my Chosen before Rhiannon had grown quite old. *I realized she had repeated her earlier words.* She had a daughter, but as sometimes happens, the child had grown up with no affinity for my service.

I found I could breathe and think again, and now that her image wasn't as clearly discernible, I was able to focus on what she was saying.

With her passing I Chose Rhiannon as my next Incarnate, but she was just a child, toddling amidst her elders. So my lesser Priestesses cared for my Temple until my young Chosen came of age. *I heard no reproach in her voice, only the fond amusement of a parent toward an errant child.* They allowed the flowers to thrive and the Temple to become less than I desired it to be. I knew my Chosen One would restore things to order when she came of age. What I didn't know was that the Priestesses who nursemaided her had indulged her so much that they caused damage within her which could not be so easily undone.

Let us witness her ascension ceremony.

The Goddess's hand waved and the scene below us shifted. We now floated suspended over a lovely clearing within the forest that surrounded the temple.

"It's the clearing with the two ancient trees," I said.

Yes, Beloved. It is a holy grove. Tonight we witness the celebration of Beltane, the season after Rhiannon's first womanly courses.

Hugh bonfires were placed all along the edge of the clearing. Around each fire young men and women danced and drank—no one had on many clothes (which was typical for a

Rhiannon-led ceremony), and everyone seemed to be having a riotous good time. Music swelled into the night and I felt my heart begin to beat in nameless anticipation.

Beside me the Goddess's laugh tinkled like a flowing brook. You feel the call of Beltane even now, do you not, Beloved?

"I sure feel something." I hesitated then added, "Something good."

Epona's laughter filled me with unspeakable joy. Happily, I studied the glade. Next to the little stream and very near the huge twin trees a tent had been erected. It reminded me of something romantic and beautiful out of The Arabian Nights. *It had a domed top and five sides that angled up to swirling mini-domes. There was a hole in the middle of the structure, and a steady stream of smoke lifted into the otherwise clear night sky. The flap that covered the entrance to the tent was closed securely, but light escaped from inside, lending the chartreuse fabric a magical glow.*

Observe, *the Goddess said as we descended through the ceiling of the tent.*

A single fire burning in a brass tripod in the center of the tent lit the interior with a flickering tongue of flame-colored light. The floor was richly carpeted with woven golden mats. The only furniture was gigantic piles of velvet-covered pillows, all dyed the bright crimson color of new blood.

"I said I won't drink it!" the girl's voice snapped. I grinned as I recognized the voice. It was me—or rather Rhiannon—as a teenager. Trust me; I'd know that smart-alecky tone anywhere.

"But my Lady, the Chosen One always drinks of the Goddess's wine before the ascension ritual." The sweet voice of a very young Alanna sounded exhausted and worried. In the

dim light I could see well enough to appreciate the incredible workmanship of the decorative goblet that she was offering her mistress. Then Rhiannon roughly knocked it from Alanna's hand. Rich red liquid rained on the golden carpet.

"I am Goddess Incarnate. I do as I choose, and I choose—" she hissed the words, foreshadowing her adult cruelty "—not to drink the potion."

"My Lady," Alanna tried to reason with her. "The Goddess's wine allows the ceremony to be pleasurable for the Chosen One. That is why Epona requires her Beloved to drink of it. It is only of you that the Goddess thinks."

"Ha! Epona thinks of her own pleasure and of controlling me. Concern for me has very little to do with what moves her." She sounded sullen. I remember using that tone with Dad once when I was a teenager. It had had something to do with wanting to stay out after curfew. I also remember very distinctly that he had promptly grounded me. His exact words were, "Shannon Christine, you're grounded until you're a better human being." Unfortunately for Rhiannon, I didn't see any evidence of her dad (or mine for that matter), or anyone who could stop her from being such a damn brat.

"My Lady, you are the Beloved of a Goddess, Her Chosen. She wants you to follow the path that is best for you," young Alanna continued, obviously distraught.

"I refuse. I prefer to keep my wits. Now leave me and let the ceremony begin." Rhiannon made a haughty gesture of dismissal. Reluctantly, Alanna collected the goblet and backed slowly from the tent.

I watched the young Rhiannon intently. With jerky movements she stood and began pacing back and forth over the small floor space that wasn't filled with cushions. She ran her hands absently through her hair, and I gave a start at the familiarity of the gesture. I'd had the same habit for thirty-plus years. It was a surreal experience, observing this mirrored shadow from the past. She was wearing a golden robe that had only a slit for her head and two armholes. It tied together in the front, but every time she moved it floated open to reveal her firm, naked body.

"Ah, youth," I muttered, appreciating the sleekness of fresh womanhood.

Rhiannon's hands suddenly rose to cover her ears, like a child trying to block a parent's words.

"No! Get out of my head! No one tells me what to do! I will have it my way, not yours!" she screamed into the empty tent.

I realized that she must have been yelling at Epona, and my gaze shifted to the mistlike figure beside me.

Always headstrong, *the Goddess whispered sadly.*

"Tell me about it," I agreed. I had certainly backed myself into many mistakes through my stubbornness (example: my starter husband, a man Dad had been dead set against me marrying), but I realized that though I had made mistakes I had also learned from them and grown because I'd been given structure and discipline, two things it appeared Rhiannon had been severely lacking.

Then the door to the tent was thrown aside and a remarkable figure entered. He was a tall male, human in every aspect, except on his shoulders sat the head of a horse.

"What the…?" burst from my mouth.

Do not fear. He is a human male. The head is that of the last stallion to mate with my Chosen mare.

"You kill the stallion afterward?" I asked, horrified. I was thinking sympathetically of Epi's mate.

The Goddess's voice sounded amused. He is sacrificed painlessly only after he has become old and infirm. Until then he lives the cosseted life of a beloved Chieftain.

I took a deep, relieved breath and continued watching. Rhiannon had quit her frenzied pacing and had taken her hands from her ears as the man entered the tent. He strode purposefully toward her, but Rhiannon took two quick steps and backed away from him. This seemed to confuse the man, and he halted near the fire. Rhiannon and I studied him. The firelight was kind to a body that didn't need dim lighting to look good. He was gorgeous—a man very obviously at the peak of virility. Naked except for a small leather triangle slung low on his firm hips, his tanned skin glistened in the flickering light. He was breathing hard, and his muscular chest rose and fell powerfully. He looked like he had just walked off a field of battle. And he had definitely been victorious. I felt an erotic ripple of feeling in response to the seductive male image he represented so well.

"Where did you find him?" I whispered.

The male was chosen from my private guard. The right to usher My Chosen One into womanhood is a great honor.

So it was through a fertility ritual that Rhiannon ascended to power. I wasn't sure how I felt about that. My eyes found Rhiannon again. She wasn't even sixteen yet—and by her lack of response she must be a virgin.

She has remained untouched, as tradition dictates. *As usual, the Goddess anticipated my questions.* That is why she should have taken the potion. It allows the veils between worlds to be lifted. I enter my Chosen One and the passage to womanhood is a pleasurable one. But she usurped my will, therefore she must pay a price for that disobedience.

Epona's tone was not harsh or judgmental. It was resigned and sad, like she wished it could be another way.

Free will is not always an easy thing to bear.

I watched as the stallion-headed man once again moved toward Rhiannon. This time she backed away so quickly that she tripped on a cushion. Falling, she started to scream, but with a movement almost impossibly swift, the man leaped to her side and caught her in his arms, twisting so that when she fell she landed across his chest.

Her scream changed into a snarl.

"Do not touch me!" she spat.

Instead of obeying her he circled her shoulders with one arm, pulling her next to him and holding her securely to his side. With his free hand he parted her golden robe and began to explore the intimate parts of her soft, young body while he pressed her more firmly against his body. I saw her face grimace in horror as it inadvertently rubbed against the embalmed horse head.

She was trembling, but not with desire.

"I order you to unhand me!" She tried to keep her voice steady, but raw fear made her sound even younger than her years.

The man ignored her. Instead of letting her escape him, he reached between his own legs, ripping the leather covering away to expose an impressive erection.

"Why doesn't he stop?" I asked breathlessly.

He cannot. He has taken the God's potion, and the spirit of Cernunnos, Animal God and Hunter, lives within him. He must mate with my Chosen One to insure fertility for Partholon. My Beloved, you felt the call of the ritual when we entered the glade. Rhiannon's ascension ceremony should have been filled with pleasure and desire, instead of horror and pain. There is no way to stop it. *The Goddess's voice was hollow.* Not even my Chosen One is allowed to endanger Beltane and the fertility of Partholon.

The rape continued and our spirit bodies ascended through the domed ceiling along with the echoing screams of Rhiannon's pain.

We floated silently far above the forest. I wondered what I would have done at her age. Yes, I had been stubborn and willful, but I hadn't been raised a cosseted, spoiled goddess whose every whim was indulged by nursemaids and slaves.

I knew that I would have taken the potion.

Observe the consequences, Beloved. *As the Goddess spoke she waved her hand before us and the sky shimmered and rippled as if a stone had been thrown onto the smooth surface of a lake. When it cleared, images solidified and moved in front of us.*

"It's like a movie screen," I said in awe.

Observe, *the Goddess repeated.*

I watched closely as scene upon scene flashed against the night sky. Rhiannon was growing older, so her appearance matured over the course of the vignettes, but that was all that matured. All of the images focused on sex. Sex with many different men in many different places and positions. The only factor that stayed consistent was that in each scene Rhiannon remained icily in control. Sometimes she would even stop in the middle of the act and order the man out of her sight. Sometimes she used a whip on her partner, even when it was obvious that he didn't enjoy her sadistic play. I watched as she coupled with countless men, even when it was apparent to everyone involved that she received little pleasure from the act.

She does not allow herself pleasure. The act of lovemaking is a thing of darkness for Rhiannon, so that finally love itself became only darkness for her.

A thing of darkness—it was an insightful description. Time passed before our eyes and Rhiannon's sex acts became more and more twisted, which seemed to reflect what happened to her personality as she gave in to the brokenness within her.

"I'm surprised she didn't get pregnant," I said.

My Chosen One can only conceive if she mates with the High Shaman I fashion for her.

At least that was some relief. I could only imagine what a horrible mother Rhiannon would be. Talk about Mommy Dearest.

The images changed once again and I felt a physical jolt as I recognized the form of a young centaur flash into the screen. ClanFintan approached Rhiannon and bowed to her. They were alone in the throne room of Epona's Temple. I loved seeing my husband's youthful image. He was not nearly as tall and muscular as he would grow to in adulthood, but he had the fine features that would be the foundation of what he would become. His shoulders were wide and his chest was deep. His jaw was already molded into strong, firm lines. His eyes were the same, dark and almond shaped, but they shone with naive pleasure instead of adult wisdom. He looked like an innocent, miniversion of his adult self.

"Well met, my Lady Rhiannon." His voice was so boyish that it held only the shadow of the deep velvet base it would attain in years to come.

"I am informed that it has been foretold that you will become a High Shaman," Rhiannon's voice purred, which made my hair stand on end in warning. It didn't have a similar effect on young ClanFintan.

"Yes, my Lady. So it has been prophesied." He sounded proud and eager.

I remembered how guarded and withdrawn he had been when we had first met, and I wanted to leap into the screen and throw my arms around him, shielding him from whatever hurtful things Rhiannon had planned. But Epona held up a mist-shrouded hand and I controlled my impulse.

Observe, Beloved.

Rhiannon stood, and then walked languidly down the steps that led from her throne. She slowly circled the young centaur, who stood almost motionless, curiously observing her.

"You might do very well." Her voice was seductive and she moved close to him, letting one hand trail from his human shoulder down his chest to where man met horse. Then she continued the caress all the way around his body, walking with slow, sensuous steps. I could see the centaur's skin ripple and twitch in response.

"I believe, my Lady, that we will do very well together." His voice had deepened seductively. "I, too, am pleased that Fate has decreed that someday we can be mated."

Rhiannon's sarcastic laughter rang mockingly. "I was not speaking of mating, you fool. I was speaking of amusement."

Before ClanFintan could reply, she reached up and unpinned the brooch that held the diaphanous material of her wrap around her body. She shrugged her shoulder in a movement that I had performed myself for this same centaur. Then she stood naked in front of him.

I saw ClanFintan's breath deepen, and when he finally spoke, his voice trembled. "I am not yet a High Shaman. I cannot perform the Change into human form, my Lady."

Again that mocking, poisoned laughter. "I have been with

many human men, but I have never been with a centaur. If you could attain human form I would not find you nearly so interesting."

I could see his young brow furrow in confusion as she stepped into his arms, her body already undulating to a rhythm she alone could hear.

I closed my eyes. "Stop! I don't want to see any more of this!" Anger, betrayal and jealousy warred within me.

Observe, Beloved, *she repeated.* There is only one scene left for you to witness.

I opened my eyes slowly. The screen had changed again. I didn't immediately recognize Rhiannon's bedchamber. Hundreds of candelabra illuminated the room. A bier raised well off the floor had replaced her huge bed. On top of the bier lay a flat mat of tightly woven rushes. Rhiannon lay atop the mat. She was naked, and the small swell of her abdomen was easy for me to recognize.

"She's pregnant?" My mind whirred. I studied her closely. She couldn't be much older than she had been in the last scene I had witnessed. My Chosen One can only conceive if she mates with the High Shaman I fashion for her. *Memory of the Goddess's words whispered through my mind. If she was pregnant it had to be ClanFintan's child.*

But the young ClanFintan had yet to be made a High Shaman. By his own admission he could not perform the Change into human form.

My stomach clenched at what her ripe belly implied.

"Drink, my Goddess." The hypnotic sound of the words made me blink tears from my eyes and refocus on the scene.

The unmistakable form of Bres had entered the room. He was obviously much younger than the man I'd seen recently. I was surprised to note that his lean body held a kind of sculpted elegance. I could imagine him being used as a model for Calvin Klein in those black-and-white photos that show semi-naked people lounging on a beach.

Guess he didn't age well. How tragic.

He held a goblet filled with thick red liquid to Rhiannon's lips. She drank greedily. I noticed her eyes had a glassy look that suggested she had already done quite a bit of drinking.

Not good for the baby, I thought.

Her head lolled back and Bres moved to the foot of the bier. He put the empty goblet down on a small table that stood next to him. Then he picked up a long, thin, wicked-looking object. It reminded me of a crochet hook, only it was longer and the top of the hook had been carved into a barbed point. He turned to face Rhiannon's feet, which were about chest level with him.

"Now you must come to me, my Goddess."

Without speaking, Rhiannon scooted down toward him while she bent her knees and spread her naked legs.

It looked like she was getting ready for a bizarre Pap test.

With leather thongs that I had not noticed before, Bres tied her ankles in place. I could see that Rhiannon's hands were gripping the edge of the mat so tightly that her knuckles were white.

Rhiannon's legs had fallen open, and her sex was clearly visible, as was the soft mound of her belly. For a moment Bres's unnaturally bright eyes studied her exposed body, then with one hand he spread open her labia. With his other hand he inserted the evil-looking instrument deeply into her vagina.

Rhiannon's body tensed and jerked spasmodically. At the same instant the candles began to flicker wildly, like a vengeful Goddess had just loosed a breath of warning.

"No!" Rhiannon screamed, spittle flying from her pale lips. "I will not be used! I will choose! I will choose!"

As her tirade ended, Bres jabbed the hooked barb far within her writhing body, and in one swift motion he twisted and pulled it back out. With it came a gush of clear liquid tinged with blood. Quickly he wiped his hands clean on his thick robe and moved to the head of the bier.

"Now you will expel it." Gently he wiped tears and sweat from her face. She buried her shaking head in the curve of his arm. "The juice of the poppy will ease your pain. It will be finished soon."

The scene rippled and faded into night sky.

Tears were streaming unheeded down my ghostly cheeks. "But you said she couldn't get pregnant unless it was by a High Shaman. ClanFintan wasn't a High Shaman yet. He couldn't even change into human form."

A High Shaman is not made, Beloved, he is born. As such, ClanFintan was a High Shaman from his first breaths.

"She killed his baby," I said in disbelief.

As she orchestrated the death of the child, so too died her ability to feel compassion or mercy for others. Ruthlessness and self-indulgence consumed her, and I was compelled to sever the link between us. Soon guilt destroyed anything else left of good within her. And in place of that good, true evil began to take hold.

"So she really isn't Your Chosen." I still felt shaky and nauseous.

I withdrew my favor, thus allowing her to exchange herself for you, my Beloved.

"Then why did you let me get pulled back to Oklahoma. Why am I not still in Partholon where I belong?"

Rhiannon and the darkness she dallies with must be stopped. I cannot allow her to loose Nuada's evil upon your old world.

The night sky rippled again, then split and opened to expose the frigid blackness of the time portal.

"Please tell me how to get rid of Nuada and stop Rhiannon." I felt panicky as my soul started to move to the tunnel.

When the time comes you will know, Beloved. Remember that Rhiannon has lived her life filled with a hatred of her own making, so hatred cannot vanquish her.

"I don't understand, Epona! What does that mean?" My voice sounded shrill.

Think of what you have witnessed this night. With knowledge comes wisdom and power.

My spirit body was sucked into the dark tunnel. This time I squeezed my eyes shut and held my terror in check. It will end soon it will end soon it will end soon was the mantra that kept going through my mind.

And I was spit out into the snow-filled sky above Clint's cabin. I opened my eyes as I drifted softly down through the ceiling of the cabin and hovered silently above the bed. My body was still curled on its side, and I appeared to be sleeping contentedly. Clint lay next to me, still dressed in jeans and a T-shirt. He was above the covers, so our bodies weren't touching and he had pulled a quilt over himself. His eyes were closed and he was breathing deeply. My heart did a ridiculous little flip-flop at the sight of him.

Allow yourself to love him tonight, Beloved. *The Goddess's voice was back in my mind.*

"But I'm married to ClanFintan," I said inanely.

He is the mirror of your mate, Beloved. He, too, was born to love you.

"But—"

He needs you, My Chosen One…

The Goddess's words blew from my mind.

I opened my eyes. The fire had burned down to a warm glow. I studied it and thought about Epona's words. It didn't take me long to make my decision.

And I rolled over to face Clint.

At my movement his eyes opened in concern.

"What?" he asked, starting to sit up.

"Shush." I reached out and touched his arm. "Everything's fine."

He lay back down, running his hands over his eyes in his habitual waking gesture. "Another dream thing?"

"Kind of—this time I saw the past."

"What do you mean?" He was fully awake now, and he rolled onto his side to face me.

I grinned at his expression. "It's pretty bizarre, isn't it?"

Clint smiled and tapped me on the end of the nose in a gesture that mirrored ClanFintan completely. "It does take some getting used to, but I think we manage. What did you see this time?"

"The Goddess showed me Rhiannon's past. I don't think Epona did it to excuse Rhiannon's behavior. I think she did it so that I could understand her better."

"And do you?"

"Yes," I said thoughtfully. "And I feel sorry for her."

His eyes widened in surprise. "Really?"

I nodded. "It could have been me. Change my upbringing and I think I might have become what she has become." I laughed without feeling any humor. "It's actually a little scary."

He pushed a curl back from my face. "But you didn't become what she is."

"No, but don't judge her too harshly, Clint. She's much more like me than either of us would have guessed. You have to realize that at one time she was just a kid, a scared kid not prepared to handle what happened to her."

He snorted a very ClanFintan-like sound through his nose.

I touched his cheek gently, allowing my hand to rest against the rough skin of his day-old beard. Something within me prompted me to say, "Promise me that you'll remember to pity her."

He looked a long time into my eyes. "I promise." he said softly.

Without stopping to think about what I was doing, I leaned forward and kissed him lightly on the lips. "Thank you."

"You're welcome." His voice had gone deep and his body was suddenly still. I didn't pull away from him, and our faces were very close.

Again, I leaned forward and kissed him; this time I lingered. He made no move to deepen the kiss, but he parted his lips and let me explore his mouth at my leisure.

"I like the way you taste," I whispered against his lips.

"Shannon my girl..." The endearment was a moan as I rolled against him, pushing the thick layer of covers down so that I could fit my body to his.

Our legs were entwined, and I loved the way my bare flesh felt against the heat and roughness of his jeans. My hands slipped under his T-shirt and I leaned into our next kiss so I could explore the ridges of his back. My fingers found the long scar that ran almost the length of his back. Consciously I pulled energy from within me and let it snake out through my fingertips, willing pain away from him. I felt the rush of warmth as an erotic tingling of sensation.

In response, Clint's arms trembled as they wrapped around me and he moaned into my mouth.

"Does that feel good?" I whispered.

"Oh, Goddess—" his voice was shaky and rough "—if only you knew how good."

I pulled his shirt off and let my lips and tongue roam down his chest to the hard expanse of his belly, all the while running my flaming-hot fingertips lightly along the edge of his skin, stopping whenever I sensed an area of pain or injury.

Finally, my teeth pulled at the button of his jeans, and I looked up into his passion-glazed eyes.

"I think you're overdressed," I teased.

"I live to obey you." He smiled as he quickly divested himself of the rest of his clothes.

"Just one of my faithful minions?" I laughed as I snuggled against his naked body.

"My middle name is Sacrifice," he murmured as he bent to reclaim my mouth.

I responded to his kiss until the top of my head felt dizzy, then I pushed him back onto the pillows. He looked confused.

"Please let me love you tonight," I said simply.

"Oh, my sweet girl..." He cupped my face in his hands. "Don't you know I can refuse you nothing?"

I swallowed back tears, and in answer I moved my mouth down his body.

His breathing was deep and ragged when he pulled me to him. Instead of kissing him, I sat up and slowly pulled his sweatshirt from my body, then I slid my panties down my bare thighs. His eyes were smoldering as he watched me straddle him. Gently, he cupped my heavy breasts in his hands.

"They're really sensitive right now," I whispered.

He kissed my enlarged nipples gently. "I'd never hurt you."

"I know, Clint. I know." I pulled him against me and wrapped my arms around his broad shoulders.

I began rocking in an ancient rhythm that Clint matched with perfect understanding. As our tempo increased I noticed Clint's aura begin to glow its jeweled luster. Then the silver of my own aura became clearly visible around me. As we moved toward climax the two auras merged and swelled, causing the feelings that were rippling through my body to suddenly intensify to an almost painful level.

Clint's eyes shot open and he locked his gaze with mine. His hands found my hips and thrust deep within me, again and again, holding me steady. The night exploded around and within us.

I drifted in and out of sleep circled by the shelter of his arms.

"That's never happened to me before." Clint's voice sounded raw and vulnerable, and wide awake.

I tilted my chin up so I could look into his eyes.

"The thing you did with your fingers," he continued. "You made the pain go away, but more than that, you..." He shook his head in wonder. "It was..." He traced my lips with his fingertip. "There are no words in any world."

"And our auras merged." I hesitated, not really wanting to ask but needing to know the answer. "Did that happen with Rhiannon?"

"No." Clint's voice was firm and had a slight edge to it. "None of it happened with Rhiannon. Only you, Shannon. Only you. The things she did to me..." His voice faltered. "She held me with an unnatural, perverse power. It was dark and wrong. I hated myself for wanting her."

"Shh," I whispered, pressing my finger against his lips. "It's over now. That part of your life is over."

His eyes were bright with unshed tears as he bent and kissed me deeply.

I felt his erection pulse and stir. Slipping my hand between our bodies, I caressed the length of him, loving the sensation of soft skin stretched over hardness.

Then I felt it. The slight indentation of scar tissue running the length of his shaft. I felt myself go cold at the thought of what this scar had to mean. The Chicago park flashed into my disbelieving mind. I saw the glint of light off the sharpened blade, and the crimson drops staining the snow-covered ground.

My eyes flew open in horror to find Clint's eyes closed in pleasure and peace; a gentle smile curved his lips as a moan escaped from between them.

Heal him, Beloved.

With the whisper of my Goddess's gentle urging echoing in my mind, I stroked him, willing health and healing and light to pass into him and to chase out the perversity and twisted pleasure and darkness with which Rhiannon had scarred him. In Clint's healing I found my own joy. Again, I took him inside my body, this time with a deeper gentleness and more complete understanding. I held nothing back from him, and as we made love I felt Epona's presence as if she was sanctifying our joining. Against my closed lids I could see the magical shimmer of our aura's pulsing as they merged together, filling the small cabin with light and beauty and the warmth of a goddess's love.

Much later he held my face within his hands.

"I love you," he said simply.

I closed my eyes and rested my head on his shoulder. "I love you, too, Clint." I knew it was the truth. I loved both of them—ClanFintan and Clint. They were two pieces of the same whole. And it broke my heart to think about leaving Clint, just as much as it made me ache with longing for ClanFintan when I thought about being parted forever from him.

Oh, help us, Epona. I breathed a silent prayer into the night.

Sleep, Beloved. The ethereal voice drifted through my mind and I felt submerged in liquid weariness. Through the layers of encroaching sleep, I could feel Clint's hand trace the same path ClanFintan's hand had traced innumerable times before. He caressed the length of my body from behind my bent knee, up the back of my thigh, to the small of my back and down. My last conscious thought was that I was no longer going to be surprised at their unerring similarities.

3

I awakened slowly, and in the first lazy moments of consciousness the entrapping arms that held me spooned against the hard heat of a warm male body confused me.

Then I remembered. *Ohhhhh,* Clint…

I'm pretty sure I blushed, but embarrassed or not nature would not wait, so I quietly slid out of his arms, found my/his sweatshirt (it was under the bed) and tiptoed across the cold morning floor to use the facilities.

I glanced in the bathroom mirror. I looked disheveled, bed-headed and (quite frankly) well and truly laid. What the hell had happened last night—I mean, besides the obvious? I had touched something deep within Clint, something that cried painfully out to me in its need to be healed. And the mingling of our auras had been utterly amazing.

Why had it just happened with us and not with Rhiannon (or, my mind whispered, with ClanFintan and me)?

The Goddess had directed me to love Clint. It was an awe-inspiring thought—that Epona was using me in this world as human balm.

I shook my head at my reflection. I'd just made love, several times, with an incredibly attractive man with whom I had fallen in love because, basically, he was the clone of my husband (who was stuck in another world/dimension). But I wasn't a divine healer, was I? Wasn't I still just me? Was anything else bordering on delusions of grandeur and Rhiannon-like thinking? And shouldn't I feel guilty? Shouldn't I go out there and tell Clint I'd made a mistake last night? I am, after all, a married woman.

No. I hated it when friggin women did that kind of morning-after shit. I've always wanted to scream at the movie/TV/book/or various messed-up girlfriends, YOU MADE A DECISION, NOW LIVE WITH IT! Please—that's exactly why I never liked King Arthur's Guinevere. She screws up (pardon the pun), sleeps with her husband's best friend, causes the fall of a kingdom, then she doesn't have the guts to make at least one man happy, so she joins a friggin nunnery and escapes from all of *her* problems, leaving everyone around her in a slavering mess. How incredibly spineless.

"Well, damnit, I'm not spineless," I told my mussed reflection. "And Clint needed me. What Rhiannon had broken, Epona let me fix. I won't be sorry for that, and I won't second-guess it."

After my toilette was complete I padded quickly (it was really cold) back to bed. Clint looked young and sexy, with a nearly obscene amount of muscular chest showing amidst our tornado of quilts and comforters.

Well, I may not be as experienced as Rhiannon, but I certainly knew how to awaken a man with a smile. And since I'd decided to love him while I was here, I may as well go all out.

"Oh, God, Shannon. You're blowing my mind." Clint's morning voice was rich with passion.

I wanted to correct him and explain that it wasn't his mind I was blowing, but my mother had taught me it was impolite to speak when one's mouth was full…

…Much later I was stretching lazily, and he was nibbling on the side of my neck, which reminded me.

"I'm hungry. Really, really hungry."

"You've certainly worked up the right to an appetite this morning, Shannon my girl." He kissed me on the forehead and jumped out of bed, pulling on his jeans and shirt. "Why don't I whip us up a real Oklahoma breakfast while you take a nice hot shower."

He didn't give me time to answer, but started toward the kitchen, definitely a man with a purpose.

"Oh…" He paused and called back to me, "I put the number to your dad's hospital room over there by the phone in case you wanted to check on him." And he disappeared into the kitchen.

I had to find my/his sweatshirt again (imagine that). Then I was pleased to hear Dad's voice sounding stronger and less under the influence. Seems Mama Parker was due to arrive at any moment. Dad reported that the doc said he'd probably be going home tomorrow, which was a good thing because he was damn tired of hospital food and bedpans.

The kitchen floor was still cold as I hurried past. Clint was busy frying something that smelled exquisite (it is an unspoken rule that an Oklahoma breakfast has to include several fried foods to be "authentic"), but he called, "Did you get ahold of your dad?"

"Yeah—he's fine. Going home tomorrow with Mama Parker."

I heard him grunt a reply as I headed eagerly for my long hot shower. After I soaked under the steaming rivulets, towel dried and re-dressed in the clothes I'd worn the day before (which Clint must have slipped inside the door while I was luxuriating in the World of Hot Water), I took my time applying Rhiannon's ultra-expensive and ultra-complimentary makeup. My mind whispered that I needed to look "together" for whatever today brought—an uncomfortable slice of the future I wasn't willing to ponder at that moment.

My hair was drying into a mane of red ringlets when I entered the kitchen escorted by a cloud of hot-shower mist.

Clint welcomed me with a heart-melting smile and handed me a loaded plate.

"Good morning. I'm glad you're hungry."

"Good morning and good Lord! Did you think I was a lumberjack?" I could only stare at the mound of messy scrambled eggs (that's eggs scrambled with green peppers, mushrooms, onions, bacon and cheese), home-fried potatoes (*fried* is the key word here), sausage patties (fried) and biscuits (ladled with real butter and honey).

"It's good for an expectant mother to eat." He still had that wonderful smile on his face.

"If I keep eating like this I can expect to be twice my size by the time I am a mother," I grumbled, but that didn't stop me from digging into the delicious, fatty mess.

When I came up for air, I noticed Clint was watching me intently.

"What?" I sputtered, taking a gulp of hot tea to clear my mouth.

"I wonder if you can ever know how happy you made me last night…" He paused and the intense look melted into a boyish grin. "And this morning."

"I—" I started to respond by reminding him of the reality of our situation, that I was still going to return to Partholon and ClanFintan. But I couldn't say the words. I didn't know what would happen to him after I left. I didn't even want to think about it. I just knew that for our time together I felt compelled to bring him happiness.

"I'm glad," I whispered.

He reached across the space that separated us and took my hand. Raising it to his lips, he turned it so that he could kiss the spot where my pulse beat strongly against my skin. For a moment I saw the painful reflection of reality in his eyes, and then I pulled him to me and kissed his sensuous lips.

He knows. The words sank into my mind and I felt an unexpectedly protective surge. I wanted to scream, THEN HELP HIM! MAKE HIM NOT LOVE ME! But I knew it couldn't be, and, in a growing part of my mind I recognized the fact that I didn't want him to change. I wanted his love.

Perhaps in a way I was as selfish as Rhiannon.

"Your turn!" I chirped, forcing my thoughts away from the morose. Before he could resist I pushed him toward the bathroom. "I won't put anything away. I'll just wash and dry and leave it stacked in a mess. Don't worry—" I gave him a final shove "—you can still pick up after me." Chuckling, he disappeared through the door.

Under normal circumstances I don't enjoy cleaning up dishes. Let's face it, twenty-four-hour maid service is one thing that is very appealing about the life of being a Partholonian Goddess Incarnate. But this morning I relished the mundane, homey ritual. I liked scraping the plates and dipping them in the soapy water (Clint must be part of the anti-dishwasher sect, too. I can't image that except for him and my parents they have much membership, though.). Ignoring my words to him, I neatly stacked the dried dishes, pots, pans and utensils. Then my nose led me to find the trash can that nested under the sink.

"Phew! Smells like something died in here—last week." I held my breath and tied off the white Hefty bag, pulled it out of the waste can and strode quickly to the front door, where I shoved my feet into Clint's huge boots. "I'll just set you outside the porch and let Clint worry about where you'll go from there," I told the stinking plastic bag as I opened the front door.

The moment I stepped out onto the porch my body became very still. Something was wrong, very wrong. The texture of the air seemed to have changed. Yes, it was still snowing, now even harder than it had since the blizzard had begun, but it wasn't the whiteness that was so disconcerting; it was the intensity in the air. Where before the covering of white had made the forest look well dressed and ready for a gala event, this morning the layer of snow had become a white shroud drawn across the face of death.

I dropped the bag and stumbled quickly to the tree line.

Pressing my hands against the bark of the first tree I reached, a medium-size hackberry, I closed my eyes and concentrated.

"What has happened?" I whispered earnestly.

Evil comes, Beloved of the Goddess. The tree's voice was distant and sounded strained.

"Is it here right now?" I looked wildly around, feeling the skin at the back of my neck crawl.

It has entered the forest. She is calling it.

"She!" I yelled. "You mean the one who perverts Epona's will?"

This time the tree's voice sounded stronger. *Yes, Chosen One.*

"Where is she now?"

Within the sacred grove.

"Thank you!" I patted the bark and tried to ignore the nervous churning in my stomach.

Be vigilant, Beloved of the Goddess.

"I'll sure as hell try," I mumbled as I scrambled, shivering, back to the cabin.

Clint stood in the doorway, fully dressed and still pink from the shower. "Is it time?" he asked woodenly.

"Yes." I hustled past him, filling him in as I kicked off his boots and reached for my own. "I knew something was wrong as soon as I stepped outside. The tree confirmed it. Rhiannon's in the clearing."

"And Nuada's on his way there to meet her," he finished for me.

I nodded.

Suddenly he seized me by the shoulders and forced me to meet his eyes. "You don't have to confront her. I'll go. I'll tell her what she wants to hear, that I never really wanted you. That I finally realize the only woman I want to be with is her. I'll explain that you were so upset when you found out I chose her that you went through the divide back to Partholon. You can leave in the Hummer right now. Go to your dad's. The trees will tell you when it's safe to come back, and then you can re-enter Partholon." He smiled sadly. "I doubt if you ever really needed me to return. You have enough power yourself."

"What about Nuada?" I asked quietly.

"When I join with her she won't need him anymore. I'll convince her to send him back to hell or wherever."

I shook my head slowly. "You know that won't work, Clint. Rhiannon is beyond reason. She might be placated enough to leave me alone if you return to her, but she'll never have enough power." As I spoke, I reasoned through things that I'd been shoving into the back of my mind. "Rhiannon didn't just wake up a couple of days ago and decide to pull Nuada over here." My eyes narrowed as I considered this. "For several weeks before you called me back I had been overwhelmed with depressing thoughts. I even imagined I saw weird shadows just past the edges of my vision." I gave a sarcastic snort. "When I realized I was pregnant I decided it was probably just hormones acting up and making me ultra-emotional, but I don't think so anymore. I think Rhiannon has been calling more than just Nuada to her. She's been messing with the evil of Pryderi. It took Rhiannon quite some time to awaken Nuada, and during that time he, and the dark power she was summoning him with, was being drawn to me instead of her, maybe because Partholon is closer than this world to wherever his death had banished him. My guess is that Pryderi's evil helped to cause the Fomorian war, and now it's helping to resurrect Nuada."

"I don't doubt what you're saying. All I'm saying is that Rhianon could still send him back."

"Maybe, but you know she wouldn't. From my trip to witness the past I learned one thing for sure—Rhiannon is a control freak. She has to believe she is in control of every aspect of her life, and to her way of reasoning, Nuada's power would just be one more tool she could use to maintain that control. It wouldn't matter to her if that power came from evil." I shook my head again. "No, we go together and we get rid of Nuada. Dealing with Rhiannon is secondary."

And then I have to return to Partholon where I belong.

I didn't say the words aloud, but I saw the knowledge reflected unspoken in Clint's eyes. Without hesitation I stepped into his arms and drew his lips down to mine, kissing him deeply, trying to tell him with my mouth the words I wouldn't allow myself to speak. How sorry I was. How much I wished it was different—and how much I wouldn't change one moment of last night.

"Dress in layers," Clint said, handing me his favorite sweatshirt. He watched with a possessive smile as I pulled it on over the shirt I already wore.

"Got an extra pair of socks?" I asked.

He nodded and retrieved another pair for both of us. We dressed methodically in silence. I glanced under my lashes at him. Is this how he looked when he used to put on his flight suit and head out to enter the cockpit of his fighter jet? Had he fought in Desert Storm? His face looked stern but serene, like nothing could bother him. Like he was used to going into battle. There were so many things about him I didn't know—so many things I'd like to discover.

"I want you to wear one of my coats." He pulled two

thick, down ski-type jackets from the coat closet. "You'll need to have plenty of room to move."

He handed me one of the coats, then reached back into the dark recesses of a high shelf in the closet. He grabbed something black and heavy, pulling it out with a metallic thump. I heard a click as he shoved a clip into the gun's handle.

He felt my eyes on him and turned slowly to face me.

"Promise me you won't do it," I said stonily.

He hesitated, searching my eyes.

"I couldn't bear it if you killed her." Just thinking about it made my heart feel like it might beat out of my chest.

"I swear to you that I will draw none of her blood." His voice took on a singsong quality, as if he has intoning a spell. The air around us shimmered, and for a moment I felt a presence like the beating of hummingbird wings.

"Thank you, Clint," I said solemnly.

"Dress yourself and let's get going." The gun fit in a black nylon holster, which was attached to a belt. Clint slung it around his hips with a brisk movement that said this was not the first time he had carried a gun.

I zipped my coat and pulled on my gloves and hat. "Ready," I said. My voice sounded too loud.

"Remember, I'll always love you, Shannon my girl. Wherever you are."

His kiss was hard. Then he opened the door and we stepped into the deadly quiet of the morning.

The deep snow was like walking through water. The fat, cotton-like flakes had morphed into the steady stinging beads that were snow mixed with ice. There was no wind and the icy crystals quickly covered our hats and shoulders with a slick film. I was relieved when we entered the heart of the forest. There the enormous limbs of the intermeshing trees, though naked in their winter hibernation, served as a canopy to shield us from the worst of the storm.

And I was gratified when the ethereal echo of the welcoming whispers began.

We greet you, Beloved of the Goddess!

Hail, Epona!

Welcome, Chosen One!

The path widened and I was able to walk next to Clint. I wrapped my arm through his.

"Are the trees talking to you again?" He smiled down at me.

"Can you hear them, too?"

"No." He held a branch back so it didn't smack me in the face. I let my fingers trail over it, loving the surge of warmth that melted through my gloves. "The forest doesn't speak to me like it does to you."

We had a long walk ahead of us and curiosity was gnawing at me. "Clint, you told me that you had always liked the forest and camping and stuff like that." Yuck, I thought. "But you didn't tell me exactly how you came to be so in tune with the forest. How did you discover you could draw energy from the trees if they don't talk to you?"

Clint took a deep breath. He suddenly seemed stiff and withdrawn. I untangled my arm from his so I could squeeze his hand and tug imploringly at him. "Please tell me. I need to understand."

He took another deep breath and finally squeezed my hand back. "Well, Shannon my girl, it's not something I like to talk about, but maybe you should know."

I raised my eyebrows at him, afraid if I said too much he'd have second thoughts about talking.

"After my accident I was in the hospital for about six months. Then rehab seemed to go on forever. Friends who had at first come to visit regularly quit coming by, or when they did they acted jittery, like they felt guilty for not wanting to be there." He barked a self-effacing laugh. "Hell, I didn't blame them. Who wants to hang out with an invalid in the hospital? After a while I was alone."

"What about your family, your mom and dad, brothers and sisters?"

"They live in Florida."

"No girlfriend?" I tried not to grind my teeth.

"I had one, but it became unmistakably clear that Ginger had only been interested in dating a fighter pilot, not a broken-down ex-flyboy."

I looked at him and almost laughed out loud. He was strong and handsome, the antithesis of a broken-down anything. But, then again, what can you expect from a woman named Ginger? Please.

"No ex-wife who came sniffing back around?" I sounded like a prying bitch, even to me.

"Sure, she brought my son by the hospital for a little while." He smiled sadly. "I thought she was being kind, but pretty soon it was obvious that she liked the publicity and the attention. When my fifteen minutes of fame ran out, so did she."

"You still loved her?" I hated that I felt so damn jealous.

"No, we married way too young and as we grew up we grew apart. The divorce was mutual and amiable." He shrugged. "But I could have used a real friend when I was in the hospital, and it would have been nice if there had been at least that much left between us."

The resignation in his voice made my heart hurt, and something he'd said surfaced through all the unspoken questions that were whirling around in my mind, impatiently waiting for me to ask him. He had a son.

"What about your son?" It made me feel odd to think about Clint having a child. Part of me wanted to be glad he had someone, and another part of me felt very jealous. Again.

He blew a long breath through his mouth. "Not much to say about Eddy. We don't get along. I've never understood it, but it always seemed the harder I tried to find something in common with him, or to figure out ways to get close to him, the more he withdrew from me. I used to blame his mom, but that's not fair. The boy and I just don't speak the same language."

I didn't know what to say. I found it hard to believe any boy wouldn't be thrilled that his father was a fighter pilot, and wouldn't rush to emulate him.

He moved his shoulders restlessly. "It used to eat at me, and after the divorce I tried to force him to spend time with me. He had just turned thirteen when I had the accident. I was in bad shape for so long I didn't see him for months, damn close to a year. When I finally left the hospital he acted like being around me scared him. I couldn't figure out why. I still can't figure it out. So I stepped away."

Clint paused and seemed to collect himself. When he started speaking again instead of his voice being tinged with guilt, he sounded like he'd come to peace with himself. "He's eighteen now. A young man. Last I heard he joined a rock band. His mom called me not long ago. She's worried about him, seems he's into drugs. I tried to talk to him and he shut me out. Again. Basically, he knows where I am, and he knows my door is always open to him if he's willing to get help. Maybe one day the part of me that's inside him will wake up. I'd like that, and I think that no matter how tough he pretends to be, he would, too."

"One thing I learned from ten years of teaching is that sometimes even good people have messed-up kids," I said quietly.

Clint squeezed my hand again and continued, "So, about two years ago I found myself alone. I couldn't fly fighters anymore. The friends I'd known for most of my life were uncomfortable around me. I didn't know what to do with myself." He paused to help me over a drift that was blocking our way. "I was on a fishing trip, staying at a lodge not far from here. Fish weren't biting, of course, so I pulled the boat to the shore and decided to hike up the side of a cliff and do some deep thinking."

Clint's voice died and we walked on in silence.

"And that's when you found out you had an affinity with the trees?" I prompted.

"Yes," he said slowly. "But only after I tried to kill myself."

"What!" I stopped walking.

He wouldn't look at me, but tugged at my hand so I had to keep walking to keep up with him.

"The deep thinking I did led me to the conclusion that I had no damn reason whatsoever to live. So I pulled out my rifle and leaned against the trunk of a huge oak, trying to find some way to blow my head off." His voice roughened as he remembered. "And the tree spoke to me. I haven't heard one that clearly since. I thought I was going nuts at first, but with its voice came such a—" he hesitated, searching for the right words "—a feeling of acceptance that I had to believe."

I understood exactly what he meant. "What did it say to you?" I asked quietly.

"It called me Shaman and told me to awake."

Clint was blushing adorably as he hurried to finish his story.

"So I pulled all my money out of the bank, cashed in some CDs and bought this place. And made new friends." This time his laugh was free of sarcasm. "Mostly old Indians. There're a lot of Choctaw who still live in this area. They try to keep the old ways alive. I'm learning how to help them, which usually means driving them to the doctor, or to the store for supplies, but sometimes it means just sitting and listening."

"You have people to take care of, too," I said to him.

"I guess that's something we have in common."

I didn't respond because it wasn't myself I had been comparing him to—it was the other High Shaman in my life.

"So you don't actually hear the trees speak anymore?"

"I just feel them. Sometimes they put ideas into my mind, or warn me of a storm. Once in a while I'll stumble onto an especially ancient tree, like the ones in the grove, and I can hear it whisper the word *Shaman*." His face radiated the joy of that single word.

The word that had saved his life.

"Anything else you want to know, my Lady?" He bowed me past another low-hanging branch.

"Yes—I want to know what it's like to fly an F–16."

His face took on a faraway expression. "Shannon my girl, the power…it's unbelievable. And it's all at your fingertips. It becomes a part of you. The cockpit is a glass bubble. You can see all around you. No sides, no boundaries. Imagine that the visibility is like you're flying on the end of a broomstick." He laughed. It was a joyous sound.

"Is that some kind of crack about me being a witch? I'll have you know I'm a Goddess Incarnate, and we don't use broomsticks to fly." Please. How gauche.

He continued speaking, pointedly ignoring my quip. "The view is like you're hanging out there in the air, and the jet becomes an extension of your body. You become pure power."

I blinked in surprise. "Like when I channeled the energy of the trees through my body?"

"Yeah, probably something a lot like that. It's bigger than you. You're just along for the ride."

"And what a ride!" We smiled at each other like gleeful children and once again linked arms, moving ever closer to the heart of the forest.

Soon the path took an abrupt right turn, climbed steeply and narrowed. Looking around, I realized I recognized this distinctive area. We couldn't be far from the grove. I let Clint go ahead of me, and as he turned to give me a hand up, his foot slid off the side of a snow-crusted rock.

"Damn!" he cursed, catching his balance by twisting his weight around, arms flailing. I saw a flash of pain cross his face.

Scrambling up after him, I said breathlessly, "Hey, I thought I'd healed you from that back pain last night." Hadn't I? That's what it had seemed like to me.

Regaining his balance he grabbed my hand and pulled me up next to him.

"Shannon my girl, it wasn't my back that you healed." Then he turned and started quickly down the narrow path.

I hurried after him. I hadn't healed his back? I was sure that I had felt pain beneath my fingertips. I remembered focusing the energy within me through my hands and into him, and he had responded—I was sure of it.

He needs you, My Chosen One.

Epona's words came back clearly to my searching memory. I stomped after Clint, my mind whirring. What was happening to me? What was I becoming? I hugged myself, feeling suddenly insecure and frightened.

A Goddess speaks to me. And, more than that (as if I needed more), it was apparent she was using me to impact people's lives, not just in an ancient world where they were used to that kind of thing, but here in the good old US of A.

But I'm not a spiritual leader or valiant modern-day Joan of Arc. I'm just a misplaced English teacher who is in love with one too many men/horses/whatever.

A wordless sound flowed across my mind, tickling my senses like the sweetest laughter imaginable.

Joan was impetuous, too.

Oh, friggin great. I'm being compared to Joan of Arc.

"If memory serves me correctly, Joan didn't end up too well. You know," I whispered into the air, "arrested and tried for heresy…blah…blah…burned at the stake."

"Did you say something, Shannon?" Clint called over his shoulder.

"Just complaining about the weather," I yelled back, scrambling to catch up with him.

We rounded another sharp right turn just as I rejoined Clint. The trail had widened a little and I could walk beside him again. He took my hand and we continued doggedly forward. Every few feet I'd reach out and let my hand brush against the nearest tree. I thoroughly enjoyed the feeling of warmth and homecoming. The contact with the ancient forest filled me. Looking around, I soaked in the beauty of the untamed wilderness. Just this one little path—we move off of it and we'd be smack in the middle of a forest as deep and thick as any I'd seen in Partholon.

Distracted by the joy I felt immersed within the forest, I didn't notice Clint's tense silence.

I drew in a deep breath. "Jeesh, even the air smells different out here. It's cleaner, more alive." When Clint didn't respond I elbowed him. "Come on, you have to feel it, too."

He responded with a preoccupied grunt. He's such a guy.

Not letting him spoil my Marlin-Perkins-Mutual-of-Omaha-Wild-Kingdom moment, I gawked at the forest. The overhead tangle of snow-covered limbs lent us the facade of traveling through a canopied world. Even though some of the icy crystals escaped the clutching branches, it still appeared that we were encapsulated in a winter wonderland. Kind of like being trapped in one of those snow globes. Weird, but not altogether unpleasant.

"This place is just damn lovely," I said with my usual delicate vernacular.

"Shush," Clint shushed me.

"Wh—" I started to question him and his free hand covered my mouth.

I shut up but glared at him. He took his hand slowly from

my mouth, and pointed off to the left of our path. Putting his lips against my ear, he whispered, "Snowmobile tracks."

I blinked in surprise. Sure enough, not far from the path were the clear tracks of two snowmobiles. They shadowed the path for a few more feet, before crossing over it and continuing into the forest to our right. Again Clint's mouth was against my ear. Not that I minded.

"This is where we leave the path. Those tracks are heading directly to the grove."

I swallowed as we left the path, following the well-marked ruts. I thought back, trying to remember how long the walk had been from the path to the grove. It hadn't seemed very far. Granted, it hadn't been snow-packed and had been much easier to walk through a few days ago, but it couldn't be much farther. I glanced at Clint's stony profile. We needed to get something straight. I stopped and pulled at his arm till he bent so that his ear was close to my mouth, then I whispered urgently, "I want to be alone when I confront her."

Clint sucked air and I was sure he was getting ready for some kind of Fighter Pilot Military Guy Tirade (if I were a guy this would be a pissing contest). I shook him and let him get a good look at my face. He stopped trying to speak and gave me the universal look for "Go ahead and say whatever you have to say, which will definitely piss me off."

I continued whispering. "Let me talk to her face-to-face. You may be surprised at her reaction. Maybe seeing me will be such a jolt that I can talk some sense into her."

He looked skeptical.

"Remember how egocentric and self-centered she is.

Don't I look just like her?" Well, I added to myself, actually, she was looking lots better than I was last time I saw her, but… "She might be so shocked or intrigued or whatever, when she sees me that I can reason with her."

He grunted the male sound for "I don't like it but you get your way."

"You can hide at the edge of the tree line. If things get crazy you'll be close enough to help me out of whatever mess I've gotten myself into."

He smiled at my words and turned his head, catching my lips off guard with a quick, endearing kiss. "All right. We'll do it your way," he whispered.

"Good," I said.

"Your way at first," he mumbled.

Mr. Have To Have the Last Word and I crept forward, moving slowly and trying to be as soundless as possible. When Clint stopped I didn't need any prompting to stay quiet. Silently he mouthed, *the tree line,* then he pointed to a thick area of trees only about twenty feet ahead of us. Through their tangled branches I could barely make out a break in the forest.

Clint elbowed me and pointed to a nest of what looked like wild black raspberry bushes. They stretched around the side of the clearing, just inside the tree line. They were only about waist high, but the snow had carpeted them so that they reminded me of blobs of cotton candy, only prickly.

"Those berry thickets are all around the outside of the grove." Even though Clint's lips were pressed against my ear, I had to strain to hear his words. "I'm going to make my way around until I'm closer to the two trees. That's probably where she'll be. Doubt if she'll notice me in the shadows once she gets a bead on you."

I didn't like the sound of that, but I stayed silent.

"I'll be close enough if you need me. I hope."

I kissed him quickly and stood silently while I watched him step outside the snowmobile tracks and begin making his way stealthily around the tree line. When the forest swallowed him I squared my shoulders and marched forward, no longer making any attempt at silence.

"I'll be needing your help now, Epona," I said aloud.

I couldn't be certain, but I thought I heard the limbs of the trees closest to me rustle in response.

I stepped through the tree line and into the knee-deep snow that covered the grove.

5

The first thing I noticed was the amazing green of the pin oaks. Even seen through the steadily falling snow, the vibrancy of their healthy middle-of-the-summer foliage was quite a shock. The eerie familiarity of the area clouded my eyes, and for a moment all I could see was how distinctly this place mirrored the grove in Partholon. Of course, the snow was all wrong, and the mechanical tracks didn't fit…

…My eyes followed those tracks until they found the two vehicles that had made them. They had been left riderless beside the little stream that twisted and spilled though the clearing. I looked beyond them and let my eyes travel from the green of the oak leaves down to the moss-covered trunks, and then to the two people near them.

Rhiannon stood close to the tree that grew on the left

side of the brook just outside of the vague outline of what looked like the same kind of melted circle she had cast in the grove in Chicago. The circle encompassed both trees and the area of the brook that ran between them. The unmistakable shape of Bres huddled directly in the middle of the circle. He was on his knees, facing Rhiannon, whose back was to me. I could see that his chest was bare, which made me feel cold for him. I peeked quickly down, hoping the rest of him was covered. I breathed a prayer of thanks to my Goddess; he had on a pair of jeans. If his head had been raised he would have easily seen me, but his head was bowed and his hands were clasped in front of him as if he was deeply in prayer.

The thought of what he might be praying to made my stomach clench.

Rhiannon wore the same red-fox coat she had been wearing in Chicago. Well, she'd worn it for a little while, anyway. I started walking toward her, muttering through gritted teeth, "Damn, I hope she's not going to get naked."

Surprised she hadn't noticed me yet, I studied her as I approached. She, too, had her head bowed. Her hair was loose and stood out in an untamed mass that swirled halfway down her back. I touched my own wild curls, wondering if that's how I looked to other people. The beanie-like hat I had pulled down over my ears didn't allow for much hair flamboyance, though.

A furtive movement at the far side of the clearing drew my attention away from Rhiannon. I could just catch a glimpse of Clint's khaki green hat through the hedge not far from the two trees. I smiled, trying to telegraph silently to Clint that I appreciated his good positioning. Then I quickly recomposed my face. With my luck Rhiannon would choose that moment to notice me. She'd know instantly what that foolish grin meant. I wasn't entirely sure why I didn't want her to know Clint was with me, but I knew it was wise to trust my instincts; often a Goddess guided them.

My attention refocused on Rhiannon. Her hands weren't clasped before her, as were Bres's. Instead, she held them out from the sides of her body, fingers pointed down and palms open but slanted, like an upside-down victory V.

Upside-down victory. In Rhiannon's opinion that would be me triumphing over her.

"Hope that's prophetic," I muttered.

The sound of my voice carried clearly across the silent glade. Rhiannon spun around. When our eyes met we froze. We were only separated by a few yards of space. Snow fell in sparkling crystal beads all around us, like a goddess was shaking white glitter from the clouds. Even though it was not yet noon the sky had darkened, intensifying the otherworldly feel of the ancient place.

Rhiannon and I blinked at the same moment. I was just thinking that she had on too much makeup when her bronze-glossed lips parted. The voice that emerged was mine, but it had Partholon's lilting accent.

"You are not as attractive as I."

That sure as hell broke the spell. "Really?" I quipped. "I was just thinking you have on too damn much makeup and it makes you look older than I look."

One of her eyebrows shot up and she crossed her arms in a gesture I automatically mirrored.

"Why are you here, Shannon?" She got right to the point.

"I think you and I need to talk." Shit, this was weird.

She smiled, and laughed softly. "And why would I wish to speak with you, *schoolteacher?*" She drew out the title like it was an insult.

Don't get mad, I told myself. Take a breath. Cool down.

"Lots of reasons. We seem to have many things in common. I thought it'd be interesting to get to know you." I hadn't expected to say that, but my intuition was telling me to get her talking.

She narrowed her eyes, making fine lines appear over her otherwise flawless face. (Note to self: don't squint.)

"I have no interest in getting to know you." But something about the tone of her voice said she wasn't being entirely honest with me.

Or herself. The words fluttered through my mind.

"Oh, please!" This time I laughed. "You have to be as curious as I am. Look at us! We're the same. Frizz out my hair, peel off some of your makeup, give me a big fur coat and we'd be mirror images." I uncrossed my arms. "You have to have a few questions you'd like to ask me. I know I have a zillion I want to ask you."

"What is a zillion?"

"There! That's a question. A zillion is an American slang term for lots and lots." Before she could say anything I jumped in. "Now *I* have a question." I motioned in the direction of Bres, who was still kneeling in the middle of the circle. He seemed totally oblivious to my presence. "What the hell is boyfriend doing over there?"

Rhiannon's expression, which had relaxed momentarily, shifted into sly guardedness. "Bres is not my boyfriend. He is my servant, bound to me by blood. He is doing my bidding."

"That sounds very *Dark Shadows*–like, but you're not making much sense. How about putting it in current-day American English so I can understand you?"

I thought for a second she was going to explode into one of the Rhiannon fits I'd heard so much about from Alanna, but apparently she mentally regrouped because instead she simply said, "Very well." With a bronze-tipped manicured nail she pointed to Bres then made a graceful, sweeping arch with her arm, like she was encompassing the area that surrounded us. "Bres is readying himself for The Call."

That didn't sound good.

"I still don't understand."

"I forget that you are ignorant of the ancient ways, and that it is only in appearance you mirror me," she said condescendingly. I felt my teeth set. "I am calling forth a protector, and Bres will be the vessel it inhabits."

"Good God!" I sputtered as the meaning of her words came clear. "Do you think Nuada is a fucking bodyguard?" I felt chills shudder the length of my body.

"Nuada!" she snapped. "That is the name the spirit has used. How do you know this?"

"Because I helped kill him back in Partholon! He's not some kind of benevolent protector, he's pure evil. You've called alive the spirit of the leader of the demonic creatures that almost destroyed your old world."

"Then this Nuada is very powerful?" Instead of being shocked she looked thoughtful.

"Rhiannon, he's evil. He won't be anyone's protector. He destroys lives not saves them." I knew by the satisfied expression on her face that I wasn't getting through to her. I took a deep breath and added, "He killed your father."

"You lie!" her voice snapped.

"I'm sorry. I hate telling you this way, but your father's been dead almost six months. I watched it happen. The Fomorians overran MacCallan Castle. The men weren't ready. They didn't stand a chance." I paused to stop the shaking in my voice. Having almost lost my own father recently I empathized deeply with Rhiannon's loss. "Epona took me on a Magic Sleep and let me witness it. He fought nobly, taking down dozens of those creatures with him. He died a hero's death."

Rhiannon's face had drained of all color.

"When you called Nuada into this world he came through this glade at the same time I did, so he found me instead of you. He went to my home." I spoke the words clearly and slowly. "He almost killed *my* father."

"Lies," she hissed. "You tell these lies because you can not bear the thought of me being more powerful than you."

"I don't give a shit how powerful you are, you moron!" I spit back at her. "I don't even want to friggin *be* in this world. I'd be back in Partholon by now if you hadn't resurrected that damn creature and brought him here. The only reason I'm still in Oklahoma is because I need to clean up your mess. Again."

"You will not speak to me like this." Her voice had gone flat and dangerous. Even her expression had shifted into something that looked like no reflection my mirror had ever shown me. She was suddenly a very foreign being.

"Look, Rhiannon. You're not in Partholon anymore, and I'm not one of your bullied slaves. You don't scare me and I'll speak to you any damn way I want to speak to you. I wanted to be nice to you, especially after Epona showed me what happened in your past to make you so damn hateful."

Rhiannon's body jerked like I'd struck her, but I kept talking.

"But you're not making this very easy. I think your problem is you've never been told no, so you blundered through your spoiled brat of a life screwing up at every turn. Now you're a selfish, hateful bitch. Under normal circumstances I'd leave you alone to plow your way through several divorces and hope you eventually come to realize you need some serious therapy, but the problem with that is you've gone over to the friggin Dark Side and somehow managed to unleash a malevolent, crazed being into this world. Shit, Rhiannon, in case you don't know it," I said sarcastically, "it doesn't usually blizzard in Oklahoma. It's unnatural, just like the magic you've been working." I took a step closer to her. "Now I want you to friggin send that damn creature back to hell or wherever so I can get back to where I belong."

"I will send the creature—" Rhiannon's voice was cold and tightly controlled. "To where he belongs. Watch and learn, schoolteacher."

Abruptly she turned from me and with a wordless shout she raised her arms over her head. Bres's silent prayer suddenly became audible. The words were unrecognizable, but my body's reaction to them was intense. The hair on my arms stood on end and I felt power surround me as if we had been caught in the middle of an electrical storm. Then Rhiannon's lilting accent joined Bres's harsh, guttural voice. She stepped closer to him, but I noticed she was careful not to cross the melted circumference of the circle.

Without raising his head he reached toward her, unclasping his hands. An object nestled against his open palm.

Even in the gray light of the snow-filtered day the blade glittered dangerously.

"Oh, friggin great," I muttered, readying myself to either rush forward and knock the blade from his hand, or hide my eyes like I was watching a scary movie. While I was still deciding which I should do, Bres raised his face, and I was horrified to see his features change, shift, reform like he'd been incompletely fashioned from unfired clay. First his mouth and nose closed, appearing to be seared shut, and then his eyes glowed and glared. Then they weren't eyes anymore, but cavernous black holes, and his mouth was a fanged horror. His face changed again, and I was staring at the most incredibly beautiful man I'd ever seen. I blinked and swallowed bile, and he was once again skeletal Bres.

Rhiannon didn't react at all to his awful transformation. She took the knife from him, and in two quick, jerky motions like she was some kind of demented, bad-spelling Zorro, she slashed a huge red X across his chest. Instantly blood began seeping from the wounds and trickling down his bare skin.

At the appearance of the blood, the tempo of their litany increased dramatically. From the corner of my vision the movement of a dark shape flickered. Turning quickly in the direction of the shape, I felt my stomach clench. My own blood went cold.

The inky blackness surged forward. Rhiannon must have sensed his presence because she turned, too. When she saw the oil-like shape her eyes narrowed and the words of her litany changed, but still the only thing recognizable about it was the creature's name.

"Nuada eirich mo dhu! Nuada eirich mo dhu! Nuada eirich mo dhu..."

It went on and on, like a stuck record. I watched as the blackness that was Nuada began to rise up and solidify into a recognizable form. Talons grew from appendages that resembled hands. Legs separated with a quiver and took on humanoid form. And wings spread. His face rippled and a mouthlike maw opened to form words.

"Female," the words gurgled from his throat. "I am here at your bidding."

His attention was focused on Rhiannon. He didn't seem to notice my presence.

"I honor your obedience…" Rhiannon's voice was seductive. "And now I further command you to inhabit the body of my servant."

Something that may have been laughter bubbled from his horrible mouth. "You have the power to awaken me, female. But your pitiful blood offering is not enough to command me." He slithered closer to where we stood. "You have been a fool. I have no desire to be your servant, but I do desire to taste of you."

With unexpected quickness, Rhiannon lunged forward and grabbed my arm.

"What the hell are you doing!" I yelled, trying to pull away from her and still keep an eye on Nuada, who kept moving closer to us. At my shout he halted.

"I see there are two of you," his voice whispered. "All the better, females. All the better." His laughter hissed.

Suddenly Rhiannon pulled me roughly into her, and in the same swift, sure movement she brought up the hand that held the stiletto. Then everything happened very quickly, like someone had pressed a giant fast-forward button and our lives responded. I felt a searing pain in my side, and something sharp crunched sickeningly against my rib.

My thoughts fluttered wildly. Oh, Goddess! Has she killed my daughter? My body went numb and I felt nothing except the damp warmth of blood. My knees were weak. Through the odd humming in my ears I heard Clint's agonized shout.

Cruelly Rhiannon slashed the material that had been my coat, and with a great ripping sound she tore through the layers of clothing that were already becoming red soaked, exposing the deep, ugly wound high on my left side. I felt like I had been turned to stone as I watched her pink tongue snake out and lick the blood from the knife blade.

At the sight of my blood Nuada's body quivered and jerked spasmodically.

"Now I command you!" Rhiannon's voice sounded magnified as it echoed through the glade. "With this blood you are bound to me—for it is as if I sacrificed my blood and my body—the blood and body of a Priestess, Epona's own Chosen. You must obey." I felt my knees give way, but Rhiannon's unnatural strength held me erect so that I was still facing Nuada. "Enter my servant!" she shrieked.

At her final command Nuada's body lost all semblance of form, and pooled black and poisonous against the clean whiteness of the snow-covered glade. The oily blackness that was Nuada surged forward, entering the circle at the same instant Clint burst from the tree line. It covered Bres's chanting body. The slick surface quivered for a moment, then Bres's body absorbed Nuada. His chanting stopped and slowly he lifted his head. Bres's eyes opened. They glowed red.

"Shannon!" Clint's voice sounded far away, but I could see that he was just feet from me. I tried to answer him, but Rhiannon hurled me at him with a snarl.

"I should have known you would be here."

I felt Clint's arms enclose me, and he dropped to his knees, trying to cradle my body protectively.

"What have you done, Rhiannon?" Clint's voice broke and he pulled frantically at his scarf, then balled it in his hand and pressed it against the bleeding wound in my side.

"And I should have known you would choose her," Rhiannon's voice dripped with sarcasm. "You have always been weak. I pray that your daughter will be born with my strength."

I felt Clint jerk as if she had slapped him. "Daughter…no, you couldn't be."

Rhiannon laughed. "Of course I could be. Though I haven't decided yet whether I'll actually keep this child or not."

Clint shifted me in his arms so that he could free his right hand. I felt him unzip his coat and reach within. When his hand emerged it held the gun. His aim was rock steady as he pointed the muzzle at Rhiannon.

Her body went very still, and I saw her eyes flicker back and forth from Clint to the man-creature that crouched motionless within the circle.

"I should have killed you the night I realized what you were." Clint sounded calm and rational, totally at odds with the bizarre situation.

"But you could not kill me," Rhiannon purred. "Instead, you played our little games. Do not pretend you do not still remember the feel of your hard cock as it entered my body and pounded into me over and over…and as we did other things in the dark of the night. Remember how your blood spurted with your seed as you let me slice open that throbbing cock, and then orgasm in my mouth."

Clint's arm tightened around me when he answered. "Until last night I would have said you were right. I have been haunted by the things we did together…" Clint's eyes flashed to Bres's still form. "…All of us. But no more. I've been healed of you and your filth." I could feel his muscles tense as his hand tightened around the gun. "The best thing I could do for this world would be to put you, and any child you conceived, out of your misery."

It took a tremendous effort for me to force my hand to move to Clint's arm. At my touch his eyes found mine.

"Remember your promise." My voice was stronger than I imagined it would be. It sounded ethereal and otherworldly, like it hadn't emerged from my body at all. "You gave me your oath."

Clint's jaw clenched and I watched him war with himself. Slowly, he lowered the hand that held the gun.

Rhiannon's mocking laughter surrounded us.

"Weak! Always weak. What a broken, pitiful shadow you are of what you might have been. You are no threat to me." Still laughing, she turned her back on us and stalked to the edge of the circle.

She stopped inches from the melted snow. The Bres creature devoured her with his red-glowing eyes.

"Nuada…" The name rolled seductively off her tongue. "You did not think me powerful enough to command your obedience. Now who has been the fool?" Rhiannon's breathy voice demanded.

"I have been the fool, mistress," the voice of the man who had once been Bres echoed liquidly.

"And who will you now obey, Nuada?" she prompted.

The newly inhabited body twitched spasmodically. The answer was almost a snarl.

"I will obey you, mistress." The words were subservient, but his tone was dangerously condescending, as if he spoke to an overindulged child.

Suddenly Rhiannon's hand shot out, striking the body that held Nuada viciously across the face. I noticed that when her hand broke the space above the circle the air appeared to ripple, like she had to force her hand through an invisible barrier. Instantly a thick red welt, much more pronounced than a normal open-handed slap should have produced, puckered the pale skin of Bres's face.

"You will learn the proper way to speak to me. And I will enjoy teaching you that lesson."

I felt Clint stiffen at her words and glanced at his face. It was set and hard. It was obvious he, too, had been privy to Rhiannon's perverted instruction.

"This stops now," he said with finality.

Still holding me, he shrugged out of his coat, and then one-handed pulled his thick sweater quickly over his head so that he wore only his jeans and a T-shirt. Quickly he propped the sweater behind my back so that my head and shoulder didn't have to rest against the snow-covered ground. Then he laid his coat over me. It was still warm with the heat of his body.

His movements had caused the creature's gaze to waver from its mistress, and seeing that she no longer held its full attention Rhiannon whirled around, eyes slitted dangerously.

When she saw Clint standing there her expression shifted from war-ready to amused.

"Did you, too, need another lesson in obedience?" she goaded.

"Not likely," Clint answered as he raised his gun and sighted. I took in a deep, painful breath to yell at him to stop, but the instant before he squeezed the trigger he shifted his aim from Rhiannon to the creature within the circle.

The sound of the shot was deafening, but it didn't cover the shriek of madness that tore from Rhiannon's throat as a crimson-ringed hole blossomed in the middle of the Bres creature's forehead.

"No!" she screamed as the body crumpled to its knees then fell heavily forword, exposing the bloody crater that just seconds before had been the back of Bres's head.

Rhiannon tore her eyes from the body of her servant and stared at Clint. When she spoke, spittle flaked from her bronzed lips and she looked vaguely disoriented. "You killed him. You should not have been able to harm him within the power of the drawn circle."

Clint shrugged his shoulders and met her wild gaze evenly. "It would probably help in the future if you remembered that this is Oklahoma. You're not in Partholon anymore, and bullets don't give a good goddamn about a circle of melted snow."

"Especially when they are wielded by a High Shaman," I added. Clint and Rhiannon blinked at me in surprise. My side felt like it was on fire, but my voice was amazingly strong (which I thought might either be a good sign or a sign I was having a last-minute adrenaline surge before dying tragically).

Behind Rhiannon I saw movement. Bres's dead body twitched and writhed, calling our attention back to the aforementioned circle. With a sickeningly wet sound the liquid darkness that was Nuada pulled free and lifted from the corpse.

"Oh, shit," I said.

Rhiannon's twisted smile answered my words. Her laughter bubbled hysterically and I understood suddenly that she must be totally mad.

"What will your bullets do against this, Shaman?" she sneered. Then she faced the creature. "You are still mine. My blood still holds you." She pointed a shaking finger at Clint. "Destroy him."

6

Slowly, the pool of darkness responded to Rhiannon's command by drawing itself up. As I watched in horrified silence, it began to solidify once again and the evil mound took on shape and form.

Struggling, I pushed myself painfully to a sitting position. I needed to get to a tree, any friggin tree. Plan A would, of course, be to get to one of the ancient pin oaks; I knew the power they held. But they were within the circle, and Nuada was between them and me. I looked frantically at the tree line. The nearest tree was probably a hundred feet away. Looks like it was time for Plan B.

Grinding my teeth together I tried to stand, and fell immediately and painfully back onto my butt. Seems my legs weren't going to cooperate. I opened my mouth to call Clint, and closed it again.

Clint was standing very still. He was lifting his arms slowly up and away from his body. I could hear that he was chanting, but I couldn't decipher the words.

I looked quickly from him to Rhiannon. Her attention was focused not on Clint (or on me, for that matter). Instead, she was moving methodically around the circumference of the circle, crooning the words *mo muirninn* to the re-forming creature as if it was an endearment. Every few feet she took the pointed toe of her leather boot and drew a sharp cut in the skin of the circle. When she had broken the circle in one place, she made her way around several more feet of its melted circumference, where she repeated the bizarre procedure. All the while she kept up the crooning.

Then Clint's words became audible to me and my gaze flew back to the Shaman. His aura was shimmering in a jeweled light that pulsed wildly around him, and he appeared suddenly so strong and powerful that the sight brought tears to my eyes. He was standing with his legs planted shoulder width apart. His arms were now almost straight above him. His hands appeared to reach up into the air as if he was calling the sky down upon us. His head was tilted back in the way ClanFintan had positioned himself as he called the Change to him.

Clint's voice had taken on a singsong quality totally unlike the chants I had become familiar with in Partholon. Instead, his words were punctuated with a deep, primitive beat that I could feel pulsing through the air around us. I listened intently.

> "I command a power not to be explained in simple words.

I call the spirits that support the world, the weather, all life.
I command not by words but by storm and snow and rain and the fury of the wilderness untamed.
I call the spirits that men fear, always among us yet infinitely far away.
I command with a voice so fine and gentle even innocent children cannot be afraid, for I hold the power of growing trees, the murmur of leaves rustling, the rays of the sun and the bud breaking into blossom.
I call you forth to me through the wind."

Clint's body turned to his right.

"I call you forth to me through the rain."

Again, he turned.

"I call you forth to me through the fire."

With his next words he completed his own circle.

"I call you forth to me through the earth."

As his words ended Clint's arms dropped and he peered around him as if he was just awakening from an overpowering dream. The blue of his aura was still glistening, but I saw nothing changed about him or the area that surrounded him.

Oh, Goddess, I prayed silently. If whatever he was doing

didn't work, help me get to the trees so that we stand a chance of defeating Nuada. With that thought I pushed my legs underneath me and began trying to scoot my way to the tree line. I glanced up to keep a check on how far away the elusive safety appeared.

And I blinked in confusion. Rubbing my eyes, I was sure my vision must be screwed up from my wound. Forgetting about Clint and Rhiannon, and even Nuada, I stared at the line of trees and brambly bushes that ringed the ancient clearing.

No, it wasn't a trick of my eyes. It was magic. This time it was pure Oklahoma magic.

My eyes traveled around the elliptical clearing. It was happening all around us. From within the forest, shapes began appearing. Regally, one by one they stepped out of the sheltering trees and into the grove, ancient men with faces so wizened with time that they appeared ageless. And for every living man there appeared with him the spectral, glowing shapes of several others. At first they were hard to identify as individual entities because they blended so well with the white and gray of the ever-falling snow, but the ring of ghostly warriors kept striding forward. The closer they came the more clearly I could distinguish their features.

The old men approached us, and as one they began a rhythmic chant. I couldn't understand the words, but the sound pulsed with the same primordial beat as Clint's invocation. The dead warriors did not speak, but they moved forward with lithe steps in time to the elders' call. I distinctly saw the plumed regalia of long-extinct battle dress rise and fall with each of the warrior's movements.

The ring of warriors, both living and dead, moved forward, like a noose tightening.

I tore my eyes from the incredible sight to look at Clint. A wonderful, pure power radiated from him and he, too, had joined the elders in their rhythmic chant.

I shifted my gaze from him to Rhiannon. She was oblivious to everything except destroying the circle of her own making and crooning to the creature within it. She had almost made her way around to her starting point. I looked at Nuada and saw that his slick, black body had completely reformed. He was a living shadow of the creature ClanFintan had defeated. He prowled back and forth, his attention focused on the small section of circle Rhiannon had yet to break.

I felt something brush the air around me, like someone had waved a feather duster over my body. The hazy shapes of two warriors passed so close to me I could have reached out a hand and touched their pale fringed shirts.

Greetings, Chosen One.

Several spectral thoughts invaded my mind, sounding totally different than my Goddess's bell-clear voice.

We thank you for your remembrance.

I blinked in surprise. These must be the spirits of the warriors from Nagi Road, the lost warriors. I stared in slack-jawed amazement as they followed the living elders to the edge of the melted circle.

Rhiannon's booted toe broke the final section of the circle and she stepped back with a triumphant shout, colliding with the shriveled form of the nearest elder. Shock made her feet unsure, and she almost fell, but the old Indian's strong arms held her upright.

"Stand aside, Sorceress." His voice was like the rustling of autumn leaves. "We have work to complete."

Rhiannon wrenched herself from his grasp. She looked wildly around, her wide eyes taking in the ghostly army. Its ranks had swollen until the spirits of the dead warriors filled the ancient grove.

"Do as the Shaman advises, Sorceress." Nuada's voice slithered over the last word. "I shall complete what you left undone."

But before his black-taloned feet could leave the damaged circle, the chanting of the elders had begun anew. This time there was an urgency and tension to the words. The beat had intensified until I felt my heart echo its pounding.

Nuada's dark maw opened to expose his pointed fangs and he snarled at the company of spirits. Then his eyes narrowed and he found Clint.

"There you are, Shaman." He sounded infinitely dangerous. "Now we will finish this between us."

The instant he broke free of the circle I felt a change ripple through the warriors. From all around me they gave voice to long-dead battle cries, which lifted unerringly skyward and echoed off the heavy clouds. As one they surged forward, tightening the circle of their own making.

Nuada paused before the wall of imposing spirits.

"The dead have no hold on me." Nuada gestured with one claw imperiously back to Bres's empty corpse.

"That's where you're wrong," Clint said slowly and distinctly. "Bres was an aberration from another world. And as such, he held no power over you. Those who surround you are the spirits of dead warriors, protectors of this forest and this world. I have awakened them—" I heard the gentle smile in his voice "—much as they once awakened me. Now we banish you and your evil god forever from this place in which neither of you belong, back to your realm of darkness."

With a reptilian hiss Nuada lunged toward Clint. Calling forth speed a living warrior could never hope to emulate, the first ghostly being blocked the dark creature's path and slashed out at him with the dead blade of a hatchet. Instead of passing harmlessly through Nuada's body, it sliced neatly into the dark flesh. Before the echo of Nuada's agonized scream had faded, the section of cut flesh turned to ash and dissipated into the snowy air.

A thousand extinct battle cries shrilled against the tree line as the ghostly army surged forward, enveloping Nuada's shrieking body. Soon I could see nothing but a writhing form cloaked in the angry spirits of warriors.

And then there was silence.

With the glimmer of forgotten dreams the warriors disappeared. Where Nuada had stood all that was left was a small ash-covered indentation in the white carpet.

The snow stopped falling.

"Shaman, do you have further need of us?" one of the ancient men asked Clint respectfully.

"No, my friend. Thank you." Clint's aura still framed him in a haze of sapphire.

But the elder didn't turn away immediately. Instead, he spoke solemnly to Clint. "My heart feels joy because the wound within the White Shaman has been healed." His words were enunciated beautifully, as if each separate syllable held a secret meaning of its own. Then the old man's eyes narrowed and he stepped closer to Clint, looking intently at the younger man. For a moment it was easy to imagine he was seeing inside Clint's soul.

The ancient Indian's brow furrowed into caverns of worry. "Think, my son." His scratchy voice sounded infinitely sad. "Be quite sure that is the path you would travel. It is a long one."

Surprise flickered over Clint's face, but it quickly cleared. "Thank you, Great One. I will remember."

"I will see you again, White Shaman. Until then, goodbye, my son," the old man said as he turned and made his way silently from the grove.

"Goodbye, father," Clint replied to the age-crooked back. Then his attention turned to me and he moved quickly to my side. He crouched down, pulling me close.

"Do you think you can walk?" he asked quietly.

Within his embrace I felt suddenly warm, and some of the piercing pain in my side faded.

"No!" Rhiannon screamed as she hurled herself at Clint, knife held up ready to strike.

But Clint reacted too quickly. He stood to meet her maniacal charge, and with the ease born of a true warrior's confidence he deflected her blow, twisting her wrist until the knife dropped harmlessly to the snow.

Still holding her wrist, Clint bent to retrieve the weapon, then spoke to Rhiannon with grim finality. "It's over, Rhiannon. I will tolerate no more."

"You!" she sputtered. "You! As if you could dictate the actions of a Goddess." Her voice was ugly with loathing.

"I would never assume to dictate to a Goddess, but you are not a Goddess." I was surprised by the gentleness in his voice.

"Lies!" Rhiannon yelled. "I am Epona's Chosen, Beloved of a Goddess, Her Incarnation. And I am pregnant with a Daughter of Epona."

"No," I said quietly into the empty silence that washed against her words. "You used to be her Chosen One, but you aren't now."

"I suppose you think *you* are," she hurled at me.

"Yes." I took a deep breath and shifted my weight slowly so I could meet her eyes. "Yes, I am. I didn't ask for it. At first I didn't even want it, and I don't pretend to know everything I should about it." I squared my shoulders, ignoring the pain and the new rush of wetness the movement caused. "But now I embrace it. Partholon is my choice."

Before Rhiannon could respond with her twisted reasoning, I asked, "What do the trees call you?"

She paused and seemed to consider the question. "The trees? They are here to reinforce my power, to make my magic greater."

I shook my head wearily. "They don't reinforce your power. You've been siphoning power from the land, yes, but the trees are not willingly giving it to you. Rhiannon, you've embraced Pryderi. That means you have betrayed Epona."

"Epona is selfish and jealous. She tries to bully me into only worshipping her, but I've always made my own decisions. Why should I stick with one goddess when there are many from which to choose?"

"What do the trees call you?" I repeated the question slowly, as if I was talking to a very dense child.

"They call me nothing," she snarled.

"They welcome Shannon by name as Epona's Chosen One," Clint said softly.

"No!" Rhiannon whispered.

"Yes." His voice had hardened and she stared at him as if she wanted to reach into his mind. "I have witnessed it.

Shannon is Epona's Chosen. She has been recognized in both worlds. And she, too, is pregnant with the true Daughter of Epona." She shook her head disbelievingly in jarring movements from side to side. Clint continued relentlessly. "The Goddess speaks to you no more. She has not spoken to you for quite some time. You know what we say is the truth."

She stood there, wordlessly shaking her head, and I saw myself mirrored within her. I saw everything that I had ever feared. All of my insecurities and hurts were suddenly reflected in her expression.

"I am sorry, Rhiannon." I spoke kindly to her. She was broken and I felt no victory in it, only sadness and a sense of loss.

Clint withdrew his hold on her wrist. She backed away from us through the vestiges of her circle and past the body of her servant, until she tripped on the bulging root of one of the ancient oaks. When she fell she did not get up. Her sobs washed through me as if they were my own.

Once again Clint crouched down beside me.

"Well, Shannon my girl, are you ready to go home?" He sounded resolute.

I couldn't seem to find my own voice, so I just nodded.

"First you better let me take a look at that wound."

I closed my eyes and pressed my head into his shoulder as he removed the blood-soaked scarf from the hole in my side. I sucked air as he prodded the cut.

"Sorry, love." He kissed my damp forehead. "It's a nasty cut, but it looks like your rib took the brunt of the blade. Let's see if I can fix this so that you don't bleed to death."

"That'd be nice," I said faintly.

Clint wrapped my scarf around my torso to secure the makeshift bandage in place. I tried not to make much noise, but the truth is it hurt like hell and I couldn't help whimpering.

"Do you think you can walk?" he asked when he was satisfied with his work.

"If you help me," I whispered.

"I'll always help you." He touched my cheek and his lips gently met mine. "That's what I'm here for."

Putting one arm around my shoulders and the other under my elbow, he hoisted me painfully to my feet.

"Oh, shit, that hurts." I was panting hard and sweat had broken out all over my body.

"I know, Shannon my girl, I know," he said as he helped me take baby steps forward. "Almost there—once you get to the trees you'll feel better."

I had a vague realization that we had passed Rhiannon, who was a silent shape curled into a fetal position at the foot of the closest oak. Then I was at the base of the giant tree. Clint leaned me gently against the cushioned velvet of the moss-covered bark.

Welcome, Beloved of Epona, the Goddess's Chosen One.

The words sounded wonderful. "Hello," I murmured, pressing the side of my face against the soft moss. "Please help me. It hurts so badly."

We hear you, Chosen.

With the words came a sudden rush of warmth that surged the length of my body. Like a shot of morphine-laced adrenaline I immediately felt soothed and invigorated.

"Oh, thank you, ancient one." My breath came easier as my body responded to the tree's healing power.

"Better?" Clint's hand rested on my shoulder.

I nodded at him.

"Good enough to change worlds?" His voice didn't waver, but it sounded oddly hollow.

I looked into his eyes and I suddenly knew if I said no, if I said let's wait until my wound has healed, I'd never go back. I'd stay here forever and be this wonderful man's wife and the love of his life.

It must be your decision, Beloved. Yours and the Shaman's.

I closed my eyes and leaned heavily into the tree. "But there's really no choice," I whispered the words to my Goddess. In this world I was an English teacher and a daughter. And I could be wife to a man who loved me very much.

In Partholon I was a symbol of security and the evidence of a Goddess's promised benevolence and fidelity.

Deep within my abdomen I felt a fluttering like the tiny wings of a young hummingbird, reminding me what my decision must be.

I opened my eyes and smiled sadly at Clint. "Good enough to change worlds," I assured him.

He nodded his head once. "We know what to do. I'll help you straddle the stream, and I'll mirror your position on the other side. You concentrate on calling ClanFintan."

Rhiannon's mocking laughter sounded strained. Clint and I turned to look at her. She was still curled at the base of the tree, just a few feet from where we stood. Her hair was a wild tangle and her eyes were glassy and unfocused.

"You cannot return."

Her words chilled me.

"Of course I can. I almost did before. It was only Nuada's appearance that messed up the transfer."

Now the laughter was mingled with sobs. "You know nothing, *Chosen One!*" she said sarcastically. Then she seemed to collect herself. She wiped her eyes and sat a little straighter as her words continued. "You can call your centaur mate to the grove, and perhaps you can even touch him briefly through the magic of the trees, but you cannot return to him without a blood sacrifice." She tossed her head in a way that reminded me disconcertingly of myself. "Ask your Goddess, if you don't believe my words."

Clint closed the few feet between them and crouched down next to her, much as he had done for me earlier. Again I was surprised by the gentleness of his voice as he spoke to her.

"Rhiannon, I did not need a blood sacrifice to bring Shannon here. I just called her and she came."

Rhiannon's head swiveled so that her face was very close to Clint's, as if she was a child sharing a secret with her playmate.

Or a lover sharing a secret with her mate.

"I did it." Her whisper carried in the stillness of the empty grove. "I was calling Nuada. I had been calling him for many passages of the moon. I could feel him but I could not draw him here, even though I was making the proper blood sacrifices. Something was holding him."

"You killed someone that night?" Clint's voice was infinitely sad.

"Yes." The word hung in the air between them. "That is how you were able to complete the spell to call her here." She looked at me then, and instead of her eyes being filled with the hatred I had seen before, they looked empty and tired.

"And the day Nuada actually came here?" I prompted.

"I sacrificed another. This time Nuada came into this world easily at my call."

"She can't be telling the truth," I said nervously.

Clint didn't look at me, instead he touched Rhiannon's tear-stained cheek with one hand, while he rested his other palm solidly against the trunk of the pin oak. Shutting his eyes, he seemed to close in on himself. His aura pulsed so brightly I had to shield my eyes. When the light was gone, he was looking at me. His expression was infinitely sad.

"She's telling the truth."

"Well, if we need blood, I have plenty of that dripping down my side!" I yelled my frustration.

Rhiannon shook her head slowly. "It must be a death. I learned that lesson well in Partholon. Pryderi taught it to Bres and Bres taught it to me." I was surprised to see her face pale until it was almost colorless. "The Triple Face of Darkness revels in death."

I remembered the stories Alanna had told me about Rhiannon's botched experiments during the time she was attempting to exchange worlds with me. Alanna had made it clear her "experiments" had met with horrible deaths, and I had come to know too well the evil of Pryderi.

"Fine. We'll get an animal." The thought of slitting some poor creature's throat in sacrifice made me feel a little sick, but it was worlds better than the alternative.

"It is not enough." Rhiannon was staring at me. "You must sacrifice a human for a human to move through the divide."

I looked at Clint for help. He only nodded slowly in agreement.

I felt my shoulders slump.

Never able to go back. I was never able to go back. The reality of it was crushing. I closed my eyes and felt my silent tears mingle with the damp moss.

How is this a choice? I sent the angry thoughts to my Goddess. *If this was the "rule" then the "choice" had little to do with what Clint or I wanted.*

The decision to return was yours, Beloved. The choice to send you is the Shaman's. The confusing answer passed lovingly through my mind.

I heard movement beside me and opened my eyes to see Clint standing next to me, so close his right side almost touched my wounded left side. He had pulled Rhiannon with him and he still held her tightly by the wrist. She wasn't struggling, though, but stood quietly beside him. The thought struck me how strange the three of us must look, Clint flanked by two mirror images.

I looked questioningly at Clint. His eyes were filled with deep sadness and resolve. It frightened me.

"This is my choice, Shannon. Never forget that—I do this willingly."

Before I could question him he turned to Rhiannon. His voice was deep and soothing.

"I can't leave you alone here. You know that." His voice made the words an endearment. "That's what went wrong to begin with. You were left alone too often, and there was no one to really guide you."

Rhiannon didn't answer him, but her eyes widened and her head made a jerky, nodding "yes" motion.

Clint smiled kindly at her. "I won't leave you, or our daughter, alone again. Ever."

Then he turned back to me. "I understand now. Remember you asked me to pity her? But it's not pity she needs. It's compassion. She needs to be cared for, to be watched and kept safe somewhere she can't hurt others or herself, including the child she carries. She is, after all, just a broken part of you." He touched my cheek. "How can I help but love her, Shannon my girl?"

Clint's hand dropped from my cheek and it reached into the deep pocket of his down-filled coat. When it reappeared it held Rhiannon's stiletto.

"Clint?" I asked, unable to keep the fear from my voice.

"Shush," he said quietly. "It's all decided."

He pulled Rhiannon close to him, letting go of her wrist to loop his arm around her shoulders so he could press her firmly against his side. In one quick movement he reached up and brought the blade to rest against the soft flesh just under his left ear. Before I could move he slashed downward, slicing the skin of his neck and the two major arteries that lay so close to the surface there.

"Clint!" I screamed. My mind rebelled, not wanting to believe what he had just done.

He dropped the blade and pressed his now-empty right hand against the side of the tree. His head fell forward and his forehead rested against the trunk. Blood pulsed down Clint's body, covering Rhiannon and him like a crimson cloak. She was sobbing wildly and trying to wriggle out of his iron grasp. I moved to touch him but his eyes froze me in place.

"Don't," he croaked. "This must be."

I saw his eyes close and his aura pulsed wildly. He took a tremendous rattling breath. When his mouth opened, two words came out in a deafening shout that echoed from one world to another.

"CLANFINTAN, COME!"

The moss-covered bark beneath my bloodless palms quivered. I watched as Clint pushed forward and the tree swallowed part of his left shoulder and Rhiannon's struggling body. With a Herculean effort he managed to turn his head so that our eyes met. His face was colorless except for spatters from the river of red that pumped in a thick torrent from his neck. His hand shook as beckoned to me.

"Come," his mouth formed the soundless word.

I grasped his already cold hand and allowed him to pull me within the tree.

All sounds ceased and time suspended. It was as if we had plunged under a deep layer of water. Clint struggled forward, leaving a trail of blood in his wake, pulling the two of us with him. I couldn't breathe and I couldn't think. Panic shrouded me.

Think of ClanFintan! The Goddess's voice was a rope to which I clung. Instantly I obeyed her.

I made myself block out the gruesome sight of Clint and Rhiannon. I ignored the stabbing pain in my side and the suffocating weight that pressed in on me. I thought of my mate. His scent and the taste of his hot skin. His ready laugh and the way he tempered his strength with gentleness. I thought of the fact that he was the father of my unborn child.

And the thick darkness in front of me began pulsing with the blue of glistening sapphires. But the color wasn't coming from Clint. He was no longer in front of me, nor was he holding my hand.

I looked over my shoulder. Both of Clint's arms were wrapped around Rhiannon's body. She was facing him and he was pressing her against his body as if they were lovers. I watched Rhiannon's arms come slowly up and wrap themselves around his shoulders as she returned his embrace. Blood surrounded them, but instead of dimming his aura the crimson mixed with the pulsing sapphire until it created a new color. Purple—a deep, brilliant purple. I felt a start of recognition. It was the color that framed my silver aura.

He must have sensed my gaze because his half-lidded eyes focused briefly on me. His lips trembled and I saw them form the familiar endearment *Shannon my girl*. Then his eyes closed completely and his head turned to bury itself against the wildness of Rhiannon's hair.

I felt the darkness around us begin to solidify and I turned my head to the place I had last seen the pulsing blue light.

A hand was there, reaching into the hardening darkness. Without another thought I grabbed it and held on with everything within me.

The tree expelled me in a rush of liquid. I lay on the ground and drew in a shaking breath, moaning at the agony in my side. Coughing painfully, I gagged and vomited violently. My eyes wouldn't focus and there was a horrible ringing in my ears. I knew my breath was coming so quickly that I was hyperventilating. My body felt as if it was simultaneously freezing and burning.

I must be in shock, I thought detachedly.

I couldn't see and I couldn't hear, but I screamed in pain as a pair of strong arms lifted me from the ground. A familiar rocking motion pounded through my body and it seemed I was being hurled through space. My head fell forward onto bare skin and I recognized the scent of sweet grass, horse and warm man.

I'm home, I thought before I slid down into the abyss of unconsciousness.

7

I was in a place of great darkness, and my first thought was surprise that it wasn't painful.

Hadn't I just been stabbed?

I didn't feel like it. Actually, I didn't *feel* anything.

This must be a coma, I thought with the same detachment with which I had earlier diagnosed my body's shock.

There was a brief sensation of settling, like a flock of birds coming to rest. Then more of the dark nothingness. It should be frightening. But it wasn't. I'd always imagined a coma victim as living consciousness trapped in the suffocating cage of a nonworking body, perpetually wanting to scream but unable to communicate with the outside world.

Well, I certainly couldn't communicate with the outside

world, but it didn't seem so bad. It was kind of comforting, like a warm bath when you've had the flu and now your aches and pains have been soaked away. A nice place to stay for a while, which, as we all know according to Oklahoma vernacular, can be a heck of a long time…

Shannon my girl.

The endearment shook the dark solitude I'd settled into so comfortably. Who was it? The question tickled at my consciousness. The words sounded familiar, and they brought with them both positive and negative connotations.

Too hard to concentrate…too much effort…

Shannon my girl! You have to wake up.

Clint. The name popped into my disjointed thoughts. An image of strength and comfort came with the name recognition, followed quickly by an overwhelming sadness.

Clint was dead.

Part of each of us lives forever.

My mind struck out wildly, remembering the flash of a cruel blade and the rush of his lifeblood.

No! I retreated from the memory back into comforting darkness.

You can't give up. You can't let it all have been for nothing.

It's too hard. It was easier to simply float on the tide of blackness.

So, you'll kill your daughter, too?

That's enough. Now he's gone too far. My anger stirred up specks of light against my closed eyelids.

The fog that covered my memory lifted and my thoughts became more my own.

Of course I would never kill my daughter. Who the hell did he think I was, Rhiannon?

And with that thought I took a deep breath. Pain spiked through my side.

That's my girl... The voice was fading fast.... *Live for me, Shannon. I want you to live*....

I felt as if I was rushing up out of a well of darkness, being sucked through a pain-spike tunnel of light.

My mouth felt really dry. Jeesh, I was thirsty.

My eyelids fluttered and the world blurred like I was trying to peer through a carnival mirror. I blinked rapidly, attempting to bring anything into focus. Well, at least I was out of that Goddess-awful tunnel.

I took another deep breath.

Oh, shit, that hurt.

Speckles of haloed light crossed, uncrossed and multiplied. Nothing held still.

But blinking rapidly was starting to help. The pinpoints of light divided again, then stayed put.

Oh, I realized, *candles*. Lots of them. The room was dark except for zillions of candles. Dozens of huge candelabra were filled with dripping pillars, and there were even more mounds of thick candles set ablaze on sconces that protruded from the smooth marble walls. I heard a crackling sound. And a fire burned brightly—in a hearth.

The room felt pleasantly warm. Actually, except for the horrid pain in my side, a terribly dry mouth and a hot heaviness on my left thigh, I didn't feel too bad. A little disorientated, but not too awfully bad.

And the room was certainly familiar, my muddled thoughts reported.

You are home. The clear voice of my Goddess sang within

my mind, chasing away the clinging effects of unconsciousness.

My eyes traveled fondly over the room I now easily recognized. My bedchamber. In Partholon! In reality I knew I had only been gone a little over a week, but it felt like decades. My room looked much as I remembered it, except I didn't usually light this many candles, and there were normally fragrant bouquets of flowers covering any flat surface that would hold still long enough for my ever-busy nymphets to decorate it.

Well, it was almost winter. Maybe they couldn't find anything that was blooming. Goddess knows it couldn't be from lack of trying, those little teenagers were perpetually in a state of rushing hither and yon (I have hypothesized that they do so because they are usually so scantily clad that scampering is about the only way they can keep warm). The dreadful lack of flowers was probably driving them crazy. I should remember to tell them a couple nice pieces of artwork and some fragrant candles would do just as well for decoration during the colder months. Goddess knows I hate a stressed handmaiden.

But what the hell have they put on my thigh?

I looked down at the offending object and felt my heart quicken. ClanFintan was lying on the floor beside the huge down-filled mattress we had nicknamed our marshmallow. His head was resting against my thigh. His face was turned away from me. From the deep, constant rhythm of his breathing I knew he was asleep. I smiled softly. He always looked bigger in real life than he did in my memory. Wonder why that was. My hand was shaking as I reached out and touched the thick mass of his black hair.

His head jerked up and whirled to face me.

How could I ever have imagined living without him?

"You have awakened?" His voice sounded gravelly.

Tears choked me and I was unable to speak. I nodded.

He pulled his human torso slowly upright, studying me intently. "Who are you?" The words seemed to be torn from deep within him.

For a moment I was stunned. Then I felt my brow furrow. Who am I? I looked closely at him, wondering if he'd been in a battle recently and had received a head wound, which would account for his moronic question.

Except for having dark circles under his expressive eyes and looking a little thinner than usual, I couldn't see any sign of injury. There did appear to be more gray in his hair than I remembered, but that could be a trick of the light. He certainly looked like the same guy/horse/whatever.

I took a deep breath and winced in pain, which didn't help my tone when I answered him.

"Jeesh, I'm me! Who the hell do you think I am, friggin John Wayne riding in with the cavalry? Shit, I've been through hell to get back here and you don't even know I'm me?" Men in any form are the ultimate goobers.

At my words his face broke into a wide smile that radiated pure joy.

"Shannon!" His shout of celebration would have been deafening, but the cheering of the throng, which at that instant burst into my room, drowned it out.

Alanna led the way, followed closely by a gaggle of squealing handmaidens. My heart did a little skip at the sight of her. *She's alive,* my mind assured me. *She's alive.* And she was carrying an armload of roses that were bursting with bloom.

Well, there are the flowers my room's missing. I really wish Alanna would let the teenagers do the menial household chores. She's supposed to be The Boss when I'm not around.

Before the group reached my bedside, the handmaidens dropped to the floor in graceful curtsies. I noticed they were all smiling even though tears streamed down their faces.

"Hello, girlfriend," I said to Alanna, ashamed my voice cracked so badly.

Alanna pressed the back of her hand against her mouth as she tried to hold back a sob. With the other hand she clutched the bouquet of roses to her chest. Then the sob burst into laughter.

"Oh, Rhea! We knew you had come back to us when the roses started blooming again."

I gave her a quizzical look, worried that they'd all gone a little crazy while I was gone.

ClanFintan answered my unspoken question. "With your loss the flowers would not bloom. They withered and died as buds. In mourning, the sun hid itself behind clouds. Even the birds did not sing." He raised my hand to his lips.

A chill traveled down my spine as understanding of the enormity of what his words meant penetrated my mind. And with that understanding came the clear knowledge that I had made the right choice, as had Clint.

Partholon needs her Beloved.

Alanna handed the nearest nymph the roses, wiped her eyes and hurried to the head of my bed. She touched my forehead with a shaking hand and smoothed back my errant curls. Bending gracefully, she kissed me.

"Welcome home, my Lady," she said through her tears of joy.

"Welcome home, Beloved of Epona!" echoed the happily sobbing nymphets.

But I had eyes only for my husband.

He leaned forward and very gently took me in his arms. "Welcome home, my only love." The velvet of his voice covered me and every particle of my soul rejoiced.

EPILOGUE

"If the mare begins to act nervous, we leave. Immediately," ClanFintan proclaimed for the hundred-zillionth time.

"Okay," I agreed innocently.

"I do not jest about this matter, Rhea." He said severely, then continued to mumble, "I do not know how I let you convince me to return to this Goddess-forsaken…"

"Talking to yourself is a sign of old age," I said brightly, trying to maintain my perky facade.

He snorted through his nose and gave me a long-suffering look. I reached forward and ran my fingers though Epi's waterfall of silver mane.

"You're not nervous, are you, beautiful girl?" I crooned.

Her ears flicked back attentively and she whickered a reply.

"See! Epi says everything's okay."

ClanFintan was having none of it.

"Stay alert!" he snapped at the two centaurs that cantered easily alongside us.

I looked at Victoria and Dougal and rolled my eyes, but they were too busy scanning the forest for booger monsters to pay any attention to me.

"Epona said we were in no danger." I repeated the words that I had said so many times they had become like a mantra.

"Hurmph!" ClanFintan said succinctly.

"We enter the forest here." The Huntress's voice was strained and serious. Before she turned to lead us off the path, she pulled her crossbow from its resting place across her back and notched an arrow in the sight.

Dougal and ClanFintan unsheathed their wicked-looking claymores.

Epi and I sighed and followed them into the heart of the forest. A healthy kick against my right rib made me shift in my seat and I smiled softly as I rubbed what I was sure was the heel of a tiny foot jutting out of my swollen belly.

Two months had passed since I'd returned to Partholon, and it seemed as if I'd quadrupled in size. I had certainly recovered from my aversion to food. If it didn't run screaming from me I ate it.

It was late January. The winter had been mild and it looked like Partholon would be enjoying an early spring, but today the air still held the chill of winter, and I was glad of the ermine-lined cloak Alanna had insisted I wear.

ClanFintan pushed his way through the sparse winter foliage so that he and Epi and I were side by side again.

"I do not understand why you cannot be satisfied with the rituals you have been performing each full moon in remembrance of the Indian warriors." His accent gave the word *Indian* a lovely mystical sound.

I had kept my promise to the forgotten warriors of Nagi Road. Every full moon my maidens poured libations of wine and honey and danced joyously in remembrance of their bravery. I hoped that somehow they knew.

But today wasn't about those warriors.

At first I had been unable to think about Clint at all. I had to force him from my mind. The thought of him entombing himself with Rhiannon had been another open wound I could not bear touching.

As time passed and the wound in my side healed, so, too, did the horror of what Clint had done. I began to be able to think of him without being drowned in grief.

The first Partholonian snowfall smelled of him.

Birdsong reminded me of him.

Each time the soul of a tree called to me I heard the echo of his voice.

And I could not make love to my husband. He called the Change to him only once. When he stood before me in human form, all I could see was the image of Clint. Grief overwhelmed me. I couldn't make my tears stop. ClanFintan shifted quickly back to centaur form and comforted me wordlessly within the shield of his arms.

He hadn't attempted to make love to me since. And I haven't asked it of him.

The centaur cleared his throat and I realized he was waiting for my answer. I met his eyes.

"Today is for Clint, not for them."

"I thought you brought libations for the souls of the dead warriors." My husband held my gaze.

"No," I answered him hesitantly. As usual I found it difficult to talk to ClanFintan about Clint. "I brought them for Clint's soul. It's time I faced this. His sacrifice deserves to be acknowledged."

"As you wish, Rhea."

"What if he can somehow tell?" My voice cracked. "I haven't been back. I didn't even get to thank him." My eyes pleaded with ClanFintan to understand.

"I thank him every day," the centaur said quietly.

I nodded tightly, afraid if I said anything else I would start crying. I had given ClanFintan an edited version of what had happened while I had been in Oklahoma. I had left out some parts to save him pain, and other parts to save me pain. But he understood that Clint had given his life to send me back to my husband and the world to which I belonged.

And without ever acknowledging it aloud, I was sure he also understood Clint had loved me. And I him.

Recently I had felt the growing need to return to the ancient grove. It was a pilgrimage I needed to make. After two months I hoped I had healed enough to face my memories and my losses; and, ultimately, to give myself closure.

Maybe I could even forgive myself.

"We have reached the clearing," Victoria's strong voice called back over her shoulder. Dougal followed her, then came Epi and me with ClanFintan by our side.

I pulled Epi to a halt and called to Victoria. She and Dougal paused and looked curiously back at me.

"I need to go first," I said simply. Before their arguments could be spoken I held up my hand to silence them. "The

Goddess has assured me I am safe." And she had. Epona had even encouraged me to make this trip. As ClanFintan opened his mouth to protest, I pulled out my trump card. "Would I do anything to harm our daughter?"

"I will be beside you." His tone said it wasn't a question.

I nodded agreement.

"Victoria and Dougal, stay close." The two centaurs nodded and waited in tense silence for us to lead them into the clearing.

I closed my eyes and we passed through the tree line. Very slowly I tilted my head up and opened my eyes. The verdant leaves of the twin giants filled the sky. Even now, after I knew what to expect, it was a shock to see them fully clothed in green after traveling through a forest of naked limbs. There was a light breeze and the graceful foliage swayed rhythmically. As we approached, I let my eyes travel down their massive length to the moss-covered trunks.

And a color rippled at the edge of my vision. For an instant I felt dread squeeze my throat, but quickly I realized it wasn't a dark, oily shape that I was seeing. My gaze fell to the forest floor and I gasped in surprise.

"What is it, Rhea?" ClanFintan snapped, worry thick in his voice.

"Oh," I breathed happily. "It's nothing bad. It's wonderful. Look!" I pointed to the ground. The entire clearing was carpeted with small blue wildflowers. They were everywhere, and as we rode through them they gave off a sweet, heady perfume.

It was like the entire grove had been sprinkled with sapphires.

"I do not remember these being here before." ClanFintan sounded disgruntled.

"They weren't. They're new." I felt a rush of emotion. The grove hadn't forgotten him. This was the forest's tribute to him.

We drew near the trees. ClanFintan lifted me gently from Epi's back. I unlatched the saddlebag that rested over her withers and took out a skin filled with honeyed red wine. Then I turned to face the trees.

I swallowed my fear. There was nothing here that could harm me.

The pin oaks were more beautiful than I had remembered, so tall and regal and strong. I knew which tree I needed to touch. The blue flowers swished softly against my boots as I approached it. Near the base of the tree I suddenly stumbled over a protruding root, and ClanFintan's sure arms caught me before I could fall.

Oh, Goddess. This is exactly where Rhiannon had stumbled and fallen.

"Are you well, Rhea?"

I realized I had stopped breathing, and made myself draw a deep, steadying breath. Then I squeezed his arm reassuringly.

"Just visiting old ghosts," I said softly before I stepped carefully around the root.

The ancient tree was enormous. Five men couldn't link hands around it, and its twin that grew on the other side of the small stream that separated them was just as imposing.

Uncapping the wineskin, I began pouring it against the base of the tree. I continued pouring as I made my way slowly around its enormous circumference.

The words came to me quite suddenly and with a trembling voice I spoke them, falling easily into the rhythmic chant.

"I remember you as the wind that breathes upon the forest,
The murmur of leaves rustling,
The rays of the sun.
I remember you as the power of trees growing
And the bud breaking into blossom.
You are in my thoughts whenever I praise
All that is noble and true."

I had completed a circle of my own. Tentatively I rested my palm against the tree's aged surface. I didn't have to see my husband to feel the tension radiating from him.

Welcome, Chosen One. The aged voice was familiar.

"Hello," I whispered. Then I spoke hesitantly, "I come…I come to…"

You come in remembrance, Beloved of the Shaman.

My body jerked in surprise at the title. ClanFintan stirred restlessly at my side.

"Yes, I come in remembrance."

I feel that you are in pain.

I closed my eyes on sudden tears. And I'd thought this wound had healed. What a fool I'd been.

"Yes," I said simply.

The Shaman wishes you to hear a message, Chosen One.

My heart beat wildly. Clint was going to talk to me?

Prepare yourself. The thought rumbled within my mind.

I tensed in expectation of Clint's message and what came nearly caused me to yelp in surprise. Through my open palms flooded peace. No words, no message that was spoken or even thought within my mind. Just an overflowing of peace. The tingling within my hands reminded me of another night little more than two months before, when healing had flowed from a Goddess, through my hands, and into his body.

I finally understood that his sacrifice hadn't changed that healing. It had intensified it.

"Thank you," I sobbed. "Oh, thank you, Clint."

My eyes had dried when I turned from the tree.

"Are you well, Shannon?" ClanFintan asked. My mate rarely used my real name.

I realized that the eyes that searched mine were asking volumes more than a simple question.

I moved to his side and he wrapped a protective arm around my shoulder. I pressed myself firmly against him.

"Yes, ClanFintan. I am truly well." I returned his gaze steadily and welcomed the flash of joy that crossed his handsome face as we understood that for the first time since I had returned to Partholon I could speak those words without feeling the taint of pain or guilt.

"Then let us go home, Shannon my girl."

At the sound of the familiar endearment my eyes widened, but he was already bending to cover my lips with his own and he neatly stifled the question my mind was forming.

Some things are better not questioned, Beloved. The Goddess's musical voice drifted softly through my mind.

She was probably right, as usual.

So instead of questioning him I returned my husband's kiss with the enthusiasm of a long-absent lover.

Our arms entwined, we walked back to where Epi and our centaur friends waited. The sweet smell of sapphire-colored flowers hovered around us like a blessing, and Epi's full-throated welcoming neigh mixed with the rustling of the oaks' rich foliage until the glade echoed with the magic of life reborn.

* * * * *

Don't miss the next installment of P. C. Cast's enthralling PARTHOLON *series.*
Divine by Blood is coming Fall '07!